SOORA SUN

BOOK THREE OF THE EMBERJAR

VERONICA GARLAND

SOORA SUN

Imprint: Independently published

ISBN- 9798388342416

SOORA SUN

SOORA SUN

SOORA SUN

DEDICATION

For my mother, for all our mothers, and for you.

'May the golden light of the sun shine upon you
for all your days.'

CONTENTS

BLACK

Chapter 1

It had been three weeks. Three whole weeks. I had endured the week of mourning observed by the people of the Outer. Seven days for every colour but all I saw was darkness. Each day I had been to the place where he now lay, buried. Gladia had made sure there were oils and coloured flowers for the observance days of the first week, but I did not use them. There was nothing there to mark his death. In Kashiq he would have had a clay dome but here, in Oramia, it was not done, even for a man of Kashiq as he was. A boulder lay on the earth to mark the burial and to prevent the place being used until he had fully returned to the Goddess. I had his plant parchments and pens, and I wrote letters to him and burned them, leaving the ashes at his grave. Nobody knew what to say to me. Nor I to them. I was not comforted by Bellis's gentle statements about his return to the Goddess, nor by Tarik's assurances that he had not been in pain when he died, nor by Achillea even, who knew what it was like to lose someone she loved. After all, they were not me and what they felt was not the same as what I felt. Mostly, I felt angry. I was angry with the Goddess for his death, for making me meet him and love him for a whole age and then taking him away. I was angry with Tarik for not having a physic that could cure him. I was angry with Benakiell and Gladia for living longer than him. I was angry with Achillea who seemed to have recovered from her own losses and wanted only for me to feel happy again and who was, in any case, distracted by her three children who ran and played and laughed with abandon, shrieking with excitement as they swung from the Paradox tree. I was angry with myself because I had never been blessed by the Goddess and had his children. Most of all, I was angry with him. I was angry with Ravin.

It was Ravin who had been on his way back to Mellia when he had apparently fallen and hit his head on a rock. At least we thought he had, for he had been found only the next morning by Tarik who had gone out to look for him when he had not returned. He found him, barely able to speak, his head swollen, and his brilliant mind retreated to some dark pit from which it never emerged again. I nursed him for a week. I bathed him and fed him poppy juice for the pain and gave him all the physic that Tarik could bring me. He could not eat and could only sip at honey water. There was nothing we could do about the fever and, one day, he was suddenly not there. Tarik and Achillea gave me poppy juice to make me sleep when it happened, but it could not dull the pain I felt in my heart, and the raging anger I felt. I had lost so much and the one person who could have helped me, as he always had, was the one person who would never be there again. It was a paradox which my mind played with constantly, like winding Gladia's embroidery silks and then tangling them up again.

SOORA SUN

I saw them all watching me. They did not know what to say to me because I reacted with either anger or dull acceptance to everything. I was not there to bury him. Tarik and Benakiell took him while I slept and returned him to the Goddess. I did not want to think of his soul being shattered into tiny pieces and remade into others. He had himself told me that this happened when we die. I wondered, sometimes, how many people had had to die for all their characteristics to have, by chance, ended up in the one person he had been.

He was never perfect in the purest sense, but he was perfect for me. He loved me with all my own imperfections and never sought to change me and I loved him in the same way. We had made plans together; the sorts of plans young lovers do. We would marry when we had children, in the Oramian way. We would begin a scribing school in Kashiq, but just over the border from Oramia and we would teach Oramians secretly how to read. We would have two children, one of each. My children would both learn to be BeeGuards. Such silly little things we used to promise ourselves. The children never came and where once I had never even thought that I wanted them, their absence became a heavy weight for us both. Ravin would read scrolls endlessly when we visited Arbhoun, trying to find some plant or physic or tale of how to be blessed by the Goddess with children and we tried them all. I even, reluctantly, tried to petition the Goddess through prayer, and asked Achillea to heal me with her songs. Perhaps the Goddess knew my heart was not in it and punished me for my lack of faith. Gladia was some comfort to me, although even she had, of course, had one child when she was very young. Nevertheless, having lost that child to the Temple, she never had another, and I had felt her pain on many an occasion.

3

She told me I should stay busy and that it would happen when it was meant to happen. It never did. None of them knew what to say to me now. It had been three weeks since Ravin had died and although I sat here, dull and aching, I could not talk to them. They knew me and him too well and their own grief spilled over me.

I wanted to talk to somebody who knew me a little but not well. Who did not know Ravin as my friends did. They were all mourning him too and I believed I could not place the burden of my grief on top of their own. Bellis and Maren already had to try to care for Jember who was as angry as I was, and as one just starting in his second age of childhood, at fourteen, he did not know what to do with it. Achillea had had to try to explain Ravin's death to her children who saw him as an uncle. Tarik, who held his grief to himself like a heavy blanket, saw Ravin as his brother, a replacement for Ambar. Benakiell had looked upon him as a son, a curious, clever man just like him. Gladia loved him for his humour and his charm, and because he loved me. I needed to be on my own.

So I took to waking early in the morning and walking. I wandered aimlessly about. I belonged nowhere. Not here in Mellia, even though it was the closest thing to a home village that I had, and not in Pirhan either. Ravin and I had moved to Pirhan after Achillea and Tarik's first child Lisu was born. It was only across the river, and we soon became regular traders across the bridge. Achillea and Tarik remained in Gabez in our old home with Lisu and later Elleni and Amir. But my home in Pirhan was tied mercilessly to Ravin and I could not go back there, not yet. I would have to explain to all our neighbours what happened to Ravin, and I still did not have the words for that. Achillea and Tarik had asked me to go and stay with them in Gabez until I was ready to return to Pirhan and had even offered to go and pack up our things in Pirhan and bring them back to me in Gabez so that I could stay with them for as long as I wanted. But they were too kind to me, and their kindness broke me even more. It was as if my heart had been laid open by Ravin's death and now their kindness felt as if they were sprinkling salt on the wound.

Walking alone in the creeping light of the gold-tinged morning was reassuring to me. There were no people, only the plants and the trees, the mountains and the rocks and the small river which continued their lives regardless of my pain. The birds continued to sing, the flowers continued to bloom, and the sun continued to emerge each day at dawn ready for another day. Seven days of walking every day had brought me an uneasy peace and allowed me to discover a small rocky outcrop some way out of the village, to the west.

I had found a place to sit, on a large flat rock. It faced east, into the rising sun and I had to scramble a little to get up to it. The grass was quite long at this time of year, but up on this rock you could see over it to the mountains in the distance. A small, golden beetle crawled over it on its way, unmoved by the size of the obstacle, doggedly climbing upwards. I put my finger in its path and after a slight pause, it climbed over that too, its carapace gleaming in the sun, reflecting all the colours of the Goddess like a jewel.

'Ah, Talla. Always with an eye for the smaller things of our world.' A familiar voice broke the silence. I looked up from the beetle and then down to the foot of the rock where Ambar stood.

'Are you surprised to see me?' That smile of his quirked at his lips, and his eyes crinkled. Before I had had the chance to answer him, he had hoisted himself up the rock and landed next to me, as light and silent on his feet as ever. I had no response to his question. I was, of course, surprised to see him. I had not seen him since he had married Lunaria seven years ago. A whole age in Oramia. Much had happened in that age. I shrugged without reply.

'What, no sharp retort, Talla? No remark about me being gone so long or about how well my agreement with Gladia has developed? No interest in my life as Vizier of Oramia? Besides, what are you doing out here so early? Ravin will be wondering where you are!'

My face must have shown some part of the deep dragging pain I felt when he said that. In the land of Ambar's mind, Ravin still lived. How I envied him that, for, as soon Ravin died, that land in my own mind was changed forever. My mind was as dense and choked as an emberjar full of ash that had burned for too long without tinder. I knew that, as soon as I spoke and told him about Ravin, in one more mind, Ravin would be dead, and I was reluctant to do so, for it seemed to me that Ravin remained more alive while more people thought it so. I had thought I could not weep more but the Goddess, who gives us tears to wash away our pain, let them run silently from my eyes and drip equally silently onto my netela. Ravin had given me that netela. He had returned from the market in Pirhan one day, not long after we had moved there. He had thrown it over my head, grinning, and drawn me close to him and kissed me under it as he had done when we first met. It had been made of a deep burnt orange silk, embroidered with six sided shapes like honeycomb. It had been carefully stitched in silks which ranged from deep red to a light golden yellow, in all the shades of honey you might imagine. 'For the best BeeGuard and the sweetest honey,' Ravin had said as he gave it to me. These small memories which came to me, unbidden, were the hardest, and I sat mute and still, unable to form the words to speak.

Ambar looked at me, his forehead etched with lines of concern.

'What has happened to Ravin? Why are you so sad? Has he hurt you?' It was in some ways typical of Ambar that he might think Ravin could have hurt me, for nothing was further from the truth. Yes, I was hurt, and it was because of Ravin, but he had not chosen to die. In faltering words, I explained to Ambar what had happened, knowing that this news would alter his mind's picture of Ravin forever. He grimaced as I told him of Ravin's death and burial. After I had finished telling him everything, he turned to me and asked me what I would like to talk about. I was taken aback that he did not rush to offer me his words of solace or a well-honed epithet or saying of the Goddess which might bring me comfort in my sorrow. The people of the Outer were experienced in dealing with death and had many small rituals and sayings which were made to bring comfort. It was common for them to visit the Empath at some time after the death of a loved one, so that the Empath would take on the weight of their sorrow and they might find the strength to continue. Although it was now two ages since I had left the life of the Temple, I had not been raised to know what it was like to love someone who then died. If one of the old Priestesses died, we were told she had returned to the Goddess from whom she came, that her journey was now with the Goddess, not towards the Goddess as it had been in this life. No one wept, there were no ceremonies, another Priestess would take her role, and because we did not love, we did not grieve, for sorrow is another face of love. I had found love with Ravin and now I had found sorrow in his loss, but I was not comforted by ritual or by kind intentions. Now, I know

7

that time builds bridges over the deep ravines of grief, but then I did not, and I only wanted to have some moments in the day when I did not, in thinking of Ravin, suddenly learn of his death again as I realised my loss. Ambar had asked me what I wanted to talk about, and, at that moment, I only wanted to talk of something which was not Ravin.

'Tell me of your childhood in the OutFort,' I said, choosing something which could not relate to Ravin. He had been a Kashiqi and had known nothing of the OutFort save what he had learned from me. Ambar turned to me and smiled, his eyes crinkling.

'Always seeking more knowledge. You are the only one I know who would ask me such a thing. Lunaria, the Queen, shows little interest in the OutFort or indeed in my childhood.' He looked away briefly. 'Let me see what I can tell you. I will start from the earliest memories I have, but I can only stay for a short while before I must go back and join my OutRiders who are in that direction.' He waved vaguely to the west, to a small stand of scrubby trees. 'And I am sure you must return to Mellia too. But I will return tomorrow morning and we can talk some more, if you want to. It can be our secret.'

I nodded, barely aware of what I was agreeing to, and, as he began to talk to me, for a short while, I forgot my grief, as I learned about the childhood of a small boy in the OutFort.

'I do not know anything of my parents any more than you do. As young children we were told by the OutCommanders that we had been chosen to defend the Queen and her land and, since we were all raised there from an early age, we did not know anything about parents. The OutCommanders acted as our fathers and our mothers, I suppose. I do not remember a great deal from my earliest years but, from what I saw later, the youngest boys were looked after until they were halfway through their first age, at around four or so, by the oldest OutRiders, those who could no longer fight or craft armour or weapons; they were called Guides.

When you told us about your life in the Temple, when we first met, it struck me that we had very similar childhoods in many ways. And yet we boys never knew until we were older that there even existed another kind of person, women.' Ambar laughed. 'It sounds so unlikely now and yet it is still the case. In that first age, we played games which the Guides thought would help us when we became OutRiders. We had balls made of stitched cloth and cotton and then heavier ones of wood which we would try to aim into a basket which they put further and further away. Later, they would give us straight sticks to aim at targets on trees. We used to play at riding horses on large tree trunks and those who looked after us made real leather saddles and bridles for those tree trunks so that we could practice climbing into the saddle and holding the reins.' Ambar's eyes looked far away, back into his own past, as he remembered his childish games.

'Every year when we were little, they would put us into a new group of boys so that we did not become too attached to anyone, so that we did not make friends. We were told often that our only loyalty was to the Queen, and we had to learn all kinds of sayings and repeat them when we woke and before we went to sleep. As we reached the end of that first age, we used to go out and hunt for lizards and other small animals and insects. We would go out in groups of six, with our Guide, and we would have to learn which animals were good to eat and how to catch them. We also had to learn to be quiet for long periods and the Guides would beat you if you made the slightest noise. Nobody wanted to be beaten after the first time. That was a quick lesson for us and stood us in good stead later when we had to move quietly.'

I thought back to how soundlessly Ambar and indeed Tarik could move and how useful it had proved to be. They could listen in to people talking without anyone knowing they were there and silently move into positions from where they could attack enemies. They could stalk and kill animals for food and observe the movements of those they were watching. I recalled how Ambar had often, in the past, crept quietly until he was close to me and had even just watched me without me ever realising he was there. He had been taught this skill from a very early age and kept it all through his life. And yet, I had been taught in a similar way to clean and to do stitching and so forth and it never felt as though those were my natural skills like tending to the bees was. I was drawn to the bees as if I had known how to look after them from being a small child. Unbidden came the sharp memory again of Ravin giving me the netela and calling me his sweetest honey and I could no longer hear what Ambar was telling me of making armour. He saw from my face that my grief had returned and hastened to tell me that, in any case, he needed to go now because his men would be waiting for him. He would return to the same place the next morning at dawn if I wanted to talk with him some more about his childhood. And with that he slipped away, demonstrating again his ability to move quickly and noiselessly away. When I looked up, he had disappeared into the grass as if he were never there.

For all that my grief had returned, it had been a more restful time for me than I had experienced since Ravin's death. Just sitting there listening to Ambar's childhood had taken me out of the current landscape I was in, where every conversation or memory or even object reminded me of Ravin and then, an instant later, of his death, into a new land. It was somewhere that small boys chased one another with sticks and threw balls into baskets, where they rode on tree-trunk horses. I pictured Jember as a little boy and how he would follow after Benakiell, importantly doing his work. Now he was older, he was still eager to learn these tasks, but he saw it now as a preparation for adulthood rather than a joyous activity. I wondered when we first realised that our childhoods were only the precursor to a life of working. Perhaps it came with the realisation that we would eventually die. Children have so many other things to think of that they rarely sit and ponder their own existence as we do when we get older. And what a gift it was to have those years in which we were unaffected by it.

I made my way slowly back to Mellia. The sky was a deepening blue, vast and unending and the Paradox trees formed solid silhouettes against it, their expansive branches making shelters from the sun. I arrived at Gladia's dwelling just as she was putting coffee into her coffeepot. She looked at me, her forehead furrowed with concern.

'I was wondering when you were going to get back from your walking. You need to sit down and drink some coffee. I have just made flatbreads and there is some of Maren's honey to have with them and then I would like to talk to you about the ...' She looked around us to make sure we were alone. '...Angels. It is coming to the time when my agreement with Ambar on the Angels will be over if he so chooses, which he probably will. Do you still have that scroll that Ravin wrote?' She stopped for a moment, realising that she had brought up his name and that each time someone said his name it made me wince or weep. This time, however, I felt cushioned from it because I had just

spent the time with Ambar when my mind's torment
had been stilled, and I replied, keeping my voice
steady.

'It is in Pirhan, with the rest of our things. Do you
need it? Is Ambar coming to see you?' Without
thinking, I had not spoken of my meeting with Ambar
that morning. It was one small thing that I could keep
to myself and think about that was not about Ravin.
Gladia passed me a clay beaker filled with steaming,
black coffee and a flatbread that was still warm. She
had liberally applied honey to it and the warmth was
making it melt and slip. I had had no interest in food
since Ravin's death although I still ate it, mindlessly, as
we had always done at the Temple where food's only
purpose was to aid us in our work, not for the pleasure
of eating it.

'He will no doubt turn up soon. It would be unlike
him to forget an arrangement which allowed him the
power to end it. It is an age since the agreement was
made because Lisu is almost seven now and she was
not yet born when we agreed with Ambar about the
scrolls. Clever Ravin to think of that!' Her voice trailed
off slightly as she realised that she had mentioned
Ravin again, but in customary Gladia fashion, she just
carried on with what she was saying.

'Only, I will need it if he decides to stop the
agreement. We made a bargain after all, and I would
not have anyone say that Gladia does not keep her word
even if they could say it about Ambar! Maybe Achillea
and Tarik can find it if you describe where it is, since
they want to go back.'

She stopped again, and this time it was because she
had told me what Achillea had not; that she and Tarik
wished to return to their home and were only still here
because of me and what had happened to Ravin. With
three young children to look after and all the trading

they needed to do to keep them fed and clothed, Achillea and Tarik both worked hard. Now that Lisu was entering her second age, Achillea would be teaching her the essential skills that all Outer children learned; making a fire, planting and tending to crops, making a flatbread and a stew and knowing and gathering fruits and spices. In addition to that, she would have the chance to try her hand at some of the professions available to women in Oramia. From the moment her sister and then her brother were born, Lisu had loved to care for them and already helped Achillea to tend to them. Achillea thought she might work as a Birthmother like Maren, but as a child herself she would begin by learning to look after babies and small children while their mothers were busy before being able to join a real Birthmother in her third age of childhood. It was convenient for Achillea that Lisu could learn on her own siblings.

Gladia looked at me.

'You will have to go back sometime, Talla,' she said gently. 'Whenever you go back, it will give you pain. But until you feel that pain, you cannot heal it. Best to go soon while Achillea and Tarik are with you so they can help.'

I shook my head. 'I will go back soon and find your scroll, Gladia, I really will, but I would rather go on my own. Walking in the morning on my own helps me with my thoughts and I am feeling stronger now. I will talk to Achillea and tell her and Tarik that they can go back to Gabez whenever they choose. I will stay here with you for a few more days and then travel back to Pirhan. It may be that Ambar has forgotten about the scroll completely.' I knew, of course that he would not, but since he had said he would meet me again the next day, I thought I might tell him to wait a little longer before

he visited Gladia to allow me to return to Pirhan to get
it. I wondered what he would choose to do.

'Here is Achillea now.'

I turned to greet her as she walked up the path to
Gladia's dwelling, Lisu skipping ahead. She was
holding Elleni's hand as the little girl walked carefully
along the path and was carrying baby Amir in a cloth
slung on her back. Even from here, I could see that she
looked tired. Achillea had not changed greatly in the
past seven years, though perhaps that was only in my
eyes, the eyes of a friend who does not notice the marks
of time. She was plumper and softer and had less time
to attend to her hair braiding and her perfumed salves
and her jewellery. Her voice was as musical as ever and
she often sang to the little ones. She sat herself down
with a thump on the dusty mat and fanned her face
with the side of her netela, shifting the cloth sling that
Amir slept in so that he lay, covered in the cloth on the
mat. He was only a few months old, and he stirred only
briefly when she laid him down, his little lips puckering
up and silently sucking at an invisible breast.

Becoming a mother had been more difficult for
Achillea than she had imagined. As an only child
herself, she never had to care for younger siblings and
as a young woman had never spent much time with
other young women who had babies, so she had
imagined a life where babies were quiet and biddable
and easy to deal with. Despite her weariness, you could
see her pride shining out and she and Tarik were
equally besotted by the children. Tarik worked hard all
the time, and every year he would travel to Arbhoun
again and go and work at the honeygold mines and
then with the metal itself. He would bring some of the
ornamental pieces he made back to Oramia with him
and made very good trades in the markets of both
Gabez and Sanguinea. He and Ravin had often worked

together on such things after they had made the
Orange of Kashiq, and Ravin had designed intriguing
boxes with sliding compartments and ornamented
locks and keys which Tarik had hammered out from
the metals he mined. Tarik had never stayed for long in
Mellia. He perhaps felt that he did not belong there, in
the place where Achillea grew up and the place where
she had met Ashtun. He was the man she had loved
first before he died in her defence at the Court of the
Queen. It was Tarik who had killed the OutRider who
had killed Ashtun and sometimes I had wondered
about that. It must have made Achillea draw closer to
him, that he had tried to avenge the death of Ashtun so
immediately and with so little thought for his own
safety, but perhaps, even then, Tarik had been swayed
by wanting to protect Achillea. Tarik liked to live in
Gabez, the place where he and Achillea had first known
they loved one another, and the place which they now
called home. It was also further away from the Queen's
Court and Ambar, his erstwhile comrade.

Gladia fussed over the little girls, giving them dried
figs to chew on and little cloth dolls she had sewed out
of scraps of fabric in her spare time. She had
embroidered their faces with smiles and big eyes. They
were made of a patchwork of fabric which looked
familiar to me, and I looked carefully at the one that
Elleni showed me.

'That cloth looks very familiar to me,' I commented
mildly to Gladia, amused that she might have thought
that I would not have noticed that she had used my old
drabcoat, the patchworked brown and grey dress in
which all Temple Maids were clothed until they became
Priestesses. I had left it in Mellia years ago, shortly
after I fled the Temple and had wondered where it
might have gone but had assumed it had been burnt or
somehow destroyed. Gladia evidently felt that it was

safe to cut it up without asking me about it, and, of course, it was.

'They do look a bit drab, though, don't they, Talla?' she said, her eyes twinkling at me. 'I think we might have to stitch some robes for them. What do you think Lisu, Elleni? What colours would you like? I can stitch you a robe each for your doll before you go.'

Achillea looked at me.

'Gladia told me you are ready to go home now,' I said, in answer to her unspoken question. 'You will be happy to get back home again and have a bit more space than you have in Cassia's old dwelling.'

'It will be good to get back home again,' she acknowledged. 'But we will stay here with you for as long as you want us to. We cannot think of returning without Ravin, ourselves, so we cannot imagine how you feel yourself.' Her big eyes filled with tears, and mine filled too, but I stared resolutely into the distance until they were steady.

'I will return in a little while,' I said. 'Perhaps I can come and stay with you before I go back to Pirhan to sort out his things.'

'Are you sure you don't mind?' I could feel her relief. And, whilst grief needs company sometimes, it also needs its own time and space. She and Tarik had lost their dear friend too, and without me being there, they would be able to take that grieving time for themselves.

'When will Uncle Ravin come back?' asked Elleni suddenly, looking at me with that concentrated look children sometimes have when they know they have asked a difficult question. Lisu smacked her hard on the arm making her wail and move to her mother's side.

'Uncle Ravin is not coming back,' said Lisu sternly. 'He is dead now. Why do you think the grown-ups keep crying? You are such a silly little girl.' She turned back

16

to me. 'But don't worry, Aunty Talla, we will look after you, and one day the Goddess will bring all the best bits of Uncle Ravin back in someone else. Uncle Ravin told me that himself, and he knew more than anyone else I know! Except Papa!'

I smiled at her, although it took some effort. The Kashiqi belief in Asmara taking the qualities of a returned soul and giving them to other souls was one which Ravin firmly believed in, and he often thought he saw the special qualities he had known in his mother in other people. Now, I wondered if I would ever see someone who would smile in the same way as him or who would stroke his beard absently while he read a scroll, or who would hold a pen almost in an embrace as he used it, or who would make me feel weak with longing when he traced his thumb along the lines of my jaw. Perhaps one day I would see someone walking in the same jaunty way he used to, or someone who wore a similar blend of perfumed oils, or someone might drop their left eye at me, that special trick I could never do despite trying very hard.

'You are right, Lisu,' I agreed. 'And Ravin had so many best bits that the Goddess will have to bless many people because of him.'

'Come now,' said Gladia. 'Come and choose what colour robes you would like for your dolls, girls. I will have to stitch quickly if you are going to leave early tomorrow.' She bustled off with the two girls eagerly following her, their disagreement soon forgotten. Achillea and I sat quietly, drinking our coffee, enjoying a few minutes without the incessant questions which her children always asked. Amir stirred on his cloth but settled himself back again. I looked down at him, marvelling at how each tiny part of him was perfect. The ache in my heart for a child with Ravin swelled inside me, and I pushed it down.

'Can you watch him while I go and get Tarik's tunic? I was hoping Gladia could repair the stitching on it before we go back. If she is going to be sitting here sewing most of the day, she may as well do some for me as well as for the girls.' Achillea smiled at me. 'We all have to take advantage of help when it is offered, but sometimes we have to ask for it too.' She was right, of course, but I still wasn't ready to share my grief with anyone, nor ask for their help. Time was the thing which affected everything; grief lessened, love grew or ebbed away, children grew, people died, and babies were born. I could not ask for Achillea's help but I could give her mine and a few minutes with Amir was not much to ask.

'Of course,' I said. 'Walk as slowly as you like; he is sleeping quite peacefully here, and in any case, Gladia is just over there with the girls.'

After she had sauntered away, I looked down at the sleeping infant. He was still sucking slightly in his sleep. I stroked his plump little hand which was grasping the end of the piece of cloth which he had been given to chew and to play with. I gently put my little finger into the palm of his other hand and his fingers tightened around it. I never tired of this little trick which I had first discovered when Jember was a baby and when I had precious little interest in such things. Nevertheless, it intrigued me that, even in their sleep, babies instinctively grabbed onto things so fiercely. Perhaps the Goddess made us so that, even as babies who know nothing, we want to hold that which we love very tightly. Amir's grip tightened and a frown crossed over his sleeping face; he winced and woke up suddenly, crying. I stroked his arm, trying to soothe him, but he wanted to be picked up.

I stood up with him, still awkward in how to hold a baby. I had held Lisu and Elleni as babies a few times, but it seemed a long time ago. Luckily, Amir could hold up his own head and was happy to look around him as I soothed him and then talked to him about the garden and what I could see. Once he was quiet again, I sat back down with him but kept him cradled in my arms, enjoying the uncomplicated warmth of him next to me. I leaned against the broad trunk of the Paradox tree and closed my eyes, feeling the bark of the tree through my robe. Amir, by now, was making contented little noises as he sucked on a corner of his piece of cloth. He smelled sweet, which was not always the case. Achillea must have been making some new salve scented with jasmine, the perfume of Flavus. She swore by a beeswax salve for soothing the skin of a baby, but, being Achillea, she wanted it to smell good too.

A butterfly flew by, hesitating in the air as it chose a flower and then pausing to rest while it fed. Amir stretched out his hand to it, imploring it to come closer, but it swerved away, and after a little while, his head drooped and he fell asleep again, nestled into me as I sat against the tree. It was a blessing to me to feel the uncomplicated warmth of another person next to me, to feel his heart beating close to mine. He was unaware, I supposed, of how much he was giving to me. This was perhaps a sign of love, even from a small child: that one could be revived and replenished by the company of another without them even realising that they were giving you something. My eyes drooped and I slept, up against the tree, waking only to the muffled giggles of the little girls who had returned looking for their mother and had instead found me and their little brother fast asleep.

Chapter 2

The next morning, I awoke, as usual, when the soft grey of the night melted into the pale pink of day. I once again went for a walk, feeling somewhat refreshed by my more restful sleep of the night before. Achillea and Tarik were going to leave later in the morning. They could not travel back to Gabez with any speed since they had the children with them and were planning to break their journey twice. Tarik would carry Elleni on his shoulders for some of the distance, but they were limited by how far Lisu could walk. It was a long walk back for them and I could see why it might have been easier for me to have gone back with them as I could have helped to carry some of their things for them. The bigger the family grew, the more difficult it became to move around with the same freedom. Gladia already complained that if she wanted to see the children then she usually had to walk to Gabez herself to see them. She really wanted them to move back to Mellia but Tarik and Achillea liked to live in Gabez; in Oramia but close to the border with Kashiq so that they could enjoy the opportunities of both lands. I could imagine that there might come a time when they simply would not make the long trek back to Mellia anymore. If only the people of the Outer could have horses, people could move around much more freely and those that were young or old could travel further or more quickly. But in both Oramia and Kashiq the horses were reserved for the soldiers and those who governed. I had sometimes seen some people who had made bags for goats to carry on their backs which could be filled with goods and thus lighten the load. If you were accustomed to looking after goats then I supposed it would be useful, but otherwise the extra effort of looking after the goat might not be worth it. Goats seemed to have independent minds and often strayed in search of fresh grass or other interesting items. When Jember was young, Gladia used to call him a goat affectionately. Now he was older, he was less forgiving of the assortment of names she liked to call him.

It would be some time before the others would be stirring and packing up their things so I decided to walk out again to the little stand of rocks some way out of the village where I had met Ambar the previous day. I wondered if he would be there again today. When I got there, there was nobody to be seen and I climbed up onto the rocks and looked out over the plains. The land of Oramia looked different from the land of Kashiq; it was greener in general as the trees were spread out over the red earth in small scrubby stands, and further in the distance near the mountains, the trees covered the slopes of them in thick stands of forest. Ravin had been fascinated by the difference between his land and mine. Kashiq was hotter and drier, with miles of sand and sandstone pillars divided by the steep gorges which the rivers had carved their way through. All the settlements in Kashiq were based around the rivers and the springs of water which made their way to the huge expanse of water at the eastern edge of Kashiq, from whence the sun would rise each day. Ravin had never seen it before and neither had I, but both of us had cherished a wish to see this vast water one day. Now it would never happen. There was an equally vast supply of tears within me, for they fell again now as I thought of Ravin. He had been so much a part of me that there was very little that I could think of that did not contain some element of him. I brushed the tears away and tried to concentrate on something else, moving the small pebbles on the top of the rock around, balancing them on top of each other.

'If you are building a wall, I must tell you that I think you are going to fail,' came a dry voice behind me. Ambar was climbing up the rock lightly, like one of those goats I had been thinking of earlier. He sat down and smiled warmly.

'Here we are again,' he said as he settled down.

'You can learn a lot from a pile of pebbles.' Ambar picked up a few in his hand. 'In the OutFort, they were our first lessons. It all began close to the end of our first age, I suppose, so we would have been around seven years old. We had to go out and find what we thought would be the best pebbles, fifteen of them, and bring them back to those who taught us. They did not tell us what the pebbles would be used for, because that was the first test, really. Some chose them for their uniform colour or size or texture and tried to make a matching set. Some spread their bets and made a few different sets. Some picked their pebbles very quickly and raced back with them. Some chose by their function – would they be good for building with, or for using in a catapult or for sanding down a rough piece of wood or honing to a sharp blade. There was a great skill in those OutRiders who taught us when we were young; no less than those who taught us as young men to be soldiers and to ride horses and to make armour. They could see our nature by the stones we chose; those who would be warriors and those who would be craftsmen, those who would make tools and those who would be adaptable and useful in any situation. Then, from that set of pebbles, we had to choose a set of five, our favourites, and the rest were all put together in a big pile in front of us. We were then allowed to look at the stones in front of us which had been discarded by others and have three turns to swap one of our original keepers for a better stone. There were those who changed their mind about their group of pebbles and those who merely spotted a slightly better example for their set. There were also those who did not change their group at all. I was one of them.'

This did not surprise me at all. Ambar had, in all the years I had known him, always been very sure of himself, and rarely diverted from the path he had assigned himself. He had single-mindedly pursued Lunaria because he believed that was his destiny and he had then again pursued a path which meant that she married him. I wondered if he was made happier by Lunaria or by the fact that he had achieved the goal he had set himself.

This game with the pebbles was a clever task by the OutRiders. The Priestesses had not done anything similar with us that I could remember. Ambar continued.

'Then, those who were guiding us gave us a short time to carefully examine our pebbles. There were only five stones in our sets, of course, but we were told to get to know each stone well. Then they took all the stones from a group and mixed them together well. Then we had to find the same stones with which we had started. For some, it was easy, for those who had collected a set of distinctively coloured stones, for instance. Those who had chosen other qualities like weight had to pick them up to try to gauge which was theirs. We took it in turns to choose one stone until they were all divided up again. Inevitably, some had chosen a stone which had originally belonged to another, and at this point we had

23

to negotiate for the return of our stone to try to get back our original set. Our guides could make choices about us based on this too. Who would try hardest to get a stone back which he believed to be his? Who would give up easily and who would use the process to actually try and change one of the stones in his set which he believed to be deficient? Who was clever, who was sharp eyed, who had a good memory, who was cunning and who was good at talking? There were many lessons which could be learned about oneself and about others through this task.'

I was intrigued. This small and seemingly insignificant game of children could give real insights into their character. I wanted to know more about it. 'What happened after that?'

Ambar laughed. He reached into the small leather pouch he always had strung to his waist, along with his quiver. The pouch itself was well worn and softened by age, unadorned and functional. All the OutRiders had them. Tarik still had his although he did not ever wear it, and it had been put away many years ago. Ambar sorted blindly with his fingers in the pouch without looking and drew out a handful of small pebbles.

'We had to keep them. Many times, after that day, we had to play similar games of choice and observation until we really knew our stones well. When we entered our second age, we learned to craft with leather and made the pouches we keep them in. An OutRider has to be very observant to progress well through the ranks. There is a place for every man in the OutRiders, but only the best become the leaders. The stones are there to remind you of the importance of every small thing about the men you lead and about the work you do. It is only through looking that we see.'

He opened up his palm and showed his stones to me. I leaned over his hand, poring over them and marvelling that he had kept them all of this time. His set of pebbles were graded by colour, from black to brown to orange, yellow and white. They were all small, round and smooth. I wondered if the OutCommanders had bags of different kinds of stones they dropped for the boys to find, for these pebbles seemed nothing like the ones we found on the ground here in Oramia.

We in the Temple had never been permitted to possess anything of our own. Even our clothes were specifically made so that they could fit a woman of any size and shape – at least when we were Temple Maids and were clad in the drab. If you became a Priestess, you were given a veil made only for you, which became yours forever. But, growing up, everything was shared; clothing, combs, even the dormits where we slept were changed every so often to prevent us from becoming attached to one situation. It seemed that the OutFort had had a different approach and had encouraged the men to have attachments to things to teach them how to improve their characters. Having the objects had reminded them of the lessons they had learnt. The sun was creeping up the wall of the sky and I thought I should return to Mellia before I was missed. I realised that I did not want anyone coming out to look for me and finding me here talking to Ambar. As I stood up, I explained to Ambar that Achillea and Tarik were leaving today to return to Gabez.

'And what of you, Talla?' he asked, 'Are you returning to Pirhan at the same time?' I was, perhaps, not surprised that he knew where I lived, but a little disconcerted. One of the reasons, which I had never really explained to Ravin, for choosing to live in Pirhan was the warning given to me by the fortune teller after we had given the Orange of Kashiq to Ambar. I had thought we might be safer there than in Oramia, for surely they would not send anyone to harm us in another land? I must have looked perturbed, because Ambar hastily told me that he only knew I lived there because he had overheard Gladia saying so.

'I will return there soon,' I answered. 'I need a few more days on my own before I can go back there.'

'After Tarik and Achillea have left, I will see Gladia,' said Ambar. 'I will come this evening. And then I too must go and spend some time on other things.'

I felt a twinge of disappointment that my distraction would soon be gone. I had been hoping not to have to occupy myself contemplating my return to Pirhan which I would find exactly as we had left it, full of Ravin's things. His scrolls would be packed neatly into his sandalwood scroll box which kept the insects from eating the plant parchment scrolls. His spare carrysack would be hanging on the wooden peg by the door. By the fire would be our twin clay jars, one for his minty Kashiqi tea and one for my strong Oramian coffee. On our sleeping mat would be the cushions we slept on, and they would carry with them the scent of my lost love. Thinking of these things made my tears swell in my eyes and overspill onto my cheeks. Ambar looked at me, concerned.

'I am sure you will not miss me so much,' he joked awkwardly, patting my arm. And then, even more awkwardly, 'I am sorry, that was an ill-thought jest. I am sorry again for your loss. I wish with all my heart that I could do more to ease your pain.'

He left shortly afterwards, reminding me that he would come to see Gladia that evening, and I walked back to the village, to bid farewell to Achillea and her family as they began their journey home.

Chapter 3

I said nothing to Gladia about Ambar's plans to see her that evening and did my best to attend to the numerous jobs that she had set aside for me. Gladia believed that keeping busy would be the best way to occupy my mind and to stop me from thinking too much about my life with Ravin and what I had lost. She had devised a long list of tasks, and it occurred to me, as she told me what I needed to do, that this would not only benefit me, but also Gladia who was kindly allowing me to do all the tasks she did not wish to do. This made me smile wryly to myself as I pondered on the thought that the Temple and Gladia had both come to a similar conclusion: that occupying the body was a sure way to distract the mind.

The tasks however had to be carefully matched to the person doing them. It had to be something that occupied both mind and body just enough to keep it focused on the task rather than on other things. When I had been a Temple Maid, I had been assigned to cleaning duties which did not occupy my mind at all and let it wander freely, puzzling things out. Consequently, I had discovered some things and uncovered others which I might not have noticed had my mind been more occupied. Gladia, I discovered, was intent on filling my hours with both sorts of tasks. She had become adept at setting small jobs which could be achieved easily by the Angels who were left for her to train and care for. This left Gladia free to talk and to stitch. She had taught many of the women how to stitch and to cook and to grow simple crops in their gardens. Some of them remained in Mellia, but others decided to leave and go to live elsewhere. Often, they went to the bigger towns where it was easier to settle as an unknown. It was hard for Gladia when they left, for they rarely returned to her. I looked back at myself and the ways in which Gladia and Benakiell had looked after me and taught me the ways of the Outer when I had first left the Temple and was grateful for all that she had taught.

There were beehives to empty and gardens to clear and beans to harvest. There were pomegranates to pick and coffee to grind. There were marigold petals to pick and cover with hot salted water for orange and yellow fabric, and turmeric root for bright orange and deep yellow, darkberries for purples and blue, and an assortment of barks for browns. There was a weaver in the village and he and his son needed their cloth dying because it sold better at the markets and, of course, to Gladia and her fellow stitchers. But Gladia liked to dye her own stitching threads too and tried to keep the darkest and brightest colours for herself, so that her embroidery patterns stood out well. I wondered if Lunaria was still stitching now that she was Queen. I doubted that she had much time for such things, but then what did a Queen really do? From what I had seen, her role seemed to be to maintain the systems which had been set up through the ages to keep the power in the hands of the Temple and the OutRiders, and to act as a figurehead who could make binding announcements on such issues as how much tax must be paid at the markets. I had no patience for stitching and would often stab my fingers. Gladia could not

28

understand how I could have such good control over a reed pen when I was scribing but not over a needle. In truth, Ravin was a far better stitcher than I was, and his fingers were more agile and dextrous than my own. He had made tiny chains out of silver wire when we had been rebuilding the Orange of Kashiq and even Gladia had been impressed by his skill whilst still warning him that he was not permitted to be a stitcher in Oramia where it was reserved as a woman's job. He had laughed and told her he would make sure to only sew when he was on Kashiqi soil. Though there, of course, he was under the guidance of Rao, the God of learning, reading and scribing not Maliq the God of crafting. It was all so complicated, especially for those like me and Ravin who liked to try out many different types of skills and to learn new ways of doing things. In both lands it felt as though it was a way in which people were held back from achieving too much or maybe even thinking too much. This was the sort of thing that Ravin and I used to like to puzzle our minds over when we chatted at night together by the fire and the sharp pain of missing him spiked in my heart. I paid close attention to beating the cloth down into the dye, sprinkling more salt to fix it and then beating it down again until the pain lessened, and I felt able to move on to the next task.

I sat with Gladia to eat in the evening. She had not asked me to cook the food, unsurprisingly. My friends all knew that I was a functional cook and had no skill at all. I always believed that perhaps it was because I had been raised in the Temple. In the Temple, we Maids were fed in a very functional way. The Priestesses knew that we needed to be well fed to work hard but did not see that pleasure in eating was important and delivered food that was plain and tasteless. They did not add herbs and spices to the food, nor allow us to eat honey unless it was in a physic of some sort. We were allowed coffee, for again, this was seen as something which helped us to work harder. They did add powdered berries to flavour the coffee every day which we were told was a gift from the Goddess. I preferred the strong Oramian coffee of the Outer without its blessing of berries. We had to eat everything we were given to eat and drink what we were given to drink. Nobody even acknowledged that different people might enjoy different kinds of foods. We did not know then that, while the Priestesses seemed to eat just the same food as us, they had other food brought to them in their rooms later. I had only discovered this myself when I had masqueraded as a Priestess when we were searching for Lunaria.

Gladia had made a spicy bean stew for us with onions and warming cinnamon and chillies, and tomatoes and pumpkin. The usual flatbreads had been made and cooked on the flat plate over the fire. The fire glowed under the pot of stew. Since Ravin's death, I had had little interest in food and had only eaten functionally, as I had in the Temple, but this evening, after all the jobs, I felt hungry for the first time and ate my food with relish.

Gladia looked at me appraisingly, her head set to one side, her dark blue netela slipping on her plump shoulders. As she had grown older, she had become fonder of the darker colours, and I wondered if different colours meant different things to you as you aged. Perhaps those who favoured a light yellow when they were young would only wear dark purple when they were older? Gladia herself said she thought the darker colours suited her more, but Achillea had whispered to me that it was because the dark colours made her look less solid and rounded. Her eyes glinted in firelight.

'You seem a little brighter today, Talla. Perhaps all that hard work is good for you?' She chuckled, showing me that she was teasing me. 'It's good to see you eat with more appetite, you have got quite thin over the past weeks. I may be wrong, but I think you feel better now that Achillea and Tarik have gone back to Gabez?'

She was right. Achillea only wanted to help me, but her sweet sympathy and her continuous references to Ravin kept the wound in my heart open. I did not want her not to talk about Ravin, but I didn't want her to talk about him either. Both options brought me pain, and, in the end, it was easier for me if she wasn't there. Tarik bore his own pain quietly, but I knew how much he had been pained by Ravin's death. They had become very close friends, almost brothers, and it was an enormous loss to him. Ravin had become almost like a brother, just as Ambar had been before he had gone off. As his friend I wanted to comfort him, but I could not take his pain along with mine. It was as if I was carrying a very heavy carrybox and someone wanted me to take even more weight in it. I felt disloyal to my friends for feeling better without them there and was relieved that, for once, Gladia had not offered me her opinion. Perhaps it was because she had already endured much sorrow herself in her life that she could understand my own. I was just trying to form an appropriate response to what she had said to me, when there was a quiet rustling noise and a figure melted out of the darkness and came to sit at the fire. It was Ambar who had come, just as he had said he would.

'I greet you, Gladia,' he said courteously to her, as he took his place close to the fire with no ceremony. 'I have returned to Mellia to discuss with you the agreement we made a full age ago, regarding the...' He paused, to think of a different word for the Angels. '...orphans you care for, who are left for you.'

31

Gladia snorted rudely. She had no time for Ambar, and although she had negotiated the care of some of the Angels with him, she did not trust him, and had often said so.

'How has it been working for you, our arrangement?' he asked, continuing to speak smoothly and disregarding her interjection. 'It is time to look again at what we agreed upon. There are changes that must be made if it is to continue, by order of the Queen.'

We both looked at him, surprised by the mention of the Queen. Lunaria had professed herself shocked when I had first told her of the abhorrent practice of the Angels, young women supposedly released from the Temple at the time of Choice and instead recaptured by the OutRiders and used for their physical pleasure and as forced labour for the building of Temples and OutForts. But when she had become Queen, her priority was to maintain the systems and traditions which had been set into being by those who ruled before her. It was more important to her that everything should stay the same as the Goddess had first ordained it – or perhaps it was Ashkana who had started it. She did not want to hear about the Angels, but she did not care much about them either. It seemed to me that, in her mind, if they had been dismissed by the Priestesses, they were somehow not as valuable or important to the Goddess and nor, by extension, to her.

Gladia frowned. 'What changes does she want to make and why?' She had expected that Ambar might want to change the agreement or even end it, but not that the Queen herself might intervene. Gladia knew that she held no sway over the views of the Queen at all.

Ambar looked down into the fire. He was married to Lunaria and was also her envoy, her Vizier. In the end, it was Lunaria who decided what might happen.

Sometimes it was Ambar who charmed her into agreeing with him, but she also took counsel from her DreamReader, Silene. The way that Ambar had described it, Silene did not trust or like him, and took every opportunity to influence Lunaria with her foretellings and her dreams. I had long thought the old fortune teller who had given me such a dark future a full age ago had been Silene herself. There again, I reminded myself, she had told me that I would need to flee with my children, and I had none of them and nor was I likely to, so she was wrong. Ambar drew a breath.

'The Queen does not think it prudent to continue the arrangement exactly as it is.'

'Perhaps it would not be *prudent* to continue with the so-called Angels at all,' retorted Gladia. 'It is abhorrent and wrong. Surely there must be another way?' We all fell silent.

'There is another way, which the Queen prefers,' replied Ambar, quietly. 'From now on, when an Angel is delivered to you, they will not know anything of what has gone on before. They will remember nothing at all of what has happened. The arrangement may only continue if you do not ever speak with those who come to live here about their past lives as Angels. They will not remember, and it will be distressing to them to learn about it. You must instead tell them that they have been ill through being with child and it has caused them to lose their memories.'

Gladia opened her mouth indignantly to speak, but Ambar continued to speak.

'I know this is not what you want, Gladia, nor you, Talla.' He turned to me, and his gaze softened. 'I owe you a debt of gratitude for your assistance. It is for this very reason that this new home of yours for them may continue. But it must surely be better for the Angels to have no memory of that which they find distressing?

Imagine if there were a means by which one could forget difficult times in one's life, and not feel that sorrow or suffering.'

I leaned back so that my netela fell over my face. The thought that there could be a way in which to forget the kind of pain which sat so heavily in my heart was suddenly very appealing to me. Perhaps it could take away my pain at the loss of my beloved. But that, I realised quickly, would mean that I would have to forget all about Ravin too, and give up on all of my happy memories as well as the ones which caused me pain. It was not normal to not feel a painful memory. It was almost like living the event again. I thought of Bellis and the other women whom Gladia had cared for over the past seven years. Then again, surely, they would not want to remember any part of their life as an Angel?

Gladia was clearly thinking about the same thing. She frowned, and the lines on her forehead and around her eyes creased deeply. She opened her mouth again, and once more Ambar spoke first.

'There is no negotiating this, Gladia. I must either have agreement on this or it will all come to an end, as I am sure you were expecting anyway. If you agree, there will be fewer of them. They will have little memory of their life as an Angel when they come to you. The things they learnt earlier in their lives, like cooking and cleaning and simple skills of life like that they will know, but they will not know any detail of where they have been or who they are, aside from their name and that they have been serving the Goddess. You can tell them they have been ill and are now recovering and then accustom them to life here.'

I could see Gladia trying to make sense of this. If she objected, then that would be the end of the agreement she had struck with Ambar an age ago. The women she cared for had become her main interest in life and she did a good job of preparing them for their new lives. But before, they had spoken with one another and with Bellis about what they had experienced, and they had mostly found a sort of acceptance of it and a relief that they could commence a new life. How far would she have to change things to make it work? Bellis and Maren both knew Ambar, and both knew that it was he who arranged for the women to be left at Mellia. What would Gladia be able to say to them about this new arrangement?

'And how is this achieved?' she asked finally, her mind still turning. 'How can you make someone forget something so powerful and so painful?'

'It is a new physic,' replied Ambar. 'When it is given, a person forgets the hours ahead of them. It is a simple thing, but, in the end, it is surely kinder to not remember. It does them no harm.'

Gladia gaped at him. 'I have never heard of such a terrible thing; it cannot be real.'

Ambar laughed. 'It is certainly real. We have used this physic for some time now, in truth, and it works well, and with no other effect.' I wished that Tarik was still here now. His knowledge of herbs and tinctures, tonics and salves was extensive, and if this physic were real, he might know of it. Though, as Ambar had said it was new, perhaps it would be new to him too.

'It comes from far away,' said Ambar. 'It is from the Isles of Soora. Those who live there are bound to the Goddess and spend their time making all manner of useful physic.' He looked away. I had not heard of this place nor its inhabitants, but it was clearly known to Ambar, and I wondered in what ways the other things they made were useful.

Gladia looked dubious. She knew that Ambar was either going to walk away or she would have to agree to his terms.

'I will have to agree. You give me no choice after all. But it does not please me. I do not believe that the Goddess herself can be pleased by it either.' She got up abruptly, the movement of her robe pushing a puff of air towards the fire and making it flare. 'And furthermore, if I am not happy with how these women are, I will stop the arrangement myself. It was only ever to help them to escape and live a normal life. You should go now. We do not need you here anymore.' Gladia set her chin firmly and turned to go towards her dwelling, leaving me with instructions to wait until Ambar had left before storing the embers in the emberjar.

Ambar shifted uncomfortably, aware of me staring at him, my distaste scribed on my face.

'It is not of my doing,' he protested finally. 'I did not choose this. It was Lunaria who decreed it. She has ... distaste ... for what occurs with the Angels. And yet she wishes it to continue because the Goddess apparently decreed it through Ashkana. It is scribed at the Temples and in the dreams of that woman, Silene, the DreamReader. To her, it is kinder to the Angels that they should not remember how they are used.'

'But how do they understand when they become heavy with child?' I asked finally, still trying to understand this new development. 'If they do not remember being with a man, how can they know?'

'Lunaria has said that when it becomes clear that they are with child, they are told that the Goddess has blessed them and that this is part of their life. Because their babies come from the Goddess, they are returned to the Temple to be raised there. They live in a different dwelling and when it is the time for them to give birth, they have the physic again and the baby is born and returned to the Temple without any trouble, and the Angels return to work.'

'That is cruel,' I retorted, the anger rising in me, white hot. 'How could she do something like that, and even more, how could you let her?

Ambar slumped down. The dark shadows from the ebbing fire flickered on his face. He looked both disappointed and strangely bereft.

'It has come to the time when the Queen needs to give birth to her heirs. You have known, from the first time we met, that the Queen's destiny is to produce a daughter as the heir to the throne, one who will maintain the lineage and way of life that has been going for so long. Her own mother, the Lady Paradox, gave birth to DoubleSouls, as you know. But Lunaria is not blessed by the Goddess with children and Silene counsels her that the time is coming. It is she who has come up with this physic plan. She has twisted it round so that Lunaria believes that if she does this, she will be even more blessed by the Goddess and have a child of her own. That maintaining the old ways is what the Goddess wants. Furthermore, she tells Lunaria that it may be my fault, that perhaps I am not, after all, destined to father her children. In fact,' he laughed sharply.' Unless the Queen is with child in the next year, she will take a new husband. She assures me it is nothing to do with whether or not she loves me, but for the love of the land and the Goddess.'

He stood up suddenly. 'I have said too much, forgive me. I am sorry to burden you with my own troubles at this time when you have so many of your own. It has been good to see you again, Talla. I wish I could see you more often, but it cannot be.' He shrugged a little sadly. 'I hope that your pain lessens, and that your life is rich.' Before I could reply, he had gone, as he always did, ebbing away into the darkness without a sound. Automatically, I stood up and began to take out the embers to put in the emberjar for Gladia to use the next day. You could not tell that they were hot just from looking at them, but rather you would need to touch them to feel their true heat. So it was with people. You could not tell, just from looking at them, who they really were.

I made my way to my sleeping mat and lay down, my mind turning over what I had just learned. I was angry, but there was also a strange and nagging curiosity about such a physic that could make you forget what might occur. I wondered if one took it, if it could provide a service to those like me who wished to forget their pain. Or perhaps there was another stronger form that could make you forget what had happened? But no, if I were to possess such a thing, it would make me forget everything. Not just the death of Ravin, but also every good thing that had happened since I had met him, every good feeling he had given me, every time he had made me laugh or kissed me or told me about something he had discovered from reading old scrolls. I would even forget what he looked like. This would surely be far worse than me being sad because he was no longer with me.

Could it really be true that something could happen to you, and you would never know that it had happened? Was it truly as Ambar said, and that this was done out of consideration for the Angels? This I did not believe. That was merely the story he had decided upon to justify it to me and Gladia, and maybe even himself. Gladia and I and the others had seen the effect of the OutRiders use of the Angels on the women who came to Gladia to be cared for and on Bellis herself. It had been through Bellis that we had first learned of the despicable truth behind the tales of Angels building

Temples in one night and the real reasons they were kept for the OutRiders. We had also learned that they were the Maids who had been discarded from the Temple by the Priestesses: those not chosen to remain as Priestesses were released into the Outer and recaptured by the OutRiders for use as Angels. The Temple and the OutFort, it seemed, worked together on this system since both gained from it. I resolved to speak more to Gladia about it at another time. Eventually I fell asleep and dreamed strange dreams about drinking the physic and it making me remember everything rather than forgetting everything. Waking up, I wondered which might be worse.

Chapter 4

Gladia was quieter than usual the following day. She frowned when I asked her if she had thought more about what Ambar had said. Of course, she had done nothing but think about it. But what could she do? She could not go to the Court of the Queen and demand that they stop. She could do nothing for the Angels except what she had been doing already.

'We cannot all change everything to how we would like it to be. All we can do is to try and make small changes for the better. If I asked some of the women who have been here in Mellia, even those who have left for a new life somewhere else, if they would choose to be able to forget what had happened to them, or to never know what had happened to them, they might choose the forgetting.' She looked at me sharply. Her short hair was flecked with grey now, and her eyes were lined with the folds of wisdom. 'All we can do is see what happens when the first of these women who forget is left with us. I assume they will remember their time in the Temple but not their time as Angels after they leave, so I will have to tell them that this is what happens to some of those who leave the Temple, that they begin a new life in the Outer. After all, we managed with you, didn't we?' She chuckled suddenly, remembering those early days when I knew nothing about life in the Outer, and I found myself smiling too, recalling when I first arrived in Mellia as a drab, as they called us, and of meeting Benakiell and Gladia and Achillea for the first time. It seemed both long ago and only yesterday.

While Gladia pondered what to tell Bellis and Maren, who were the only other ones in Mellia to know about the arrangement which had been made, I walked down to the gardens where the sun was already beating down on the flatbread grain and the tomatoes and pumpkins. Each day, when it got to its hottest, the plants seemed to hang their heads and droop, unable to cope with the intensity of the sun and then the cool of the evening and the absence of those bright rays would restore them. The balance of life seemed more evident to me these days. There could not be bright sun without darkness, nor searing heat without sharp cold. There could not be forgetting without remembering or sleeping without waking or grief without love.

I took a flat basket and began to harvest some of the grain so that it could be ground to flour later. It was back breaking work. You had to bend down to the stems of long grain grass and cut them off at the ground and then put them in the basket to be threshed later. When I had first arrived in Mellia, there had not been much grain grown, as there were not many people in the village, and many people preferred to trade other things which were easier to grow and harvest and exchange them for the grain at the market in Sanguinea. But Gladia had thought it a good idea to teach the women how to be able to grow all their own food, and besides it gave them more to do. Gladia and Ashkana were perhaps not so different, I thought, amused suddenly by this thought. Both were fond of telling others what to do and of holding them accountable if they got it wrong, and both firmly believed in the value of hard work, though, certainly in

Gladia's case, it was usual for that hard work to be done by others. I bent down again and was grateful for the focus I gave to the harvest, because it stopped me from thinking about other things. Eventually, when the basket was full, I trudged with it to the threshing floor and tipped it out onto the smooth clay floor, ready to be threshed.

Benakiell had supervised the construction of the threshing floor at Gladia's request. He still came back to Mellia three or four times a year but most of the time he lived in Kashiq, with Shira. She did not usually accompany him when he came back to visit, preferring to stay in her own land. She always sent cakes for Gladia with Benakiell when he came, and Gladia looked forward to them almost as much as she looked forward to seeing Benakiell, now resigned to the fact that he would never see her as more than an old friend. He had returned to Kashiq shortly after Ravin's death. He guarded the pain of his loss to himself. First his apprentice, Ashtun, had been killed by the OutRider and now Ravin, with whom he had spent so many pleasant times discussing the finer points of dwelling making and ingenious inventions, had died. He had said to me, before he left, a few days later, that he felt that it was wrong for such a young man to die when there was he, Benakiell, an aging man with a permanent limp, still alive. Like me, he did not want to share his grief, but to nurse it, as a mother nurses a child.

Angrily, I pushed the pile of grain so that it spread itself over the smooth oiled clay floor and left it so it could dry there for a few more days before it could be threshed. What was I really doing here? What was I getting out of being here, apart from spending more time on my own? Surely, I could now just go back to Pirhan, without telling Achillea that I had returned, for a week or so and spend time by myself in my own dwelling without having to be in Mellia or in Gabez. Gladia was now preoccupied with the questions in her mind about how long she would be able to continue working with the Angels, and how she would deal with women who had no memories of what had happened to them. It seemed unlikely, now that he had delivered his message about the Angels, that Ambar would return to Mellia, and he would probably not be seen again for some time. I had enjoyed meeting him and talking of his time at the OutFort as a child, but that time was now over.

I could not see how we could simply talk again when he had so suddenly changed our knowledge of the Angels and what now happened to them. I felt almost as if I heard the voice of one of the Priestesses who were in charge of us when we were young; brisk, and firm and with an expectation of being obeyed.

'Get on with your work, Maids. You are not here to ask foolish questions, nor to expect wise answers to them. The Goddess, bless her name, does not expect questions nor give answers. If answers are needed, they will come through your work.'

And yet, there was, in the emberjar of my mind, so long a place of gentle warmth since I had met Ravin, a glowing shard of angry heat. I could not see how this new development would change things. For surely, the Angels were still women, no less than I was, or Achillea or Gladia or the Queen herself. How could it be right that they could be used and yet be unaware of being used? But if this physic of forgetting could truly make them forget and feel no pain, was it not a good thing? And then again, was it not a very dangerous thing, because there may have been some part of the OutRiders which prevented them from visiting the worst pain on the Angels simply because they knew it would be remembered. Now, they could do anything they wanted to the Angels without fear of reprisal. I could not think what could be done to stop this happening, nor what the consequences might be for the Angels. If it were to suddenly stop, a Maid from the Temple who had been taken by the OutRiders to be an Angel and who was already taking the physic of forgetting would suddenly find herself in a position of great horror. Would that not be even worse? These questions with no answers chased their tails furiously in my mind. I had had enough. I would leave and start travelling back to Pirhan. I would tell Gladia that I would try to catch up with Achillea and Tarik, although I had no intention of doing so. Since I would, from now on, be on my own, with no Ravin and no children, I should begin to accustom myself to it.

I wanted to be on my own so that I could cry without someone trying to comfort me or talk me out of my grief. I dropped the basket onto the floor of the threshing area and walked back to the dwelling. There, I hastily began to parcel up the things I wanted to take with me. Luckily for me, it had been one of those trips where Ravin had brought a large quantity of things with him to Mellia to trade and so there had been little room for his own things. I took with me his robe and trousers and briefly held the robe to my face to breathe in his scent. It was already fading. I had slept with it after his death, and that familiar scent was ebbing away. I could not preserve it and soon enough, although I might crave it, I would not be able to conjure it up, only to know that it was not there. Achillea and Tarik had taken some of the tools and less important things back with them and so there was little left for me to add to my own bundle: the clothing, his beard comb and his scented oil, his metal nibbed scribing pens and his rolls of plant parchment, and the little bag of dried fruits which he carried everywhere with him and often absentmindedly chewed on while he scribed or drew or considered a new invention. Inside the pouch were dried figs and dates, sugared orange rinds and honeyed almonds, salted pistachios and dried darkberries. I took one piece, imagining it as a gift from Ravin.

'Take another, Talla,' I thought I heard him say, 'You know you want to.' And so I did, and the sharp yet sweet taste of the sugared orange mixed with the soft, heavy sweetness of the date. It did not take me long to bundle my things together after that and then I went to find Gladia to tell her I was leaving.

On the way, as I walked down the path, I saw Jember aiming rocks at a tree. He was using his sling, and apparently aiming for some small target scratched on the tree. I had not spoken much with him since Ravin's death, and now I hesitated. He had always got on well with both Ravin and Tarik, and was a bright youth, curious and eager to learn. He had also sought out their company. Living as he did with two women, his mother Bellis and her partner Maren, he felt the need to spend more time with men, and since Benakiell was seen less frequently in Mellia these days, he had looked forward to the times when we visited. I called over to him and he turned, startled. I walked over to him and asked him how he was. He shrugged his shoulders in that way that is common to all as they move into the Third Age of childhood. He was taller than me now, well built for his age. He still had those long curly eyelashes I remembered from when he was a little boy, though, and in happier times, a ready and mischievous smile.

'I miss Ravin,' he said, simply. He was the first person who had said that to me. Concerned as they were for my feelings, and not wanting to upset me, they held in their own feelings of grief and loss. And yet to me, it was worse not to know that they too were missing him, that they too felt his absence as much as they had felt his presence. Jember had not yet learned to not always say what he thought, and his comment was a blessing to me, even though of course it made me sad too. He aimed another stone at the tree and shot at it, the rock glancing off the bark and leaving a scratch along it. He glanced at me, a little shyly.

'Do you want to have a go?' He proffered the sling and a handful of stones.

'Tarik told me that this was what he used to do at my age,' he explained. Having heard Ambar's description of life for the boys of the OutFort, I could imagine them all honing their skills with their slings, perhaps using those pouches of treasured pebbles. I took it from Jember. I had never used one before. In Oramia, only the men used them, and it was not one of those skills which was taught equally to men and women. Jember did not seem to have learned this, however. The sling was made from a back patch of soft leather and long cords of braided bark. It had been well used since Benakiell had first made it for Jember when he was still only a small boy. As he got older, the length of the sling cord was increased, which in turn increased its reach and power. Jember selected a stone from a small pile he had gathered next to him and showed me how to place the stone and then pull through the cords and loop one cord to my finger and hold the knotted end of the other.

'Just let go of the knot when you want the stone to be thrown. As long as you have the loop round your finger, only the stone will be thrown, not the whole thing.' Jember smiled at me. I had been in a hurry to leave, and yet here I was, being taught how to use a sling by a boy, instead of getting on my way. But he missed Ravin as I did and I wanted to share this time with him, as Ravin would have done, with interest and concentration, always intent on learning something new.

The first few times I released the knot at the wrong time and the stone flew away in the wrong direction, but once I had worked out where I needed the sling to be in the air before I let the knot go, I began to enjoy the focus it brought to my mind. It was a good way to occupy myself, an activity that needed both my mind and body to work together in companionship and one in which there was no space for thinking of anything else. Eventually one of my rocks hit the tree I had been aiming at and I turned triumphantly to Jember.

'You see! You can do it! Now you will just have to practice until you can aim for a smaller and smaller target.' Jember congratulated me and turned to find more stones, but I stopped him to explain that I would have to go, that I was now planning on returning to Pirhan for a while. His face fell and he kicked out at a bush bad-temperedly. 'Why does everyone I like want to leave me? Benakiell seems to spend more and more time in Kashiq with Shira who he never brings to see us anyway, Ravin is dead, Tarik has gone back to Gabez with his own son, and now you are leaving too!'

I was surprised by his outburst. I had not realised how much he wanted us around him, especially the men, and then I realised that, without a father, he relied on these men to talk to and to guide him. There were other boys in the village, but he did not mix much with them, nor with their fathers. His mother, Bellis, had always kept him close to her when he was a small boy, and now that he was older, he only had the close relationships that he had been allowed to make then. Perhaps he had always thought of Tarik and later Ravin as being like his unknown father might have been. Now that Tarik and Achillea had a son of their own, he must have felt left out, and he had lost Ravin too. If only Ravin could have known that there was a boy who thought of him as being like a father, it would have made him so happy.

'I am sorry, Jember,' I said. 'I will be back to visit you soon, or perhaps you can come to visit me and see Tarik and Achillea in Gabez.' Jember's eyes lit up at my impulsive suggestion and I added, cautiously, 'If Bellis agrees, of course.'

'I am nearly a man,' said Jember, pushing his chest out a little as he did when he was a small child. 'She cannot make me stay here forever.'

'There is time enough to be grown up,' I said. 'Now you had better practice hard with that sling and I will do the same. When I next see you, I will be better than you!'

Jember snorted. 'You will never be better than me!' He hastily began to collect more stones to practice his aim. I waved to him and set off to tell Gladia and leave for Pirhan.

Chapter 5

The place where I chose to stay the night, on the way back to Pirhan, was a well-known stopping place for travellers. There were a few Paradox trees and some large rocks clustered next to a small stream. There were usually a few people there, but not today. I did not often travel alone except to the markets, but I had sometimes gone to Gabez from Pirhan when Ravin had been travelling away himself. Since I had met Ravin, he had almost always been with me on longer journeys, and it felt strange to be on my own now, even though that was what I had been longing for. I coaxed the embers in the emberjar back to life and made a small fire, just big enough to heat up some water for coffee and warm a flatbread. I ate and drank mechanically, my eyes half watching the flames as they crackled and spat, their golden light making the shadows dance. I thought back on my conversation with Jember and smiled wryly as I realised that I would have to either trade for a sling at the market or make one of my own. Ravin would have loved the challenge and would, no doubt, have spent weeks reading scrolls about different kinds of slings, in order to make sure he had the best advantage. Perhaps I might do the same; I would need something to occupy my mind.

I had tied my cloth to a wooden frame which a traveller had made and left. This was often done, especially by those who travelled frequently. It afforded some shelter from the wind and the rain in the season, and from the sun during the day when it was hot. Since I was on my own, it felt safer for some reason to be inside. I heard the noise of someone walking closer to me. Perhaps there was another traveller after all, although it was late, and the stars had risen in the sky like sparks from the fire.

'Would you like some company?' A familiar voice spoke softly in the darkness. Startled, I looked to my left and there, melting out of the shadows as usual, was Ambar. He remained where he was until I told him to come and sit down. I was still angry with him over the new plans for the Angels, but it seemed to me that the plans came more from Lunaria and her Dreamreader, Silene, than they did from Ambar. He did have power and a certain degree of sway over the Queen and her decisions, but, like everyone else, in the end, it was her choice.

Also, I did feel safer that there was another person there with me, even though I was not given to flights of imagination about the dark. To me, the night had always felt kind and enveloping, and besides, it was never really so dark at night that one could see nothing. Coming from the bright light of the day, it sometimes felt like one would never see clearly again but if you allowed yourself time to adjust, gradually you could make out shapes and tinges of light from the moon and the stars. I looked around me for signs of the OutRiders who normally accompanied Ambar at a discreet distance but could see and hear nothing. He saw me looking.

'They are down the hill,' he said, waving an arm. 'Do not worry about them.'

I could not think why I should worry about them while Ambar was there anyway, so I dismissed them from my mind. I added water to the coffee on the fire and then realised that I had only one drinking vessel with me and explained that to Ambar.

'I do have a small flask with me with something to drink in it anyway,' he replied. 'You can try some if you like, although I warn you that it is very strong. It is something else from the Isles of Soora; it is a kind of honey drink, honeywine they call it.' He reached to his carrysack and drew out a small flask made of honeygold and embossed with the sign of the Queen, that same symbol that had appeared on the brooch that had been left pinned to my blanket when I was left at the Temple as a baby. The central honeycomb shape was in some sort of reddened metal, just like the brooch had had a dark red central stone. I looked at him dubiously. He laughed.

'I will drink from it first so that you know it is not poison,' he reassured me, still chuckling. 'Though why I would want to harm one of my oldest friends, I cannot tell you!' He took a mouthful from the flask, rolled it round his mouth and swallowed it. Leaning closer, he wiped the neck and offered it to me. I could smell a sweet, honey scent on it which enticed me. I reached for it and took a tentative sip of the liquid inside.

It filled my mouth with the taste of honey and fire rolled into one. Just as I started to think that it was too sweet, the feeling of fire would intervene, and then, in turn, just when that was becoming too powerful, the sweetness of the honey taste would take over. I could see why Ambar had rolled it around in his mouth, because doing so prolonged the pulsing contrasts of flavour. I wondered how it was made and asked Ambar.

'I have no idea,' he admitted, frankly. 'It has clearly got honey in it but what the other is, I cannot tell you, only that it is not only in the mouth that it has that surprising impact. Later, it makes you feel happier and warmer inside too.' I looked down at my cup of coffee which suddenly seemed unappealing. Ambar took another drink from the flask and passed it to me again. This time I took a longer drink, and again the sensation of the strange honey drink filled my senses.

'Shall I tell you more about growing up in the OutFort?' asked Ambar, after we had shared the flask several more times. I felt pleasantly warm and peaceful, though my mind seemed to think more slowly. I did not want this feeling of warmth to go, nor did I want to be on my own when Ambar left. Sometimes, Ravin had told me stories of Kashiq when we lay on our sleeping mat at night, and his voice would fill my mind with tales of the gods and goddesses and with fables of how the animals came to be made, and all manner of other stories. Ravin was as good at drawing stories with his words as he was at drawing pictures with his pen. Often, I would go to sleep while he was still talking to me and would pass seamlessly from his story into a dream of my own making. Ambar, too, had a warm voice to listen to and I did want to hear more of what he said.

He began to tell me of some of the smaller things that he did at the OutFort. I would have liked to have known what they told the boys about women and about the Angels, but Ambar told me instead of being taught to cook and to find food off the land. Whereas in the Temple we had learned to grow crops in the gardens, each set out with the colour of the day, in the OutFort, they were taught to be able to find things to eat from wherever they were, as well as growing crops. They learned the plants of the Outer and which could be eaten or how to prepare them. They learned which foods could be dried in the sun and which must be eaten immediately. Of course, everyone knew how to make a fire from an emberjar, but they also learned how to make fire without an emberjar by using sparking rocks. From being quite small boys, they learned to use the sling and the bow to kill small animals to eat. I intervened at this point.

'I am going to learn to use a sling! Jember showed me what to do before I left Mellia. I am going to practice until I can beat him!'

'Are you indeed?' Ambar laughed out loud, his white teeth gleaming in the firelight.

Indignantly I turned to him, ready to defend my right to use the sling, even though it was not a job for women, when I realised that he was teasing me. He reached once more into his carrysack and drew out a sling. It was beautifully crafted, with embossed leather patterns on the cradle for the stone and multicoloured plaited leather cords. He handed it to me and picked up a small stone from near the fire.

'Show me how you would prepare to shoot it. But don't let go of the string. I am not sure I trust your aim!'

I took the stone and placed it into the cradle. My fingers fumbled with the cords. The honeyed drink made me move as if I were in honey too, slow and sticky. Eventually, when I had rested it where I wanted it, I pulled the strings tight through, sliding one finger through the loop in the cord and holding the knotted end between the other fingers.

'Come here and let me show you a better way.'

Ambar moved around so that he was behind me and reached around me and over my shoulder to position my fingers differently. He mimicked how to let go of the knotted thread and it was a quicker, more intuitive way of doing it. He kept his hand on top of mine and briefly, I leaned against him, relieved to be able to depend on another person, if only for a while.

'I wish I could forget,' I said, dreamily, the honey drink slurring the edges of my understanding. 'I wish I could forget everything, just for one night. Maybe you are right, maybe it is better to forget things that should not happen than to remember them. Ravin should not be dead, and I would like to not remember that, if only for a little while.'

'But you would not remember that you had forgotten,' said Ambar, gently. Obstinately, I disagreed.

'My heart would know, even if my mind did not recall,' I insisted, the tears beginning again. 'Where can I get this physic of forgetting? Is it safe? Have you tried it before?'

Ambar reached to his pouch and pulled out a small, stoppered cylinder, once more made of honeygold. This time without the symbol of the Queen.

'I have some here,' he said. 'I have not tried it myself, but I have seen others who have. If you want to take it, I will stay with you.'

'But then it *will* be remembered, won't it?' I asked slowly, trying to understand. 'If you are here, you will remember for me, and then what will be the point?' Somewhere in my mind, a thought was glowing, but it was too elusive for me to grasp. 'To be truly forgotten, it must be forgotten by all.'

Ambar looked at me again, his face half in the shadows and half in the dancing firelight.

'Why not?' He murmured, half to himself, and his words drifted over me like woodsmoke.

Then, turning to look me in the eye, he said, 'I will take it too. There is enough here for both of us.' He poured some of the bottle's contents into my cup of tepid coffee and waited for me before he raised the bottle to his own lips and drank it at the same time as me.

Then we sat for some time by the fire, unable to find the words to say. I began to feel tired and yawned. Ambar moved next to me, and, without thinking, I leaned against him, tired of holding myself up on my own. He put his arm around my shoulders and, as I leaned my head against his shoulder, lay his own head on top of mine.

Chapter 6

A bird call woke me. It repeated the same few notes over and over again, wanting to speak and yet not knowing how to make the words. I opened my eyes and saw the sun through the faded red cloth above me and wondered where I was. The travellers' camp. Of course. I was on my way back to Pirhan. I lay under a cloth I did not recognise, a heavy green cloth which smelt faintly of cedarwood and cinnamon. I struggled to my feet, my head swimming, and my tongue thick in my dry mouth. Why did I feel like this? I made my way out from the cloth frame to find a fire already lit and a pot of water heating up. There was no sign of anyone else. It felt as if I were still in a dream. I sat down, befuddled, by the fire and made coffee through force of habit.

The bird continued to call until I thought it would never stop. It prevented me from thinking clearly. Every time I felt like I had grasped my mind, the bird's call would interject, and I would be cast adrift again. I drank the coffee slowly, realising that it was not my usual coffee, but a much richer variety. I looked around me and saw nobody else. I stood up and scanned the horizon in every direction, but it was empty, save for occasional small trees which jutted out of the red dust and the rocky outcrops. I looked east towards the sun and Pirhan, and the golden light showed me that it was shortly after dawn. My mind, bewildered, was trying to tell me something. But I felt curiously peaceful, as if I had been rested by sleeping for a very long time, so I sat down again by the fire, savouring the coffee, and chewing absentmindedly on some dried fruit and nuts which had been left in a small wooden box by the fire. Who had left me these things? Was it Ravin?

Ravin. He was dead and buried. The knowledge came to me as if from far away. Everything in the emberjar of my mind was as if it were covered in a thick layer of fine, powdery ash. My mind had been softened and blurred around the edges and when I tried to grasp at thoughts, they kept sliding away from me. I reached into the small box and took out the last few pieces of dates and almonds, along with something else which lay at the bottom of the box. I lifted it out and held it up. It was a small pendant made of honeygold. It was in the shape of a sun, with a smooth circular centre and a ring of thin rays of different lengths, made from silver wires which had been cunningly inserted into the central disc. Ravin would have liked to have seen it, I mused, and he would have worked out how to make it himself. I turned it over thoughtfully, but it had nothing engraved on either side. It reminded me of the bee pendant I had once been given by Ambar.

Ambar. He had been here last night. I remembered seeing him here, by the fire. I tried to recall what we had talked about, but I could only recall something about using a sling and how Ambar had hunted with one when he was a boy. Later, I remembered drinking something sweet and potent with him and then nothing more. I shook myself, trying to make the memories fall better into place. 'Try and remember,' I urged myself, out loud, my voice sounding oddly loud in that quiet place, just like the insistent birdsong. Remember. I was trying to, but I had forgotten what had happened. Forgetting. Ambar had told us about a new physic of

57

forgetting, something taken by the Angels so that they forgot the difficulties in their lives. I had wanted it. I thought I remembered taking it. It was in a small metal flask. I wanted to take it to forget that Ravin was dead. I did not want to constantly remember what I had lost. Had I taken it? I recalled, as if in a shaded echo, that Ambar said he would take it too. But where was he now?

He must have left the heavy green cloth over me, for it was not mine. He it must have been who had left the coffee and the box of fruit and nuts for me, and the pendant of the sun. But why had he gone? And if we had both taken the physic, how would I ever know what I had forgotten? The day before, it had seemed very important to me that everything should be forgotten, and now my mind wanted nothing more than to remember. I began to slowly put the things away with the rest of my bundles which were as I had left them. I did not know what to do with the things which Ambar had left but thought I would take them with me. Perhaps I would meet him on the way ahead.

I finished off the coffee and filled up my emberjar before covering the remains of the fire with dirt to quench the flames. I took down the faded red cloth I had used as a cover over the wooden travellers' sleeping framework and folded it up, feeling the warmth it had already absorbed from the sun which now shone brightly. I folded up the green cloth too and wondered idly why it was green. Did the OutRiders also have an attachment to the colours of the days? They never wore colours when they wore their leather armour, but perhaps they too were assigned a colour for their birthday by the Priestesses. After all, the OutRiders came from the babies abandoned at the Temples too. Next time I saw Ambar, I would ask him, along with other things which I now wanted to know, like if he knew what had happened last night. The box was pushed into the top of one of my bundles, and the sun pendant was put in my underpocket to keep it safe.

I checked the fire was out, put my carrysack on my back, hung the other bundles off my shoulders and set off on the path to the east, towards Pirhan. As my head got clearer, I knew my plans remained the same: to go back to our dwelling in Pirhan and to spend some days there on my own before letting Achillea and Tarik know that I was back. I had told them that I would go to their dwelling on my return from Mellia, so they would assume that I was still in Mellia with Gladia, and Gladia would assume that I was in Gabez with Achillea.

My mind worked at what had happened during the time I had forgotten. It had been the evening, and I had been staying at the travellers' rest place when Ambar arrived. I recalled faint snatches of conversation between us, me mentioning Jember teaching me the sling and Ambar telling me how he had used it in the OutFort. I remembered the taste of honey, in a drink. Ambar telling me he would take the physic too. And then, it was as if I were trying to look down a dark well. There were faint shadows and soft echoing noises, but nothing was clear. No doubt I had just fallen asleep, and so had Ambar, and then he had left before I awoke. But I could not ever know. Perhaps he had wandered off and then woken up and not remembered where he was. I had no way of finding out unless or until I saw Ambar again, and that was always at a time of his choosing, not mine. Nevertheless, despite my concerns in the light of day, it did seem as if I had lost a small amount of the weight of grief that I had carried around with me since Ravin's death. If nothing else, the physic had been a powerful inducement to heavy sleep.

BROWN

Chapter 7

Ravin had arranged for me to have some beehives
made in Pirhan. He had got to know our
neighbour, a man named Gurshan who let me
keep them in his orchards, in the Kashiqi way. He grew
oranges, mostly, but also jasmine, for the oil, and the
honey made by my bees was sweet and fragrant.
Gurshan let me keep the bees there in exchange for
some honey when I harvested it. I had grown
accustomed to the clay pipe hives of Kashiq, and each
year, when it was the feast of the Goddess, Ravin would
arrange and trade for a new pottery cover for me, of his
own design. There were five of them altogether, each
with a different image: an orange, a bee, a scroll, a tree,
and a sun. The sun was the last one I had received from
Ravin, and he had drawn the sun so that it was right in
the centre of the cover, with the door for the bees in the
middle of the sun. I had with me several small clay jars
in which to put the honey. Pirhan was right on the edge
of the river, and one of the main occupations was
working with clay. The potters, under Maliq's

guidance, took the clay from the riverbanks and shaped all manner of different vessels which they traded very successfully, especially in Gabez, which lay only a short distance away over the river in Oramia.

As I bent down to scoop some of the honey out of my draining tray, I felt sick, my head spinning. I put the clay jar down carefully, and sat down, my stomach turning over the coffee and flatbread I had eaten earlier. I had also eaten a handful of walnuts, and perhaps it was those that had made me feel unwell. I dipped my finger in the honey which had dripped through the wooden grid on which the honey was resting and ate it slowly, waiting for the feeling to pass. Honey always seemed to soothe me when I felt unwell, and the feeling soon faded, and I carried on with my work.

I had still not decided what to do, nor where to live. My best friends all lived in Oramia, except for Benakiell but he was a long way to the northwest of Pirhan. On the other hand, the man I had loved so much, Ravin, was from Kashiq, and I couldn't help feeling that staying in Kashiq would make me feel closer to his soul. I was going to go and visit Achillea and Tarik and the children in Gabez. I had been back to see them once, a few days after I had returned, just briefly, to tell them that I would be going back to Pirhan but that I would come and see them again soon. I was planning to visit the next day once I had harvested the honey so I could take it over the bridge to Oramia to trade. I also had some of Ravin's tools to take to Tarik, since he would make more use of them than me. I had a basket of oranges which Gurshan had traded with me for some more honey and which I knew I could trade in Gabez.

Once the honey had dripped down into the tray, leaving the beeswax honeycomb at the top, I poured it carefully into the clay pots I had brought with me, and stoppered them with plaited palm leaf stoppers. The honeycomb I rolled into a ball, squeezing out the rest of the honey, and wrapped the beeswax in a cloth I kept for that purpose. The empty tray I added a little water to and left by the beehives as a gift to the bees. It may have been fanciful, but I believe that they knew that I meant them no harm and were happy to share the honey with me, especially when I left them something, and soon the bees were crowding round the tray, drinking up the honey water with alacrity.

The dwelling was dark and cool when I got in from the trip to the orchard, and I was grateful for the respite from the sun. My eyes were still dazzled green with the sun's bright light, and I tripped over the corner of one of Ravin's baskets of parchments. In the Tower of the Wise, in Arbhoun, and in other cities of Kashiq, parchments on which wisdom of various kinds and stories and poetry were scribed, were kept so that all who could read could share freely in what the scribe had sought to say. Ravin had his own collection of such scrolls and parchments, some scribed by him, some scribed by me, and some scribed by others which he had acquired or traded for. There were five baskets in all, and Ravin had sorted them into groups according to what was scribed on them. They were all important to me because they were important to Ravin, and, as I had finished my packing, I decided to read through some of them.

Since I had got back from Mellia and the unsettling interlude with Ambar and the physic of forgetting, I had not been assailed by the heavy waves of grief which had at first crippled me. It was perhaps that the pain of the initial injury had now passed, but I was still not, and never would be, the same person that I had once been. I was getting accustomed to a life where a part of me was missing, as if a limb had been cut off. I could, of course, live my life without that limb, but it would always be more difficult, and I would never feel quite as whole again. I wondered whether the physic had helped. Seeing Ravin's recognisable script made me feel as if he were still there, and I thought of what a gift it had been to me that I could read what he scribed, that I could know again his thoughts and ideas almost as if he were talking to me. To be able to read the scribings of another was like a memory, something which became real. The scribings were like Ravin's memories, held forever and by reading them, they could become my memories too.

I picked up the nearest basket, the one I had almost tripped over, and carried it out to the courtyard where there was still cool shade, but also light from the sun to help me to see the scrolls. Some were neatly rolled and tied, but others were on small scraps of parchment. The one thing they all had in common was that they had all been scribed by Ravin. His tight, unadorned scribing was another part of him which brought back memories. From watching him scribe at the Tower of the Wise in Arbhoun where we had first met, to sitting in this very courtyard. Both of us sat with a pen making notes on different things: I scribed about the bees mainly and Ravin would often read scrolls scribed by others and then take out of them the information he needed and then scribe it for himself. I picked out the first piece to try to work out what this basket might concern. It had on it a drawing of some islands, or so it seemed. Certain places had been marked on it, along with mountains and forests. I had seen such things before, drawn by travellers for others to follow and reach the same place. Ravin had titled it at the bottom. 'The Isles of Soora'. I blinked, surprised by the coincidence of Ravin having a parchment drawing of the very same place that

Ambar had mentioned. It was almost as if he had known that I would be curious about it.

There were five islands altogether and they lay in the huge body of water at the very eastern edge of Kashiq. They may have been the very last pieces of land in that water for there was nothing else evident on the map, save a small section of the Kashiqi coast. I wondered how anyone got to them and assumed it must be on a boat like Benakiell's which I had been on once, and that time had been enough for me. Unlike the rhythmic movement of a horse, which I had ridden on several times many years ago, the movement of that little boat on the water had felt uneven to me and somehow uneasy and unpredictable. There were little houses drawn onto the map in different places and a bigger settlement drawn on the main island of Soora. Ambar had said that the physic of forgetting was made on the Isles of Soora by those bound to the Goddess. But why had Ravin copied this picture and kept it? I laid it to one side and selected another parchment scroll. This time it was closely scribed, again by Ravin, for I recognised the neat way in which he laid out the notes he took from other scrolls he had read.

I read through it. It was some notes about certain plants which grew only on the Isles of Soora and their uses in physics and tonics. I looked at them with interest, wondering if they were what the physic of forgetting was made from, but the notes suggested Ravin's interest was in a tree called the Osh tree, which grew on the island of Oshana. I looked back at the drawing of the islands and saw that Soora was the middle island and that Oshana was the furthest island to the east. I read on.

'Osh bark can be made into a tonic which is given to those women who want a child and whom the Goddess has not blessed. It can be taken every day for a week at sunrise before eating or drinking for the best effect, beginning on the day of Soren. It sometimes only needs to be taken for a week before the Goddess will bless the woman. If she is not blessed by the Osh tea and does not become with child after the first month of use, the Goddess's blessing can be enhanced by her husband using the tea also. Osh bark should be collected at a full moon on the day of Soren and crushed before steeping for one week in honey water.'

Beneath these notes, evidently copied from some other scroll or parchment, were more notes in Ravin's hand. Would it be more effective, he asked, if the remedy was taken at the same time of day? Was there a way to acquire this tonic beyond going to the Isles of Soora? Who was the person who had made the original notes, and why? And another shorter note to ask me about honey water and what effect it might have if bark were steeped in it. I had become caught up in this, and I addressed my mind to this question as if I might be able to answer Ravin when he next walked through the door. Perhaps the Osh bark was very bitter, I surmised, or perhaps the honey caused it to release the tonic contained within.

There were several more parchments within the basket, all relating to the Isles of Soora or to remedies which could be taken to make it more certain that the Goddess might bless a couple with a child. I had not known that Ravin had been so busy doing all this study to try to make our dream of having our own child come true. It was typical of him that he would do this, try to find out the answers he wanted and then come to me to explain things. I wondered whether he had been planning to tell me his findings when we returned from Mellia. I imagined that we would have read his notes together and then worked out how to get these tonics from the Isles of Soora in the hope that they might work. It appeared, after all, I reminded myself, that at least one of their other tonics was successful, since I still had no memory of what had happened on the night that I had taken a draught of it. I felt a little sick again at the thought of it.

Reading Ravin's notes had offered me a glance into an imagined future. It could not exist and yet it already did in the emberjar of my mind. It was something which never failed to absorb me; the way that our minds could make and remake events which had happened in the past or were yet to happen in the future almost as if they only existed within our minds. Even if you took a single event witnessed by many, they would all have a different truth to tell about it, each one convinced that their version was correct. But an imagined future with Ravin, however I told it, was impossible. Perhaps I would take the parchments to show to Achillea and Tarik when I went to visit them. An idea began to form in my mind.

I needed something to occupy my mind, to keep it from curving in upon itself, like a snake eating its own tail. Seeing these parchments of Ravin's felt like a message from him to me, a suggestion to me that I should see if I could travel to the Isles of Soora. Yes, it would be a long journey, and I would have to make it alone, for everyone else that I knew was preoccupied with living their own life. But perhaps I could find out more about these plants and maybe even trade for some of the tonics and bring them back with me to study.

Tarik had knowledge and skills of physic, although mainly it was the ones used in the OutFort for injury and he had little knowledge of physics for women, although after three children, he was now learning some of the herbs which offered relief from sickness for Achillea, and together they had made some new tonics and salves which Achillea could trade with the women she knew. Although they still lived in Oramia, they visited me in Pirhan often, and whenever they did, Achillea would visit the Place of Prayer and pray to Soren for her guidance. She sang with others for events in Pirhan, and would sometimes take the salves and tonics there, much of the singing being related to healing in Soren's name or praying for a blessing from the Goddess. She had sung for me before, a song asking for the Goddess's blessing of a child for me and Ravin, but I had found it unsettling and somehow shameful to have my deepest wish sung about out loud. My own thoughts and worries were loud enough inside my head.

There were more parchments to read in the basket, many of them on a similar theme. I had not realised that it had taken up so much of Ravin's thinking. We had spoken of it, but it did not seem to me as if there were much to be done. I wondered whether it was because I had been brought up in the Temple and had escaped it, whether the Goddess was punishing me for taking my fate in my own hands perhaps, but Ravin pointed to the Angels and how being from the Temple did not stop them from having babies. I had tried to put it all out of my head, but it was clear that for Ravin, the search for understanding had gone on. There was a small piece of parchment caught at the bottom of the basket. I recognised my own scribing. I picked it out, curious about what Ravin had kept that I had scribed. It was my account of the warning given to me by the fortune teller, she who I later thought to be Silene, the Dream Reader of the Queen. She had warned me:

'You have journeyed a long way, but it is short compared to where you must now go. You are loved, but that will change, for love is fickle and cannot be trusted. There is one who seeks you out, but he will bring great danger if you ever see him again. Harm will befall your children and all you know if you do not flee this land. You must protect them from those who seek to destroy you. Remember the Goddess in all you do, for she will see your actions and judge you. Your destiny was scribed before you were born.'

I read it again. It was some years since I had last seen the actual words she had spoken, although I remembered it. It was one of the reasons, although I never told Ravin, that I was happy to follow his suggestion that we should live in Pirhan, in Kashiq. Although it was very close to Oramia, it was in another land and so I felt we were safer there. As time had gone on, the warning had drifted from my mind, and I had assumed that the parchment I had scribed it on was lost. But Ravin had saved it here, in his basket of notes. The woman had foretold that I would have children, not just one child but more than one, and here I was, with no children nor yet a partner to share them with. When I had received the foretelling, seven years ago, I had surmised that it was Ambar who was the one who sought me out back then, to find the Orange of Kashiq. And now, he had sought me out again. I read the words again more closely. It said I was loved but that love could not be trusted. That much was true. Not even the deep love between me and Ravin had been enough. She had warned that harm would not only befall my children but also those I knew if I did not flee the land of Oramia. Great harm had indeed befallen Ravin, and it had happened while I was in Oramia.

Shocked, I read it once more. Although I did not have children, it felt much more real to me now than when it had first been told to me, and perhaps the part about the children was just meant as an emphasis, to underline the warning of danger that could befall all I loved. Journeying to the Isles of Soora would certainly be a long way, longer than I had journeyed to go to Arbhoun before I had got the foretelling. The more I pondered on it, the more it seemed that my finding this was some sort of message, given to me mysteriously, like the silent language the bees used to tell one another of the flowers. I would go and visit Achillea and Tarik and explain it to them and then I would pack up my things and begin to journey to Soora. Perhaps this was the destiny which was scribed for me before I was born.

Chapter 8

The dwelling was full of noise when I arrived. Achillea added to the noise with various instructions and pleadings especially to Elleni who was too small to understand the consequences of her actions and too big to be restrained as easily as baby Amir, who was, in any case, a contented child who lay and gurgled, occasionally babbling in response to Lisu waving a toy at him. Tarik seemed not to be in the dwelling.

Even so, there was more noise than usual coming from the area outside the dwelling. There were the quiet measured tones of Tarik, though even they sounded a little more forceful than usual, and the louder tones of another man and then a sort of pleading voice which sounded like Maren. But how could Maren be here? I looked at Achillea queryingly.

'Elleni, stop it! Lisu, why don't you take Elleni to your room, and you can play with these old netelas quietly! Amir needs a sleep and I need to talk to Aunty Talla. If you are good, Aunty Talla will tell you a story later.' She rolled her big eyes at me comically. I smiled at the two little girls who danced about uncertainly for a little while, and then took the offered cloths and ran off with them, scarcely able to believe their luck.

Achillea fanned herself with her own netela. It was a hot day, and the noise somehow made it hotter.

'What's happening?' I whispered.

'It's Maren. She is here with Jember.' So that was who the other voice was, and it didn't sound like a happy voice. Jember had never been to Gabez and had certainly not mentioned it to me when we had spoken before I left Mellia. Achillea looked both concerned and exasperated the same time.

'Jember? But why? What is wrong with him?'

'He found out. About Bellis. He asked about his father, too many times perhaps or in too much detail. The story she had told Jember about his father dying before he was born did not hang together well enough anymore, and eventually it was too much for her, so she told him. Now he is determined to speak to Tarik about it because she told him about Tarik, too. Maren said that the burden of keeping everything hidden had become too hard for Bellis. I understand that, but now the burden is on others. Tarik is trying to talk to him out there at the moment, but he is very angry. Maren came with him because otherwise he said he would travel here on his own, because he did not want to be with his mother either. He is very angry with her too. He needs to see an Empath. Or one of Soren's listeners. His anger is boiling over everywhere at the moment, and I am just trying to keep the children out of his way.' An anxious tear escaped and trickled down her cheek, which she brushed away and continued.

'He said the most terrible things to Tarik. You know how much Tarik tries to leave behind his life as an OutRider. He accused him of all kinds of things and wanted to fight him, even. What happened to Bellis was not Tarik's fault and yet Jember is trying to say that it is.'

'I will go and speak with them,' I replied firmly. My own discussions and my weariness would have to wait. We had always suspected that the day might come when Jember found out that his father was an unknown OutRider who had used his mother when she was an Angel. There would never be a way of finding out who his father might be, nor, I supposed, would anyone want to find out such a thing. To try to explain a system which allowed such a thing would be an impossible task, but perhaps I would be able to help to answer some of Jember's questions and accusations.

'I trusted you and you have failed me!' Jember was shouting now, the words fired as if from a sling shot. 'Men like you did bad things to my mother and then she lied to me, and I thought of you and Ravin as being like my father, and I thought he would be proud of me if he had still been alive, and now I find that he probably is still alive, and he doesn't know or even care about whether I am alive or not! I spent years of my life hoping to become more like my father when what I was told by my mother about him being kind and brave and clever was all a lie! I don't know who I am anymore!'

Maren moved forward towards him to try to soothe him, but he turned on her too.

'And you, all you care about is her, my mother! What about me? Who cares about me? She probably isn't even my mother! I was probably just thrown out by whoever had me, dumped on the Temple steps or something! You always said you were there at my birth, and yet that's probably a lie too!'

Maren's lip quivered. She had always done her best to help Bellis to raise Jember in the way she wanted to, and even though she had not necessarily agreed with Bellis's embroidered tale of a kind, brave husband who died tragically before Jember was born, she went along with it out of love and concern for Bellis, and out of a desire to keep Jember happy. Tarik was waiting patiently for Jember's mind to stop being clouded by the smoke from such angry embers.

I stepped forward. Jember whirled round, about to start on me too, but I spoke first.

'Jember, that is enough. I can assure you; Bellis is your mother. I was there when you were born and you made as much noise when you were born as you are doing now, so it is definitely you!' Tarik's mouth twitched in the beginning of a smile, and Jember paused, as if trying to come up with something more to say that he had not already said. I seized my chance and continued.

'Ravin always said this day would come, and come it has. Both him and Tarik have always loved you and helped you along the way. We knew that you needed to see good men doing good things so that you too could learn to be a good man. Did you know that Ravin also had a difficult time at your age?'

Mute now, Jember shook his head.

'Come here and sit down next to me,' I offered. 'I am tired from all the walking I have done to get here from Pirhan. Maren, why don't you go and talk with Achillea? Those children will drive her to distraction and a story from their Aunty Maren will be just what they need, and will keep them away from here for now, while Tarik and I talk to Jember.' Maren smiled with relief and went inside the dwelling. Tarik quietly stoked the fire and put the pot of water on it to make coffee. I sat down gratefully in the shade near the wall and Jember flung himself down near me. I could see the smeared tracks of tears down his cheeks, long dried but still leaving their mark.

'When he was your age, Ravin ran away from his home village too,' I began, feeling a pang that Ravin could not have related this story himself. 'But, unlike you, he was not running from a loving family and a village who loved him and a slave-driving grandmother like you have.' I smiled at him, teasing him about

Gladia, whom he loved dearly, despite her bossy nature. 'Ravin had to leave at a terrible time in his life. His father had died before he knew him, so, just like you, he grew up with his mother. But then, when he was your age, his mother also died and then his elder brother threatened him and told him that if he did not join the Defenders of Yael, who are the soldiers of Kashiq, like the OutRiders here, that he would kill Ravin himself! Imagine what that must feel like! So, from that day, Ravin had to leave Galdin, the place where he had grown up, and travel far away. He was lucky that he found someone who wanted to look after him and care for him, and who taught him much of what made him the man he was. He would have understood your pain, Jember, but he would also have reminded you how lucky you are, for your mother loves you, as does Maren. We have all known you since you were born and watched you grow. Ravin did not have that, but yet he grew into the wonderful man who we all loved.'

Tarik poured the boiling water into the coffee pot and the strong smell of coffee drifted upwards. It did not have its usual effect on me, and I thought how much I might prefer a cup of Kashiqi mint tea instead. How strange it is that we always seem to want what we do not have.

Tarik spoke. 'You know, Jember, you are actually very lucky. Before you get cross with me again, let me finish. You have heard how my dear friend Ravin had a similar life to you, even down to him having had a father who was a soldier, and who he never knew. But at least you both had a mother who loved you. I grew up with nobody, no parent who loved me so much that they tried to make my life easier for me. I grew up knowing that I had been abandoned by my parents and, as you say, dumped on the Temple steps.' He

74

smiled wryly. 'We know that you have many questions that you want to ask. Some things, we will be able to answer, but others, you may never know. But remember, it is the same for everyone; we cannot know everything. But I can tell you something about the life of an OutRider and Talla can talk to you of other things you may want to know about your mother.'

Jember looked from Tarik to me and back again, uncomprehending. It was clear that, although Bellis had told him about Tarik and his former life as an OutRider, she had said nothing about her own history as a Temple Maid and then as one of the Angels, the slaves made by the Temple for the OutRiders. I sighed. Were not half stories always worse than whole stories? And yet, now Bellis was not here, we would have to tread this path carefully, for her story was not our story to tell.

'Why not start with you,' I suggested. 'What did your mother tell you, exactly?'

Jember frowned with the effort of trying to recall exactly what Bellis had said to him. I understood how hard it was. I had lost count of the times when something had made me so angry that the smoke from its fire had obscured anything else that was said. And where it was forgotten or unknown, the mind wove its own tale from a miscellany of threads.

'I was asking her about my father,' he began. 'When Ravin died, it made me think of my father, because I have never had one and yet I always thought of Ravin and you, Uncle Tarik, as being like a father might be. So, I decided to ask my mother more about him, what his name was, where he came from, how they met and so on. I had in my mind that I might go and travel to find his family one day so I could see if I was like them. I always feel like there are parts of me that my mother does not understand, or even parts that she does not like and that maybe those are the parts which came to me from my father's line. She has always refused to tell me more, saying that he died before I was born and that it hurts her too much to talk about it. But it did not make sense to me anymore. I am in the Third Age now, and even you, Talla, can talk to me about Ravin and he only just died. Sorry,' he added, as he saw me wince. 'But how can it still hurt her almost fifteen years later? And then I asked her why she never told me anything about him, what he liked to do and things like that, and she just shouted at me that if I wanted to know what he did and liked to do, I should ask Tarik since he used to be one of them, the OutRiders, and that she had no idea what his name was and didn't want to know and that she hoped I would never meet him and that I should never talk of it again.' Jember looked miserable.

'And then what happened?' asked Tarik.

'I just kept asking questions. I just want to know! You must know how angry it makes you not to know things. If you know things, you can understand things, that's what Ravin always used to say. I just wanted to find my father, and to have someone be proud of me! Benakiell used to say that to me, but now he spends all his time in Kashiq with Shira, and Ravin is gone, and you have your own children, and you will always love them more. So, I told her I would come here to Gabez, and I would ask you about it and I just put some stuff in a carrysack and left but then Maren came after me and talked to me and she said she would come with me. She told me that the OutRiders are bad people and that it was an OutRider who was my father and that my mother did not even know him or his name and that he forced himself on her. She said my mother could never trust another man again for the rest of her life, and that all the OutRiders were the same. But I still don't understand. You have all been lying to me since I was born! Even Ravin must have known and yet he never told me, or even gave me any advice about how to talk to my mother about this. I don't know anyone else like me, I don't think, and then I thought about all the women who Gladia looks after, along with my mother and Maren and they often come and then have their babies, and there are never any fathers for their children either. Am I one of them? Will they all grow up like me?' Fresh tears tracked their way over his smooth, brown cheeks adding to the marks left by previous tears. Jember was such a tall boy that sometimes I forgot that he was not a man, but still a child; though capable of a man's work, he was not yet capable of adult thinking.

Tarik's face carried its usual calm appearance. Placidly, he added another stick to the fire and moved the firestones slightly. I knew that he was giving himself time to think of the right words to say. We had all done as Bellis wanted, right from when Jember was born, but although we probably always hoped that it would never arise, there was surely no doubt that it would. We should have talked about it more between all of us, but we were all concerned not to upset Bellis. She had seemed so happy and settled in her life in Mellia with Maren and Gladia and helping Gladia with the Angels who were delivered to them.

'I think that we need to talk to one another as men,' Tarik said to Jember, smiling slightly. 'You are, after all, almost a man. Where I grew up, the Third Age was known as the Age of Manhood because they always said it would be then that it would be determined what kind of man you would be, what your skills and qualities and indeed weaknesses would be. So, I will ask Talla to go inside to talk with Maren, so that she can find out more and also, because it is very hot out here and I am sure that Talla would like a rest in the shade of the dwelling, after walking here from Pirhan.' I nodded agreement, and went inside, leaving Tarik with Jember. I would have liked to have stayed, to have heard what Tarik might say about his life in the OutFort. He didn't like to talk about it much, although he may well have discussed it with Achillea. I had talked to Ravin about some of my life in the Temple which I had never shared with the others. We allow those we love into the darker places of our souls sometimes, knowing that their light will make things easier to see and to understand. I had heard the stories from Ambar more recently and I wondered now whether he talked to Lunaria about his early life at all. It seemed unlikely.

Inside, the girls were still playing games with the old netelas, dressing up and making tents out of them in their part of the dwelling behind a curtain. Achillea sat with Maren, feeding little Amir. He suckled as he slept, his chubby little fingers grasping Achillea's netela, making contented little snuffling noises. Maren looked up anxiously as I came in.

'How is he? Is Tarik talking to him? I need to know what he says to him. I don't know how to manage this. Bellis has told him so little, and I knew this day would come but it brings her such pain to talk of those times that we just don't. It builds up inside her and Jember was asking so many questions that it was as if a thread had been pulled too tight in one of her stitchings and snapped. And now we will have to unpick it all and start again, resew that which was ruined, and know that the thread is shorter now.'

It was a good picture Maren drew, this comparison with sewing. Gladia had taught Bellis well and she was an adept stitcher; her neat, even stitches never seemed to waver. But I wondered now how many times she had unpicked what she had done and resewn it to make it look better, and how many times she had changed the words she wanted to say to Jember to make things look better.

'Can you tell me what Bellis has told Jember? Because from what he was saying out there to Tarik, it doesn't sound as if she has told him the full story even now, and I am worried that Jember will come home, and things will be even harder.' I asked.

Maren's eyes fluttered and she blinked several times. She had always blinked a lot especially when she had been blinded and it was a habit which returned especially when she was worried or tired. She sighed.

'Things are so much easier when they are small children.' Achillea looked at me at this point and rolled her eyes, imagining no doubt that things could not possibly get more difficult than to be looking after three small children. 'When Jember was younger, he just accepted what he was told, and it didn't seem to bother him. He spent time with other men like Benakiell and Tarik and of course Ravin. But now, since Ravin's death, he has done nothing but ask about his father, what he did, what his name was, where he came from, on and on and on. It has been relentless for poor Bellis. He asked so often and in so many different ways, that she started answering differently and then not knowing what was meant to be the real story. And of course, none of it was the real story, because it was too hard for her to tell him. Can you imagine what it might be like to tell your child he was made not out of love but violence? That you knew nothing about him and had never even seen him. All she knows is that it was an OutRider. Any of the OutRiders we see at the market in Sanguinea or wherever we are, any of them could be his father and we would never know. But for Bellis, every time she sees them, she is reminded of this, and it will not go away. Working with the other Angels who come to Mellia is sometimes helpful to her, to know that she

79

is not alone, but also sometimes it hurts her more. And now, Gladia has told us they will be coming to us with no memory of what has happened to them, from some new physic they have, and all Bellis has ever wanted is to forget that time, but Jember is of course a constant reminder...'

Maren's voice trailed off as she realised that it seemed as if she were blaming Jember for the current predicament, even though he was blameless. He did not know when he asked the questions that it would cause his mother so much pain, and nor could he have been aware that even his existence was difficult for her.

'Bellis loves Jember more than anything,' Maren said, fiercely. 'She just doesn't know how to tell him or whether it will make him love her less. She fears that more than anything. Before I left with Jember, in such a rush, she told me to look after him and to keep him safe, and to ask you, Talla, to talk to him. You can talk to him without it hurting you like it hurts Bellis, and because you have known Jember since he was born. I am too much like Bellis,' she added ruefully. 'I, too, was put through much pain by the OutRiders, and I, too, have lost much to them. I am sorry to put this burden on you, Talla, so soon after Ravin's death, but I do not know what else to do. Can you talk to him?'

It had become very difficult. Jember had been told many stories already about his early life, told with the best of intentions. But those stories themselves had become a burden, both to him and to his mother. You might think it would be better to tell him the truth, but he was still a child, albeit one who was learning to become a man. And unless we were all utterly complicit in the story we told, he would find out that he had been lied to once more. But I did not know what Tarik would tell him from his side. It felt that in removing the burden from Bellis, we would be placing it on Jember, and none of us wanted that. I was suddenly weary and then nauseous, the sour juices turning my stomach over until I had to rush outside where I was violently sick. Ravin had always said that the ills of the mind often became the ills of the body, and perhaps the thought of all that Bellis had been through had made me ill.

I returned inside and apologised and explained my hasty departure to Achillea and Maren. They looked at each other strangely, but before they could speak, Tarik came into the dwelling, having left Jember out in the courtyard to tell me that Jember had some questions for me. I asked Tarik what he had told Jember.

'I have answered his questions as best as I can,' he said. 'I have told him that it was indeed an OutRider, who forced himself on Bellis, who is his father, and that he is unknown and always will be. I have told him that I was also an OutRider but that I am no longer, that I can tell him something of what it is like to be an OutRider. I have not,' he turned to me, 'told him about the Angels, about how his mother was used, not just by one but by many. I have not told him of how the Temple and the OutFort conspire with one another to make more Temple Maids and Angels and OutRiders with their poisonous system. That is too much to bear for one who is still a child. It is hard enough for him to learn that he will never know anything about his father and that his father could have inflicted such pain on his mother. We must carry this burden ourselves for Jember for now. I do not think that Bellis will want him to know these things yet.' We all looked at each other and nodded agreement. Inside, I wondered whether I would be able to face all this questioning without having to tell any lies. If Jember asked me directly, I was not sure how I would respond.

'He wants to talk to you, Talla, about his mother. He regrets already the things he has said to her and says that he wants to try to understand. Perhaps if he hears from another woman, and one who has known his mother since before he was born, he will believe it more. He is much calmer now, but he wants to know about his mother. He believes that you will be truthful with him, and I have assured him that you will.'

I went out to the courtyard. The sky was that deep blue that came with the hot weather. There were not clouds in the sky yet, for it was not the season of rain, that would come in a couple of months. The leaves on the small date tree growing in the courtyard hung limply, for there was no breeze. Jember was throwing small pebbles against its trunk.

'What do you want to know?' I asked. He turned and smiled at me hesitantly, unsure if I were angry with him.

'I don't know,' he began, uncertainly. 'Uncle Tarik has explained some things to me, and I know she was trying to protect me from the pain of knowing about who my father was. It's a good job I don't know who he is,' he continued fiercely. 'Because if I did, I would kill him for what he did. Tarik has told me that whoever he was, he will never even know that I exist and that I will never find out who he is, so I should try and not think about him too much. Uncle Tarik told me that if I ever need a father to talk to, I should think of him as being like a father to me. That made me feel better. And I do understand better why my mother lied to me, that she was trying to protect me, but I want you to tell me more so that I can look after her better.' He pushed his shoulders back and, in an instant, I was reminded of him when he was a small boy and the way he used to strut around the village proudly, pretending to be a man. I smiled at his earnest attitude. 'Tarik said he first met my mother when they found her, after she had been attacked. Do you know more?'

'Your Uncle Tarik helped to rescue her from her attackers,' I answered. I did not mention Ambar. I told Jember how his mother had been found, but not the reasons why she was being pursued by the OutRiders, nor that she was an Angel. I confined myself to answering his questions and told him honestly how his mother had been traumatised when we found her, and how Achillea, Gladia, Maren and I had helped her to recover from her ordeal, at least physically.

'Why did you lie to me?' he asked. 'Why did you all tell me that my father had died before I was born and that he had been a brave and good man and all that?'

'Surely you must see that we could not speak of this to a little boy?' I replied, gently. 'A child is not ready to bear these difficult things in their heart. Telling you what we did meant that you did not ask your mother too many questions, for it made it hurt again whenever she thought about what had happened.' Jember nodded, apparently understanding our intentions.

'Does she hate me?' he wondered, finally, his voice breaking.

'No,' I answered firmly. 'She loves you. In all of the difficult times your mother has had, she has always loved you. She believes that the Goddess sent you to her to help her, and she always has done.' I hoped that I spoke with conviction. I sensed that it had become harder for Bellis as Jember was approaching manhood. A baby or a small child who was relatively powerless and dependent was a different prospect to an independent and curious son who was intent on finding out about his ancestry.

'I don't know who I am, anymore,' said Jember, in frustration. 'I thought I knew what my place was in the world, but now I don't. And I don't feel like I can ask

83

questions back in Mellia, because nobody wants to answer them.' He balled his hands up into fists, the anger still there. He needed an outlet for his feelings, or a way to hold them in check, and it seemed to me that he needed to be more occupied than he was in Mellia, doing odd jobs and helping out with some of the dwelling making when Benakiell returned periodically. It was difficult in Oramia for a mother to guide a son into a choice about their choice of work, or for a father to guide his daughter, because all the different types of work were allocated by virtue of whether you were a man or a woman. In Kashiq it was easier, for they were allocated according to which of the gods and goddesses you wanted to be guided by. Living in Mellia meant that Jember only had the chance to see a few of the choices he could make.

'When I go back, my mother will not want to talk to me about anything,' said Jember. 'She will worry that she has upset me and then she will say nothing and that will upset me more. I just can't help feeling that she blames me for what my father did.' He turned to me again, as another thought hit him. 'Surely I will not grow into one like him? But Gladia is always talking about how children are like their parents and that they take their essences into themselves and mix them up and sometimes you can see from looking at a child what his parents look like or act like. What if I look like him? What if somehow I am going to end up behaving like him?' He looked at me forlornly. I looked back at him. He seemed so familiar to me, but I tried carefully to work out what aspects of his appearance might come from his mother. His long curling eyelashes for sure, and the way his hair caught the sun. But in truth, there was more that was different than was the same. His skin was of a darker tone than Bellis, and he was taller and more muscular even at the age he was than her.

84

Bellis had always spent long hours thinking and dreaming, even at the Temple where we had thought her lazy. Now I knew that she spent much of her time, even now, in prayer or thoughtful contemplation of the Goddess. Jember was a young man and had always been full of energy, always wanting to be busy doing something. Without the outlet of hard physical work, he would get irritable and angry.

'Your mother cannot be reminded of him,' I reminded Jember, forgetting that he did not know the details of how the Angels were hidden from the OutRiders who used them. He looked at me sharply.

'She must have seen him surely,' he responded.

'No, she didn't,' I answered quickly. 'She told me that she never saw his face.' That was true. Jember's face fell again.

'So, nobody can even tell me what he might have looked like, and what parts of me come from him?'

I acknowledged the truth of this. We sat in silence for some time. Jember had run out of questions. I leaned my head against the smooth clay and Paradox oiled wall and thought how tired I felt. Perhaps I was just trying to catch up on all the sleep which had evaded me when Ravin died. Though since I had returned to Pirhan I had been sleeping much better.

Tarik looked out into the courtyard, to see how we were progressing. I waved him over and told Jember to go and greet his cousins and Achillea in the dwelling. I hoped he would also apologise to Maren. I told Tarik what I had told Jember, and what I had not.

'I feel that he needs time away from Bellis,' I said. 'He needs to be doing something, to find a work that he loves so that he can build himself up more. You know what it is like to be defined by something you can do nothing about.'

Tarik nodded. 'We could not change where we came from, nor the manner of our births any more than Jember can. His mother will always love him but nonetheless, he is a reminder of a difficult time for her, and while he is asking questions and searching for who he is, it will be hard for her. I have an idea though.'

I listened as Tarik explained that there was a man who worked on the eastern side of Gabez, who he often worked and traded with, who was looking for an apprentice in his wood carving trade. The one who was taken on would have to learn how to cut the wood, and then how to carve it into boxes and carryboxes, spoons and combs. The more skill they learned, the more he would teach them. This man, Durkin, had no sons of his own to pass his trade on to, and had been looking for some time for a lad in his third age who might want to become a wood carver.

'Durkin has a room at his dwelling ready for an apprentice. Jember would have a place to live and food and the chance to help Durkin with trades and eventually a chance to trade his own work. What do you think? Do you think Jember could be a wood carver?'

'It will depend on whether he wants to leave Mellia and his mother, won't it? And even more, whether she wants him to do this or not? She is still his mother.'

Tarik smiled wryly.

'I forget about these things sometimes. Of course, Achillea usually explains everything to me, how things are done in the Outer, but some things I never considered before. You know as well as I do that we worked hard from this age without parents. In the OutFort, it would not be long before Jember would be learning to fight and kill at this age. Besides, we would be here for Jember if he wanted to visit us. We don't have space for him to stay here, and anyway at his age, he does not want to have small children running around him all the time. Besides, I think Achillea would kill me if I brought another child into the house at the moment, she is kept too busy with the ones we have!' He smiled and his eyes crinkled at the corners as he thought of his wife and children. Despite her protestations, Achillea loved having all the children around her and she and Tarik seemed to have made the perfect match in one another. His contentment bit at me sharply. So many things which I never even used to notice had become more important since Ravin's death. I swallowed down the acid feel in my mouth.

'Let us ask Jember and Maren,' I suggested. 'He can speak for himself, and Maren knows and loves Bellis; she could give us an idea of how she might react.'

We spoke to both of them as we all ate our evening meal together out in the courtyard. The heat of the day had not yet eased, and the cooking fire made it hang around us even more. The smell of Achillea's pumpkin stew, full of herbs and spices drifted around us. The baby lay sleeping on a cloth next to his mother, oblivious to the chatter around us. The girls were occupied with eating. Maren frowned at the suggestion at first, but then considered it in more detail.

'We would miss Jember, and we would never want him to leave if he did not want to. But we have spoken together before about him finding his path in life, and how he might need to leave Mellia to do so. We just did not know how it could happen. We had hoped that if Benakiell had returned to Mellia for longer, then he could have been apprenticed to him, but this seems like a good idea. Bellis would want him to return home often though, and he will need to come home with me first to talk about it with her. In the end, it is up to Jember though. It is his path to make in life and he must decide where he wants to go.' She looked fondly at Jember who was twitching with excitement at the idea of this new adventure.

'I really want to,' he said firmly. 'I can see Uncle Tarik and Aunty Achillea whenever I like, and I am sure Tarik would not have suggested this man if he did not respect his work.'

'Nor,' reminded Tarik, 'would I suggest you to him if I did not think you would work your hardest for him. It will be me who is blamed if you cannot do the work, or if you leave before the end of your apprenticeship. Durkin is a good craftsman, and he knows his craft. You will learn well from him if you listen carefully and don't try to be too clever.' He turned to Maren.

'I can introduce Jember to Durkin tomorrow so that they know one another. It may be that Durkin will want to test his skill and his hunger to learn. If that is successful, then you should go back to Mellia so that, if Bellis agrees, Jember can get started straight away.' Maren nodded her agreement and Tarik took Jember to the part of the courtyard where he worked on his crafts and gave him a small block of wood and a chisel so that he could practice before he met Durkin.

Achillea looked meaningfully at Maren and then at me. I could not imagine what they had discussed about me when I was out in the courtyard, but it seemed I was about to find out.

'How are you feeling?' asked Achillea. I sighed. I knew that my friends were worried for me and my health since Ravin's death, but sometimes it was tiring that they asked me so often.

'I am fine, Achillea. I have good days and bad days, but that is to be expected, or so they tell me.'

'I was concerned when you were sick earlier,' she murmured. 'Have you eaten something bad, or been with one who is ill, or taken something to make you sleep that disagrees with you?'

'No,' I replied. 'It is nothing. Probably I am just tired.' I did not want to mention that the physic Ambar had given me had made me feel sick, because, in truth, I had been sleeping better since I had taken it, and in any case, I did not want them to know that I had been talking to him, or that I had taken this strange physic which stole my memory.

Maren took up the cause. 'Is the Goddess blessing you with every moon?'

I looked at her blankly for a moment before realising what she was asking.

'Not since around the time that Ravin died,' I answered. 'But Gladia told me that it was normal for the Goddess to rest a woman at difficult times in her life.'

'That is true. But there is another reason sometimes that a woman is not blessed with every moon and that is if the Goddess has given her a full blessing.'

Achillea clapped her hands unable to restrain herself. 'Oh Maren, do you think it could be true? All these years she has been waiting, and then it is left for her as a parting gift from Ravin? Do you think it could be so, Talla? Can you tell, Maren?'

I felt suddenly lightheaded. I bent my head down and breathed deeply, away from the smoke of the fire and the sultry heat. It did not make sense to me, this suggestion of theirs, that I might be carrying a child, that which Ravin and I had longed for, but which had not appeared, but part of me suddenly felt relieved and hopeful. Perhaps, rather than forgetting that which caused me pain as I had tried to do by taking the physic of forgetting, I needed to remember Ravin. What better way could there be to always remember someone than to have a part of them in a child? And then I thought of Bellis again and saw how it could work both ways.

'Would you like me to try and feel your belly? asked Maren. 'I might be able to tell by now, but it is not always easy to be sure.' I nodded mutely. Maren got up and I followed her inside the dwelling, into Achillea's room where a hanging cloth kept it private. Achillea promised to keep the others away.

I lay down and Maren asked me to raise my robe. I felt suddenly vulnerable, even though this was an old friend. There was something about lying down, exposed like that which made me feel open to injury. Maren rubbed her hands together with some Paradox oil and then gently felt my belly. I shut my eyes, feeling her moving her hands firmly over my belly, stopping and then starting again.

'I cannot tell for sure,' she said. 'But I think I feel something. We will know better in a month's time when, if you are blessed by the Goddess with a child, we will be able to see your belly grown. She pulled down my robe again and I sat up, unsure what to say or how to feel. Being presented with an uncertainty was difficult. Maren patted my hand.

'But you should also know that it may just be because you are tired and grieving, so do not raise up your hopes. I will not speak of this to Gladia or to Bellis unless you wish it, yet, for there is nothing sure to say. Achillea will know well enough if you talk to her what signs to look for beyond the sickness. It does not seem easy to explain if this has happened, for it is unusual for it to only show itself now. But your grief may have masked it.'

We returned to the courtyard. Achillea kept trying to catch my eye queryingly, but I paid all my attention to the girls who came to ask me to tell them some of the stories I knew. From my initial scorn, I had grown to love the works of Scholar Finzari, and his simple, moral tales set in the orchards or the gardens of Kashiq, and his poems extolling human virtues such as bravery or kindness. He had scribed many short poems as teaching tools for children.

'The   wise   white   owl   sat   in   a   tree
These wise words she said to me:

Speak a little,
Listen more
Save the words
In your mind's core.
See a little.
Learn to do
Save these words
From me to you.'

Elleni clapped her hands with delight and Lisu solemnly repeated the words after me until she had learned the words for herself. She was quick-witted, with a good memory, and I enjoyed teaching her. I felt sure she could learn to read and scribe, but Achillea was not convinced that it would be a good thing to do. She was, after all a child of Oramia, not Kashiq, and in Oramia no child learned to read; in fact, no person of the Outer learned to read. It was different in Kashiq where I lived, not too far away. It was strange to think that how one grew and what one ended up doing or learning or enjoying was driven so much by an accident of birth, whether one was born in this land or the other.

Later, as we sat around the dying embers of the fire, enjoying the cooler breeze which had finally arrived, I asked Tarik if he knew of the Isles of Soora. Despite the possibilities that Maren and Achillea had planted in my head as surely as a date seed, I still wanted to try to find out more about the place which Ravin had tried to find out so much about in the weeks before he died.

'I have not heard of them,' he answered, scratching his head thoughtfully. 'But you say they are beyond

Kashiq? I do not think the OutRiders nor yet the Temple can reach as far as there, surely? There must be some path of trade which leads from there to Oramia.'

I knew from what Ravin had scribed that it had to do with some kind of herb or plant, but also, from what Ambar had told me, that they also made physic there that was used by the Queen's Court. Which surely meant that the Temple and the OutFort had at least some connection with it, if only through trade. But I still had not shared my encounters with Ambar with anyone. While I was thinking about this, Maren surprised us all by speaking up.

'Hortensia, the one who trained me as a Birthmother, she learned her art at Soora. I am sure that is what she said. She had come to Oramia from there when she was a young woman, so that she could work as a Birthmother and to train other Birthmothers. She never spoke very much about her life when she was young, for she was in her Fourth Age when I last saw her, after the birth of Lady Paradox's DoubleSoul children, the birth of the Queen as we now know.' I asked her what else she knew about the Isles of Soora or about Hortensia herself, but she seemed to know very little. I had observed before that Maren's memories of the time before she had been blinded by the OutRiders were as clouded as her sight had been, as if smeared with oil. She remembered all that Hortensia had taught her about her work delivering babies safely, and caring for them and their mothers, but knew curiously little about the woman who had taught her.

'What did she look like?' asked Achillea, ever fascinated by such detail. 'Did she resemble one of Oramia or one of Kashiq?' How did she wear her hair? How did she speak?'

Baffled, Maren tried to answer these questions but had little to give. We learned that Hortensia was shorter than Maren who herself was quite short, that she was well built and strong. Maren had no close recollection of her appearance and said she never saw her without her netela or in anything other than normal Oramian clothing. She spoke softly and slowly but that was how Birthmothers were taught to speak, to soothe the worries of the mothers.

'I would like to find out more,' I said. 'It was important to Ravin and so it is important to me. He was finding out about these islands and never got to share his knowledge with me. Perhaps I should go to the Tower of the Wise in Arbhoun to try to read more about them.'

'That is too far to go for you on your own,' said Achillea firmly. I knew that she wanted me near, especially if what she and Maren had suggested came true. But I did not think it was true, it seemed too farfetched to me, and in any case, a journey would give me something to think about, to take my mind off my grief. I said nothing in response, reluctant to make promises.

'There is one I know in Pirhan,' said Tarik. 'He is a metalworker and trader. He trades with people from all over Kashiq. He may know more about Soora than you could find out in Arbhoun. They say his metalwork can even be found in the Court of the Queen. If there is any kind of precious trade from the Isles of Soora then he would know, for sure.'

'That's a good idea, Tarik.' Achillea saw an opportunity to be both encouraging of me and to prevent me from journeying on my own to Arbhoun. 'Talla, you can ask him all your questions. Maybe Ravin even spoke to him about it, and he can tell you more. What is his name, Tarik?'

'Khadar. Everyone around there knows him.'

Chapter 9

There was a taste in the air. Something you could smell and yet taste at the same time, the sharp musky scent of metal. It reminded me of when you bit the inside of your cheek and it bled. All around me was the sound of metal being worked. There were loud, low noises and lighter, bell-like notes. Men were making pans and knives and needles and chains, large keys and small rings, intricate jewellery and hoe blades. Kashiq was not a place where one's work was defined by whether you were a man or a woman as it was in Oramia. Instead, one's work was defined by allegiance to one of the six gods and goddesses of Kashiq. The one who guided crafting was Maliq and there were many who were skilled in crafting, both men and women, but almost all of those who worked the metal were men. Perhaps they liked the power they had over something which seemed so hard and impenetrable, and the way they could bend it to their will.

Kashiq was rich in metals. It was as if the plants and trees which were so much more common in Oramia had, in Kashiq, turned into different kinds of metals which grew underground like plants. In Kashiq, metal things were used all the time and by everybody, whereas, in Oramia, only small items were permitted beyond the Queen's Court and the OutRiders. One could own a knife to cut reeds or prepare food, an axe to cut down trees or a hoe blade for your crops. Small jewellery items traded from Kashiq, and needles were also permitted, but if you tried to take large metal items or the metal rocks into Oramia, they were always taken from you when you came into the country. It was the way that the OutRiders got a lot of the metal they used in their armour and weapons.

I headed for the uppermost corner of the market area. Like all Kashiqi markets, the metal market was based around a square, divided into smaller squares, with each trader keeping to their place. Those who were working the metal, whether it was to make fine, long wires or intricate inlaid boxes, or casting shapes using beeswax as we had done with the Orange of Kashiq, worked around the central square. On an already hot day, the heat of the many small fires used to soften and melt the metals shimmered in the air. I asked a woman who was trading fine Kashiqi jewellery if she could tell me where to find Khadar, the trader Tarik had told me about.

'Khadar?' She looked at me curiously. 'You must be rich in trades to seek out one such as him. Are you sure you would not rather trade for something of mine, this pin for your netela perhaps? It is said that in Arbhoun all the fine ladies are wearing these now.' She showed me a ring with a small slit in the side and a long pin which slid around it on a small loop. You could hold the two sides of the netela together by pushing the pin through the cloth and then moving the ring around, so the pin rested on top of it. It was an ingeniously made thing, and I knew that if Ravin had seen it, he would have wanted to get one for me, or learn how to make one for me. Regretfully, I shook my head but told her that I might come back later when I had something to trade with me. I asked her if she was interested in trading for honey, but she shook her head and directed me to where Khadar could be found, already turning to her next potential customer.

Khadar was a short, powerfully built man. His arms bulged with muscle, and he stood near his wares, arms folded across his chest, looking out over the market from his position right at the upper end. Only the most determined would come this far for their metal boxes and keys and intricate mechanical devices but it seemed that he was well-known for there were plenty of people looking at his goods. He had a couple of apprentices working for him who were letting people know what trades would be viewed most favourably, reading off a list which had been scribed, perhaps by Khadar himself. I edged towards him.

'See the apprentices if you want to trade,' he said brusquely. 'They will decide and then we can do business.'

I smiled at him as sweetly as I could. Which was probably not very effective because I was tired and hot. 'I am not looking for trade, but for Khadar, with whom I wish to speak.' I had learned from Ravin that Kashiqis set great store by long and complicated speech. 'I have heard of his great skill at metalworking but also of his travelling all over this land, and I am searching for information about a place where he might have traded, somewhere so far away that only a trader of his high status is likely to know.' I was proud to have managed this speech without my customary rolling of eyes or cynical tones. Khadar looked at me appraisingly.

'I am he. Who has given you my name as one who knows so much and has travelled so far?'

'There is one who was a close friend to one I loved. His name is Tarik, and he lives in Oramia in Gabez. He knew Ravin, and he suggested your name as one who might know something of what Ravin was searching for.'

'Ravin? You should have said you knew Ravin! Where is he? I was waiting for him to get back to me about something and then he just seems to have disappeared. Perhaps he found a different way to get there?'

It had already happened so many times, this point where I would encounter someone who did not yet know of Ravin's death and who still believed him to be alive. I wished with all my heart that I was that person. Unlike many other things, it did not really get easier with time, and I, who had been perfectly normal only a minute before, suddenly began to weep, silently. Khadar looked at me, alarmed by the tears dripping down my face.

'What is it? Come this way.' He beckoned me towards a small cloth lean to tent where he had some colourful cushions set out in the shade, and a pot of Kashiqi tea. I followed him, trying to compose myself enough to explain my story to him – or at least as much of it as I wanted him to know.

I told him of Ravin's death. His brow creased. Now that he was away from the trading stall, he relaxed and looked much friendlier. He expressed his sadness at the news and then asked me if I would be going instead of Ravin to the Isles of Soora on his trading vessel, since he had already traded with Ravin to allow him to travel there. I looked at him open-mouthed.

'Ravin was very persistent. He really wanted to travel to the Isles on the next trade boat that went there. It will take almost a week for you to get to Safran, where the boats sail from, in two weeks' time, on the day of Flavus. But do you wish to go, in your condition? I can offer you some good metalwork objects instead of the journey on the boat; you could put them aside for the little one when it comes.'

I looked at him. How could it be that he could know about the possibility of the baby? He laughed and his eyes crinkled up at the corners.

'I hope I do not speak wrongly. My wife is also similarly blessed although the baby will come sooner than yours, I dare say – at least according to the Birthmother. It must be a comfort for you to know Ravin left something of himself behind for you when he returned to the Goddess. But if you do go, at least you will know that you will be well looked after there by the women of Soora, for it is they who began the teaching of all the Birthmothers in our land, and they care for many women – for a price, of course.' He rolled his eyes. 'They drive a hard bargain, those women. They have what everyone wants; the special wisdom of the Birthmothers, the plants which only grow there, and which make all manner of Physic, the metals that can be found there on the island of Orish, and the honeywine. For such things, they can trade whatever they want, as I told Ravin when he first told me of his plan to go there. What did he seek?'

I stumbled over my words, trying to take in all that Khadar had said. I wished I could ask Ravin what he had been planning but could only guess. It seemed that he had secretly been looking for a way for us to have a child and that he had hoped that he would find out some answers on the Isles of Soora. It was a sour truth that, now he was not here, I might both find out the answer and have a child. But part of me wanting a child was bound to Ravin and our life together and now things were different. I explained to Khadar that Ravin had been very interested in learning, was guided by Rao and often travelled to find out new things, and that we had been interested in the plants they grew and if they could be used with honey.

Khadar raised his eyebrows at me. 'You will not be able to trade for any of those plants,' he said. 'The only trade for those is with the Oramians, your own kind if I am not mistaken. The women of Soora do not trade with anyone else for most of them. I do not think you will learn anything new there; they hold onto their secrets tightly. But I do not know. They may look on you more favourably since you are a woman; they trade with men, but they do not trust us, and no man can stay there longer than a week.'

'Are there no men on these islands at all?'

'Well, there are the men of boats, who live and work there, but there are not so many. They live mainly on their boats, I think.' One of Khadar's apprentices approached then and asked him about a complicated trade, and I could see that it was time for me to leave. I would have to decide what to do. I assured myself that I could still not go if I wanted. After all, Ravin had already traded for the place on the boat. Hastily, I got up and thanked Khadar for his kindness, and told him that I would take Ravin's place on the boat.

'And what of the other space, the one he intended for you, I guess? Shall I see if I can get you some small trades for that space?' Khadar waited impatiently for my answer. I was again surprised. So, Ravin had intended to take me with him. It made my heart full that he had not meant to keep this as a secret from me forever, but only as a surprise for when we returned to Pirhan. I understood now why he had been anxious that we should return to Pirhan no later than we had planned, for it would have given us the time to plan and make the trip. Now, because of all that had happened, there would be no planning and I would have to make an immediate decision. I could not think of anyone who would come with me on the trip. Achillea would have been my first choice, but she needed to be at home with her children and in any case, remembering how she had hated the movement when we had been on Benakiell's boat, I doubted that a journey on a boat would entice her. Nevertheless, I did not want another stranger taking Ravin's place, so I thanked Khadar again and promised to return the next day. I needed to get the details from him of where to go to find the right boat once I got to Safran, the town on the coast near the Isles of Soora but I did confirm that I would be keeping both the places on the boat.

Later, sitting outside, in the shade near our dwelling, I began to read again the various parchments which Ravin had gathered together in the basket, including the one which had on it the drawing of the Isles of Soora. There was not a great deal more there which I had not read, just some notes scribed by old travellers about the dangerous rocks on the southern coast of Kashiq and on the south of the island called Aman, the smallest of the islands. The notes said that it was a holy island, sacred to the people of the Isles of Soora. There were also some notes Ravin had scribed, about the honeywine that was made there and a question about whether my knowledge of the bees could be traded for knowledge of the physics. It was a possibility at least, and I decided to take with me several gourds of my best orange blossom honey, and some honey which had thin slices of orange peel steeping in it. The orange peel gave the honey a lovely flavour and then, by the end of the time of steeping, the pieces of orange peel were saturated with the sweetness of the honey and were delicious. I carefully added the information which Khadar had given me about the different islands to the drawing and rolled up the various scrolls of plant parchment relating to Soora. I tied them and then untied them again and added the scroll on which I had scribed my memory of what the fortune teller had told me in her warning. I had only a few days before I would need to set off for Safran, in order to be sure of getting them for the day of Flavus in ten days' time.

Chapter 10

It was the day before I was due to start my journey. I had chosen a few things to carry with me, always being aware that now I would have to carry everything myself. I had two large water carriers made of leather and waxed hard with beeswax. The deserts of Kashiq could be dangerous if you did not carry water, although there were often fellow travellers on the same routes, especially the tracks between towns which were well used for trade. The towns and cities of Kashiq were, without exception built where there was an abundance of springs and underground water for wells to be dug, so they could be easily replenished each day. Likewise, food for a couple of days at a time must be carried, as well as items for trading. I needed a change of clothes and a couple of netelas, my small gourds of honey and beeswax and the rolled scrolls. There seemed a lot, but luckily I was now practiced at carrying loads back and forth and had always been strong, in any case.

I loosened the ties on either side of my robe, which I wore, Kashiqi style, over trousers while I was in Kashiq, and by itself when I was in Oramia. It was in deep red, similar to the colour of Ravin's headdress, which I had brought back with me, along with his other clothes. The robe was one which could be tightened or loosened using ties which were attached at the front and back and tied at the sides. I had always been able to tie the ribbons right back, but now I needed more space. I was still unwilling to think about the possibility of a child, even though it was becoming more evident. I had not been back to see Achillea and Tarik, mainly because I would have to talk about it and for now it was difficult for me to accept. It had been so long since Ravin and I had first discussed it and it was still something which I associated with him. Before I had met him, I had never had the slightest inclination to have a child, nor had I ever believed that I could have one, since in the Temple none of the Maids or Priestesses were ever blessed by the Goddess in that way. There was a definite change in the shape of my body now, though, a rounding and a softening which I recognised from the times when Achillea had been with child. Even Khadar had recognised it. If I can just make this trip to Soora, I whispered to the emberjar of my mind, then it could be true. Because if I did, then it would make it true; it was what Ravin wanted. And yet, there was a nagging doubt in my mind because I had not felt the sickness until after Ravin had died. Perhaps it was the grief that masked it.

'Talla, are you there?' Achillea's voice called through the courtyard. I had no agreement with her that she would be coming to Pirhan, and my first thought was that something bad must have happened, but her voice sounded light and cheerful. I went out, a little cautiously. Standing there was Achillea with Gladia, of all people.

'Well don't just stand there,' said Gladia grumpily. 'It's hot out here, and I need a drink.' I looked at Achillea, and she returned my look with a sunny smile.

'Isn't this lovely, Talla? Gladia decided to take a trip to visit us in Gabez to bring Jember once Bellis and Maren had said their final farewells, and then, since Jember wanted to start his work straight away, Gladia thought it would be nice to check up on you, especially after she had heard from Maren.' She looked at me pointedly. 'I thought you would be coming back to see us sooner.'

I ignored her hints. 'Where are the children?'

'Tarik is looking after them today.'

'For the sake of the Goddess,' interrupted Gladia. 'Can we please get into the shade so that you can offer one of your elders a drink of water?'

I led the way into the dwelling. This would disrupt all my plans. I had meant to send a message to Achillea and Tarik as I left on my journey explaining to them what I was planning. By the time they had got it, I would be gone, and they would be unable to stop me. I could not let Achillea stop me from what I needed to do. If I could get to Soora, this child could be real.

'I see it's true then,' said Gladia, fanning herself with her netela, and looking at me appraisingly. 'Maren was right. You will have a part of Ravin even now, after he has gone. You must be very happy, Talla.'

'Will you move back to Oramia, Talla?' asked Achillea brightly. 'You could come and live in Gabez again, near us, so we can help when the baby comes.'

I did not know how to act. I wanted to get rid of them so that I could continue with my plans, unchallenged, and yet I also really wanted to just sit quietly under a Paradox tree and feel at peace with the world. This was a long-cherished dream of mine and I had confessed it to Ravin, once, who had roared with laughter when he heard it.

'You were not created to sit under a Paradox tree, Talla, nor to be at peace. That is for others to do. Remember we always want what we cannot have or cannot do, it makes the wanting more acute. You will only sit peacefully under a Paradox tree when you are an old lady in her Age of Wisdom, and I shall be sitting beside you, reading to you the story of our lives and our children.'

I caught my breath.

'I cannot. I do not believe that it is true that the Goddess has blessed me with a child, even though people have told me so. It seems too painful to be a blessing to me, somehow, that Ravin should have died and never known that he was a father. I am sure he would not have died if he had known. I need some time to get used to the idea, on my own, I think.'

Gladia looked me up and down again.

'Seems strange you didn't start being sick until after you left Mellia. Though you do seem to have the right sort of size to be for three months, about halfway through, I suppose.' Gladia seemed to have done a lot of discussing about women's appearances at various stages of having a baby. I supposed it must have related to all the work she had done over the years with the Angels, who usually appeared with bellies of various sizes. Still, I didn't like the idea of being discussed in this way and ignored her.

'Would you like some of this fig and almond cake?' I asked instead, attempting to deflect the attention. Gladia could always be distracted by cake, which was a novelty in Oramia, though common in Kashiq. It was not the sort of thing that traders brought back with them to Oramia, for it did not keep for many days, especially when it was hot, and in any case, most traders had other more important things to trade for. I offered her the biggest piece.

'I will go back to Gabez soon,' said Achillea suddenly. 'I should not leave Tarik for too long with the children, they will drive him mad.' She looked at me pleadingly. 'Perhaps Gladia could stay with you, and you could bring her back tomorrow?' I could tell that she wanted me to rescue her. Gladia was a dear friend, but she could be overwhelming, and the children got very excited and then she ended up being very stern towards them. But Gladia couldn't stay here, and I couldn't take her back on the next day because it would add too much time to my planned journey. I tried to think swiftly, but Gladia was too quick for me.

'Am I not wanted here?' Her voice raised at the end of the question accusingly. Achillea turned to look at me in surprise. After all, it was Gladia whom I had clung to after Ravin had died. Gladia was the closest person to a mother that I had ever known. What could I possibly want to do that would stop me from looking after Gladia for a day? Frustrated, I replied hastily.

'Of course, you are. But I am going on a journey in the morning, early, and I cannot change it.'

'Where is this journey to?' asked Achillea suspiciously. Perhaps she remembered my talking about the Isles of Soora. I sighed.

'I am going to the Isles of Soora from Safran. There is a space on a boat for me in two weeks' time. Ravin planned it before we went to Mellia, and I only found out about it recently. I have to go because it is the last thing Ravin arranged before he died. I will not take too long, a month at most, and then I will be back here.'

Gladia snorted. 'You are having a child; I can tell you that without being a Birthmother. In a month's time, you will certainly be convinced. But travelling all that way doesn't seem sensible to me, and on a boat. I never heard of such a thing.' She tutted and shook her head.

'You can't go all that way!' said Achillea. 'You need to be here with the people who care about you!'

'I am going.' I was firm and their opposition was making me feel more and more obstinate. Why should I not go to the Isles of Soora? If I was having a child, it was a normal thing, and not something to stop one's life. I often saw women at the market trading things and carrying big loads when they were very close to giving birth.

'She will do what she wants,' said Gladia finally. She turned then to speak to Achillea, so I could not see her expression. 'You go back to Gabez now, Achillea. I am quite capable of walking back over tomorrow morning when Talla sets off on this trip of hers. In fact, I will probably leave before her, since I am always awake with the first rays of the sun. It will give me a chance to talk to Talla and it will give her the chance to go off on her journey.'

I looked at her suspiciously, but her round gleaming face was impassive. A crumb of cake clung to her lower lip. I looked at Achillea, but she too seemed unconcerned, and agreed to meet Gladia back at her dwelling the next day. I could not think how to express that I simultaneously felt annoyed by their concern and annoyed by their lack of concern, so, instead, I went to find some more coffee. When I returned, they were speaking of Jember and Bellis's reaction to him leaving Mellia.

'He is very excited to be making his own way now,' said Achillea. 'Durkin is a strict but fair man, according to Tarik, and he will give Jember a good training as a woodcarver.'

'Bellis could see that it was the best way for them both, but she wept long and hard after he had gone. I hope that one day she and Maren might come together to visit him in Gabez, when he has settled down into the pattern of life.' Gladia turned to me. 'She wanted me to tell you of her gratitude for helping to answer some of the questions she could not, about what happened. I think it was easier for her when the Angels were not coming to us unknowing, as they do now. It is as if their pain, or the pain they would feel if they knew what was done to them is passed on to her, since she does know their pain. Ambar really has put us in a difficult position this time.' She sighed. 'Life seemed easier in the old days before we got caught up in all this.'

'But think of all the women you have helped, Gladia.' Achillea was always one for looking on the brighter side. 'Their lives at least are better. Look at Bellis and how much she loves and depends on you. It is as if she is the daughter you lost to the Temple.' Gladia nodded and smiled. I felt a momentary sharp anger. Why was it always Bellis who was thought of thus? Why could Gladia not see me or be reminded of me in these same words? Why could I not remind her of the daughter she had lost to the Temple? I went out to blow some life into the embers of the fire to boil the water for the coffee. If I had been on my own, I might have started having second thoughts about my prospective journey, but somehow, now that I had told Achillea and Gladia of my plans, it made them more real, and not something that I could step away from. In a curious way, their opposition to my plans just made me want to fulfil them even more.

Later that evening, I told them a little more about what I planned to do when I got to the Isles of Soora, about the learning that Ravin had done and what I wanted to find out about the physic that they made there. I did not mention the physic that Ravin had been looking at which made it more likely that you would have a child. In any case, it seemed unnecessary now. Instead, I talked about how perhaps one could encourage the bees to make honey from the plants which had the healing properties and thus make honey into a physic itself. Achillea was very interested in this, as I had known she would be, and immediately began coming up with ideas of which would be the ideal plants to use in this way. Gladia sat quietly for much of the evening while she stitched. She did not need much light to see what she was doing, for she was just stitching around the edge of a netela and not following a pattern. Her hands were well practiced in this, and she stitched unerringly, straight lines of tiny, even stitches. She was using a bright yellow thread, the colour of the sun, on a netela which was a light blue, and was sprinkled with tiny flowers in the same yellow. I praised her sewing, and she beamed, pleased with my compliment.

'Are you sure I cannot teach you to stitch, Talla? You used to be very good at making designs for me when we first met.' I recalled the patterns I used to draw for Gladia, using a piece of parchment and a pounced pattern. In more recent years, she had asked Ravin to do her some drawings to copy onto her netelas and many of them had become favourites. Ravin had been good at making pictures of flowers and leaves and birds, but also in making patterns with shapes. I could wield a pen much more accurately than a needle, and my stitching was functional at best. Even Lisu, Achillea's daughter, could stitch with more skill than me. The Temple had taught us the basic skills and then selected those who showed promise for more training and teaching. Perhaps if they had given more training and teaching to those who found it difficult rather than those who found it easy, I might have had more interest in such things. I laughed.

'I think I will stick to the bees, Gladia; their sharp needles never sting me like your needles do! But if a child is born to me, will you stitch its headband? I would l like there to be remembrance of Ravin and this will always have him with us.' Gladia's face softened and she agreed that she would indeed make the Kashiqi headband for my child if one was born.

'I wish you wouldn't go,' said Achillea. 'But I know you will always do what you want to do, despite what everyone says. It is something admirable, though infuriating. But I must get back now, to get over the bridge to Gabez before the night's bell.' The bridge between Pirhan and Gabez was closed at nightfall, and a loud bell was sounded a few minutes beforehand so that the traders could all return. 'I will meet you back at our dwelling in the morning, Gladia,' she added, looking at Gladia meaningfully.

'I will see you out,' said Gladia, heaving herself up. 'Talla, why not go and brew some more coffee for us, and perhaps another piece of that cake since I will be gone in the morning!' The bridge reopened each morning with the first rays of the sun, and although I intended to begin my own journey early, it would likely not be quite as early as Gladia intended. She had always risen with the sun and gone to sleep early too. She walked outside with Achillea, and I could hear them talking quietly, no doubt about me and their concern about my plans. Sometimes, even all these years later, I still struggled with the interference of others in my own plans. At the same time, I was grateful, often, for their advice and their concern. Love seemed to me to be a thing of position; each person had the perfect place for their loved ones to be: some kept them very close and others further away, and the ones who knew and loved you most, somehow knew the exact place to be.

Chapter 11

I awoke with a start. The sun was coming through the opening, high up in the wall, which let in the light. Perhaps it was Gladia leaving? But when I pushed aside the curtain of my room, it was clear that Gladia had already left for Gabez. She had left me the netela she had been finishing off. It was typical of Gladia that she would leave a gift, quietly and without drawing attention to it. She liked to be in charge of conversations, and to tell everyone else what to do, but she gifted things quietly, as if to show a different side to her. I picked it up and held it close to my face. It smelled faintly of jasmine and was warm from lying in the patch of sunlight. I decided to take it with me on my journey and put it over my hair. I had also taken Ravin's headband and used it now for myself. Nobody would know that it was not mine by birth, and it would make me feel as if some small part of Ravin was with me on this journey to Soora.

I took the path south out of Pirhan. There were already quite a few travellers on the path, many of them were metalworkers heading towards the honeygold mines at Darsoun. I would be turning from the path long before then, however, and going east into the risen sun, heading towards the town of Bariz where I could spend the first night. Ravin and I had been to Bariz once. It was right in the middle of the land of Kashiq and had, like all Kashiqi towns, been built around a spring. It was surrounded by hills, and you could see them faintly in the distance, even from near Pirhan. I squinted into the sun and continued to walk. I no longer felt sick and having this journey to aim at made me feel more alive and focused than I had done for a long time. If there was a baby, then it would be a wandering soul if this trip were anything to go by.

I walked alone but keeping other travellers in sight. There were no trees around, only the shifting sands which formed their own hills and mountains. The path led between their soft mounds, on harder sandy stone. I wondered if it had been worn down to this rock by thousands of travellers over the years, or if it had always been there. There were sandstone pillars and outcrops here and there and it was at one of these that I sat in the shade for a rest and a drink and some dried fruit. There was no one else here and I leaned gratefully against the cool of the rock. Looking down, I could see the little pits of the sand lions and remembered the time that Ambar had shown me how to capture the little creatures, telling me how he had done the same thing as a child in the OutFort. They were cunning creatures, antlions, waiting patiently for the fall of sand into their trap which signified a fallen creature to be attacked. I touched the edge of the pit with a stray piece of dried shrub. There was no response. Perhaps its owner had moved into another dwelling. I touched it again. This time there was a twitching at the bottom of the pit. I tried to capture it, but it was too fast for me.

Looking up, I could see a small group of travellers heading for the same shade as me. Luckily, it was a large outcrop and there was plenty of shade to share. I wondered if any of them were heading to Bariz, or even to Safran. Travelling loosely with others might be a good plan. There were a few pebbles scattered about on the ground. Some were the rough, crumbling pieces of sandstone that littered the landscape near these pillars. The sand built up into these tall piles of sand which became rocks, and then, with the passage of time, became sand again. It seemed life was a constant process of constructing and then deconstructing and then remaking. Ravin used to tell me that the only way to understand how anything was made was to take it down to its key parts and then rebuild them. Perhaps the Goddess was trying to understand the world.

I ate a few dried apricots. The dry sun of Kashiq was perfect for drying fruit and it didn't have time to rot before it was a well-preserved dried fruit that could last for many weeks. They even dried out thin strips of meat in the same way, after rubbing it in salt and spices. I preferred a spicy Oramian stew but could see that dried meat made more sense. You could put the dried meat into a sort of stew or soften it in boiling water before you ate it. It was only made at the hottest time of the year, and the very thin slices were laid out on flat rocks for only a short while before they were dried or cooked by the sun. Then they were packed away in small gourds of salt and spices and honey to preserve them.

'Are you going to share those apricots with me, or do I have to get my own?' Gladia flopped down next to me and fanned herself. I looked at her in disbelief. What was she doing here? She was supposed to be back in Oramia by now. Talking to Achillea and the children, lecturing Jember, planning her return to Mellia. But not here. I opened my mouth, but I didn't know what to say.

'You are wearing the same sort of face that Jember wears when he is asked to do the chores,' she commented drily. 'Did you really think that we would just let you go off on a mad trip to an unknown place and do nothing? It was clear that you had no intention of staying at home, so the safest option was for one of us to come with you. It couldn't be Achillea, so it has to be me. Even though you might have thought I was getting too old for such things, I am plenty hardy enough for a journey. I might make a lot of noise and fuss about it, but I usually get things done, and I nearly always succeed in what I plan.' She looked at me. 'So don't bother trying to talk me out of it or try to send me back or anything else. You are as stubborn as I am, but I have had more years of practice.'

Mutely, I held out the soft basket of apricots and Gladia took a few and placed one in her mouth, chewing it thoughtfully. I expected to feel angry with her for ignoring my plans and for making me take on her plans instead, but, curiously, I felt only relief that someone would be there who knew me and who knew Ravin and who wanted the best for me. Although what Gladia thought was best and what I thought was best were not always the same thing, I reminded myself. It might be a good idea to explain to Gladia what we would be doing on this journey and that she would have to follow my lead if she wanted to join me. I had a strange feeling in my belly. A fluttering, bubbling feeling. It came again. As light as the touch of a bee's wing on my cheek. It was the movement of a living thing, quite unlike anything I had ever felt before, for it came from inside my skin not outside it. I dropped my hand to my belly. Gladia fixed me with a glinting eye. The feeling came again, and this time I thought I felt it from the outside with my hand as well as from the inside.

'The baby is moving, isn't it?' said Gladia smiling. 'Now will you believe that it is coming?'

'I cannot. It just does not seem real to me. I feel as if I should have known that such a thing had happened, that there should have been some instant sign from the

Goddess. If only we had known, then maybe it would have given Ravin strength to go on fighting to live. I do not know if I want one without the other,' I said.

'Perhaps it was Ravin who gave you the strength to have this baby,' said Gladia pensively. 'I do not understand it myself. Why does the Goddess bless people with a child who should perhaps not have one, those like the Angels, who would be better never being blessed in this way and yet never blesses those, like me, who had only one child and who never had the chance to raise it?' She looked at me defiantly. 'It is a strangely unkind Goddess that can bless a woman with a child and then, when she has to give it up to the Temple, to the Goddess herself, cannot bless her again.'

'Perhaps it is no more than chance,' I replied. 'Perhaps we give the Goddess too much gratitude. After all, the bees are similarly blessed, even though they have no Temple as far as we know. And so is every other animal and bird, and creeping creature. Perhaps it makes us happy to think that the Goddess is thinking of each of us, especially if we seem to be chosen for happiness.'

Gladia looked at me. Her eyes glinted, but she said nothing, reaching instead for her leather water bag and drinking from it. She was wearing a netela in purple which seemed quite simply decorated compared to the ornate ones she usually chose. It was decorated with yellow circles and discs of different sizes. She wore it, as I did, over my head to protect her from the hot sun, as all Kashiqis did. This was not usual for Gladia; normally she proudly ignored Kashiqi traditions, insisting on maintaining her Oramian style of dress. I looked down and saw that she was wearing the loose trousers of Kashiq too.

'I thought I had better dress like someone from here, so it looks like we belong together. I shall be your

mother as we travel, I think. It would make sense.' She
nodded her head wisely and then said, with a sparkle
in her eye, 'It will allow me to give you lots of advice
and tell you what to do in front of others and you will
have to listen. It will be very enjoyable for me. Tell me
more about what we are looking for and what you think
you will find on these islands which cannot be found in
Oramia?'

Resigned, I told Gladia what I had told Achillea and
Tarik about what I had found out about the place we
were going to. I also told her what Khadar had told me
about the Birthmothers being trained on the Isles. I
told her that the best Birthmothers came from there
and travelled out into other lands and that Hortensia,
the one who had trained Maren, had come from there.
Gladia listened carefully and nodded a few times
thoughtfully. Then she took one more drink and
suggested we should continue our journey since we had
a long way still to go. Although my plans had been
changed by her appearance, I was glad of her company
while we walked. She told me that she and Achillea had
agreed on the plan together and she had, in any case,
already told Bellis and Maren that she would stay away
for about a month. I wished again that they could all
read, as I could and told Gladia this. She surprised me
with her answer.

'I agree with you, Talla. I really think that this
scribing is not for the likes of me to learn or to do but
it would make everything so much easier if I could just
send a message to Achillea or Bellis with my words in
it as if I were speaking. Otherwise, the wrong message
might be sent by accident. I will never learn it properly
because I am too old and stubborn to take lessons, but
I would like to learn to read and scribe a few words
which I can use as messages. Of course, that would

mean that the people I was sending them to would have to learn them too, though...'

'Well, I could show you how to scribe and recognise only a few words,' I replied, not wanting her to talk herself out of this new development. 'Then you and I can send messages to each other, even if nobody else can. We can think of a few things we might want to send as a message, like "I will come in a week" or "Please bring cake".'

Gladia laughed at the last message and agreed that message would be well-used. I hoped that once Gladia saw how useful it could be to say things exactly to another person, even when you were far away from them, that she might want to learn more and learn how to read and scribe properly, for teaching her to recognise and scribe a few phrases was really no different to the methods employed by the OutRiders where they sent pre-agreed symbols to one another, as we had once done with Ambar. I could not understand why Ambar did not learn to read, but he had told me that it was not considered appropriate for him to know how to read when Lunaria, his wife and Queen, could not. Which in turn made me wonder why she did not learn to read, for she was the Queen of the entire land, and we were all, in some way, under her command. In fact, why did not all the Priestesses and OutRiders learn to read and Scribe, instead of continuing with their practice of having a designated Reader at every Temple and OutFort?

We continued to walk at a steady pace, I was walking slower than I used to, but it was more restful to walk at this pace anyway. For all of her puffing and sighing, Gladia had great stamina and was used to walking long distances with ease. It was hot though and we stopped in every small patch of shade we could find and were grateful to get to Bariz as the sun started to slip below the horizon. The sky was a light golden colour, almost the same shade as the shifting sand beneath our feet, as we got to the travellers' dwellings which were situated just as you came into the town. We could have chosen to sleep outside, using a cloth for a tent, but however hot it got during the day, it got much cooler at night, and, in any case, Ravin had warned me of the scorpions which lived in the grainy sand and rocks, and of their propensity for finding warm bodies lying on the sand. He had himself been stung by one as a youth, after accidentally rolling over onto it in the night. He described the pain of the sting as being a hundred times worse than a bee sting. Although I had still never been stung by a bee, I had seen their effect on others, and had no wish to try out a scorpion sting.

The dwellings were basic rooms with two sleeping mats and a large clay pot of water, a fireplace and a cooking pot and plate. We traded a few small items we had brought with us for that purpose; some fresh oranges and almonds from Pirhan and some small salves. Bariz itself was famed for its dates and there were date palms everywhere. There were large groves of them surrounding the town, irrigated with water from the spring when it was the time for them to fruit. It was said that the hot sun and the dry sand made the perfect date; plump, sweet and juicy, and they were certainly delicious. Everywhere around Bariz, there was evidence of the dates they were famed for, from the shade shelters and roofs which were thatched with the leaves of the date palm to the brooms made with old flower stalks to the sweetmeats and cakes which abounded. There were some very large dates which had had the seed removed and which were stuffed with crushed nuts and dried fruit. In the more northern towns of Kashiq that I had been to, the stuffing would have been mixed with honey to bind it, but here, where the date was the king, they used something they called date honey, where the sweet pulp of the date had been mixed with water and orange juice to make something sweet and viscous. I would have preferred honey myself.

We sat out in the evening, under the waving fronds of a palm tree, the warm breeze moving over us gently. I was happy that Gladia had come with me, that I had someone to talk to or perhaps also to be quiet with, for the company of one with whom one can be silent cannot be overestimated. She sat stitching in the half light of the lantern. She was not doing embroidery but was just stitching the narrow hems around the netelas she had already sewn, and she did not need to see to do that. She had done it so many times, her fingers worked without her mind seeming to.

'Ambar came to Mellia again a few weeks ago,' she said. 'I don't really know why, unless he thought you would be there. He was asking questions about the Angels that we have cared for, the ones who do not remember. He wanted to know if they all still forgot everything. It seemed very important to know whether any of them remembered anything. Why do you think that is?'

'I do not know.' I thought of what Ambar had told me about the Isles of Soora being the place where they got the physic of forgetting. I wondered if they used it on other occasions, and why they made it in Soora in the first place. I thought back to the night that Ambar and I had taken it and I knew that I could never tell Gladia that I had taken that physic. Some of what I was thinking must have shown on my face, because she shot me a sharp look.

'Has he said something to you about it?'

'No, I have not seen him since we were in Mellia. I do not expect to see him at all. I was wondering how they knew it would work, and if they were told how long it would work for. After all, at the Court of the Queen, they can keep giving it to the Angels, but once they leave them with you, you cannot and will not be giving them more. Perhaps they are worried that leaving the Angels with you is no longer a good idea and that it might be better to keep them all.'

Gladia frowned.

'Surely they would know how long it lasted for?'

I agreed that it seemed unlikely that they had not been told this, but, at the same time, if it lasted forever, then those who lived in the Isles of Soora would only ever be able to trade with new traders for it and it had sounded as if the OutRiders traded often for the physics from the islands. It was only a short while ago, but I really regretted pleading with Ambar to give me that physic. There was something very unsettling about not knowing anything about what had happened, even though I had probably just gone to sleep. I would not choose to do it now, but I could not change the past, however much I might want to. We always think we would change many things about the past, but we are already changed by the past when we think that. We look back on the past having already learned its lessons.

Gladia was concerned at the thought that the women she and Bellis cared for might start to regain their memories after a while. It would surely come as a worse shock to them to start to recall these things suddenly than if they were reliving an event which they already knew had happened. We talked back and forth about this for a while but there was no solution possible from where we were. In any case, we were both tired and needed to leave early next morning for the next part of our journey, so we took it in turns to bathe with some of the water which had been left for us in the dwelling and quickly went to sleep. It was a mark of how tired I was that even Gladia's stertorous snoring did not cause me more than momentary irritation.

Chapter 12

It took us three more days of travel to finally reach Safran, the town from which we would get the boat to the Isles of Soora. The landscape was much the same, and the towns we visited were also very similar to Bariz. Ebdil was bigger, Galdin was smaller. But they were much more interesting to me because Ebdil was the place where Ravin had stayed when he had left home, where he had lived with Hurkim, his beloved teacher, the one who taught him all he knew and who gave him his thirst for knowledge. It was many years since Hurkim had died and I did not know of any other's name who might have known Ravin. As we walked through the small market, I tried to see in my mind what Ravin might have seen. Ravin had always told me that a place was made by the people who lived in it, rather than the buildings or the location of the place and had never talked much about the place of Ebdil. He had never told me that so many dates were grown there, but I did remember him saying to me that there were no bees there, that the dates grew without the help of the bees, and that I would not want to live there. He was right. It seemed strange to me that there were no orchards there as there were in Arbhoun and the other more northern Kashiqi towns.

Galdin was a smaller place, though bigger than the village remembered by Ravin. It had no doubt grown in the years since he had been there. I looked around curiously, trying to imagine Ravin as a small boy running around the dusty paths between the dwellings, or chasing about with the other boys. Gladia and I watched as a small group of five boys played some game involving chasing one another armed with a long, whippy strand from a date palm. Try as I might, I could not decipher the rules, and eventually assumed they must be changing them as they played. I thought then how much we rely on the rules of the games we play in life not changing. If the rules for living were changed as often as in this game, we might not be so shocked when things happened which we did not expect. Gladia followed my gaze, smiling at the little boys.

'It doesn't seem long since Jember was playing games like this and now he is living away from his home and learning to be a woodcarver.' She sighed. 'All it does is remind me how quickly the years seem to pass. You will find that for yourself, Talla, when the little one is here. No sooner will it be born then you will see it grow so fast you will barely remember when it was so small. Do you think you will have a boy or a girl?'

It still seemed important to me that I could not acknowledge directly that I would have a child soon. The emberjar of my mind seemed to want to burn with two fires. I knew from what I had observed in myself that it must be true, and yet, I still felt that until I got to Soora, where Ravin had wanted me to go, I could not say it out loud in case it was not true, in case the rules for this particular game had been changed without me knowing.

'I do not know,' I replied, which was true. Gladia was not satisfied with this vague response, however, and pressed me further.

'Well, if you could choose, which would you prefer to have?'

'I don't know,' I repeated, genuinely unsure. The Goddess blessed you with a child, surely it was not for you to have a preference, any more than one could wish one was younger or older or taller or shorter. 'It is the choice of the Goddess, is it not?'

Gladia glared at me. 'It is not like you to be so reliable on the so-called choices of the Goddess, Talla. Surely you are not trying to put me off my question? I will always get an answer, it just takes a little longer sometimes to get it!'

I laughed out loud. She was right. Of all the people one might hope to put off finding out an answer, Gladia was the one who you would never succeed with. I decided to answer her in general terms.

'Well now, looking at Achillea's children, the girls seem to be both louder and livelier, and little Amir seems to sleep and smile a lot, so perhaps a boy is more peaceful. On the other hand, remembering how loud and lively Jember was as a boy, perhaps a girl is less trouble...'

Gladia smiled. 'I think you will find that they all have their qualities and their failings. It will be interesting to see, and even more interesting to me to see you as a mother, Talla, because, in truth, I never imagined you having children. You and Ravin seemed very happy without them, unlike Achillea and Tarik who never seem to stop having them!'

Ravin and I had never spoken with anyone about our wish to have children, preferring to keep it to ourselves, and so I did not blame Gladia for her conclusions even though I found them a little hurtful. Reminding me how easily Achillea and Tarik were blessed by the Goddess just served to make me think that perhaps I had disappointed the Goddess in the way I lived my life. It was the only reason I could hold on to. Ravin had never seemed to care about it as much

as I had, and yet, now he was dead and I could not talk
to him about it, I had found out that it was something
that very much occupied his mind. That hurt me too.
The emberjar of my mind crackled.

'Just because you did not think of me having
children does not mean that Ravin and I did not want
them. You, above all others, must know what it is like
to want a child and not to have one. More than anyone,
you know what it is like to have a child but then to have
them taken away, and to long for one but never to have
one. It is the same for me, Gladia. Now that it seems
that I will have what Ravin and I yearned for, I can only
think that it might be lost to me, that the Goddess will
change her mind.'

Gladia was silent, but I could see her lip trembling
and I regretted saying what I had. There were few
things that could make Gladia weep, but the thought of
her lost daughter was one of them, even now, so many
years later.

'I am sorry, Gladia,' I said, hastily. 'I spoke unkindly
to you.' A tear trickled down my cheek. Gladia patted
my hand.

'Of course I know how it feels. I just did not know
that you felt it too. And you will be luckier than me, I
am sure, for I never knew my child before she was
taken away. She is real to me, but not to anyone else. I
live with knowing that she will never know how much
I wanted to keep her and how much I have thought of
her over all these years. If there is a Goddess, I hope
that she has heard my earnest prayers for my daughter
and kept her safe.' She smiled at me. 'She would, of
course, be older than you by a long way; I was very
young when she was born. But sometimes I think that
the Goddess sent you and Bellis to remind me of what
my own daughter might have been. I'm glad she did.
Now, let us find some food in this place and then sleep

for we have yet more walking to do tomorrow, and my old bones are getting weary.' She heaved herself up and brushed the fine sand off her robe, making a cloud which caught the last of the sun's yellow rays.

The travellers' dwellings in Galdin offered a meal along with the use of the dwelling, depending on the trading, and Gladia had traded some of her stitching. They were quite plain netelas by Gladia's standards, but they were pleasing, in tones of orange and yellow. Since we had first coloured cloth years ago, Gladia had continued to collect and use the marigold flowers which gave those tones, and her garden back in Mellia was now full of marigolds. It was by far the easiest of the dyes to make, aside from brown, and was so bright and cheerful that people could not resist it. It was the colour of the sand which blew all around and of the darker sandstone pillars further west, where we had come from. Here in Galdin, as we got closer to the Isles of Soora, the sand was becoming lighter in colour, almost the colour of honeygold.

'We have a good chicken stew tonight,' said the woman who was in charge. She smiled at us. There was a wide gap between her front two teeth which made her smile seem even wider. She wore one of Gladia's yellow netelas as a Kashiqi headdress, with an embroidered green band. She handed us each a clay dish of stew and a flatbread and then took one for herself, having served all the travellers who were there. She came to sit next to us and asked questions of us as all do of travellers. Where we had come from, where we were going, what work we did, what trades we made and so on. She praised Gladia's netelas and then asked conversationally whether either of us had been to Galdin before.

'No.' said Gladia cheerfully. 'But we knew someone who lived here once.' I glared at her, not wanting to talk about Ravin to strangers, especially in the place which he had grown to hate. He once told me that his happy memories were all of people, and his sad memories were all tied to places. 'Stay with the people who make you happy, and leave the places that do not, and somehow, you will end up in the best place.'

'What was their name? I might have known them. Are they still living somewhere else in Kashiq?'

'His name was Ravin,' answered Gladia, speaking for me because she knew I could not. 'He died not long ago, after an accident. He was her husband.' She pointed to me. It was not true that he was my husband because we had never married, but it was as if we were.

'Ravin! Did he leave here long ago? His mother was of Yael. She cared for my own father when he was dying. She brought him comfort as he left this world.'

I told her that this did sound like Ravin and his family and explained that he had left Galdin when he was only fifteen, leaving quickly because of his brother. She frowned.

'I only knew that the boys left after their mother died. The older one was already one of the Defenders of Yael and I assumed the younger one went to be one too, with his brother. It would have been a way of keeping them together, wouldn't it?'

I wondered if Ravin had ever considered this, that his brother, who he saw as trying to force him into a career in which he had no interest, was only trying to keep the two of them together. I wondered whether his brother would tell the story in the same way that Ravin had. I nodded and smiled at the woman, who told us that nobody had ever seen the brother again, anyway but that she could probably find somebody who had known Ravin's mother. I smiled again and declined the offer. I could not see that it would make any difference to anyone, and from the eager way in which this woman chatted about things, it would not be long before the news of Ravin's death would be common knowledge in Galdin. Gladia praised her stew and the talk turned to recipes and cooking before we headed off to sleep.

Chapter 13

Safran was a town like no other I had yet encountered. It was built at the edge of a huge expanse of water, bigger than anything I had ever seen before. Ravin had read me the scribings of one called Bashtar who wrote poems and stories about this water called the Great Sea.

> *'Silken smooth in the morning*
> *Fast moving at dusk;*
> *The Great Sea brings life to many*
> *And death to many more.'*

As we had approached Safran, we had seen this water, shimmering between the sand and the sky so that it almost looked as if it were floating. As far as your eyes, squint shut against the bright sun, could see, there was a line of shimmering blue ahead of us. Gladia stood still and looked in amazement at it.

'Bless the Goddess! So much water! They must never be thirsty!'

'But you cannot drink the water,' I said. 'I read it in a scroll once. The Great Sea is full of salt; to drink it would only make you thirstier. The people must drink water from the rivers and springs like everyone else.'

Gladia gaped at me, disbelieving. 'Well, what is the point of that?' She snorted and her indignation made me smile.

'Just because you can read scrolls doesn't mean you can laugh at me not knowing things,' she said, wagging her finger at me, but her mouth was twitching into a smile too. It was exciting to be somewhere so different to any of the other places either of us had been to before.

Safran was a busy place, bustling with the sounds of people trading and working. The main part of the town looked much like any other Kashiqi town; dwellings made of smooth mud with small windows with a shady courtyard in the middle. These dwellings were roofed with reeds, like the dwellings in Oramia, and there were sitting areas which had also been thatched in the same way, all around the streets. There were the usual palm trees growing along the sides of the paths, and a marketplace set out in a pattern of squares. That market contained a profusion of things which we had never seen in any other market, however. There were stalls which sold all kinds of fish, for a start. In Oramia, there were small fish in the rivers, and I had heard that there were lots of fish in the lakes in the north of the country, but even Benakiell had never been to them. I had eaten fish before but not often. Here, it seemed, it was the main source of meat. Gladia sniffed the air dubiously.

'This is hardly one of the scents of the Goddess, is it? It is Lilavis today and we should be smelling the sweet scent of lavender everywhere, not this strange smell! On the other hand, if these fish are all there for the catching in that big water, then they really are blessed by the Goddess with free food. With all the dates and these fish, one could live here with very little trading.'

There were people with woven sacks of fresh fish and there were also stalls where they traded small, dried fish, their shrivelled bodies emitting a concentrated pungency which almost made my eyes water and certainly turned my stomach. More pleasant was the smell of the fish which had been smoked over fires and which carried the scent of wood fires and herbs as well as of roasted fish. There were also food trading stalls which were cooking, and trading meals made with fish; there were whole grilled fish which people were taking home with them to their families, and there were fish balls, made in front of you out of flour and fish and herbs and then dropped in pots of boiling palm oil.

Large areas of the market were given over to trading reeds which seemed to be used much like the long grass of Oramia, for making roofs and large, woven storage baskets, but I wondered what else they were used for that so much could be traded. That I would only discover in the next days. The other thing, which was offered up for trade, and for which there were many visitors trading, was the salt. I had never before thought about where the salt came from that added flavour to our food in both Oramia and Kashiq. Here, it was something traded by many. It was found in both huge reed baskets lined in cloth and in tiny little cones of plant parchment with the top folded over, and all other sizes in between. We had passed by lots of shallow clay pits filled with the salty water which lapped at the edge of the land. It did not take very long, especially in the heat of this place, for the water to wisp away into the air leaving behind a white sand-like powder: the salt.

Gladia looked critically at the clothing and the stitched items which were arranged for trading. It seemed that it was not a skill which was practiced much here in Safran, and the clothes were quite plain in comparison to most Kashiqi clothing which tended toward the decorated and ornate. Gladia stopped by a place where a woman of a similar age to her was sitting, trading for a variety of clothes. Many of them were clearly older items, ones for which their owners had no need, or in the case of the children's clothes, had grown out of.

'I have a few small clothing items to trade,' began Gladia. 'They are of the best quality, stitched by me, and from the famed stitching traditions of Oramia.' I looked at her in surprise. This was the first I had ever heard of any famed Oramian stitching tradition. She smiled at me breezily. 'My friend here from Kashiq has always admired the stitching found in Oramia and often wears clothing stitched by Oramian stitchers, isn't that so, Talla?' She jabbed me in the arm.

'Absolutely!' I mimicked her bright smile and surreptitiously rubbed my arm. The woman looked at me, interested. I could see her eyes taking in the embroidery on my robe and on my netela, and then Gladia's.

'Hmm. Well, they are always good trades, that's true, but I have little other than clothes to trade here with me today, and you can't be looking for them. What are you looking for and what are you offering?' She looked up at Gladia from where she was sitting, seemingly disinclined to get up. She sat on a mat, her legs stretched out straight in front of her, her hands in repose on her lap.

'We need a place to stay for the next week and all the trader dwellings seem to be in use. As you can see,' Gladia waved her hand in my direction, 'Talla here is blessed by the Goddess and needs to sleep somewhere comfortable.' I almost smiled. Gladia was the one who was seeking the comfortable place to sleep, although of course I would not object to it, either. Gladia had every intention of using me as a potent bargaining chip. I lowered my head humbly and attempted to push out my belly further to emphasise it. The woman looked at me cursorily and then turned her attention back to Gladia.

'Well, I do have a room at my dwelling that you could stay in for the week. Nothing fancy, mind. I'll take three netelas in trade, and you'll have to find your own food. Water and coffee and dates, I will provide for the morning. I'm not bargaining, take it or leave it.'

Gladia, who was about to start the bargaining process shut her mouth and agreed to the woman's terms. She took out one netela, a regular, simply stitched one, and offered it to the woman, who looked at her suspiciously.

'We said three.'

'And three you will have by the end of the week,' responded Gladia firmly. 'We do not yet know if the room will be suitable for us. You will get another in the middle of the week and one more at the end. That's how we do business. Firm but fair.'

The woman laughed. 'Well, it's a long time since someone got the better of me! I think we will get along well. My name is Zareen, by the way. What brings you here to Safran? The only Oramians we usually see are those strange, veiled ones occasionally come to trade with the Isles, with their guards. They bring stitching to trade, too, very high quality. But they only trade with the Isles for the physics. The Soorans will trade only with what they really want or need. They seem to have everything that others want.'

'It would be interesting to hear more of the Isles,' I said, breaking my silence. 'I am Talla, and this is Gladia. Perhaps we can learn more this evening.' I looked around at the market where many traders were already beginning to pack up their goods, ready to return to their dwellings.

'We can go now,' said Zareen, suddenly springing into life, and beginning to fold up the clothing she had for trades. She carried the clothing in a palm leaf basket which she tied onto her back. 'I used to carry my children in this basket when they were babies,' she chuckled. 'It's a good use of it.' Achillea used a length of cloth to carry her children when they were babies, but it served the same function, allowing the mother to go about her daily life with her hands free to work and the child comforted by her closeness and the beat of her heart.

We followed Zareen through part of Safran, down the gradual slope, closer to the big expanse of water. I could see that the land was fringed with dark green reeds, like the ones used to make plant parchment. Perhaps this was the source of all the plant parchment used by the Kashiqis. Arbhoun alone must have had thousands and thousands of plant parchment scrolls in the Tower of the Wise. It had been a long day and we were grateful to arrive at her dwelling a short time later. She showed us the spare room in her dwelling, and we gratefully put down our bags. I was very tired, suddenly and decided to rest on the palm leaf mat for a few minutes before following Gladia outside. She was intent on finding out more about the islands to which were heading, and more about the likelihood of her being able to trade with them. She was older than me by a long way, and usually she was the first one to want to rest and be still, but it seemed that the Goddess, in blessing me with a child, had taken away some of my energy, or perhaps was sending it to the child as it grew. In any event, I closed my eyes and only woke up some time later when Gladia came in to tell me that there was food to be eaten for the evening.

'Time to wake up, Talla! That baby needs food as well as sleep you know!' Through these past years, Gladia had become someone who had learned a lot about caring for women who were with child. She had looked after many of the Angels who Ambar had left for her. He had told us then that marrying Lunaria was what he had always dreamed of, but when I had met him in more recent times, that dream seemed to have changed into a dream of her having his children. I wondered whether he would ever be satisfied, and then I wondered how I had got to thinking of him again. I had determinedly put him out of my mind since I had returned to Pirhan, and since I had found out the plans which Ravin had made before he died. But there was something glowing in the emberjar of my mind, and it would not be quenched. There was a puzzle lingering there, perhaps forgotten for now, which I needed to remember.

Later, we asked Zareen to tell us about the Isles of Soora. She told us that those who lived on the Isles kept apart from the rest of the Kashiqis, even from those who lived in Safran. It was said that the Sooran women had started living there long ago when a small group of women had laded there. Many of them were with child and had been trying to escape from a group of men who were intent on doing them harm. It was said that they had taken a small reed raft, and, in desperation, had cast off into the Great Sea, preferring to take their chance and die in the water than to be recaptured by their pursuers. They had landed on the Isles of Soora and had found that the islands provided all that they needed, including protection from those who chased them. Seeing this as a gift from the Goddess, they had vowed to remain there forever and to make the rules about who would be permitted onto the islands. Men were only allowed to visit for trade but were not allowed to stay and could only sleep on their boats. There were, it seemed, groups of men who lived on their boats, traded with the inhabitants and, occasionally, fell in love with them.

'They come here sometimes, the women who have decided to leave the Isles to be with their men. Some of them stay and live here, but most move on, on their own, after a while. They are used to their own company and do not seem able to live with men for very long. They often go out as Birthmothers in Kashiq, and maybe even Oramia, teaching their craft to others.'

Maren had told us that Hortensia, the one who had been her teacher and had delivered the babies of the Lady Paradox, had originally come from Soora but we did not know what had become of her after she had left those babies at the Temple. I asked her more about the physics and the herbs which they traded, but she knew little, telling us that they only traded them with certain groups, including the Priestesses of Oramia and the guided of Soren in Kashiq. She did, however, tell us that one of the islands was known to be the source of a variety of precious metals and stones and that this was what most of the men who lived on their ships went to the Isles to do. They transported the metals and those who traded in them to and from the island. This fitted in with what Khadar had told me and explained why he knew how to get to the Isles of Soora and could provide us with our place on the boat. We told Zareen that we were planning to visit the Isles and she snorted in the same sort of way as Gladia.

'It's a lot of effort to get there, considering that they will probably send you on the next boat back, later that day,' she said. 'You can only stay if they decide you can, not if you choose to.'

SOORA SUN

I lay awake that night wondering what it was that I hoped to find out from the inhabitants of the Isles of Soora. It seemed that they protected their privacy fiercely and it also seemed unlikely that they would tell me what I might want to know about the mysterious forgetting physic. Perhaps it would be enough for me to go to the Isles just to satisfy my curiosity about the things which Ravin had discovered, but I doubted it. Hearing the history of the founding of the islands reminded me of the Angels. They too needed to find a place of safety to have their babies and were pursued by groups of men. There seemed to be a connection between the women of Soora and the Angels, and my mind was trying to show it to me. Once there was some sort of puzzle in my mind, I had to keep working on it, like a bundle of tangled threads, until it was resolved.

As we waited for the day on which the boat would make its way to Soora, Gladia and I spent time walking around Safran and noticing the differences between it and other towns in Kashiq. On the surface, many things were the same. The markets were laid out in the same way, there were a few Places of Prayer around the town, and the people looked much the same as any other Kashiqis. Still, it felt different. The lower part of the town, beyond Zareen's dwelling, was even more distinct. The rivers which ran into the Great Sea split as they approached it into numerous smaller streams and channels, all of them fringed by the dark green reeds. Men steered small boats up and down these channels, bringing goods from the large dock that had been built where the rivers and the land met the sea.

These boatmen dressed simply in shortened Kashiqi trousers and a short tunic, with loose wide sleeves which enabled them to steer their boats with long wooden poles. They must trade for the wood for the poles from Oramia or further north in Kashiq, I mused, for there were no large, strong trees growing here, only date palms and reeds, unless trees grew on the isles of Soora. The boats themselves were made of those very same palm trees and the reeds. The wood of the palm tree was very light, and they wrapped it in bundles of reeds and bound them all tightly with palm leaf ropes. These boatmen made good trades, since anyone who wanted to get to the dock had to use their services, and anyone who wanted to transport goods to or from the Isles of Soora also needed to trade with them, either for the goods, or for the use of the boat.

I asked Zareen whose guidance the boatmen were under, and she told me that it was Maliq, the god of making and crafting. I supposed that it did require craftsmanship to make the boats, but otherwise they seemed to be general traders to me, which went against the Kashiqi beliefs. It would have been the sort of thing that Benakiell would have liked to do, I thought and mentioned it to Gladia.

'Oh yes, anything to make a good trade and to be free of the rules,' she agreed. I thought back to the only time I had been in a boat before, which had been with Benakiell, crossing the river between Oramia and Kashiq. The movement had been somewhat similar to riding on a horse, but I definitely preferred riding the horse. Even now, so many years later, I remembered those days when I had ridden on the horses with Ambar and wished I could ride them again. Gladia, on the other hand, had not enjoyed riding on the horse at all, and neither had Achillea. I wondered whether Tarik missed riding on them too. I had not told Gladia about the similarity, reasoning that once she was on the boat, she would have to stay on it until it was time to get off. Now that we had travelled together so far, I relied on her calm, no nonsense attitude, and her kind friendship to me. She really was like a mother to me, and one evening, just before we were due to leave, and just after Zareen had left with the remaining netelas due to her, I told her so.

'Gladia, I have never known a mother, and will never meet my own, since she is unknown to me, but ever since I first left the Temple, you have been in my life, and I think that I think of you as a mother. I do not know how that feels, exactly, having grown up without one, but I feel that if I need to lean on someone, if only for a little while, then I can lean on you. I know that you think of Bellis as your daughter whom you lost to the Temple, and of Jember as your grandson, but if you have any love to spare, I would like you to look on my child as your grandchild too.'

I blinked. Since the Goddess had blessed me with this unborn child, my eyes had been too full of tears. Perhaps it was only that my grief for the loss of Ravin was intertwined in my thoughts of a future with a child but without him.

Gladia patted my hand, and then rested her own on top of it. I could feel her plump warm fingers on top of mine, like a comforting blanket.

'There is always love to spare, Talla, as long as it is felt. It is like one of the springs of water in Arbhoun, endlessly providing for those who need it. You are a part of my family, which I have somehow made for myself. My daughters Bellis and Achillea and you, who have all lost your mothers have found me, and I, who have lost my daughter have found three. We are all blessed by the Goddess. And I am still wondering whether you will bless me with a grandson or a granddaughter.'

'We will only know when it is born,' I replied, still not wanting to think so far ahead. Gladia, however, had no such inhibitions.

'I wonder if the Birthmothers on Soora will be able to tell somehow whether it is a boy or a girl,' she mused. 'They probably have some herb that they can drop on your tongue, and it changes to a different colour depending on what you are having.' I laughed, imagining it.

'Anyway, it is time to sleep. We have to leave at dawn tomorrow so that we can get down to the dock where the boat will take us to Soora.' She checked over her bundles to make sure she had everything she needed and then went inside the dwelling. I did the same thing, checking that my precious gourds of honey were still well sealed and had not been cracked. At home, I often kept my honey in glazed, clay jars, but they were very heavy and not at all suitable to bring on a long journey. I traded my honey in various differently sized gourds which I grew in the garden. The small ones were used by Achillea for her salves and ointments, and the larger ones by me for my honey. I still hoped that it would be my honey which I could trade for information from the inhabitants of the Isles of Soora.

ORANGE

Chapter 14

There were small, gentle waves in the Great Sea. They tapped and poked at the sides of the boat, keeping it constantly rocking, which it was doing anyway because of all the people who were clambering on to it. It was a larger version of the small crafts which went up and down the rivers, out to the Great Sea, and who fished in the water, heaping up their catch in the flat bottoms of their boats. This boat was made of a combination of the palm wood and reed bundles which the small boats were made of and with planks of wood cut from large trees. It looked like the wood from a Paradox tree, and I wondered if that was one of the things which was brought from Oramia to trade with Soora.

We had been allowed on to the boat after the man who was in charge had examined a simple list on which names were scribed. I guessed that Khaled must have sent him a scroll to reserve our places. He pointed us to a space on the right, where nobody was sitting, and told us to stay sitting for the whole voyage.

'How long will it take to get there?' asked Gladia, apprehensively. He laughed.

'It will take as long as it takes. Depends on the winds and the waves. Not much wind so far, so it might be a longer journey than usual if the sails don't catch the wind.' He gestured upwards to a pole in the centre of the boat where some large yellow sails hung loosely from woven ropes. Then he turned and pointed to the sides of the boat where, on flat extensions there sat six sailors on each side, each one holding a large wooden paddle. 'If there's no wind, you'll be relying on them to get you there. Ready boys?'

They all nodded in assent, as a large thick rope was untied from the dock and tossed back onto the boat. The men with the paddles picked them up and began to push the boat through the water. The paddles moved up and down at exactly the same rhythm. I could see that, at the front of each side raft, there sat a man who did not row, but who gave instructions to the men, and shouted across to his counterpart on the other side. It reminded me of the way in which ants might move a large dead beetle to their nest; many small, matched movements which made moving a large object seem easy.

Gladia shuddered. She drew her netela over her head and across her face.

'I don't like this. I don't like it at all. It is just like riding a horse, except at least when you were on a horse, if you fell off, you would land on the ground. Here, if we fall off, we will land in the water and drown straight away.'

'We won't fall off,' I reassured her, sounding calmer than I felt. 'They do this every day.'

'Someone probably falls in and drowns every day too,' she retorted gloomily. 'How would we know? In fact, how do we even know that they are going to take us there? Maybe they will just take us into the Great Sea and drown us there and take all our things.' She grasped her bundles tightly. 'Well, I shan't let go of mine, if they want to drown me, they will be drowning my stitching too!'

The sailor in charge of the boat looked up from where he was sitting and laughed out loud again. He was perhaps in his fifth or sixth age. It was hard to tell, for his skin was at once lined but smooth, the crinkles in his face most apparent around his eyes and his mouth from smiling and laughing. He seemed very jovial. His head was wrapped in a dark blue cloth, tied roughly with a Kashiqi headband, but it was a much shorter headcloth than usual, with just a flap covering his neck. I could see that being in such a windy place would make wearing a long headdress difficult and, in any case, here on the water there was no need for protection from the frequent sandstorms found on land. His beard was cut short, close to his chin in the way that many Kashiqi men did as they got older and was well sprinkled with the silver light of wisdom.

'I won't be drowning you, don't worry,' he chuckled, looking at Gladia. 'Your trades aren't rich enough to make me bother!' Gladia glared at him, immediately ready to do battle.

'I'll have you know that my stitching is well known throughout Oramia!' This seemed a stretch to me. She was well known in Sanguinea, but it may have been more for her character than the quality of her stitching.

'Hmm...' The sailor scratched his chin thoughtfully. 'Perhaps it would be worth drowning you after all, then...' Gladia looked up sharply, but his face was once again wreathed in smiles, and she realised that he had been teasing her. We all laughed, Gladia rather self-consciously.

'I am Jan,' he said. 'Short of name but not of height. Who are you, and why do you travel to the Isles?'

Gladia perked up at the opportunity to chat and seemed to forget her discomfort at being on the boat. She glanced at me to see if I would answer first, but I was more interested in watching the water as the boat moved through it, skimming over the top like some small water insect, and I gestured to her to carry on talking.

'Well, I am pleased to meet you, Jan. I am Gladia. I come from far away, in the land of Oramia, where, like I said, I am well known for the quality of my stitching.'

Jan bowed from the waist. 'If the stitching is anything like as beautiful as the stitcher, it must be beautiful indeed!' I rolled my eyes towards the sky, expecting Gladia to do likewise, but instead she giggled like a young girl, and edged her netela further off her face, smiling.

'And what of your daughter here?' he asked, pointing to me. 'Is she the reason you both travel to the Isles? Are you seeking help for the birth?' I was about to correct him on who I was and to tell him my name, but, before I could, Gladia spoke.

'This is my daughter, Talla,' she confirmed. I thought back to what we had talked about the night before, and what I had told her, and felt a warmth inside me. It was the first time that somebody had called me their daughter, and it felt strange, like I had been remade. The thought made me smile at both her and Jan.

'You must have been very young when you had her,' said Jan, intent on charming Gladia. She preened, smoothing down her dress and patting my hand.

'Oh, indeed. We are going to the isles, as you say, to ask the Birthmothers there about the child. Talla's husband Ravin died before he knew about the child, and it is very important that everything is well with the child.' I did not correct Gladia's description of Ravin as my husband, for, in all but ceremony, he was. A word scarcely changed that, especially now that he was gone. She said nothing about my search for answers about the physics made by the Sooran women.

'That stitching of yours had better be as good as you say: they are very particular about who they see. Unless you have something they want, they will put you on the boat again as quick as they can. I don't suppose you will have what they really want at the moment, which is honey. I heard them talking and saying their hives are not producing enough honey for what they want, so they need to get it from elsewhere. Normally they make all their own because the bees feed off the plants which they use for the physic, but the bees are not making honey.'

I stored this information away. Perhaps I would be able to offer my knowledge of the bees to trade with the Soorans for their knowledge of the physics they were trading with the Priestesses and the OutRiders. After all, knowledge and wisdom were valuable things, and, while you could not see them, they might be very precious. Knowing where an ancient spring might be, or how to make plant parchment or how to read could help you much more than trading a wooden box or a netela. To me, it was this which was the most valuable trading commodity. The more knowledge or wisdom one had, the more people might wish to trade for it, especially if you knew what others did not.

By now, the sailors had unfurled the yellow sails and had turned them so that they caught the push of the strong breeze which skipped over the tops of the waves, turning them white and foamy. Every now and then, the sailors on one side or the other would paddle for a while, helping the boat to turn towards the islands ahead of us. As we moved along, we were followed by flocks of birds squawking to each other and occasionally roosting on the higher sail poles. The other passengers on the boat were mainly men from Kashiq who seemed, like Khadar, to be interested in the precious metals which could be found on the islands. There appeared to be no one who might be trading on behalf of the Priestesses or OutRiders of Oramia, but I could not tell. I thought back to when I had first met Ambar, at the market at Sanguinea, and how he had disguised himself as a trader and realised that any one of these traders could be an OutRider. On the other hand, I could not imagine any of the Priestesses disguising themselves as any of the other women on board. Aside from myself and Gladia, there were only three others; one of them must have also been travelling to see the Birthmothers, since she had a huge belly, and must have been close to giving birth; she was with a tiny elderly woman. The other woman had a large bundle of cloth with her. The cloth was a similar colour to the sails of the boat, a kind of deep marigold yellow. It did not seem to be made into clothes or decorated in any way, but just a large amount of yellow cloth. I wondered why they needed so much, and why it was all the same colour.

I pointed it out to Gladia, who immediately asked her new friend, Jan.

'It's the only colour the Sooran women wear. We call the islands the Isles of Soora, because the main island is called Soora, but the women there also call them the Isles of the Sun. The Isle of Rengat, where the Birthmothers live and learn, is the furthest east, and the sun rises there before anywhere else, they say. They say that the sun brings the blessing of the Goddess Soren on them. The day of Flavus, such as it is today, is the most important day of the week for them. The colour yellow is auspicious, since it signifies both Soren and the sun and so they all wear yellow, or shades of it. It gets a bit boring after a while. I much prefer the colours you are wearing, Gladia.'

Gladia looked down at her purple robe and the simple red Kashiqi trousers she wore underneath it and smoothed her hand over the embroidered hem of tiny blue flowers. Jan himself was wearing different shades of plain blue, his short, wide-sleeved robe over the short wide trousers.

'I wear the colours of the water,' he said. 'I am a man of the water, not of the land. Kashiq has endless miles of dry, hot sand and that's what the colour yellow reminds me of. I like the water, the way it changes every day, the fish and the birds and the boat and the sky.'

Gladia shuddered delicately. 'It is all a long way from my home. I think of the colours of the Paradox trees - the purple of the flowers and the green of the leaves. I would far rather be sitting beneath a tree than riding on one in the water!' Jan laughed again. It seemed that nothing could dent his good humour.

'Where do you sleep?' I asked, remembering what Zareen had told us about the men not being permitted to sleep on the Isles, and that she had said they slept on the boats. There did not seem to be anywhere on this boat to sleep.

'When all the people have left the boat, there is plenty of space for me,' said Jan. 'I keep my things in that box over there. I have some old sails which I have rubbed Paradox oil into, and I can tie them up to protect me if it rains – not that it rains very often here. I have a metal box where I can light a fire without burning the boat down so I can keep warm and make a tea. If I need to wash, there is plenty of water! This is my home. I am not tied to any one place, but go where

I wish, and as long as I keep my head down, I do as I choose. The trading means I can have sailors work for me and do the hard work.'

'Well, where do they sleep?' asked Gladia sharply.

'They sleep here too,' said Jan. 'Most of the time, I run the boat on my own, but when I am taking so many passengers and boxes to Soora, I need the extra strength of a few good men, especially when the boat is heavy. But when I am on my own, the boat is light, and I use the sails to move about.'

'Don't you get lonely?'

'Only when I meet lovely ladies like you! Now, please excuse me because I have to go and help with the sails; we will be there soon.'

He got up and went to the ropes which tied the sails and pulled and twisted them so that the sails now hung in a different direction, and then nimbly hopped down to one of the side rowing sections to speak to the men. Gladia's eyes followed him.

'Seems like you enjoy being on a boat more than you thought,' I said drily, unable to resist the opportunity to tease Gladia in the same way that she had teased me over the years. She reached over and jabbed my arm sharply with her finger and then wagged it at me.

'You can't blame him for being impressed with me!' She laughed along with me, but I saw her eyes drifting wistfully back towards Jan, now fully occupied with the steering of the boat, as we came closer to the Isle of Orish, the first of the islands. It was on this island, on the picture which Ravin had drawn, that the precious metals were found and traded. Many of the passengers on the boat wanted to get off here to do their trading.

I could see Orish to the north of us. It seemed almost barren of small plants, with strange craters rising up from the sand. It was made from light-coloured stone, almost the same colour as the pale-yellow sand which drifted over its surface, and which formed long strands on the shore. Here and there, a spindly date palm grew in the sand. The water nearest to the island was a light, shimmering blue, sparkling in the sun, quite different from the dark bluey-grey water we had travelled over to get there. The reason that Jan needed to play full attention to the sails and the sailors became clear. There were patches where the water travelled differently, and as we got closer to them, I could see that they were areas of jagged rocks where a boat could easily founder and be broken apart. Jan was steering the boat between these rocks. Gladia, who had been so anxious about drowning before, now seemed to be completely confident in Jan's abilities, and it was left to me to worry about why we had set out on this foolish journey which risked not only my life but that of my unborn child.

Then, as the boat turned, we could see a small, calm harbour with a large dock in it, similar to the one we had left behind us at Safran. It took little time then to moor the boat, and for Jan to drop a large, flat plank, which hung from the boat, into a slot on the platform. This acted much like a lock and held the boat fast so that some of the passengers could get off the boat safely. They must have all done the trip many times before, because they all walked over the plank on to the island without concern. A couple of the sailors passed over the bundles which they had brought with them for trading.

As I looked around this, the first of the Isles of Soora, from the boat, I saw that on the soft, yellow beaches near the harbour there were many drifted lines of pebbles which had been rubbed smooth by the Great Sea. They differed in size and colour, but they were all smooth and rounded, and looked just like the stones which Ambar had shown me, the ones he had kept since his childhood in the OutFort, in all the same shades. If the OutCommanders got those special stones from here, then the trading with the Isles had been going on for longer than I knew. I would need to ask Ambar about it if I ever saw him again.

Looking up, I noticed a woman, dressed in yellow, standing at the end of the walkway. She was checking the people who had landed against a list scribed on a scroll of plant parchment. It seemed that the women who lived on these islands really were careful about who they allowed onto their islands. Some travellers had only empty boxes and baskets and seemed not to have brought anything to trade, but they had scrolls with them which the woman read carefully before allowing them onto Orish.

'They get those scrolls if they have already traded things in Safran or Soora,' said Jan from behind us. 'It's easier than moving the goods from here to Soora where most of them are kept, so they just bring the note with them instead.' I could see how that made things a lot easier in some ways; much lighter to carry, allowing one to bring more empty containers if one was collecting metal or metal rocks for melting. On the other hand, could these notes not be scribed by someone who was not of the Isles of Soora? I asked Jan.

'They have thought of that. Each note has a special code on it which tells of its authenticity. Since you only ever see a few of them, it's impossible to try to work out what it means or how to scribe your own. Though many have tried!' He laughed. 'They just get put back on the boat.'

'Who puts them back on?' asked Gladia. 'Some of them are quite big men, and there don't seem to be very many women of the islands here.'

'The sailors do it,' he replied. 'We protect the women of the Isles, and, in return, they let us sail around their islands, trading and carrying passengers. They feed us and tend to us if we are ill, and in return, we do as they ask, and return those who try to take advantage of them. We will even carry them off the dock by force if they refuse to leave peacefully.'

'Would you even carry me off the dock?' asked Gladia, her eyes twinkling. Gladia's reassuringly plump and solid figure would indeed take a little effort to move. Especially if she was being stubborn, which was always a possibility with Gladia.

'I would jump at the chance!' Jan said, making Gladia chuckle and me roll my eyes skywards. 'But it won't be at this dock because we are leaving now for Soora.'

He moved off, waited for the last of the travellers who had boarded the boat here at Orish and then unfastened the plank from the platform, and began directing the sailors to turn the boat back towards the open water to the east. As we rounded the long spit of land near the harbour on Orish, we could already see the next island, Soora, ahead of us.

Chapter 15

Soora was quite a contrast to the bare, stony landscape of Orish. It was covered in forest at the western end, and low clouds hung over the forest, wreathing it and softening it. Perhaps these were the forests where the mysterious plants and herbs might be found. The boat sailed quite close to the land, and although the land itself was rocky and fringed with cliffs, there seemed to be no more rocks in the water. As we neared the settlement at Soora, we passed another island, just as close to the boat but on the southern side.

'I think that is the island of Aman,' I said to Gladia, remembering where the different islands were from Ravin's drawing. 'I wonder if anyone actually lives on that island because it looks so small and rocky.'

'It is the holy island of Aman, you are right,' said Jan from across the boat. 'They go there to get messages from Soren. They have celebrations there sometimes, where apparently they drink honeywine and dance and sing. But you can't go there unless you live on Soora, it is forbidden to us – and especially to men, apparently. Though we can still trade for the honeywine anyway, and I'm not much of a dancer!' Again, he laughed, which seemed to be his response to most things.

I thought of the honeywine which Ambar had given me months ago, on the same night that we had taken the physic of forgetting. I recalled its sweet fire and the way it had made me feel happier and more open, and I could see how it might make you feel like singing and dancing, especially if others were. Honeywine was not something that ordinary people in Oramia ever had. It would be traded very highly, if at all, and most people did not want to trade all their pomegranates for a small drink when instead they could have a soap ball, a reed knife, some sewing threads, a couple of baskets and some flour for those same pomegranates. For those who had wealth, like the Queen and her court, perhaps it was taken regularly, as regularly as coffee or Kashiqi tea.

The small town of Soora stood in a shallow cove and the whole area by the water was edged with platforms where boats could pull in. Once again, there were women waiting for the boats as they drew in and locked their walking planks to the side of the dock. Once again, they wore yellow, in different shades, like marigolds or grains of sand, individually different but together all the same. For each place where a boat might land, there were two Soorans, one checking a list of names of travellers and one checking for goods to trade and making a note on what was brought into the island. It reminded me of the scenes at the bridge between Pirhan and Gabez where the same sort of thing happened, and a proportion of all trades was taken away as payment for the privilege of travelling to trade. I could see why most ordinary people did not travel far from where they lived to trade. Items had to be of great value for someone to be willing to give up part of their hard work to one like an OutRider who appeared to do very little that was positive, at least for the people of the Outer. In Kashiq too, the Defenders of Yael, the soldiers, both men and women in Kashiq, took a third of your goods and sent them to the Council of the Wise.

Here, however, it was the Sooran women who collected the taxes, and they were not Defenders of Yael, even though we still were in Kashiq. Or were we? My head spun, trying to untangle it all.

'What happens next?' Gladia asked Jan.

'You will get off and tell your name to Sarina, the one who is waiting nearest the boat. She will scribe it on the list for the day. That list will then be passed on to Harisha who is further up, just at the end. She will then discuss your purpose of travel and she will decide where you can go next, if your trades are useful and so on. If she decides that there is no good reason for you to be here, then you will wait over there in that shelter.' He gestured toward a simple shelter built of bundled reeds at the end of the dock, where a small number of people sat. 'Then you will be picked up again by a boat returning to Safran, like I told you before. Otherwise, they will decide how long you can stay here and then they will give you a note with a code on it so that they know when it is time for you to leave.'

Gladia snorted. 'It all sounds very complicated to me. Why can they not just let people go where they wish?'

'There is too much of value here. They are only protecting what they own,' said Jan, for once serious. 'People will always try to take advantage of those who have something they want. We never think, when we see someone who has what we want, of the work they have put into making it, we only think that they have it and that we want it! Even the Oramian Priestesses are not averse to trying to take advantage of the Soorans. Anyway, you had better be moving off, it will soon be time for me to pick up my next passengers.'

'Will we see you again?' asked Gladia.

'Perhaps. If you return to Safran at the same time as me. Otherwise, it was nice to have met you Gladia – and of course, Talla.'

Gladia's face fell briefly, but she smiled in response and bent down to gather her bundles of embroidered articles, and we climbed up onto the plank and across it to the walkway. Jan had already turned to talk to a small group of the sailors who were demonstrating something with some rope, and we left to go and speak to Sarina.

There were only a few of us, the majority having left at Orish. Sarina stood, small, but composed and upright, a scroll clipped to a thin piece of wood so that the breeze which travelled around the harbour did not steal it away. She wore a long robe with wide sleeves which could be tied at the wrists or left wide, just like the sailors. It was of faded yellow, like ebbing sun on sand, and she did not wear any netela, but stood barefaced in the sun, her hair neatly braided. She wore an embroidered belt, which looked to me like a typical Kashiqi headdress and was neatly stitched with six sided shapes, like the shapes of a honeycomb. She raised her eyes to me.

'Name?'

'I am Talla, and this is Gladia.'

'I'm her mother,' added Gladia importantly. I hid a smile. Gladia was enjoying her new status. Sarina glanced at her briefly and made a note of our names.

'Purpose of visit?' I paused and then opened my mouth to answer. Once again, Gladia took over.

'There are three reasons really. The first and most important one is that Talla here is blessed by the Goddess, as you can see. She needs a skilled Birthmother to reassure her about the child. Her husband died before he even knew about this blessing, and it would mean a great deal to know that all is well.

We know that the Birthmothers of Soora are the most skilled of all. We have brought with us things to trade with you. I am a stitcher and embroiderer and have brought with me cloths you may like. Talla makes salves and creams, but her real skill is with the bees. She is a Beeguard back in Pirhan, and was also a Beeguard in Oramia, where I am from. If you need any assistance with your bees, Talla is the one who can do it for you.'

Sarina looked at me, a spark of interest gleaming in her dark eyes.

'She speaks for you a lot, your mother,' she commented. 'You can take your trade goods to that shelter over there and wait for me and I will see whether it is worth anything to us for trade. We will talk about the other things afterwards.' She scribed a curling figure next to our names on the scroll and then moved to the next people who were waiting to be checked.

We walked over to the shelter.

'Try to look a bit more delicate,' whispered Gladia. 'If you want to stay here to find out whatever it is you want to find out, then you will have to look like you need to stay here. I'm going to show her all my yellow stuff first, because it doesn't look like any other colour will do.' We sat down in the shade, outside the shelter, on a rough bench and waited for Sarina to return. I did feel suddenly very tired, much as I had when we had ridden the horses. I hadn't noticed it until I had got off the boat. It seemed unlikely that sitting down and being moved by the agency of something else might tire you, and yet it seemed to. I reached for my water gourd and took a drink.

There was a sharp poke to the arm.

'Sarina is talking to Jan,' hissed Gladia. 'Do you think she is asking him to take us off the island? Or do you think she is asking him if we should stay? What do you think he will say?'

I laughed. 'I am sure if she is asking him about you, he will give a glowing report!'

'Do you really think so?' Her face brightened at the idea.

'We'll find out soon enough,' I said. 'She is coming over here now, along with the other one.' Indeed, her small but determined figure was heading towards us, accompanied by a taller, slimmer figure. Jan had turned to escort one of the remaining passengers firmly back onto the boat.

'Right let's see what you have, then. My name is Sarina, and this is Harisha.'

They waited patiently while Gladia unpacked her stitched cloths and then turned them over, looking at the backs of them with a practised eye, and testing the seams for strength. Gladia, though she was twitching with annoyance at having to have her work judged, remained quiet.

'Some of these will do well. As you may have heard, we Soorans only wear the colours of Soren and the sun, may that light shine upon you. But there may be others here who wish to trade with you for the other colours, the sailors for instance.' The taller one, Harisha, turned to me. 'Do you have your own honey to show us your skill with the bees?'

'Yes, I do.' I took out one of my small gourds of white honey and a small wooden spoon for her to taste it. The honey was rich and almost solid, infused with sweetness and the slight scent of thyme which grew near Pirhan. Harisha closed her eyes as she tasted it, and then rolled it round her mouth before finally swallowing it.

'You have the skill, if this is honey from your own bees. Before you start scolding me for being suspicious, mother Gladia, there are many who try to trick their way onto these isles for reasons that are not related to healing or to the glory of the Goddess. We have learned to be aware of all the tricks. But we will see. We have need of the advice of a Beeguard,' she said, turning abruptly back to me. 'The bees are not making honey well enough. There seems to be something wrong; we do not know what it can be, and we need them for our plants as well as for our honey.'

'I will do all that I can to help,' I replied, feeling suddenly fuller of energy. Somebody needed me and my knowledge. At last, I felt like I could do something useful.

'They can stay for a while,' said Harisha, turning to Sarina. 'Don't put any leaving day on the list just yet. We will decide later when we have seen if she helps with the bees. I will take them up to the dwellings at the Place of Prayer to rest.' She picked up some of our bundles and swung them onto her shoulder. She wore a similar robe to Sarina, but it was a deeper yellow in colour, and it was sewn with small lighter yellow flowers. She smelled faintly of jasmine. It brought back memories of the Temple, for on the day of Flavus the Goddess was clothed in yellow and her feet were anointed with jasmine oil.

She set off north, towards the settlement, walking at a brisk pace. We followed along, looking at the dwellings and the people of the island. The dwellings were simple structures, somewhat similar to the dwellings of Oramia, but, on the wooden frameworks od the roofs and walls, instead of long grass, were bound reeds as we had seen on the mainland at Safran. At the back of the dwelling was a fenced courtyard just as there was in the rest of Kashiq, where they had their fire and kept their water pots. Many of those we saw were women clothed in yellow, all going about their business. There were also sailors wandering round in their short outfits, chatting to the women of Soora, trading and sitting and drinking and eating. They provided a flash of colour – reds and blues and greens, although never yellow. I wondered if there was an agreement between the sailors and the Soorans in that regard.

'I thought you didn't like men here?' said Gladia, looking around, probably trying to spot Jan, even though he was on his boat.

'We like them well enough. Some of the time. They look after us and we look after them. We all know our limits. If there is one of Soora who chooses to leave the island with one of the sailors, then they leave, but they do not return. Only the Birthmothers are permitted to return after they have worked in other lands, when they are aging and have a longing to return to the Goddess in the place where they first encountered her. But most of the time, we stay where we are; them on the boats and us on the land, joined by the sea.' This reminded me of Ravin, suddenly, and it made me catch my breath. He often told me of how love was like a lake or a pool of water which joined two people together like two lands. Both recognised it to be love but it was different for each one, just as the water was the same water, but different in each land. Harisha must have heard my intake of breath and seen me wince. She looked at me curiously but said nothing.

The Place of Prayer was at the edge of the settlement of Soora, set off to one side, and by the time we got there, Gladia was puffing and panting because the land rose up more steeply beyond the small town. The Place of Prayer itself was built, like the boats and the other dwellings, out of a combination of hard wood, palm wood and reeds. We did not visit the Place of Prayer itself but were led by Harisha round the back of it to where there was a row of small dwellings, made similarly of reeds and palm wood.

'You will stay here,' she said, indicating the last dwelling. She took out her scroll and added something to it. I guessed that she was recording which dwelling we had been assigned to. 'There is wood for a first fire, and some dates and flour in a basket. Beyond that, you must trade for your own food or find it yourself. The Goddess gives enough to all for their needs.' She looked rather critically at Gladia's plump appearance, still puffing after the exertion. 'Though perhaps not enough for their wants. I will be back in the morning to take you to the bees.'

'We have not agreed a trade yet for the dwelling,' said Gladia, a little grumpily, but, as always, with her eye on the trading.

'We do not trade for the dwellings of Soren,' answered Harisha severely. 'Soren is here to heal all those who come to Soora, even though they may not know that they need healing. If you want to please Soren, then please visit the Place of Prayer and trade for an offering to Soren. May she bring you the sleep of healing tonight.' She turned and set off briskly back down the path.

I looked around. There did not seem to be any other people staying in these dwellings, and aside from a few yellow figures moving in and out of the Place of Prayer, it was quiet and still. Gladia went inside the dwelling, and I followed her in. There was a neat pile of palm wood and charcoal to make a fire with, a clay pot of water and a small basket containing flour for flatbreads and some dried dates. There were also a couple of pots and clay beakers.

I felt like I had been living on dried dates for weeks and wanted something more substantial to eat. There was another small basket next to the flour basket which

I opened, and found some small, smoked, dried fish.
Whether they had been left for us by the women of
Soora or by a fellow visitor, I did not know, but I was
grateful for them. We had become more accustomed to
eating them while we had been staying in Safran, where
they seemed to be the main food of choice. In Safran,
there were large tables where the fish were dried on
palm-leaf mats in the sun. There were also smoke
houses, built of palm leaves, where small. fragrant fires
were built which smoked, with the aroma of rosemary
and thyme infusing the fish. Gladia still preferred
Oramian food; a good goat or bean stew, but even she
appreciated the fish this evening. She unpacked a small
package from her bundles and produced some fine
Oramian coffee, which we drank outside, watching the
sun go down.

Even though we could not see the Great Sea from
the dwelling, it felt different to be on the island. I felt
as though everything was vast and we were very small.
The sky was a rich gold as the sun slipped down to the
horizon, and then the clouds began to turn all the
colours of the Goddess as it dropped down further. I
had observed before that the colours of the sky from
dawn to dusk followed through the colours of the days
of the week. We sat and watched the colours merge into
each other in silence, each of us content in our own
thoughts, until the sky was a rich purply-black.
Eventually Gladia got up.

'These old bones have had more than enough for
one day. I am tired and need my sleep. You should
sleep too, Talla. If you are to work with the bees
tomorrow and we have more discoveries to make, you
will need to rest. That baby of yours will welcome the
rest too, I am sure.'

I laughed. Since I had got here, I had felt much better, and any lingering queasiness had gone. Gone too was the weariness I had felt for so long.

'I will sleep soon, Gladia. The child waits in any case until I am resting before it wakes up inside me. The only time it is sleeping is when I am moving. I will stay here until the moon is bright and then I will sleep.'

She made her way in and, after some shuffling about as she found a sleeping mat and lay down with her bedcloth, the sounds of her snoring began to hum. The fire was dying down now, so I got my emberjar and pushed the embers into it, ready to be sparked into new life in the morning. Each morning the sun rose and made his path through the lands, and each night the moon rose and made her own path. Every day they followed one another, never quite catching each other up, always looking ahead to the next day or the next night. I had heard Achillea telling Lisu and Elleni a story of how the sun and the moon had fallen in love with one another and that the reason that all the colours came in the sky at dawn and dusk was because this was the only time at which they met. Perhaps one day I would be telling my own child this story. I looked for the moon and saw her, hiding her face a little behind a lingering cloud.

'You must indeed be a BeeGuard if you look out for the moon,' came a voice out of the darkness. It was Sarina, the one we had met earlier. Her voice made me startle, but she must have just left the Place of Prayer and seen me sitting out by the dwelling by the light of the fire. She carried a small oil lamp which lit up her face.

'Greetings,' I murmured, unsure of how to respond to her remark about the bees and the moon, for I had heard no such tale before in either Oramia or Kashiq. I gestured to her to sit near me, and she lowered herself to the ground gracefully, placing the lamp to one side.

'You come from far away,' she noted. 'But I feel you are one of us, somehow. It must be the aura of the BeeGuard that shines out.' She trailed her hand across the star-sprinkled sky. 'They do say that the moon, who shines so brightly in the sky at night, is the great mother hive of the heavens. All around her are the bees themselves, the shining stars. They fly across the heavens towards the hive, eager to bring the sweetness of the world to the great hive, and the great mother, so that more will be born.' She smiled dreamily at me as she looked up into the stars. I thought this an interesting story, and one which I had not heard before. It was worthy of the Scholar Finzari, whose scrolls I had first read seven years ago. Sarina turned to look at me again.

'The child you carry is important,' she remarked. 'All children are important, of course, but I feel this one more than most. Did you know that they say that the Goddess sends down the souls of new children as bees to our land? If we care for the bees, we care for the children. If we treat them well, they repay us with sweetness and nourishment, but if we are unkind or threatening then they sting us with their pain.' She resumed her gaze of the heavens, and then reached down to the pocket she had hanging from the netela around her waist. In Oramia we had an underpocket which hung beneath our robe and was unseen by others, but here, as in the rest of Kashiq, people often had a pocket hanging on the outside of their garments. Sarina took out a small gourd and pulled out the stopper and took a drink of the contents. She saw me looking at her and laughed.

'It is honeywine. Do you want some?' She offered me the gourd, and I could smell the sweet contents. It

164

reminded me of the night I had seen Ambar when I had drunk honeywine and taken the physic of forgetting with him. It did not seem attractive to me now, and I shook my head. She laughed again and I realised that the honeywine had made her at ease and eager to talk.

'Everyone drinks honeywine here in Soora. Maybe you have not ever tried it; after all, in Oramia it is only the Queen's Court who can trade for it, and in most of Kashiq, well, the Council of Soren is in charge of it. But, you know, they cannot make it in Kashiq. Which is why it is important that our bees make lots of honey.' She took another sip and then looked at me again, her eyes suddenly sharp. 'Much rests on our honey. I hope you will be able to help us and the bees and our Soorabis.'

'The Soorabis?'

'That is the name for those women who worship Soren on the sacred Isle of Aman who make the honeywine. We are almost like the bees ourselves, aren't we, always working, birthing the young, using the honey. The Soorabis live a life of worship and prayer, and it is their intercessions that no doubt bring Soren's blessing upon us all. Without our beloved Soren and her mother, the Goddess, those women from long ago, the first Soorans, might not have lived. They do say that when they had landed here on Soora, that there were five of their number who offered up prayers to the Goddess for deliverance, and that those same five became the first Soorabis, dedicating themselves to protecting us all through prayer and healing.'

Sarina took another longer swallow from her gourd and then rose to her feet in one easy movement, picking up the lamp. She waved her hand dreamily behind her in farewell and left, walking through the night until she faded into it. Her visit made me feel slightly uneasy. I felt as I had felt in Oramia – as if I were being closely watched.

Chapter 16

That night, I slept fitfully, tossing and turning, unable to settle. When I finally did sleep, it was into a deep sleep in which I dreamed in broken images. I dreamed first of Ravin giving me the map and smiling at me in that way that still made me melt inside. But then the dream changed quickly into a memory of Tarik when he killed the guard who had killed Ashtun, and his face as he watched Achillea weeping and his face turned into Ravin's face, and then it was Ravin weeping; something I had never seen. Then Ravin came to me in my dream and embraced me and kissed me and I looked up and it was not Ravin but Ambar. And then, the dream changed again to what seemed to be a real memory, of me sitting by the fire at the place I had met Ambar and of Ambar drinking honeywine, with me, and of him kissing me by the fire.

I woke more tired than I had gone to sleep. The child within me kicked bad-temperedly and seemed to circle like an old animal trying to sleep. I rubbed my belly in an attempt to soothe it, but, in the end, I got up. Gladia was already up and about. She tended to wake with the dawn, all the more now she was older. She had once told me it was a good time of day because many others were still asleep and she could have the time to herself, to make coffee and sit by the fire.

'You never stopped groaning and shuffling all through the night. Kept me awake for hours,' she grumbled.

I almost retorted that it was her snoring which had made me restless, but I held my tongue. For a start, it was not true. It was the dream which had so disturbed my sleep that I had ended up waking Gladia, and I did not want to talk about what I had seen in the dream. Ravin and I had often discussed dreams; he dreamed something new nearly every night, often of new designs or things to try, whereas my dreams were rare and always seemed to be heavy with meaning. Often, they were full of warning and danger, quite different from the dreams that others had. Achillea had told me that she often dreamed more when she was blessed by the Goddess, but she dreamed new songs to sing, and she dreamed of delicious banquets and pretty flowers and of her children laughing and playing. Perhaps, I thought, the Goddess sends us the dreams that we deserve.

Gladia pushed a beaker of coffee into my hands, and I drank some gratefully. She had rebrewed the coffee we had used last night, which made a weaker drink. Many Oramians did this, to use up all the goodness of the coffee. I always wanted the stronger brew in the morning, as it woke me up more, but I was just grateful that Gladia had brought some with her because I had brought very little with me. I hoped she was planning on keeping it for us to drink rather than trading it.

'I wonder what they will show you today. You will probably spend all day looking at bees and such, won't you?' Gladia's eyes slipped off to the side, and I knew she was planning something she did not want me to know about. I waited patiently for more information. 'I might have a wander round the market here, see what there is to trade, talk to a few people.' I wondered if one of the people she hoped to talk to was Jan. I nodded vaguely to her, and she looked relieved, happy to be going somewhere without me, perhaps.

The Place of Prayer was already bustling with visitors, mainly the yellow-clad Soorans. They were setting out their stalls of trade for the emblems of Soren. These were small reusable trinkets which people placed around the Goddess as an offering in the name of Soora, small metal tokens, woven strips of cord which could be worn around the wrist, and, here, square pieces of yellow cloth. I pointed them out to Gladia, and, with an eye to a bargain and a trade, we walked over to the Place of Prayer to take a look at them.

They were just squares of cloth, but they had been stitched with simple pictures of the things which might bring Soren's healing. So, some had pictures of children, and some had pictures of flowers or bees, some had stars, and some had boats on the water. Gladia looked at them critically. She had brought with her some yellow cloth, and she could see that the Soorans who made these tokens were getting good trades for them. Whether they would want to trade for any made by one who was not Sooran was unlikely. Even so, they made a pretty sight pinned to a cord and fluttering in the breeze.

'Do you want to trade for a prayer to Soren for her healing?' The woman who stood next to the poles hung with fluttering squares enquired, perhaps sensing that we had come for help from the Birthmothers.

'We do not have our trades with us at the moment,' said Gladia. 'But we may return later. What will the prayer bring to us?'

The woman smiled and explained to us how their system of trading for prayers and emblems worked, here on Soora. There were ropes hung around the statue of the Goddess on which the squares of fabric, the prayers, were tied. Each cloth would be left on the rope for one day, but if more than one square was traded for, each additional square added a day more. So, if one traded for seven prayers, they would all be tied to one rope, and they would stay near the Goddess for a week.

'Each prayer square is stitched by one of the holy women of Aman, the Soorabis, who prays to Soren while she sews. When the prayers are hung near the Goddess, she hears them more clearly.'

I guessed that as soon as the prayers were taken down from the ropes, they were traded again. I wondered if those who sewed them actually did say a prayer while they stitched them. Gladia looked disappointed when she heard of the special prayers and became quickly disinterested once she knew she could not profit from them like the Soorans.

'Please go into the Place of Prayer and pray to Soren,' urged the woman. 'She will hear you even without the special prayer cloths, and perhaps you will come again with your trades later.'

We walked toward the entrance to the Place of Prayer. Like the ones in the rest of Kashiq it was a six-sided building, but here the whole place was given over to Soren, the Goddess of healing and to Asmara, the Goddess, herself. It seemed that the other guiding gods and goddesses of Kashiq were not needed here. The statue of the Goddess stood in the centre of the room, just as it did in the Temples of Oramia, but this statue depicted the Goddess in a different pose to that seen in Oramia. In Oramia, she was carved seated, her legs underneath her, and had a ring around her head. As Temple Maids, we were told that the circle around her head showed the infinity of her creation. Here, in Soora, it was the Goddess's arms which were raised above her head to make a circle. Hanging from her arms were what could be the wide Sooran sleeves we had seen around us so much, but, equally, they could have been seen as wings, like the wings of a bee or a bird. These wings or sleeves were carved with fine lines radiating down like the rays of the sun. The Goddess herself was the familiar rounded figure, except that her feet could not be seen. In Oramia the Goddess's feet were anointed with scented oils, one for each day of the week, and the scent for each day would remind us of what day it was. Here in Soora, the whole room was filled with the scent of jasmine, the scent of Flavus and of Soren.

All around us there were Sooran women seated in the same pose as the Goddess, sitting on their feet with their arms raised above their heads, their hands clasping each other to join the circle. Occasionally they would bend forward, and their arms would be rested on the floor. I was fascinated to see this since I had never seen it before in the rest of Kashiq. There, Soren was one of six Gods and Goddesses who guided different aspects of life, and all were equally worshipped. In Kashiq, Soren was worshipped in song by those who were guided by her and Achillea would often visit the Place of Prayer when she came to visit me in Pirhan. She loved to sing, and her singing was valued by those who followed Soren. Here, there was no singing, but rather a low humming sound from the voices of many murmured prayers. It ebbed and flowed like the sound of the bees. After a minute or two, Gladia left the building, and I followed her out.

We walked back to the travellers' dwelling. Gladia was not impressed by the differences we had seen. Surely the Oramian Temple was the model for other temples? That was the first kind of temple after all, was it not, she argued. I was not sure. According to the scrolls I had read in Kashiq, it had been Kashiq where Ashkana had come from, and she had fled to Oramia when her love for Lord Rao had ended. She founded the Temples there, but perhaps she had merely changed a few things from what she had known in Kashiq? Gladia was dubious. Although she had no interest in the Temples of Oramia, and kept away from them, especially given what she knew about the Priestesses and their repellent ways with the Angels, she would always support Oramia over Kashiq. 'It's what I know,' she used to say if any of us ever tried to persuade her otherwise.

Harisha arrived shortly afterwards. Her tall, thin figure strode over to us, full of energy and purpose.

'Are you ready to observe the bees?' she asked, with no initial greeting to us. Gladia looked at her disapprovingly and greeted her first.

'Blessings of the Goddess to you too, this sunny morning.'

Harisha looked at her, a curve of a smile attempting to escape her determined mouth.

'Greetings, mother Gladia,' she replied. I waited for Gladia's usually robust dismissal of being called mother Gladia, rather than sister Gladia, but it didn't come. She used to complain that it made her seem old. I realised, with a slight shock, that she was indeed getting old. She had reached her sixth age and her hair was sprinkled with wisdom. She had walked with me for days and then travelled by boat here to the Isles of Soora. I had just resolved to treat her more kindly, and more as I would normally treat an older woman, when she poked me hard in the arm.

'You are not listening, Talla! Honestly, you used to be a much better listener! I was just trying to tell you that I am going to the market in Soora later to see what I can pick up in trades while you are off with your important work.' I apologised and told her that I would see her later, while rubbing my arm. I was surprised I did not have a permanent mark there from the number of times she had jabbed her finger on it to get my attention. 'And don't you work her too hard, either!' she ordered Harisha. 'She needs rest and calm for that baby, not difficult tasks!'

'Be calm, mother Gladia,' said Harisha. 'I am forbidden from overtasking one who carries the blessing of the Goddess. But we should go, for we have to walk to get to the place of the bees. I have food and water,' she added, gesturing to the sack she carried over her shoulder. Nevertheless, I took a small gourd of water and a few dried dates in my own carrysack along with a small gourd of my white honey.

Harisha led me north of Soora on a narrow, winding path. Like all the paths on Soora, it was made of hard dirt which had been swept and cleared of surface stones and grit. The ground was dry and sandy and bare, but ahead of us I could see that the land was green with vegetation. The air here was fresh and clear; a slight breeze blew in continuously from the water, carrying with it the faint smell of fish and saltiness. As well as that, though, there was the scent of something else, something herbal and musky. We came over the top of the hill we had been walking up and there in front of me were hundreds, maybe even thousands, of the same plant. It had greyish green leaves and a few of them still carried small yellow flowers, each the shape of a sun, its petals being the rays. It was not a plant I had ever seen before, and I bent down to pick a leaf and a flower, to examine them more closely. Harisha looked at me sharply as I crushed and sniffed the leaf, and then sniffed the flower. The leaf smelled sharp and spicy, but the flower smelled of strong, musky honey.

'Sungold flowers,' said Harisha. 'The bees feed from them and have done for many ages now. We use them to make some of our physics which we trade with the travellers who have a need for them. You cannot take the flowers or the leaves,' she added, as I made to put them in my hanging pocket for later. 'It is forbidden for those who are not of Soora to take them; they are only for us.' Surprised, I let the leaf and the flower fall. The flower was so light that it was carried along by the breeze a little way until it tumbled to the dust, like a falling star.

'The hives are this way.' She led me east, towards the edge of the island, where I could see what looked like small dwellings on stilts, built of palm wood and palm leaves. They were quite unlike Oramian beehives which were made from hollow logs and hung in the trees, or like Kashiqi hives which were made of cylinders of clay and stacked up, one on top of the other. As we approached, I could hear the humming of the bees inside them. It was an agitated noise, not the calm. low vibration one heard from a contented hive at all. Harisha headed for the first one.

'The bees are not making enough honey,' she said. 'It began some weeks ago, and we cannot find out what it is that is bothering them. We have even tried new hives, but they will not use them. The plants are as they have always been, and the bees visit the flowers before we harvest them, but they are just not making enough honey.'

I looked up, alerted by her insistence on the bees not making enough honey, as if there was some special reason why they needed more honey here on Soora. I remembered Maren telling me that the bees made enough honey for themselves and enough honey for our needs, though never enough for our desires.

'Can I see them in the hive?' I asked. 'How do you get into the hive to remove the honeycombs?'

Harisha went to the palm leaf roof, which I now noticed had several woven entrances for the bees to use, and simply lifted it off and placed it on the ground. I moved closer to the hive as she walked further away. A couple of bees followed her, and one alighted on her arm and stung her. She slapped her hand on the offending bee, which in any case was now dying, and bent her mouth to the sting, searching for the sting with her tongue before pulling it out with her small, neat teeth. It surprised me that the bee would sting one whom it should presumably know well, and who would care for it. I took out my gourd of white honey and placed a little on the ends of my fingers and spread out my hands close to the top of the hive. Almost immediately, the bees emerged to my hands and began to crawl on my fingers, taking in the white honey. The white honey was known for its healing properties for both people and for bees, and it was clear that they needed it. Harisha looked on dubiously. I raised my hand and the bees that were on it closer to my face so that I could observe them better. I could feel their tiny tongues lapping at my honey-coated skin.

'Be careful,' warned Harisha. 'They are always very angry.'

'Not angry,' I replied, watching the bees as they flew off into the hive and were swiftly replaced by others. 'Hungry.'

Chapter 17

Harisha looked at me blankly.

'But they are surrounded by all these plants. How can they be hungry?'

I ignored her and moved my hands closer to the hive. The humming got louder. I peered into the hive. New wooden frames for the honeycomb had been placed in the hive but little had yet been built, and there was very little honeycomb to be seen. The hives had been very recently stripped of all their honey, presumably by the Soorans who seemed to lack the understanding of their bees that other BeeGuards might have. I looked around me. There were dozens of hives here, all neatly standing on their wooden stilt legs, warmed by the sun. Each hive had a small wooden sign next to it with a number scribed on it. The Soorans with their love of recording no doubt used these numbers to note when they had taken honey from the hives.

I turned to Harisha who was still standing some way distant, absently sucking on the place where she had been stung and watching me suspiciously, as if I were about to start stealing the bees, or perhaps their precious sungold flowers. Taking the small gourd of honey out again, I poured most of it out onto a flat stone which lay nearby. The bees came almost instantly to it, the hum changing to what seemed to me a grateful tone, lower and calmer. Soon the whole rock was covered in bees.

'I don't understand,' said Harisha plaintively. 'The bees are supposed to make honey, not eat it.'

'What do you think they live off, the bees?' I asked her, astonished at her lack of knowledge. She looked around her.

'I don't know. The leaves of the plants, maybe?'

I sighed, exasperated.

'Can I speak with your Beeguards?' I asked, changing direction. Perhaps if I could speak with those who knew, they could explain why this event had come to pass.

'We do not have any real Beeguards now, just women who work with the bees and the honey and the sungold flowers. Some of them have gone to the holy island of Aman along with the honeycomb. They are praying to Soren to heal the bees so that they will make honey again. Our BeeGuard, Kavina, the one who knew everything about them, died a few weeks ago quite suddenly. She was supposed to teach others her craft, but she never did.' Her face twisted bitterly. 'She could not bear the idea that anyone might have her knowledge of the bees; it was what made her so special. And now it seems that choice is leading to disaster. Typical of her that she would be still wanting to be the centre of attention, even in death.' Harisha almost spat out the words. Evidently this now dead BeeGuard had not thought much about a world without her in it. And yet, surely, one of the things the Goddess puts us all here for is to pass on our knowledge and our wisdom to those who come after us.

'It would be better for all of those women to be here with the bees, feeding them,' I answered. 'These bees cannot make honey with nothing to gather it from. Where have all the flowers gone?'

Harisha looked around her. Like me she could see the long stretches of the bluish green bushes where one could still see a few of the sungold flowers, but most were completely stripped of flowers. I could see that she was thinking hard about what to say in reply. I could feel my mind glowing with exasperation. What did these women think they were doing? How could they know so little about the bees? I lowered myself down so that I could sit on a neighbouring rock. It was tiring to keep standing with my increased size, and there was no need for me to remain standing, after all. The bees were still lapping up the honey from the rock. I focused my attention on them rather than on Harisha so that I could calm down. There were so many bees on the rock now that it seemed as if it were the rock that was alive, its surface shimmering and moving with the bees' wings as they took in the goodness of the honey.

'The flowers are used to make physic with,' she replied eventually, looking evasive. 'We have had requests for a lot more of this from our trading partners, and we needed to get it made. All of the plants needed to be harvested in order to get the physic we needed to trade.'

'What type of physic is it for, that you will put your bees in danger?' I asked, my ears having pricked up at her answer. Could this be the physic of forgetting, or one of the ones which Ravin had been searching for, the ones that could help to make a child?

'It is of no concern to you,' came the crisp reply.

'Well, what I can tell you that is of concern to *you* is that you will now need to bring honey here to your bees if you want to save them. You will need to mix it with water and to feed them from shallow plates until they are well fed. They cannot make the beeswax for the honeycomb without having anything to eat, and no, they do not eat leaves! They eat, or rather drink from the flowers. Any that is extra is made into honey and stored in the honeycomb in case they need it when there are no flowers to feed from, and for their children to grow in. There are no flowers to feed from because you have picked them all for your physic. And there is no stored honey in these hives either, because it has all been taken. Where has all the honey and honeycomb gone?' I was angry with this near-sighted attitude, risking the balance that the bees brought to the land for a few short-term rewards of trade.

Harisha blinked. 'The honey is needed to make the honeywine for the celebrations for the week of Soren's Sun which will be happening soon. It takes time for the honeywine to ferment. The honeycomb was harvested at the same time as the flowers.' It was now clear that somebody had made a big mistake in the timing of the harvests, probably through ignorance due to this possessive BeeGuard, Kavina. I sighed in exasperation.

'You must get back any honey which has not yet been made into honeywine. Without the honey, your bees will die, and they cannot drink honeywine. Without the bees, you will have no honey, nor yet any new sungold plants because the bees move the beedust from flower to flower to make the seeds. If you cannot get back enough honey, you will need to trade for it with your visitors. Tell the sailors to encourage honey traders who have come to Safran to make the journey here. You will have no honey made here until you can feed the bees as well as your hunger for the sungold flowers and for their honey. It is woven together like the threads of a cloth.'

Harisha stood, seemingly unable to move, trying to understand what she needed to do and who she should find. It seemed as though the answer I had given her had provoked more questions. Perhaps there would be someone else I could talk to who could understand the urgency of the situation. I looked into the hive again. Most of the bees from that hive were on the honey smeared rock. Peering inside, I could see the queen of the hive being tended to by the bees which worked in the hive. One flew in and went straight to her, feeding her with honey collected from the rock. There were a few bees working on building up the little beeswax containers in the hive. These would be filled with both honey and young bees which grew in them, much as my own child was growing inside me. Without the honey the queen could not lay eggs and the eggs could not grow into new bees. I stood up.

'We must return to the town. I hope that you will find someone there who will understand how important this is. You will have nothing to trade but the metals if you do not solve this problem.'

Harisha nodded, her eyes far away, seemingly trying to work out how to solve this problem any other way.

'We will ask the guidance of the Goddess and of Soren,' she said eventually. 'She will know how to heal the bees.'

I wished that Gladia were with us so that she could have treated Harisha to one of her disparaging snorts. But I knew that we were only here by the agreement of Harisha and her fellow Soorans and it was too important to put the bees into jeopardy. I felt as if I were trying to save someone very precious to me, as if the bees were Ravin. I could not save him, but I had the chance to save these bees and I was determined to do so.

'Is there one of the wise who follow Soren who could help us? For not only does Soren need to heal the bees, that which the bees make is healing to others, and you said the flowers are used to make a healing physic too. Soren will require us to move with much haste.' I tried to link her desire to turn to the Goddess and to Soren with the urgency I felt. Harisha nodded again. When I had first met her, down by the water's edge, I had thought her very sharp in mind. I realised now that I had been deceived by her busy efficiency. She had a busy mind, but it turned in circles and came to no end.

'Let us go then, perhaps to the Place of Prayer or to your Council of Guidance?'

She nodded her head again. Now she had an aim, she became brisk again and started to trot down the path towards Soora. I was grateful that we were now heading back down the hill, because she was moving more quickly than me, and I became quite breathless. The child inside me kicked in irritation. I stopped to catch a breath. Harisha carried on though, and merely gestured back to me, flapping her hand as if to tell me to walk as slowly as I wished. It seemed that she wished to convey my message herself, or perhaps to consult with others before I arrived. I slowed my pace. A few bees were flying behind me, eager to discover the source of the honey, and to see if there was any more. I took out the gourd of white honey and scraped it out with a stick for them, trying to work out in my mind how much honey I had brought with me to trade, and how much more would be needed to feed the bees until the new flowers emerged, for there were many hives. I did not know how long that would take. Some flowers only bloomed for a day and were then replaced, but others lasted for weeks and took weeks to reappear. Some only flowered once in a year. I knew nothing about the flowering habits of the sungold flowers. The Soorans would have to decide what was important to them; the honeywine or the bees.

When I finally returned to the dwelling, it was empty. Gladia had gone to the market as she had told me, and I sat down gratefully and leaned against the side of the dwelling, shaded by the long palm leaf fronds on the roof and slept for some time, until I heard a voice.

'Wake up, sister Talla.'

Opening my eyes, I saw that I was surrounded by a group of Sooran women, the sun shining through their yellow robes. It cast a sort of golden shadow on the ground around me. I blinked. Harisha was there too, hovering like a bee over a flower.

'This is Talla, the one who is the Beeguard. She says we need to feed the bees, but there is no honey left. Ask her your questions, Rays of Soora.' Said Harisha, stumbling over her words.

'We shall sit with you, Talla,' said the smallest of them, smiling at me kindly. 'There is no need for you to stand up. The baby no doubt needs you to rest.' She looked critically at Harisha. 'Harisha, go and fetch food and make tea for Talla. She needs nourishment, not to be rushed about all over the island.' She sat down, and so did the other four women. I did not know whether they were from the Place of Prayer or of the Council of Guidance, or some other group, but they carried with them an air of authority and power. It was the same sort of air that surrounded the Priestesses of the Temple and the OutRiders, and those of the Councils in Kashiq. There was nothing to see that was different to any other person, but just a feeling that surrounded them. Unlike other people, they knew that they had the power to make things happen.

Chapter 18

I am Estar. I am the Ray of Soora. I guide those who live on the Isle of Soora. We are responsible for the sungold flowers and for the bees and the honey. We are responsible for the sailors and the visitors to our Isles.'

'I am Dayo. I am the Ray of Orish. I guide those who live on the Isle of Orish. We are responsible for the metals mined there, and for the salt made there and all the island trading.'

'I am Layla. I am the Ray of Oshana. I guide those who live on the Isle of Oshana. We are responsible for the plants used in physic from the islands and for making and trading all physics from the Isles.'

'I am Nousha. I am the Ray of Rengat. I guide those who live on the Isle of Rengat. We are the Birthmothers responsible for the births of babies and for the training of those who travel other lands as Birthmothers, doing the work of Soren.'

'I am Mina. I am the Ray of Aman, and a Soorabi. I guide those who live and worship on the Isle of Aman. We are responsible for the brewing of honeywine and for the spiritual guidance we receive from Soren and Asmara, bless their names, and for the worship and praise of Soren and Asmara.'

They bowed their heads and intoned together a prayer or a chant.

'Soora, Orish, Oshana, Rengat, Aman.' It was only the names of the islands, but I realised they had been ordered so that their first letters spelled out the word Soora. It was a symbolic prayer, a way to show they were only one letter on their own but formed a word. I looked around at these five women, who called themselves the Rays, wondering where to begin. The one I now knew to be Nousha, who had spoken to me first, smiled at me again. I could see how her calm manner might be of value in a Birthmother. Maren had the same sort of strong calm, the kind of person who could hold you up so that you were strong enough to conquer your fear or your pain.

'Harisha tells us that you think you know about our bees,' said the one called Estar, the one responsible for the bees. She frowned. Her skin was leathery and tough, and her eyes looked similarly tough. I did not think that she would take kindly to what I had to say. I chose my words carefully but made sure to tell them what the problem with their bees was. As soon as I had finished, they began to argue with one another about who it was who was the cause of their problems.

'If it were not for Layla demanding all the flowers for the physic straight away, the flowers would not all be gone.'

'Well, if it were not for Dayo demanding all the physic be ready for trading immediately, I would not have needed them.'

'I am not the only one who uses the physic; Nousha also takes her share.'

'And anyway, if it were not for Mina, demanding all the honey and honeycomb I have in order to make the honeywine for the Week of Soren's Sun, the bees would have had honey in the hives.'

'Well, I am not the only one who uses the honeywine we make, Estar takes her fair share for the sailors, and so does Dayo for the trade.'

They all glared at one another and stopped to draw breath. I was still waiting for one of them to ask me what the solution could be for their problem and how we could achieve it, knowing that we had little time, but they were intent on finding the blame first.

'What on earth is going on here, Talla? It sounds like a crowd of children jeering at each other!'

Gladia's familiar brisk tones cut through the air. The Rays turned to look at the cause of the interruption. Gladia looked back at them, unconcerned with their power. She had always been this way. The only time I had seen her defiant spirit broken had been when she was tortured by two OutRiders just before Ambar had rescued her. But it did not seem that power and authority held much sway with her. Perhaps it was because I had been raised in the Temple, where there was a strong line of power, that I was not as outwardly defiant as she. But, like her, I was angered by their squabbling when there was a real issue of importance to be resolved.

'Perhaps they need you to sort them out,' I suggested to her, my mouth curving into a smile. 'Apparently it is more important to find someone to blame than anything else.'

Gladia snorted in her most derisory way. She looked each one of the five up and down and then turned her back on them and turned to me, instead.

'So, what have you managed to find out about this problem they have with the bees, Talla?' she asked me. 'And what needs to be done first? I will tell you about my time at the market later, I can see this is more important.' She turned to face the Rays, who were all still speechless, and gaping at her. 'You are lucky to

184

have Talla here. For if anyone can help you with a problem that seems at first glance to be impossible, Talla is the one who can untangle it.'

'She is right,' said Estar slowly. 'The Goddess knows who is to blame, I am sure. Harisha said that you knew the bees were hungry straight away.' She looked away, pained. 'I should have known, but I was so busy with all the demands from different people that I took my eyes away from where they should have been. This has never happened before, there has always been enough for everyone's needs.'

'Let us first hear what needs to be done, sister,' said Nousha, the Birthmother. 'From what Harisha said, it sounds as if we need to act on this straight away.' She turned to me and looked at me expectantly, just as Harisha herself returned with some sweetened flatbreads and a beaker of tea for me.

Gladia looked at her critically. 'And where is my coffee?' she asked and, without waiting for an answer, heaved herself up and walked heavily over to the fireplace and began to stoke up the fire under the pot, blowing deeply on the embers to make them spark into life. Nousha's mouth curved with amusement and Harisha looked uncomfortable. I sipped my tea before I started to speak. It was similar to a Kashiqi mint tea, but there was less mint in it and more of some other herb or spice, which warmed it and softened the sharpness of the mint. In Kashiq, the mint tea was often sweetened with honey to counteract the sharpness, but here it was not.

'It is made for women who are having a child,' said Nousha. 'It is soothing to both. What do we need to do first, Talla?'

I tried to order my thoughts. The bees were more important than any of the other demands, as far as I could see, and the bees needed to be fed with honey and water until the flowers might bloom again and feed them.

'How long will it take the sungold flowers to bloom again?' I asked Estar, the Ray of Soora. She told me that it would be a week or more. The hive I had looked in had very low amounts of saved honey in it, which would be used to feed the Queen of the hive who could then lay more eggs. But the eggs would have to be laid in the little beeswax cells which could not be made by the bees unless they had more sustenance.

'You must get all the honey you can find on the Isles now and take it to the beehives. Mix it with water and pour it in shallow plates so the bees do not drown. This must be done straight away, or the bees will start to die. You will need to put out fresh plates of honey and water every day until the flowers bloom again, and probably for longer. If any of your visitors have brought with them honey to trade, you must trade for it now, and tell the sailors to bring more from Safran as soon as they can. I have with me four gourds of good honey which you can start with. Whoever is in charge of the honeycomb taken for the honeywine needs to take whatever has not already been used and bring it back to the bees, for the honeycomb will provide both honey and beeswax to start the bees back again.'

The Rays of Soora looked at one another in consternation.

'But I have to trade for the fine embroidered silk and the gold threads before the week of Soren for the garments of the Soorabis,' said Dayo, looking to Mina for confirmation. Mina nodded firmly.

'We must have the cloth and the threads. It is more important than anything else you might mention. It is, after all, for the glory of Soren and the Goddess herself,' she added virtuously.

186

'Well, to make those trades, I need all the physic I can get from Layla, especially the sungold Oblak physic.' Dayo looked meaningfully at Layla. It was apparent that the physic made from the sungold flowers was the one which was the most valuable to them in terms of trade, because it was for this reason that they had harvested all of the sungold flowers at once. We appeared to be going in circles of blame again.

'You know,' remarked Gladia mildly from where she sat with her coffee. 'When I had to solve Jember's squabbles when he was younger, we started out with the things that we could change and the things we could not change. Maybe you could do the same because the longer you argue, the harder it will be to solve the problem.' She was right.

'We cannot do anything now that the flowers have been harvested. They are no good to the bees now. But the honey they already made themselves, that can help them. So where is that honey now?' I asked.

Estar spoke. 'Most of the honeycomb that was taken recently was for the Soorabis on Aman. They brew honeywine from it. Some honey and beeswax go to Rengat to the Birthmothers where they use it in salves to soothe the women giving birth. Some also goes to Layla to use in the physics they make on Oshana.'

I turned to the other Rays of Soora.

'Tell me what honey you have on the island you guide. We must organise the sailors to go and collect it as soon as possible. If you do not save the bees, there will be nothing left to trade. There will be no honeywine at all, no physics to trade and no soothing of birth pains. You may be able to get more bees brought over from Kashiq, but it will take a long time before they settle, and before you do that, you will have to grow the flowers they need to make the honey. It must be done now.'

'I have some which was taken in trade a few days ago,' said Dayo. 'A Kashiqi trader traded it for some silver and other metals, and for salt.'

Nousha likewise offered some of her stored honey, but all agreed that she should keep a third of it for the mothers she cared for. Estar had very little stored on Soora, except in small quantities but she willingly offered that, and promised to try to choose the traders who had honey above all others to land at Soora and be given favourable trades. This left us with the two Rays who seemed to require most of the honey and who were the origin of the mistake that had been made. It was clear that they both thought their claim was more important, and that the other one was to blame, but I did not care who that might be. What was more important was to get the honey back to feed the bees and restore them to health while we waited for the sungold flowers to bloom again. Once that was done, then the Rays of Soora would have to work out what their priorities for the future were.

Layla turned to Dayo. 'It is your trade demands that mean I had to get the sungold flowers in such quantities. We are trading so much of the Oblak physic that I need to keep distilling more. You will have to tell those you trade with that they must be patient.'

'But they are the ones who trade the golden silk with us for the Soorabis.' Dayo again directed us to Mina.

'We have to have it,' she stubbornly responded. 'The new Soorabis will be confirmed in the Week of Soren's Sun.' She folded her arms across her chest. The long wide sleeves of her robe hung down over her knees. Her hair was cropped short, and her face was smooth and impassive. She wore a large pendant made of silver and honeygold which seemed to be a series of circles and spheres of different sizes.

Gladia spoke again. 'So, it is you who is really the cause of all this, is it? You are the one who wants the honeywine, and you are the one who wants this Oblak physic to be traded for the cloth you want. You will have to decide which one is more important to you. Can't you trade something else rather than the physic for the cloth you want? I have cloth with me, but it is not silk. Perhaps you need to choose some different cloth this time.'

Mina looked at Dayo. Dayo shifted her legs underneath her uncomfortably. 'They will not trade for anything else but Oblak and the other physics they have always traded for. I have tried offering them metals, but they do not want them as much as the physics. They say they need them, and that it is important.'

Of course. I guessed that the Oblak physic was the same physic of forgetting that Ambar had told us was now being used for the Angels. And the same physic of forgetting that I had taken. Gladia had too, from her response.

'Surely, they can manage without this physic you speak about? What does it do that is so special anyway? And where do they come from? Can't they go to some other place which does a lot of trading like Arbhoun and find it there?'

There was a silence. Clearly there were things which we were not to be told. This only made me more determined to find out more. Meanwhile, the honey still had to be found.

'We must get the honeycomb you took for the honeywine. It is the only option left to us at this time.' Estar spoke firmly, and it seemed clear to me now that she was the leader of these Rays of Soora, the one who made the ultimate decisions about the Isles. 'We must find a sailor who can take us to Aman, to stop them from starting the fermentation. Which sailor can we use, one who will willingly sail through the rocks to Aman?'

'Why not ask Jan?' suggested Gladia. The Rays turned to look at her, surprised by the suggestion.

'Jan is a good sailor,' said Mina slowly. 'He has sailed me to Aman many times before. But he has only just sailed here from Safran; he may not want to sail again tomorrow.'

'It can do no harm to ask,' said Estar mildly.

'I will ask,' concluded Mina. 'But he can still say no. We have no power over the sailors.' It sounded to me as if she would be quite happy if Jan refused the request. I wondered how hard she would try to persuade him before she gave up. She got to her feet and called Harisha over to accompany her down to the settlement of Soora to find Jan.

Gladia got up too. 'I will come with you,' she announced firmly. 'I know where Jan is, since I just left him, and I think he will agree to do the trip if I ask him to.' I raised my eyebrows at her, but she looked the other way.

'She may be of help,' said Nousha, just as Mina was about to refuse Gladia's assistance. 'She seems to know Jan well, and she is not one of us.'

'I agree.' Estar dismissed the three of them with a wave, and they walked off. I could not believe that Gladia felt so confident that she could influence Jan after so little time, but, apparently, she did.

'We should pray to Soren while they are gone,' said Layla, looking anxious. 'We must heal our bees.' Estar and Dayo got up to accompany her, but Nousha smiled at them and told them she would stay with me, and look after me, as a Birthmother should. They left, and when they had gone, Nousha looked at me kindly.

'When were you first seen by a Birthmother? When did you first learn that you had been blessed by the Goddess?'

I told her then that I had not really been seen by any Birthmother except Maren's brief inspection, that I had not believed that I could be having a child. I told her that Ravin and I had tried to have a child for years and that the Goddess had not blessed us, and that I had found out some weeks after he died that I might be bearing a child.

'Would you like me to check?' she asked. 'I may be able to tell you more about when the child might be born, and to soothe your aches and pains.'

I agreed. Partly because Gladia was not there. I did not want her there when the Birthmother told me anything about this unborn child. If Ravin could not be there, then I wanted to be on my own. Nousha took out a small gourd of salve from her hanging pocket and rubbed it on her hands. It smelled faintly of marigolds and honey and made her hands slip over my skin smoothly. She asked me to lie down on the mat and glided her hands over my belly which seemed to increase in size every day. She slid her hands around my skin, pausing occasionally to feel again. The child inside kicked bad-temperedly at first, but, as she continued to gently rub, it calmed down as if it were sleeping.

'How many months is it since your husband died? I can try to work out from that when the child might come. Assuming you have not been...' Nousha paused, searching for a delicate way to phrase it. '...I mean...um...been with another man...since then?'

'No,' I answered briefly. 'It is twenty-five weeks since Ravin died. It is not a day that I will forget.'

'Of course not,' replied Nousha. 'The baby seems quite small, but then your belly is the right size to be about that far along. No matter, babies grow as they will, and in the end, they enter the world when they are ready to enter the world, with all that Asmara, our Goddess sends them with. You will be blessed to see your husband again in your child.'

I was not sure. I could not think that it would necessarily be a comfort to me to be constantly reminded of what I had lost, and I thought of Bellis and Jember. I changed the subject of our conversation.

'What do you use in your soothing salve, there, sister? I make salves in Kashiq using my beeswax and flowers from my garden and I have not made one like this before. It had not occurred to me before now that I could trade these soothing salves to women having babies too. My friend Achillea would have liked this salve when she was with child.'

Nousha smiled and twinkled her eyes at me. 'Well, now, I am not sure if I can share all the secrets of the Birthmothers with you, but that one I can. It is only marigolds, distilled, and honey and beeswax, with Paradox oil which we trade for with Oramia, with a little lavender and rose oil.' I thanked her for her generosity in sharing her recipe for the salve and told her of the little salves I made for dry lips which were very popular in Kashiq's dry lands.

'This could be good for trading with the sailors who live on the water,' she mused. 'The salty water often dries out the face and stings a cracked lip. Thank you, sister, I will let Layla know, for it is she and her sisters on Oshana who make all of our physics and salves.'

'Are there many physics for those blessed by the Goddess with a child?' I asked, curious to know if she might talk of those plants noted by Ravin, the ones which might make a woman more likely to have a child.

'I do know one Birthmother, Maren, but she has never really used many physics with women apart from simple rubbing salves, and sometimes honey and poppy juice when the pains are very bad. She learned her job from one who came from here, I believe, one called Hortensia.'

Nousha looked at me in surprise. 'Hortensia? There is one who lives on the island of Rengat, who is called Hortensia. She is very old, in her Age of Wisdom now. Though her wisdom is not always evident to us, for her mind is confused. She did return here from Oramia, a long time ago, perhaps five ages or maybe thirty years ago now. She was the one who taught many of our Birthmothers, especially about birthing DoubleSouls, because she had delivered several and had learned from that. It is very hard to tell when a woman is carrying DoubleSouls except if she is bigger than other women, but it is important for us all know what to do if another child is born. Perhaps she would like to hear of this friend of yours. If you are permitted, you may like to visit Rengat, when you are happy that the bees are well looked after.' She looked at me kindly. 'They do not mean to harm the bees, you know. They are unable to think beyond the things which are important to them. We all need to look at things from the outside sometimes. I am sure they will help to avert this crisis.'

I hoped she was right. Meanwhile, as we waited for the others to return, I thought about what she had said about Hortensia, convinced that this must be that same woman of whom Maren spoke, the one who had trained her and who had been with her and the Lady Paradox when Lunaria and her sister (who might be me) were born. It was Hortensia who had taken the babies and left Maren to be found and tortured by the OutRiders. It was Hortensia who had left the babies at the Temple where I had been found with Lunaria, along with a brooch bearing the emblem of the Queen pinned to my blanket. Surely Hortensia must hold some of the answers to this story?

Chapter 19

A little while later, as the sun was setting in the sky, and its golden light fell on the Place of Prayer, Mina and Gladia returned, without Harisha, who had gone back to her dwelling already. The others saw them coming and joined us. Nousha and I had not spoken more of Hortensia, speaking instead of generalities, the plants which grew on the islands and if there were any animals living here. I imagined they must have all been brought here by the women who settled on Soora. Nousha said that there were many birds, especially on Oshana which had lots of large trees called Osh trees. Birds, of course, did not need boats to travel, and there were many birds which found their food in the Great Sea along with the sailors. In fact, there was a seabird which they called the Sailor which used its large white wings as sails in the air and could often be seen whirling and diving in the sea near the island cliffs. But there were no domestic animals, for they need grass to feed on and there was not enough here. The Soorans ate fish, like the people of Safran. There were some small animals here, little mice and lizards and bats which had come ashore hidden in the bundles of travellers, and, of course, many small creeping and flying insects.

Gladia was puffing as she trotted after Mina up the path. Mina was at least an age younger than Gladia and her sturdy legs strode easily along. She looked rather annoyed.

'Will Jan take us to Aman in the morning?' asked Estar. She looked doubtful, and I was unsure myself when I looked at Mina's face, but when I moved my gaze to Gladia's face, I knew that they had succeeded by the wide smile she gave me as she finally dropped to the floor to regain her breath.

'Yes,' replied Mina, almost glowering.

'Good news is it not?' said Gladia. 'Mina would probably never have managed to persuade Jan on her own, but when I added my voice, he was very amenable.' She smiled smugly. I could see Mina struggling with a response. It occurred to me that Mina would have probably preferred Jan to have refused the trip and might not have tried very hard. I resolved to ask Gladia more after the Rays had left us for the night, but I did want to know more about the details of the trip first.

'My thanks, Gladia,' said Estar, formally. 'Mina, you and I will go on the boat to Aman, and we will bring back the unfermented honeycomb. I sent word, while we were at the Place of Prayer, to those who work with the bees and they will be using the honey we have got so far and putting it out ready for the bees in the morning, which will give us a little time to see how much more honey we need to store.'

Gladia's smile grew.

'Jan will only take us if Gladia and the other one come too,' said Mina crossly. 'She somehow convinced him that it was very important that they should be there too.'

Estar turned to Gladia. 'Why is that? Aman is our most sacred place and those who are not Soorans may not go there.'

'I don't think that Mina really wants to give up her honeycombs,' answered Gladia. 'She didn't try very hard to convince Jan how important it was. I told him that it was, and he said he would understand how important it was by whether the Rays of Soora would permit me and Talla to travel there too. Otherwise, he won't go. So, if you really do think it is important for the bees to live on your islands and continue to make the seeds for the flowers you need so much, and for the honey for the honeywine you need so much, you will be taking us. Otherwise, well, you will have to sort it all out yourselves and Talla and I will instead travel back to Safran with Jan in the morning.'

She looked triumphant. I had seen a new side to Gladia on this trip. She seemed somehow freed of worry and concern. Perhaps it was good for her to leave behind her responsibilities to the Angels in Mellia, and let Bellis and Maren do that work. She had seen Jember settled in Gabez with Achillea and Tarik and now she had met someone who seemed to take great pleasure in her company. I felt a sudden sharp pang of jealousy, even though I knew it was unreasonable. She had no responsibility to anyone except herself and was free to do as she wished. I, on the other hand, seemed to carry more and more people around inside my head. It was as if they sat around the fire of my mind and enjoyed its warmth but rarely fed it with fuel.

The Rays continued to look perturbed. Mina looked around at them, at first seeming almost smug until she realised that the others were contemplating doing as Jan wished. She tried to convince them that nothing else other than the wishes of the Goddesses Asmara and Soren mattered. She reminded them that no one who was not from Soora had ever been to the isle of Aman before, and she suggested that perhaps the crisis with the bees had been over-exaggerated by me and Gladia. Estar looked at her rather coldly at this point.

'Are you suggesting that I do not know that there is something wrong with the bees? I would never dream of telling you how to dance for Soren when it is Soren's week, and yet here you are telling me my work! Not only that, but, as you know, it is not only you who decides whether this happens or not, nor is it me, but it is all of the Rays who will decide. We will use the stones of choice and it will be decided.'

The other Rays all nodded and reached into their hanging pockets. Each pulled out a smooth, round pebble, like the ones we had seen on the Isle of Orish, and like Ambar's. One side of the pebble was white, and the other side had been coloured with ink to be black. They flipped them over and over as they pondered and then they chanted the same prayer they had chanted before: Soora, Orish, Oshana, Rengat, Aman. As soon as they had said Aman, each laid down their stone in front of them. Only Mina's was black.

'It is decided.' Estar spoke firmly. 'The boat will sail for Aman in the morning. We will see you at dawn.' She rose from her place, putting her choice stone back in her pocket. The others followed suit. Mina looked petulant, but she could see that the others wanted Jan to take us all to Aman, so she was bound by their choice.

Gladia waited until they were gone before she laughed loudly.

'You can rely on old mother Gladia to get her own way in these things,' she said, her eyes twinkling. 'Though maybe I am not as old as I felt before!'

I pondered the stones of choice as we sat and drank tea later. Gladia was saving her good Oramian coffee for when she really needed it, so we both drank Kashiqi tea instead. It was a matter of numbers, I could see. If there had been an even number of Rays, it would not have worked as a method of deciding, for there could have been an even number of outcomes, half could have chosen to agree and half to disagree. But, because there were five Rays, a choice would always be made. It seemed as good a method as any other I had seen to decide an outcome. I guessed they made all the communal decisions affecting the islands in the same way. It gave me hope that they might change some of the other ways in which they worked so that the bees would be more protected in the future. Then I began to wonder how the Rays were chosen and if there was a similar system of choosing them, or if they were perhaps chosen by Soren in some kind of way. I remembered how, in the Temple, where I was raised, we were told that at the end of childhood, the Goddess herself helped us to choose the right path. It turned out that it was all a trick. The Priestesses presented the different scrolls of choice so that the most attractive ones were the ones for the choices they had already made. So, in Bellis's case, she had selected a beautiful scroll, anticipating that it would mean she would stay in the Temple with the Goddess. In fact, the priestesses had selected her to be an Angel. So, something that appeared to be a choice might turn out not to be. But this system with the stones of choice did not rely on only a few people being able to read, and the outcome was clear, especially with only five stones to look at. I asked Gladia what she thought about it.

'It depends on who's doing the choosing, doesn't it? After all, if you had five fools making the choices, you might end up with a foolish choice. Maybe they don't choose what they actually think is the right choice, but they just shut their eyes and flip the stone. Maybe if one of them dislikes another one, they always choose the opposite choice.' She sighed. 'Well, if I had a stone of choice, I am not sure I would be choosing to be going on a boat quite so soon after we got here. Jan says it is a rough crossing, so we had better get some rest. Especially if we have to meet at dawn.'

Chapter 20

The wind was sweeping across the water, sending tiny shivering ripples over the larger waves which were crashing on the sides of the dock at Soora. Jan was already on the boat, knotting his sails into place. There were only three oarsmen aboard apart from him, who slouched on their wooden plank seats, no doubt ungrateful for the early trip. Gladia was triumphant in arriving just before the Rays did and made sure that she was the first whom Jan helped on to the boat, holding on to his hand of assistance a little too long. Only Estar and Mina came. Mina must make the journey quite regularly, I thought, but she showed no enjoyment of the trip and spent most of the time with her eyes closed as the boat made its way to Aman.

Gladia, for all her efforts in getting us onto the boat in the first place was similarly sour about the trip. Perhaps she thought it would be as gentle a trip as the longer journey to get to Soora from Safran had been, and that she might have been able to talk to Jan on the way. But this was quite a different experience.

The waves were larger, and as Jan pulled at the sails with the ropes to make them catch the wind, the boat bounced across them, like a flat stone skimmed over water. Again, it reminded me of riding a horse. There was a way in which horses moved when they were going quite quickly, and if you did not move your body in their rhythm, you would hit the saddle with a hard jolt. If you got it wrong, it was very uncomfortable, and if you got it right it felt smooth and managed. Like me, Estar moved with the boat. It was almost like a dance, a movement that was languid and then sudden and then moving regularly, almost as if it heard the beat of music or a song.

Jan was wholly occupied with the sailing. Over the noise of the grey fishbirds, which seemed to follow all the boats around in search of fish, and the wind rushing past, Estar explained to me that the route to Aman, while short, could be treacherous to those who did not know it. There were patches of sharp rocks which could sink a boat, and deep currents under the water which could drag a person far out of reach. Jan carried with him a drawing of the islands, much like the one which Ravin had left for me, but where mine had all the detail drawn on to the lands, his had more detail drawn on to the water. He had it nailed to a flat plank in the centre of the boat, and it had been cunningly waxed with beeswax to keep the ink from running in the spray of the sea. He checked on it often, marking off landmark rocks with his fingers so that he knew where he needed to turn the boat to avoid the rocks. It must have been exhausting to concentrate so hard. I could concentrate very well when it was only one thing that required my attention, like reading a scroll, but Jan was both reading the drawing and acting on what he read immediately. Jan did not look exhausted however but exhilarated.

Gladia might not have enjoyed the journey, but she did enjoy watching Jan at work. Occasionally he would catch her eye and his own bright eyes would twinkle at her and they would both smile at each other.

'Your mother appears to know Jan well,' said Estar. 'Are they related? Perhaps they are brother and sister?' I wasn't sure whether she was just making polite conversation or whether she wanted to find out more information about us. I think Gladia would have been very disappointed to find out that Jan was her brother. I smiled and told her that they were good friends and left it at that.

I felt protective of Gladia and her attraction to Jan. Why should she not enjoy his company? Being older did not prevent you from recognising those who recognised your spirit. In Kashiq, it was thought that when a person died, all the elements which made them special were redistributed by the Goddess when new children were born. So, we might recognise the humour of a loved one or the way they used to hold their pen or the way they closed one eye at us in other people who were born after they died. Perhaps one day our child might do something to show me that he or she had been given something of Ravin, that the Goddess might have saved one small part of the intricacy of Ravin's soul and given it to his child. They said that every child showed somehow who their parents were. I had often wondered who I might have got my own traits from. Did my mother hate to cook, like me? Did my father have a glowing emberjar in his own mind, like mine, which was quick to spark in anger? Perhaps my hair was like my mother's or maybe my father was good at reading. I would never know now, for there was no way of telling, and mostly I was comfortable with that. But the child within had stirred inside me and that in turn stirred my mind to return to these questions which I thought I had long left behind.

The island of Aman had been in view the whole time since we had left Soora. It was not really so far away, if it had been on land, we would have thought nothing of walking to it. But since we could not swim in the water like fishes, we had to take the boat, and we could not sail straight there since we had to avoid the rocks. We had to sail around the island to the southern shore where the rocks gave way to a small sandy cove. There was a single boat landing site there, but no waiting Sooran with a parchment and a pen to scribe our arrival. You could not see Soora from there since there was a tall and rocky mountain in the middle of the island which blocked the view. Even though I knew Soora was there, it felt very far away from us. As we got close to the landing area, Jan came to Estar.

'Since there are no Soorabis here waiting for the boat, do I have permission for one of my men to jump onto the platform and tie up the boat for you?'

Estar looked troubled and Mina shook her head doubtfully. After a brief pause, Estar nodded her head. 'Jan, you may jump out and tie up the boat and then you must get straight back on the boat. You must only walk on the wooden walkway. That is acceptable.'

Gladia looked on in disbelief. 'Why does he have to ask your permission to tie up the boat? Surely it is obvious that one of the sailors needs to do that, otherwise we will be floating around on these blasted waves forever!'

'It is forbidden for men to set foot on the soil of the holy island of Aman,' said Mina. 'They are not made in the image of the Goddess. The island is for the Soorabis. You are fortunate to be allowed here yourselves. But the Rays of Soora have chosen and here you are.' Her face puckered as if she had just bitten into a very sour lemon. 'I hope you will not be here for long. We will go and find the makers of the honeywine and get as much honey off them as is not already fermenting, and then you can leave them to their peace and prayer.' She clutched her large round pendant piously in one hand and then closed her eyes as if in prayer.

Gladia rolled her eyes at me but wisely chose not to make any further remark and instead turned her eyes towards Jan, who had brought the boat close to the dock and now leapt out and landed on it smoothly, carrying with him a length of rope. He tied the boat to the metal loop which had been fixed in the platform, working quickly and efficiently. Then he called for one of his men to throw him another rope from the rear of the boat and he tied that up too, bringing the boat alongside the walkway so that the dismount plank could be placed to link the boat and the platform. He beckoned to us to walk over the plank. Mina went first, then Estar, then me and then Gladia. It seemed to me that he held her hand for longer when he assisted her on to the plank.

'Take care,' he said, seeming to address it generally, but somehow contriving for it to also seem to be a personal message to Gladia who glowed happily. Jan himself hopped lightly back onto his boat.

'I will be back at noon,' he said to Estar. She nodded her thanks and turned to walk along to the end of the thin strip of planks on which we had landed.

'Why don't you just stay on the boat and have a rest while you wait?' asked Gladia. No doubt she had imagined herself returning for a chat part way through the morning.

'The boats may not moor here at Aman,' said Mina in clipped tones. 'The Soorabis only use the boats to transport goods to Soora and for carrying any Soorabis to the islands who need to get there. It was fortunate for you that I happened to be on Soora when this arose.' Her nose wrinkled in distaste. 'Jan will return for us at noon and then you will leave Aman. Then, hopefully, we can continue to worship the Goddess and Soren without interruption and in preparation for the week of Soren's Sun. The new Soorabis have much to prepare, and we could have done better without this interruption.'

'Well, if you had not used up all the honey and taken all the honeycomb, the bees would not be in danger and you would not have to have us here, sullying your precious island,' said Gladia stoutly. 'But since you seem to have done so, we may as well get on with the job. Where do you keep the honeycombs?'

Mina glowered at her, but I saw the edge of Estar's mouth curve upwards in amusement before she quickly replaced it with her usual grave expression.

'Let us go, Mina. We have much to do, and time is of the essence. The sooner we get what we have come for, the sooner we will be able to leave our beloved Aman in peace.' She bowed her head and raised her two arms above it, forming the unbroken circle I had seen at the Place of Prayer. Mina promptly followed her lead and the two women stood there for some moments, joined in their unbroken circles of faith. I paused for a few moments, and then started walking towards the end of the dock. It felt as though Mina would otherwise take the opportunity for some prolonged prayer which would delay our mission again. Gladia followed me and the two Sooran women brought their arms down and raised their heads in one movement and scuttled after us.

There was a long uphill path before we arrived at a large building which had been carved out of the rock of the mountain which rose up in the centre of Aman. It reminded me of the Temples of Oramia, which had likewise been carved out of stone, by the Angels. I wondered who had carved this place. Although it had been carved out of the mountain, the building was angled towards the east and was filled with the golden light of the sun which streamed through the windows. Polished metal sheets had been placed around it to reflect the sunlight into the room further. Light yellow cloths hung near the windows, and as the sun shone through them it made the floor look yellow. A small knot of Soorabis came up to Mina and Estar and they moved off to one side, presumably so that Gladia and I were excluded from the conversation. I took the opportunity to look around me further.

This was a functional place, it would seem, despite its light and decoration. I guessed that the place where they worshipped was hidden further up the mountain perhaps, or in some other less obvious place. There were a few rooms which led off from the central one and in each one there were Soorabis engaged in various activities. In one room, I could see a large frame where very thin silk had been stretched across and very thin metal wires were being tied to it. It was the shape of a half circle, and the wires were being tied to it in the places where it had been stitched already with very fine metallic thread, like the rays of the sun. These must be the stitchings that Mina had spoken of; the cloths they needed for the new Soorabis. As I walked a little nearer, to look at it more closely, Estar returned and took my arm, gently steering me away from that room and towards a different one.

'The honeycomb is through here. We may need you to examine what we have, because it is hard for us to tell what honey the bees will still feed off, and how far the fermenting has gone.'

I could not believe that this woman, who was supposed to be in charge of the bees on Soora would not even know what honey her bees could sustain themselves off. Surely, she should know these things.

As if she could read my thoughts, her face warmed, its golden tone flushed with red.

'It was not very long ago that I was chosen to be the Ray of Soora. The one who used to care for the bees, Kavina, she was very ill, but she had not wanted to teach anyone else to look after the bees except her. She was very forceful in nature and had convinced all of us that the Goddess had given her a special gift for beeguarding in a dream, and that the same thing would happen at the right time to another when it was their time to be the Beeguard. It was only just before she returned to the Goddess, when she realised that she would die, that she began to teach me how to look after the bees. I think she thought she had more time left to her. But the Goddess chooses when she takes each person and I have had to try my best to learn. I was chosen to this job by the women who live on Soora. Perhaps it was just that nobody else wanted to do it or knew anything about the bees. I did not know they needed caring for beyond giving them the hives. Kavina said it was not the kind of work that could be learned by reading a scroll, and so she refused to scribe any instructions.'

'The bees look for a balance in the world, and give a balance to the world,' I said, trying to formulate my thoughts, shocked that there could be someone who was supposed to be a BeeGuard who knew so little. 'Could you not have tried to find a BeeGuard from Kashiq who could have taught you what to do? Or perhaps asked if another BeeGuard somewhere in Kashiq had scribed a scroll? I have myself read many scrolls on beeguarding, and always keep notes on what honey comes from which hive and which flowers my bees like to visit and so on.'

'Here on Soora, we prefer to keep to ourselves,' said Estar. 'We keep to ourselves as much as we can.'

'Except when you are trading,' put in Gladia, who had been following the conversation. 'You can see that there are things that the people of Kashiq and Oramia can do better than you, otherwise you would not be trading with them for anything. So why not accept that, just as with things like embroidery and metalwork and meat, there are skills that can be traded?'

Estar bowed her head in acknowledgement but said nothing and turned instead into a large room off to the right. In the room were lots of large clay pots.

'This is where the honeywine is made,' she said. 'I was hoping that Mina would explain how it works to you so you could see what honey could be recovered, but she seems to have gone elsewhere.' She looked around vaguely and then called over one of the women who were working in the room and asked her to tell me what happened to the honeycombs before they became honeywine.

'First of all, we take the tops off the honeycombs here and let the pure honey drain out, and then the honeycomb is put in hot water and washed so that all the honey and some of the beeswax comes out. Then that warm water is mixed with the honey and spices are added along with the motherwine and then we leave it to become honeywine. It takes about a month until it is ready. It is stored in those big jars over there until we need it.' She was an older woman and seemed quite happy to tell us the secrets of how they made the honeywine. It seemed simple enough to make, but if it really was that simple, surely we would have seen it more in Kashiq and Oramia? Perhaps it was this mysterious 'motherwine' that she spoke of. I asked her about it, and she told me that as the honeywine was made, a strange sort of jelly would appear in the mixture and that at the end of the month of brewing, that would be taken out of the honeywine jar and placed into a new jar which was just being started. It must contain some special ingredient. 'It comes from the Goddess,' said the woman. 'It just appeared one day so she must have sent it. Nothing appears from nowhere unless it is from the Goddess. After all, she is the one who created everything from nothing.' She looked at me triumphantly and perhaps a little pityingly.

'All well and good,' said Gladia crisply. 'But we are not really interested in that part of things, we need the honeycomb.' The woman looked at her in disbelief and was about to speak when Estar interrupted her.

'It is important, Kanisha. Please show us where the honeycomb is.'

Sullenly, the woman showed us where there were wooden boxes in which honeycombs had been placed. I looked at them carefully and some of them were still capped. Some had the white caps which I had come to know meant they were storage areas where the bees would store the honey they intended to use to feed themselves. Lower down the honeycomb were some darker capped areas which were where the eggs for new bees had been laid. Just like the baby inside me, the young bee was surrounded in a sweet liquid which gave it sustenance until it was time to be born. I explained this to Estar who listened carefully and then told Kanisha to organise the women who worked there to carry the boxes down to the dock so they could be loaded onto the boat when Jan returned. If we could return this perfect honeycomb to the bees then, not only would they have enough honey to keep them going until the sungold flowers bloomed again, but there would also be new bees hatching to take the place of those who had perished.

As we turned away from the boxes of honeycomb, we saw some honeycomb which had been drained being mixed with water. Quickly I went over to the woman who was now stirring it around vigorously with a wooden paddle. The water was warm enough that you could feel the heat coming off it in the cool of the stone building, but it was not over hot and the honey in the water could be used by the bees. Estar asked her to stop and to put the honey water into a large clay pot which could be taken down to the dock with the other things. At that point, Mina returned and, as we were about to look at another pot of honey water, stopped the woman from doing anything with the honey water.

'You have enough now,' she protested. 'There will not be enough honeywine for the week of Soren's Sun and for all the Soorabis to dance with. Go and get more honey from Layla on Oshana. It is not fair to take all of my honey and not to take any from the one who uses up all the flowers in her Oblak physics.' She turned to me bitterly. 'You look just like the ones who trade for the Oblak all the time. Maybe you are protecting them, so that they do not suffer with a lack of their physic even while I am going to suffer for it!'

Estar listened to her outburst patiently.

'I will take some moments to pray to Soren and Asmara in your prayer room,' she said, having considered the request silently for some time. 'I am sure that the right answer will be given to me. But remember, Mina, you may not agree with the answer I get. Soren heals and the Goddess gives life, and that is our work here too. The Soorabis are here to help all in Soren's name by their actions, not just to grow nearer to Soren through prayer.'

'I will pray too,' announced Mina piously. I asked Estar quietly if I might come too, to pray to Soren for healing. Gladia's eyes narrowed when she heard me say this. She knew that it was not in my nature to do this, with my own history of growing up in the Temple. But, if she suspected that I was not being entirely honest, she didn't say anything, but just patted my hand in a motherly way and went to sit down on a mat outside the building as the rest of us made our way to a room which had been set aside for prayer.

Estar explained to me before we went in that it was a place of silent prayer, and that it was not a Place of Prayer, but just a place to go to pray when one needed to throughout the day. Mina looked at me pityingly.

'She is not one of us, remember, Ray Estar. She likely does not pray as we do. Especially we, the Soorabis, who are so close to Soren, the goddess of healing and light.' She sounded like the Priestesses in the Temple, with their smug, professed closeness to the Goddess, interpreting their own desires as the desires of the Goddess and their own power as her power. But I bit my tongue, which was twitching with unspoken angry words, and bowed my head humbly.

'She can still pray, Mina,' scolded Estar. 'The Goddess hears the prayers of all, especially those whom she has blessed with a child.' She turned into the room, and I followed, intrigued by what I might see.

The room was filled with golden light, in common with the other rooms in the building, the sunlight being filtered through thin yellow hangings at the window. Near one of the walls was a sculpture which looked just like the pendant which Mina wore. From a distance, it looked like a combination of circles and domes, but from here, I could tell that it was a simplified statue of the Goddess. This statue had the arms clasped above the head to make a circle, just like I had seen in the Place of Prayer on Soora. I wondered if this was where the circle around the head of the Goddess statues in Oramia had come from. I sat quietly on one of the floormats. Like all Kashiqi mats it had been woven from dried palm leaves. This one used palm leaves which had been soaked in some kind of dye before they were used, and had a pattern woven into it of dark red and yellow lines against the bleached bone colour of the natural palm leaf. I bent my head down to look at the pattern further and when I lifted it up, Mina and Estar were both in the Sooran prayer pose. Estar sat with her legs folded, but Mina sat back on her heels, kneeling. Both held their clasped hands over their heads and had their heads bowed down, with their chins touching their chests. They held this pose for quite some time before gradually lowering the circled arms to their laps and raising their heads. Then they repeated the process several times. I remained seated with my hands in my lap and my head bowed until Estar rose to leave.

'I hope the Goddess brought you healing,' Mina said to me, virtuously. 'I prayed for you as well as for wisdom.' I wondered if she had joined the two subjects together and prayed for my wisdom. And then I wondered if our view of wisdom would be the same and thought it probably wouldn't be.

'How did the Goddess guide your wisdom, Estar?' Mina then enquired. I felt like rolling my eyes like Gladia might.

'We will go to Oshana,' announced Estar, which surprised me. I wondered if she had been praying to the Goddess or just taking the quiet time to reflect on all her choices. Perhaps it was the same thing. Mina looked relieved.

'The Goddess has guided you well,' she murmured. 'We will have enough honeywine here now for the Week of Soren's Sun, so that the Soorabis can dance and hear the Goddess as they join our service.'

'How do women become Soorabis?' I asked, half expecting Mina to ignore the question, but she must have been feeling vindicated by Estar's decision and answered me, despite my being a stranger.

'They are called by the Goddess. Sometimes in a dream. Sometimes they want to be apart from others. Sometimes they are women who cannot birth a child and so they come to the Goddess to be blessed in other ways. The Goddess hears our prayers, and our sculptures and our dancing and singing is like food to her, it is sustaining. We give our creation back to her, so that she can create more. When a woman is sure that this is her path, after a year of living with us, she becomes a Soorabi during the week of Soren's Sun. She drinks honeywine every day of the week and she learns the dances of the Soorabi. She gains her Soorabi sleeves to use for dance and in prayer.' I nodded my head in interest. 'The sleeves are made of the finest silk and embroidered with golden threads. They are made in Oramia by the skilled embroiderers there, who also pray to the Goddess as they stitch, like us. We trade for them with honeywine, and the physics made on Oshana.'

It was clear that this was where the Court of the Queen was getting the physic of forgetting, or Oblak as they called it here. Ambar had had both the physic and the honeywine when I had met him. Perhaps the silk came from the Court of the Queen. There were huge wooden coffers there, full of silk, which I had seen myself on the one time I had been there when Lunaria became Queen. Maybe Lunaria herself even did some of the stitching on the silk; her fine, skilful stitching had been well known when she was a Priestess. If not her, then it must be the stitchers amongst the Priestesses who were doing the work.

'It must be an amazing sight,' I murmured. 'I would really like to see these triumphs of stitching. My mother, Gladia, stitches, as you know, although her work would not be fine enough, I am sure. I have always been interested in stitching myself, but it is not my skill; I am a Beeguard.' In fact, I hated stitching and had been swiftly removed from the stitching group at the Temple and moved to the cleaning group where I had stayed. I preferred to untangle the threads or come up with the patterns for another to sew.

'I can show you some of the sleeves,' offered Mina, seemingly friendly towards me now. 'You cannot see them being worn, that is only at the feasts of the Goddess and of Soren, but you can see the fine work.' She walked over to a large, carved wooden cupboard, sealed with a large lock and took a metal key from her pocket. I had seen these keys in Kashiq before. They were like levers that would push pieces in the lock out of the way in a specific order, and only one key could open the lock. Ravin would have loved that key. A tear slid out of my eye, but I brushed it away with the edge of my netela and concentrated on what Mina was showing me.

The soft yellow silk was indeed very fine. If you held it up to the light, you could see through it, like a bee's wing. On it had been stitched fine lines which held very fine wire to the silk. The lines looked like the rays of the sun. Mina held it up to the light, and against her arm so that it hung down. I could imagine how these sleeves might look, especially if they were in the sunlight, and could understand why Mina wanted to protect them. But there was more for us to do now that Estar had decided that we must go to Oshana, and she was already turning to leave. I hurried behind her, but Mina stayed. There was no need for her to leave her island now and she was satisfied with the decision that Estar had made. Perhaps Estar had made that choice just in order to be free of Mina, I thought. She certainly seemed more buoyant as we walked down to the dock.

Gladia was there, talking across the water to Jan on the boat.

'Here they come,' she said. 'Looks like we will be off soon. Thank goodness for that! It may be the home of the Goddess Soren but it's not my idea of a lovely place. Did you get all the honey you need?'

I explained that we had a lot of honey, enough for the immediate needs of the bees, but that we would also be travelling to Oshana to get their supplies of honey. To my surprise, Gladia did not protest at the thought of another boat trip but smiled sunnily at Jan.

'Looks like you will have to put up with me for a little longer, Jan!'

'It can only be a pleasure,' he protested, his face full of smile. 'And your company will make the journey even more delightful.' Gladia loved it. All his compliments were eagerly received and gobbled up as eagerly as fine apricot and walnut cakes. He must have had years of practice, I thought to myself, years of paying compliments and charming his passengers. I had never found it easy to be told good things about myself. It was frowned upon in the Temple and doing well was expected. Being paid a compliment about how I looked, or what I did still tended to make me feel uncomfortable. I had trusted Ravin's words about me because he had tempered them with little jokes. Besides, he had also spoken to me of my faults, as I had him. How I wished he were here now, to smile at Gladia flirting with Jan, and then to whisper in my ear.

Jan's sailors loaded up the boat with the boxes and large clay jars of honey which had been sent down to the dock while Estar talked to Jan about the next stage of our journey, the trip to Oshana, and when it might happen. The physics, which Ravin had found out about and which he had wanted us to find together, were there, though it seemed we had not needed them after

216

all. If Ravin had still been alive, we would not have been here at all, for the child would be proof that the Goddess had blessed us without needing the Sooran physic. But life had taken a different path. Now, I wanted to know more about the Oblak physic, the physic of forgetting, that which I had taken with Ambar.

Chapter 21

It was the next day before we arrived at Oshana. Estar wanted to get the honeycomb back to the beehives as soon as possible, so that the immediate difficulties could be lessened. She had talked to me further on the boat about the bees and how I cared for my own bees. I suggested to her that she should mark some of the frames for honeycomb in the hives, and never harvest those frames. With the Sooran appetite for noting down all transactions, I didn't think it would be long before there was a scroll for each hive and a noting down of the numbers of honeycombs removed from each hive. I also suggested to her that she scribe the ways in which the bees needed to be cared for from now on, so that they would always be looked after properly. We arranged that I would see her again once we had returned from Oshana and speak to her about this, so she could scribe it for others to use. Much of Soora was already planted with sungold flowers, so there could not be many more planted, and they grew nowhere else. The bees could not make more honey than they already were, and it would mean that there would be less honeywine and Oblak physic to trade in future. It was good to have limits. It could mean that those who traded for the physic might be willing to trade more of their goods for what they got in return if they knew the supply was limited. Privately, I hoped that it would mean that there would not be enough of the Oblak for them to continue using it for the Angels.

After a good night's sleep, we set off for Oshana on calm, silky water with scarcely a wave or a cloud in the sky. Estar had spoken to Layla who would accompany us back to the island she guided. She pursed her lips but nodded crisply when she heard that she too would have to give up some of her honey. She did not speak a great deal on the journey but carried with her a scroll which she read in deep concentration all the way to the island. I was becoming accustomed to the rise and fall of the boat by now, and, on that calm day, it was very pleasant to be gently rocked. Gladia seemed to have lost her distaste for boat trips and leaned back, enjoying the morning sun on her face, watching Jan all the while. Inside me, I could feel the child moving gently with the rhythm of the boat. It was as if I were being rocked both inside and out.

I pondered Estar's choice to take me to Oshana with her as she went to retrieve the honey. In truth, she probably did not need to go to Oshana to get any more. We had retrieved a lot of the honey which had been taken to Aman for making into honeywine. There seemed to be such a large appetite for it here among the Soorans themselves, the sailors who lived on their boats around the islands and, of course, the traders. I thought back to the honeywine which Ambar had given me, and which I had willingly drunk. I had not known anything about it then, really. It was not ever anything I had seen the need to seek out until I was seduced by the hope that it might make me feel better. And it did, but it also encouraged me to try the Oblak made on Oshana, this elixir that could make you forget. It did make me forget, but not forget what had happened to Ravin, only to forget what occurred after I had taken it.

If Ambar had taken it too, as he said he did, then neither of us would ever remember that time, it seemed.

I thought that Estar probably wanted to balance the resentments of both Layla and Mina who blamed one another for being too greedy with the honey. She did not want to be seen as favouring one over the other and so she would take honey back from both. I wondered how many times she had to do this, to balance the other four Rays of Soora so that they remained a united group who made decisions using their stones and then accepted the result. How many times did Estar choose her stone based on what she thought others might choose?

I was most interested in what was produced on Oshana though. That was what had drawn Ravin here in the first place, and I was intrigue, mainly for the suggestion that there were physics one could take to encourage or discourage the blessing of the Goddess. Growing up in the Temple, we had often heard stories of how women left their babies on the steps of the Temple because they did not want to or could not care for them any longer. And at the same time, there were women making weekly supplications to the Goddess, pleading to be blessed with a child. Surely, I thought back then, the Goddess could merely bless those who wanted babies and not bless those who did not want them. Not every woman who was blessed by the Goddess considered herself blessed. That way, there would never have been any babies left on the steps of the Temple. Now, I could see how much the Temple and the OutForts profited from these babies. They helped to keep the system going. They were brought up by the Temple, who selected those they deemed to be of higher value and released the others to be taken by the OutRiders as soon as they left the Temple. They became the Angels who were used by the OutFort as labourers who worked on the buildings of the OutForts and the Temples and who were used by the OutRiders for their physical gratification. This in turn led to many of them having babies which were left on the Temple steps and so it continued. If there were physics to stop a woman having a child, then the Angels did not need to ever have babies. But if they did not have babies the system would collapse.

I told myself to discuss this further with Gladia that evening, to see what her thoughts were. She had worked for a long time now with the Angels who Ambar had released each year, and she had seen the pain that their memories brought back to them. She had seen for herself the impact on a child of finding out the truth of their ancestry from when Jember had found out about his own father and the continual effect on his mother Bellis of what had happened to her. She would definitely be the person to talk to about this. Meanwhile, although the sungold flowers used for the Oblak physic only grew on Soora and could not be used back in Kashiq, it was possible that some of these other physics might be made using similar plants found in Kashiq. Achillea would be most interested in them.

Lapsing into thoughts of Achillea, I thought about how she had changed since I first met her. Or perhaps it was me that had changed. When I first met her, fresh from a hard-working life at the Temple, she seemed to me to be lazy and superficial. I had found myself irritated with her and with her chatter about what I saw as the more trivial things in life. But now I knew her, I knew her to be kind and generous, thoughtful and sensible. She had befriended me when I was not an easy person to befriend and had been my loyal friend ever since. Ever since I had left my childhood in the Temple, Achillea had been there for me, and now I missed her. She had become more focused on her role as a healer, one of Soren's chosen, even though she lived in Oramia not Kashiq as I did. She had understood the healing nature of her singing and had linked it to her ability to make physics and salves. She would want to know every detail of my visit to these interesting places. Gladia was a good companion, but there were things I would rather talk about with Achillea. She had had three children and could tell me what it would be like. The child within me seemed to fill all the space, and to be moving all the time. It seemed as if it rarely rested, except when it was being rocked by the boat or by my movement. I did not remember her being disturbed like this, but it may just be that I had not listened to her.

It was hard for me and Ravin that Achillea and Tarik seemed to be blessed so easily by the Goddess with children and we were not. I used to blame myself sometimes. I once told Ravin that perhaps the Goddess did not bless me with a child because I had gone against the wishes of the Temple. He laughed off my dark fears, telling me it was nothing to do with it, and that I was the greatest blessing. He was so adept at understanding me, so able to calm my fears and so able to make me smile. And now, remembering him, a tear slid out again.

'If you need respite from your thoughts, perhaps you should try the Oblak,' said Layla suddenly. 'It helps you to distance from the pain of memory.'

'I am well,' I answered, knowing that this was not the answer for me. 'I am remembering Ravin. He was the father of this child.'

'There is no shame in the Oblak physic,' said Layla, mildly. 'We only use it here in very small quantities. Just a few drops are enough to make the pain of childbirth bearable, and any pain which can be borne can be overcome. After the child is born, many women take Iskra, which returns their memory to them. But because they did not fully live through the pain, they do not remember its sharpness, they only recall it vaguely.'

My mind sparked. So, there was a way to regain that lost time when I had taken the physic with Ambar. If I could get some of this Iskra, perhaps I could put my mind at rest. But another thing was interesting me too. Layla had said they only used a few drops of Oblak at a time and yet Ambar had used a full vial of it, and they must be using a lot of it on the Angels too.

'What do those you trade with use it for, this Oblak?' I asked, trying to look as if I was just making conversation.

'It is not my job, to ask questions of those who trade,' said Layla sharply. 'You must ask Dayo. All I do is make the stuff. We did not used to make as much, but then we never used to trade it. Nousha took most of our supply for the women who were birthing. Some of it went to Mina, of course, for her rituals. Less than a year ago, a Birthmother came on the trade ships and asked to trade for it. She had heard of it from one of our Birthmothers who had trained her, out in Oramia.'

I nodded and then turned to look at the water just as Jan shouted to the sailors to turn to the west, to take the boat into the harbour on the island of Oshana. It seemed that the reach of the Queen's Court was even more extensive than I had thought, making its way even to these small islands off the land of Kashiq. How they had come to find out about the Oblak physic was still a puzzle to me despite the story of the Birthmothers.

Oshana, the most northern of the islands, looked like a green tower rising out of the water. The small settlement on Oshana, like all the other Sooran islands, was based around a harbour where the only flat land on the island was. Beyond, it rose up steeply, with a crowd of tall trees standing on the slopes, making it seem even taller and steeper. Around the highest parts of the islands hung clouds, as if caught to the branches of the trees like fishing nets. The trees made me think of Oramia, and the welcome shade of a Paradox tree. The palm trees of Kashiq never felt as solid and substantial as the Paradox trees, nor the shade as dense, but these trees seemed to be even more majestic than the Paradox trees.

'I hope you're ready for some hard walking,' said Jan to Gladia, following our gaze towards the trees and the clouds. 'I've unloaded things here before and helped to carry them up to the dwellings in the forest where they work. Its steep work if you aren't used to it.'

'Just because I am not a youngster does not mean I have no stamina,' replied Gladia quickly. 'Talla and I have often been in places where we have needed to climb, and, as you see, we are still here today, none the worse for it!' Jan laughed.

'I wouldn't doubt it! I suspect you always get what you want in the end, Gladia!' He closed one eye to her, making her chuckle.

'Made quite the impression on Jan, hasn't she?' said Estar drily. Perhaps she had captured my rolling eyes. 'He is right, though, it is a steep climb. In your condition, you should walk slowly. You don't have to come up to the working dwellings anyway, we can take the sailors up with me to carry down the pots of honey. Unless you have an interest in our physic and how we use our honey?' She almost sounded eager for me to go with her, and I wondered if she saw me as a good support in case Layla should prove as stubbornly reluctant as Mina had been.

I was determined to see what was being made here and what ingredients were used. Like Gladia, I was able to keep going for a long time as long as I was not made to go too fast. But there was no doubt that my changed body made it more difficult, and that I needed to rest more. Luckily, with Gladia there, I was less likely to be the one left at the back, and I assured Estar of my genuine interest in the physics and how they were made.

'It is good to hear of the interest of those beyond Soora in our lives and our work,' she replied, smiling. 'Sometimes we forget that there are so many other people and lands out there, and we only look at ourselves. Your visit has shown us not to shun the thoughts and wisdom of others.'

Chapter 22

Layla walked alongside me as we trudged up the narrow, steep path. She seemed much friendlier to me now, perhaps because she knew that most of the honey was already coming from Mina, who she appeared to have little time for, and not from her. Or perhaps it was because I was interested in what she had to say. I had always been a good listener. In the Temple, I used to listen to conversations I was not invited to, and from them I learned a great deal. Then, when I started living in the Outer, I learned to observe people's faces as they spoke, too. Often, I learned from these unspoken gestures. There is nothing that pleases a person more than to be listened to. I knew it for myself. To be the one whose words are being treasured is a feeling of being important. Of course, there were also people who craved that attention so much that they became dull and repetitive, never enriching themselves by listening in their turn. They were the ones to avoid. But Layla spoke of what interested me.

I was lucky to be the one doing the listening since, if I had had to talk, I would have had to slow down to breathe, but Layla was clearly accustomed to the steep path up through the thick forest, for she barely showed a sign that she was troubled by the exertion. Gladia trudged behind us, puffing and panting and sighing, but keeping up. We stopped occasionally so that Layla could show me a plant that she was speaking about, and Gladia took these breaks as chances to rest. Estar had lapsed into quiet and walked purposefully alone, a little distance from the rest of us.

The trees that surrounded us were very tall and, Layla told me, very old. Their trunks were like tall, solid pillars, lacking in branches until they were higher up, nearer to the sun. The leaves were a rich, glossy green which formed a sort of canopy over the top of us, protecting us from the sun. Not only was it shady, but it was also cool because all around the trees hung wisps of clouds making the forest damp and humid. Some of the trees had had patches of bark removed, and next to each patch was scribed a number.

'These trees are the Osh trees, the ones the island is named for. They do not grow anywhere else as far as we know. They need the heat of the sun and the constant clouds around them in order to grow. Those patches you see are where we harvest the bark which we use in one of our physics. Smell the bark.' Layla peeled off some of the bark, which was light brown, almost spongy and crumbly, with deep fissures in it and held it out to me. I sniffed it. There was a sweetness about it, like a mixture of cinnamon and honey, the scent of a delicious cake as it cooked.

'You only get that scent when the bark has been peeled off the trunk. Otherwise, imagine, the whole island would be scented by Osh bark. We number the tree patches so that we only take bark from trees that are ready. It takes seven years, a whole age, for a patch to fully replenish, but a year for the tree to be ready to be harvested in a different patch. The number ensures we do not kill the tree by taking all the bark. It would be like removing all of a person's skin.'

I had never thought of bark in this way before, but it made sense. I could also see that Layla's mind had devised a clever system for ensuring that, unlike the honey, the bark would not be overused. Perhaps if she had suggested it to Estar, their situation with the bees would not have arisen. They gave the appearance of a united group of guides, making and standing by their decisions, but I wondered now if they were really just guiding their own island and looking after it without really thinking about how the other islands interwove with it. Like pulling a thread in a piece of cloth, the collapse of one could cause the collapse of others.

'What do you use it for?' asked Gladia. She sounded interested, but I suspected it was merely a ruse to keep Layla standing still and afford Gladia a little more breathing space.

'The physic would not be of any use to you, Gladia, even though it is quite powerful.' Layla smiled. 'Osh bark tea is used to encourage the Goddess to bless a woman with a child. It seems to attract the Goddess's favour in some way. We do receive travellers who come from far away who have heard of Soora and the bark of the Osh tree. They are usually women who have longed for a child for at least an age. But the bark only works in women up to their fifth age. Beyond that, the Goddess replaces her blessings with wisdom in our elder women, as you know. And Talla clearly has no need for it.' She smiled at me and gestured towards my belly.

'Hmm...' Gladia shot me a look. 'I wish I had known about it when I was younger then. I had a child once, who I lost. I wanted another but it never happened again. Perhaps if I had had some of your Osh bark tea, I might have been blessed.'

Layla looked at her kindly. 'Perhaps. But it does not always work for everyone. Some are wounded when

228

they give birth and cannot carry a child again. And, for some people who take too much of it, it means that DoubleSouls are a more likely outcome. They are difficult births for our Birthmothers to deal with, and although of course two babies are a double blessing, they can also be a hardship. I heard that there is a scroll in Arbhoun, the city of wisdom, which tells of the Osh bark. A scholar must have taken the time to scribe it. In any case, it seems that more travellers know about it now, throughout Kashiq. But, like the sungold flowers for the Oblak, there has been a much greater demand for it in recent times, perhaps over the last year. Dayo makes too many trade promises for the physics; she is too eager to please her customers who now want physics as well as precious metals.'

This must have been the physic that Ravin had found out about and what he had wanted for us to get. This was why he had planned this trip. I felt contented that I had done what he would have wanted us to do. A small bird perched on a swaying branch and turned its head to one side as if examining me. It looked quite drab, a sort of light brown shade, until it flew off and then I saw that its wings were a startling yellow underneath. Layla saw me marvelling at it and told me that it was called the Soorabi bird, for the way in which it resembled the Soorabis and their wide golden sleeves.

'You see more of them flying around when it is the time of year to harvest the Soorai berries, because they love them. We have to try and pick them before the birds do!' She laughed. 'The Soorai berries don't seem to have the same effect on the birds as they do on people though! They produce just as many young every year!'

'That sounds as if it is some kind of physic to prevent the blessing of the Goddess,' remarked Gladia. 'I can't imagine the Birthmothers needing a lot of that.'

'You might be surprised, Gladia,' said Layla quietly. 'Having a child is seen by so many, yourself included, as a great blessing. Which indeed it is. But there are many reasons why not bearing a child is desirable too. There are those who suffer in the birthing of children and may die if they have more. There are those who already have as many children as they can care for. And there are those who know they could never mother a child properly, or who wish to work without attending to a child. But it is the Soorabis here on Soora who use it most. They use the Soorai berries to sharpen their devotion to Soren. You see, the berries stop you from even wanting to have a child. The Soorabis never feel that urge. We trade it with others who have the same need too; soldiers are often given it to focus their mind on their fighting, and I did hear that there are those like the Soorabis in other lands, like Oramia, who use the berries for their priestesses too.' She set off up the hill again, catching up with Estar, unaware of the effect of her words on me and Gladia.

'If the Priestesses use these berries, do you know about it?' hissed Gladia. 'If they can stop women from having babies, why do they not give the berries to the Angels? They could keep them working on the buildings all the time and never worry that they would be birthing children with OutRider fathers.'

'Unless...' I paused, almost unable to comprehend what I was suggesting. 'Unless they do use the berries and then deliberately stop giving them so that the Angels do bear babies sometimes. Because remember what happens to the babies that are born to the Angels? Except the ones who are lucky enough to come to you.'

'They are taken to the Temples, that's what Bellis and others have told me...' Her voice trailed off as she recognised the implications of what she had said. 'But that means they are deliberately making babies for them to harvest, like crops! They are making babies who will become Priestesses and OutRiders and Angels! They are making themselves over and over again.' Her face creased, making her look old and tired. She stopped walking for a moment, overcome with her understanding, and repulsed by it. I stopped with her. I was also struggling with what we had just learned, but I felt it was important that we did not let Layla or any of the other Rays of Soora know this just yet, until we had had time to unpick it all.

'Don't say anything to her,' I warned.

'I am not so old that I am stupid,' responded Gladia acerbically. 'These lines and grey hairs are signs from the Goddess of my wisdom, I'll have you know.' She sighed. 'I wish the Goddess would send down some real wisdom to those who seem to need it most!'

We finally reached the working dwellings in the middle of the afternoon. The curious atmosphere of the Osh forest and its soft, damp blanket of cloud meant that we arrived feeling as though we were drenched with sweat. The dwellings were arranged in a clearing in the forest, where several of the large trees had been cut down and the wood used to build the dwellings. They had been there a long time or so it seemed. Trailing mosses hung from the roofs and the wooden logs they had been made of were splashed with grey and green lichens. There were perhaps five or six separate dwellings and I saw Soorans walking around, carrying baskets of bark and fruits of different kinds, and bundles of leaves and herbs. They stopped to stare at me and Gladia, strangers who had accompanied the more familiar figures of Estar and Layla who were now explaining to them that we would need to take any honey that was not already in use so that the bees on Soora could continue their work.

'I think I will just sit down for a while,' said Gladia, as the two Rays of Soora returned to us.

'Of course,' murmured Estar. 'It has been quite a difficult walk for you, hasn't it? Galina, can you get our visitor some of your tea?' One of the women who had come to greet us nodded and wandered off towards a fireplace to find some tea for Gladia. I would have liked nothing more than to sit down with her and drink tea and discuss what we had already found out, but this might be my only chance to discover more about these physics that seemed to be mostly used by the powerful of Oramia. Not for the first time, I wished that Ravin were with us and that we could talk it through together. I smiled brightly at Layla.

'I would be so interested to see the physics you make here, especially the ones which contain honey. It is something which I do myself back in Kashiq, as does my friend Achillea. Do you use beeswax in your salves too?

Layla's eyes lit up. She was clearly someone who enjoyed her work immensely, and anyone showing interest in it was immediately important to her. Estar waved her assent, and we walked towards the first of the working dwellings. Layla explained to me on the way that there were three main dwellings where the work of making the physics was done and then two for living and sleeping in and one for cooking and storage.

'I'll show you the Osh bark first. The Osh trees only grow here, as I told you. So, it can only be made here. It began as a simple tasty tea, from the smell of the bark which is like cinnamon. The women who worked here took some to Soora, and the more popular it became, the more babies were born!' She laughed. 'The sailors must have been busy! Anyway, we always get some visitors who hope that coming to Soora might help them to gain the blessing of the Goddess, and we started to trade the tea with them, and it was a success. We soak the harvested bark here.'

Layla showed me some large clay pots which contained sheets of Osh bark soaking in water. The bark was left steeping for several days and then the dark brown liquid was mixed with honey and boiled until it was reduced down to a dark, aromatic syrup. This was then stored in small clay pots with narrow necks and carved wooden stoppers coloured red. The tea itself was made by mixing a small spoonful of the syrup with warmed water. They did use quite an amount of honey to make the syrup, and I asked Layla if they had their own hives on the island, or if they got all their honey from Soora.

She looked at me, puzzled. 'We don't have sun here in the forest like they do on Soora, or sungold flowers. Those flowers only like to grow on that strange sandy soil they have on Soora; they do not grow here in the forest.'

'But you could perhaps have the hives near the edges of the forest, near where we arrived on the boat,' I offered. 'You may not be able to grow the sungold flowers but other herbs which flower grow here, and the Osh trees themselves must flower too. You could not keep bees in the quantities they do on Soora, but you could have a few hives. You could use the Oramian hives, old logs hollowed out for the bees and hung up on ropes from a tree branch.'

Layla looked at me doubtfully.

'The Isle of Oshana does not produce honey for trading, that is the job of Soora. We try to only look after the thing our island does best. Estar would not want me to have honey hives here.'

'But surely it would be better, if so much more honey is needed by everyone?'

'It always used to work. But ever since we started trading more, things do not work as well.'

'Perhaps you trade too much?' I asked.

Layla sighed. 'Yes, perhaps. But we are of Soren, and we are bound to help those who ask for healing, whether it is through physics or honeywine or prayer, and the trading helps us to do that. We are all bound to one another. I will ask the council of Rays and see what they think. Come and see the Soorai berries now.'

We walked to another of the dwellings so that she could show me how they worked with the Soorai berries. These required no honey- in fact they required very little except to be dried. The process began with pounding the berries until they were a glistening purple pulp in a pestle and mortar. It was hard work and the women who were doing it worked rhythmically, making liquid thwacking noises as the small, seeded berries were squashed. Some raw Soorai berries lay in a basket on the side, and I looked at them carefully. They were somewhat like a darkberry, but their skin was glossy, and they were smaller. They had a pungent scent which tickled at my mind, trying to make a link. But I had never seen a Soorai berry before; they did not grow anywhere else and I had never seen them traded in markets anywhere, not even in Arbhoun, that great city of wisdom and trade.

We moved on, to a large flat table where there were flat sheets of metal being coated with a thin layer of the pulped berries. Layla told me that those sheets were placed in a clay oven with a fire at the bottom and dried out. At the next table three women were sitting grinding that dried up pulp, which resembled blood-red leather, into a powder, and it was then that I knew where I had encountered that strange, heady scent before. If I closed my eyes, the memory ran in front of them as if I were still there, but watching my own self in another land, the land of the past.

The food and drink at the Temple, where I spent the Ages of Childhood were bland and of little interest. I ate and drank then because I was hungry, and I needed fuel for my body to work more. It was sufficient for our needs. Porridge, flatbreads, single vegetable stews, coffee. Occasionally meat or fruit. Honey if you needed healing. I had become greedy since I encountered life on the Outer, and life in Kashiq, where everyone seasoned their food and added delicious herbs and spices, and combined vegetables together. They even made rich cakes and sweetmeats in Kashiq, much beloved by Gladia. The Priestesses told us that the Goddess had given us the plants to eat and that their taste was how she wanted them to taste, that if she had wanted different foods mixing, she would have made them so. There was only one thing in the Temple which had any kind of addition made to it, and that was the coffee. To the coffee was added a powder, called the Goddess's Blessing by the Priestesses. That powder was a dark blood-red and carried with it a faint scent of acrid smoke. The same scent that I smelled now. The Soorai berry powder.

I suddenly felt quite dizzy, almost as if I might suddenly fall asleep or faint. I caught hold of Layla's yellow sleeve and told her I needed some fresh air.

'Of course. The scent is quite strong in here and I keep forgetting that you are getting closer to your time. Please go and sit outside. Galina will bring you tea.'

I made my way out, holding on to the side of the dwelling as I stumbled out and sat down under the shade of an Osh tree. I breathed in the air of the forest to rid myself of the scent of the Soorai berries. I had never really thought about why our coffee had this extra ingredient in it, which, I realised now, was one of the reasons that the coffee on the Outer tasted so good to me, and why the coffee at the Temple had tasted so bitter in comparison. At the Temple, of course, we had never tasted any different, so we just assumed that was how it was supposed to taste. Now, I saw that the Priestesses were deliberately making it so that there was no chance of any of the Temple Maids ever bearing a child or even ever having a desire to bear a child. I myself had never had any feeling towards having a child for quite some time after I had left the Temple but had always thought that was just my nature. After all, motherhood was not for everyone.

All that time that Ravin and I had wondered about the reasons why the Goddess had not blessed us with a child, and the reason was the powder named the Goddess's Blessing by the Priestesses. They never wanted us to love a child or to make a child with love. Our role was to work and to worship the Goddess. And if they so decided, your role would be to become an Angel and work in a different kind of way. But some of the Angels bore children, who were then taken back to the Temples and the OutFort and, in their turn, grew through the system. But, if taking the Soorai berries had such a lasting effect, how did the Angels bear children? The answer, of course, was in that other physic made here – the Osh bark tea, which caused a woman to be more likely to have a baby. Using these two substances, the Priestesses and the OutFort could decide on when new people were needed to keep their system going. And at the top of the system was the Queen, Lunaria.

And Ambar. He had ready access to the physics that the Court traded for with the Isles of Soora, but did he know of how they were used? He knew of the Oblak, and of the honeywine, for he had shared both with me.

236

But surely if he knew about the Osh bark tea, he would have told Lunaria about it? My mind was spinning so fast that I shut my eyes, only to open them a moment later when Galina brought me some tea. Briefly I wondered what had been put in it, but it smelt only of mint and camomile. She offered me some dates which I ate, for once relishing their cloying sweetness, which I sometimes found so tedious back in Kashiq, where they were everywhere. Slowly my mind began to calm down and I started trying to slowly pull out the threads of understanding.

I had so many questions which I did not know if I would ever get answered. Did the Priestesses continue to take the Soorai powder even when they had been chosen to be Priestesses? If so, could this be the reason that Lunaria too had not been blessed with children, heirs to the throne? How did they decide when to stop with the berry powder and start with the Osh tea? I needed to know more about how quickly the tea worked to reverse the effects of the berries. The women of the Isles of Soora had made these physics with the sole aim of helping women to heal, and yet in Oramia they were being used to control them and to make their suffering worse. I wondered what their reaction might be if I told them. But if I told them, I would have to tell them everything and they might just hand me over to whoever came from Oramia to trade with them. After all, look at Mina and how driven she was to get the embroidered sleeves for her Soorabis. I didn't think she would much mind what she had to do as long as she got what she wanted. The child inside me kicked ill-temperedly, apparently unhappy with my position, which was bent forward to clear my head. So, I sat up, resolving to go and find out more. I walked over to Layla who had just emerged from the dwelling where the berries were being turned to powder.

'The scent is a little overwhelming when there is so much of it all in one place,' she said. 'You get used to it and then forget that others are not. I am sure the fresh air will have made you feel better. Estar is organising the spare honey we have, and it would appear that Gladia is resting.' She smiled and indicated Gladia who sat propped up against the sturdy trunk of an Osh tree, her head nodded down, snoring slightly. I smiled at the sight.

'You love your mother, you can see it in your eyes,' said Layla. 'Have you always been close?'

I was surprised by her comments. I had known Gladia for a long time now, having met her on the same day that I had met Benakiell, and I had, I suppose, looked on them both as parents, although Benakiell was now less present in my life, living as he did In Kashiq. I had even taken on his dead wife Velosia's name as my own family name. Had Gladia and I always been close? Not exactly. And yet, Gladia had always stood up for me, often when others distrusted me. When I came out of the Temple, I had never known what love was, or how it could arise in such a wide number of ways and in such different contexts. 'There are as many different kinds of love as there are stars in the sky or grains of sand,' Ravin would say to me. 'All are stars, but all are different. Just like love is love, but it's always different. We just don't have the words to describe it better.' I smiled at the memory of him saying that and Layla took that as her response.

'Do you want to see the last of the working dwellings here?' she asked. 'We have lots more dwellings in different parts of the forest, but here is where we make the three physics that we use or trade most; the Soorai berries, the Osh bark and the Oblak physic, the one we use the sungold flowers for.'

This was the one which I really wanted to know more about. The others had been the ones which Ravin had made notes on, but the Oblak was what I had taken, in the midst of my grief, and what the Angels were now being given to make them forget their ordeal at the hands of the OutRiders. We walked over to it and Layla reassured me that the sungold flowers had very little scent, so I would not feel faint again.

The flowers were stripped of their petals and the petals were put in large clay pots to steep for a week. The seeds from the flowerheads were crushed and also soaked in water, which made the oil in them float to the top of the water, where it was skimmed off and saved in metal vessels. Layla explained to me that the oil would otherwise soak into the clay and be wasted. The steeped flower petals were drained and boiled down with some honey into a light golden yellow syrup which was mixed with the oil.

'It is only when you mix the two together that you get the effect of the Oblak physic,' explained Layla. She was one of those people who loved to talk about her work. I wondered if that was how the Court of the Queen had found out about it, just by showing interest in Layla's work if they had met her in Soora one day.

'I wonder how they first discovered what happened when you mixed them,' I mused, looking at it.

'They used to use them for different things,' said Layla. 'We only started making the Oblak a few years ago. They were combined by accident and then, when the physic was taken by someone with the pains of childbirth, she remembered nothing of the whole day that the child was born! It came as a great surprise to her when she realised she had a child. Since then, of course, we only use small doses for women in pain. We do sometimes give more, but then we can give another physic called Iskra to reverse its effects.'

239

'Doesn't that mean the original use of the Oblak was pointless?' I asked, trying to understand how it might work, and, in a corner of my mind, wondering if I might take this antidote, Iskra, and remember for myself what had happened on the night that I took it with Ambar.

'Sometimes, when we know we have lived through something, emerged at the other end of it, and it is over, then we already have the strength to cope with our memories of it. In any case, the memories, from what I have heard, are softened, as if through age, because they were not endured at the time.'

'But what if it were given for some other great suffering that had not ended, or that was too hard to bear?'

'It is only really used for women giving birth, and usually that has a happy outcome,' said Layla. 'Of course, sometimes it does not, and really maybe it is better to not have the sharpness of those memories after all. I think that for some, whose suffering is great, Iskra is not given for quite some time, if ever. It works even after years, they say. I wouldn't know; I have never tried it or the Oblak. I never had children, nor wanted to, and the Soorai berry powder keeps it so. My interest lies in the forest plants and in the physics we make here; there is no time for anything else. The Iskra physic, for instance, is made from a plant we use to ease aching muscles, called the Moon plant because of its round, silvery leaves. One of the Soorans of the past made the leaves into a tea and found it relaxed tight, sore muscles. We had long used it for women who were giving birth to soothe their pains, or for after the birth if it was long and tiring. Like all these things, it was discovered accidentally by giving it to a woman who had been given Oblak and we found it reversed the effects of the Oblak. If you took it without having taken the Oblak, it would just relax your muscles and help you sleep. Perhaps it was Soren who guided it, and we just thought it was accidental, though. Even those of us who prefer to work with what we can see sometimes have to accept that things happen which we cannot explain yet. We always trade both the physics together, in pairs, like DoubleSouls.'

It seemed that the Soorans assumed that everyone in every land thought in the same way that they did, and that all had good intentions. As I had seen throughout my life, this was not necessarily true.

'Would you like me to give you a pair of them?' asked Layla suddenly. 'You are asking so much about them; I can sense that you are worried about your birthing time. You can take them with you so that wherever you are when you give birth, you can ease the hard times.' She smiled briefly. 'It is a long time since anyone showed any interest in my work here with the plants. If you ever go to Arbhoun, to the Tower of the Wise, perhaps you can scribe about my work here for others to read. And if you find any scrolls about plants and their healing properties, then you could send a copy of the scroll to me with a trader.' She looked wistful. 'I would like to go myself, but we do not leave the Isles unless we do not want to come back. I cannot think of living a life away from this forest and the plants and the birds that live here. I did ask another woman who came here to trade for the physics to do the same thing, but she did not ever send me a scroll to tell me if she had done what I asked, or not. She did write everything down though.' Perhaps this was how the Queen's Court had come to learn of the physics, then. One of the Priestesses or a member of the Queen's Court might have come here and shown such great interest that Layla had been flattered and had told her what she had told me. It would explain how the Court had come to hear of the more recent development of the Oblak; they had clearly known about the Soorai berry powder for many years.

I nodded assent to her offer, and she went back into the dwelling, coming back a few moments later, with two small vials made of metal, just like the one that Ambar had owned, but smaller.

'Keep them in your pocket,' she murmured. 'Estar and the other Rays do not like for anything to leave the Isles unless it has been traded and recorded. They think that our knowledge will be diminished if others know it. I think that we could learn so much more and share so much of use with others if we did, but I will never get all the white stones of assent. Take them and use them well.'

I took them and looked at the vials before I put them into my hanging pocket. They were made of metal curved into a slim tube, soldered at the sides and bottom. At the top there was a wooden stopper which had been cunningly carved so that it was narrower at the bottom and wider at the top. It was pushed down tight and then a metal loop was fixed over the top and hooked over a little peg. If nothing else, Tarik would take great interest in this locking device which I had not seen elsewhere. The Oblak tube was stoppered with red stained wood and the Iskra was stoppered with yellow wood.

'Have you ever been to Arbhoun?' asked Layla. 'It must be such a place of learning; all those scrolls to read and to scribe...please do not forget to send some scrolls to me. I do not care as much if you do not scribe about my discoveries here in Soora, but I would be so interested to read of the work of others. Now that I have shown you my work, would you tell me some of the things you said that your friend makes, the tonics and the salves. It could be that they too would be things

I could look at making out of our own plants here on Oshana.'

And so, we sat for some time as I told her of the salves that Achillea made using the beeswax and honey from my hives, the salves that soothed the skin dried by the hot sun and the sand, and the salves that protected wounds and that cleared the eyes. I also told her of the beautifying salves that Achillea made, the perfumes and the salves tinted with berry juice for the lips. Layla scribed everything I told her onto a long roll of plant parchment, muttering as she went, running through similar plants in her mind which she could use instead of the ones we used on the mainland.

'I think you might love the Tower of the Wise in Arbhoun,' I said, amused by her rapid scribing. 'You could do this all day long if you were there.'

'I like to scribe and to read of the works of others, it is true,' she replied. 'But, after some time, I tire of it. My work is not just scribed on the scrolls but is found in the living plants around me. I seek to learn about my land and my place in it. When I am in the Osh forests, I feel close to the Goddess, much closer than I feel if I visit Aman, bathed as it is in the golden light of Soren. Perhaps I am nearer to the Goddess Asmara than to Soren herself, even though I am of Soren, since I make the physics of healing, because I create my physics like she created us. The forest creates itself over and over, and it makes all it needs, except for the light of Soren, the sun. I could not imagine ever leaving it. It is peaceful here, though I do like to visit Soora when the Rays have meetings, because then I can learn from others who travel, just like yourself.'

'Do you never have a longing for a child yourself, or someone to love and live with?' I asked curiously. I never had myself until long after I had left the Temple. I had not believed that it was a part of me at all until I had met Ravin, and even then, I had never been one for fussing over babies. It had gradually crept up on me over time.

Layla looked at me blankly. 'No. I am enough for myself. The forest gives me all that I need. I may not give birth myself, but I see my physics, the plants I grow and my ideas as if they are children. I nurture them from the first spark of an idea through developing the physic right through to when I send them out into the world. In any case,' she continued briskly, 'I take the Soorai powder every day. I do not want to feel the need for those things. If I need human company, then I talk to other women who live and work here, many of whom also take the berries. If they leave, they stop taking it. Most stay. We do not have many children here on Oshana for that reason. If women who work here are blessed by the Goddess, they go to live on Soora instead, where life is more normal.' She laughed, a little sharply. 'Oshana is apparently the island where those who are a little less normal live.'

'Are you ready to return, Talla?'

Estar approached us. With her were three of the women who worked here, each holding several gourds of honey which was what Layla had said she could spare. Having her own hives would mean that she could always use her own honey and not be held back by others, I thought. And then, as quickly, I realised that it was important for Layla and the other women of Oshana not to be isolated any more from the other Soorans, that having to share resources around meant that they learned from each other and moderated each other's behaviour. I nodded and went over to Gladia who was still sitting against the trunk of the tree, still sleeping, her bottom lip quivering slightly every time she breathed out. I reached out and poked the top of her arm, using the very same movement that she had employed against me numerous times. My forefinger sank into her plump, burnished arm and her eyes sprang open, straight into a Gladia glare.

'No need for that!' she exclaimed, rubbing her arm just like I always did when she did it to me. 'I only closed my eyes for a minute! Shall we go and look at the working dwellings now?' I laughed.

'It is time to go back to the boat. All the work here is done.'

Gladia frowned at me, unable to work out if I was telling the truth or teasing her, until she saw Estar waiting with the other women and their gourds of honey, and then she stood up, blinking.

'There must be some kind of sleeping physic here, I don't usually just fall asleep. Perhaps they make poppy juice here too and put it in my tea!' This made me smile again. Gladia was well known for falling asleep at every opportunity.

'Perhaps Jan is keeping you awake late at night?' suggested Layla, with a mischievous tone in her voice. Gladia pretended she had not heard and instead sauntered over to Estar and began to walk down the path with her, making it seem that it was I and not her that was delaying our departure. I turned to Layla, but she was already heading back to her work, absorbed.

Chapter 23

Will you and Talla be returning soon to Safran?'

Estar's question to Gladia dropped into the cooler air of evening as we sailed into the harbour at Soora. The water was gently rolling, with just enough wind to keep the sails full. The sun was beginning to sink lower in the sky, and there was a golden tinge to the few clouds which drifted across. A seabird skimmed the air, seemingly moving without effort, sailing the air like Jan's boat sailed the water.

Gladia and I had not had the opportunity to talk alone since we had been on Oshana, and I did not know what her response might be. I did not know what my own response might be, if I am honest. The Isles of Soora seemed like a very different land from either Oramia or Kashiq, even though they were ostensibly part of Kashiq. My breath caught in my throat as I realised that I had felt more rested and more at peace here than in either Mellia or Pirhan, and that the reason for that was that I had no memories of being here with Ravin. If I had been here with him, my heart would have been full of sorrow, recalling happy times spent with one who was no longer here. It was not that I did not want to remember Ravin, I still remembered him all the time, forgetting that he was dead. It was more that it afforded me the chance to not tie everything that happened to his death. My mind always sought meaning, just as the emberjar always sought to spark fire. Fancifully, I thought that perhaps Ravin had known everything that would happen and had guided me here because he wanted me to be happy.

'Why do you need to know, do you want us gone?' answered Gladia, a touch sharply. 'Now that Talla has worked on so much for you, and solved your problems, you want her gone so you can take all the credit?' She snorted. 'Not yet. We will go when Talla is ready, and not before. She might choose to stay longer. After all the work she has done for you, that is only fair.' She folded her plump arms across her bosom and looked implacably at Estar. Estar looked back at her evenly.

'That is not what I meant. Of course, we are grateful. Talla was sent by the Goddess Soren herself to help us and to heal us. If it had not been for her, we would not have been able to continue. But you will need to move from the travellers' dwellings if you plan to stay, for they are made for travellers who are only staying for a week or less. The rules of the islands state that the longest any visitor may stay is three months; twenty-one weeks. There are those who have to stay that long if they might have trouble birthing, for instance. After that, you must leave Soora. Talla may have has the child by then, anyway, looking at her. Will she want to do that?'

I raised my eyebrows at Gladia and Estar and then said, 'I think I can decide things for myself. But I won't decide anything now, when I am tired and ready to sleep. Gladia and I need to talk about our plans later.' Gladia opened her mouth as if to speak but closed it again after she saw the look in my eyes. Her role as my mother was mostly welcome, but not when it came to treating me like a child.

Estar blinked. 'I am sure your mother only wants the best for you. Why do you call her by her name instead of calling her mama as most people do? I called my own mother mama right up to the day Yael took her to the Goddess, years ago.' Gladia opened her mouth to reply but I spoke first, tired of her talking for me all the time as if I were a child in their first age.

'I was raised without my parents, until I was grown, when I met Gladia. She is the closest I have known to a mother, but she did not give birth to me. We do not know who did.' Gladia subsided quietly. I hoped that what I had said had not hurt her feelings, but it sometimes felt as if she was relishing her motherly role a little too much. I was not used to being spoken for; in fact, I never had been. Ravin had never spoken for me either; it was one of the things which I cherished about him.

'I see.' Estar reflected on what I had said. 'But Gladia is still your mother in her heart, of course. And no doubt in yours. There are many who cannot give birth to their own children, but who nonetheless become parents to others, and love them. I am not a mother myself; it was not a path which the Goddess chose for me. But I am the Ray of Soora, and I care for all those who live on Soora in the best way I can. I tell them the rules, and I punish them for bad behaviour and reward them for good behaviour, just as a parent does.' She laughed suddenly. 'Imagine being the mother of so many children! I will let you rest now since we are arriving back to Soora, and tomorrow, I will come to find out your wishes. If you wish to stay a little longer, you will have to find another dwelling. There are those who will trade for the use of a room in their own dwelling.'

We had pulled alongside the dock while we had been talking. The oars dipped almost silently into the water and steered us along, and once again, Jan jumped out onto the platform to tie in the boat with those big woven ropes which hung off both boat and dock. He placed the plank that joined the boat to the land across the gap, and we made our way onto land again.

'Will you come and share food with me this evening?' he asked Gladia as she got off, holding her hand a little longer than was necessary. She glanced at me.

'I am tired,' I said. 'We need to talk but let us talk in the morning. My mind is like a spent emberjar, it is going to need a lot of sleep to make it work again!' I also looked forward to having some time on my own. So Gladia arranged to meet Jan later that evening and we made our way back to the dwelling. Gladia fussed over me when we got back, putting the pot of water on the fire for me to make a drink, and heating up some pumpkin stew from the day before for me, before going to wash. I noticed that she was wearing her other robe, having washed the first as she washed herself, and had chosen one of the netelas she had brought with her to trade. It was a pale purple in colour, dyed with darkberries in small quantities and embroidered at the edges with darker purple spots of various sizes. I thought I could smell the faint scent of lavender and jasmine too, as if she had put on some perfumed oil.

'You will no doubt be asleep when I return, given that you are so tired,' she said. 'I am tired too and will not be back late. But it will be nice to have the chance to talk to Jan when he is not running up and down a boat. Do you like this netela?' I assured her that the netela was beautiful and that Jan was sure to notice it. She pretended that she had not heard me, and left soon after, hurrying down the path with far more alacrity than she had shown on the way up to the Osh forest.

When Gladia had gone, I washed and prepared to sleep, having eaten up the stew. I untied the pocket from my waist and felt the two small metal tubes. Taking them out, I looked at them both. Would I need the Oblak to forget the moment of giving birth? I knew of nobody else who had done this, although it seemed common here on Soora. If I thought I might need it, then I could not take the antidote for it before then. But if I gave birth in Kashiq or indeed in Oramia, there would be no Birthmother to give me either, anyway. If I took the Iskra now, I might remember what happened on the night I had last seen Ambar. I rolled the tubes around in my hand. This could be my only chance to find that out, on my own. But did I want to find out? I put the tubes back in the pocket and tried to sleep, but I could not.

The presence of the tubes kept my mind awake, as if someone were blowing on the embers of my memories to reawaken them, or as if a bee were trapped inside my head, trying all the time to escape. I sat up. I could not carry on like this. I decided on a game of chance; if I pulled out the one with the red top, the Oblak, I would pour them both away and that would be an end to it. If I pulled out the yellow one, the Iskra, I would take some of it and see what happened. The Goddess would guide me.

I pulled one out. It was the one with the yellow stopper. I pulled the stopper slowly out and cautiously sniffed the contents. It reminded me a little of hyssop, the scent of Indicas, sharp and clean, almost like mint but muskier. I reminded myself that Layla had said it would only relax a person if they had not taken the Oblak and would have no other effect on them. Tentatively, I drank half of it and then paused, my mind querying my actions again. I reached over for the stopper to replace it, but I tipped my hand and most of the remaining liquid drained out onto the earth floor of the dwelling, soaking up quickly and leaving its sharp scent behind. Cross with myself, I tipped the last few drops into my mouth, put the stopper in the empty vial and replaced it in my pocket. There seemed to be no effect at all on me, and, bad-temperedly, I lay down on the sleeping mat and pulled a cloth over myself to sleep.

YELLOW

Chapter 24

Some of my mind came back to me that night in my sleep. Dreaming is always uncontrolled, the mind wanders where it will, it speaks as it wishes and it shows you pictures so vivid it is as if you were living in a different land, and in a different way.

'Why not?' murmured Ambar. I leaned against his shoulder again, knowing that I should not because Ravin would be angry, and then knowing that Ravin would never be angry again. He leaned back against the rock and lay his arm around my shoulders. He pulled out the vial again and looked at it searchingly, as if to find an answer engraved on its surface.
'Have you taken it yet?' I ask him drowsily. I feel surrounded by warmth, the air is like water. Ambar drinks from the vial, quickly as if he might change his mind. There is a faint clinking sound as he replaces it in the pouch. He looks at me searchingly, and his body is the opposite of mine, coiled and tense, his muscles poised for flight, it seemed.

'Let's forget everything together,' I say, my words trickling like honey. 'The two who don't belong anywhere.' I laughed. 'We will never remember it, so we can't forget it.' I felt as if I was pronouncing a great wisdom, but Ambar laughed and drew me closer.

'How could I forget this?' he asked me and bent his lips to mine.

My mind clouded here, as if this was as far as my memories went, but I knew it was because I had spilt the Iskra, that I must have taken a stronger dose of the Oblak than could be counteracted by the little Iskra I had taken. I was left with only vague impressions and feelings and was unsettled by them all. I felt that I had been with Ambar, that he had loved me, and then I realised I was thinking of Ravin, and the memories felt tied up in one another. You might have thought that this conflict would have woken me from my dreams, but it did not. Instead, my mind roved from one memory to another, from memories of Ambar when I first met him to memories of Ravin when he told me about love being like an orange, and back to Ambar and his face when he saw Lunaria and then again to Ravin as he lay dying. A little more did come back to me later, too, just before I woke, at daybreak.

I was lying in Ambar's arms when he woke up. It was not light yet and I was only vaguely aware that he was even there. Soft as a shadow, he rolled away from me. There was some faint shuffling. It was the strangest thing, because I was remembering things which had happened when I was asleep. Things that I should not have been able to recall because I could not see them, being asleep. Ambar looked down on me as I slept. He took off a necklace he had around his neck, under his robe, the very one which I had found in the

253

morning when I woke up and he was gone. He pulled it to his mouth and kissed it and then placed it in the wooden box. Even though I was asleep, I know he looked down at me and I know he smiled. And then he left before I woke.

But why did he wake so much sooner than me if we had both taken the Oblak physic? Was it because he was a man and was taller and bigger than me? And why did he not wait to see that I was well when I woke up? It was as if he had left so that I could not speak to him when I woke. Perhaps the Oblak had made him forget everything and he did not even remember who I was? But then why had he left me the necklace? Nothing was clearer for having these half memories and I was disturbed by the few that had come back to me. Perhaps it was just that my mind had made up what it thought had happened and I had not relived any kind of memory but had merely dreamed an ending that made sense to me. I had no means of getting more Iskra and I was afraid of what I might find out, in any case. I needed to forget what I had just learned, but the Oblak only worked if you took it before something you wanted to forget. How much more useful might it have been if you could take it after an action that you wanted to forget.

The more I thought about this, the more uncomfortable I became. There were actually so few occasions in life when one knew beforehand that something would be so painful that it should be forgotten. I could see how the Oblak could be of great value to one of Soren, a healer. There were times when one knew that pain might be inflicted; childbirth was one, the stitching of wounds and the manipulation of displaced joints another, but, it seemed to me, a person could very easily inflict all manner of ills on a person

254

by giving them it before they intended them harm, just as the OutRiders did with the Angels. I should have asked Layla if the Oblak ever wore off naturally, over the course of years, so that people might gradually realise what they had forgotten, perhaps in their dreams at first. If so, perhaps I would slowly come to realise the truth of what had happened.

Ambar would surely have access to supplies of the Iskra. Layla had said that they traded them in pairs, the Oblak and its antidote together. If the OutFort and the Queen's Court were using so much of the Oblak, there must be a lot of Iskra left, unless they poured it out. If I saw Ambar again, I resolved to ask him for it, though I doubted he would give it to me. Had he taken it already? Had he already known that he could reverse it before he took it? He had never mentioned anything about the Iskra when he had told me about the honeywine and the Oblak. Had he deliberately not told me, so that he would be able to remember, and I wouldn't? I lay on the palm leaf mat, the questions in my mind swirling round. These were threads I could not untie.

Gladia was already up, bustling around, a flatbread cooking on the flat plate over the fire, the smell of some of her treasured Oramian coffee blending with the woodsmoke.

'You must have had some bad dreams in the night, Talla. You were muttering away to yourself half the night. They do say that having a baby makes you more likely to be given dreams by the Goddess. Did you ever hear the story, when you were in the Temple, of how the Goddess was born?'

I shook my head. In truth, there were times when my mind had wandered when I was a child living in the Temple. There was so much to listen to, so many words of wisdom, scolding tales, the famous aphorisms of

Ashkana that after a time, I had learned to bow my head respectfully and then think of something else. This story might have been one I missed, or perhaps it was one that was not considered right for us Maids in the Temple. After all, hearing a story about the Goddess bearing a child might have put ideas into our heads. As I had concluded, all the Temple Maids were given the Soorai berry powder anyway and could never have a child while under the control of the Temple.

Gladia took the flatbreads off the hot plate and handed one to me, along with a beaker of coffee. The scent of the slightly sweetened flatbread, cooked with the addition of honey, mixed with the sharp strength of the coffee. I took an appreciative sniff and settled down to listen to Gladia who, for all her cynicism, knew a large number of Oramian stories about the Goddess.

'It was in the days that the world began. Mother was existence itself, without her there was nothing. In the beginning of time there was only a black velvety darkness which stretched forever, blacker and blacker. There was nothing else, and Mother longed for new life to come into being.

From the darkness her longing first brought into being a tiny spark of life, and then it grew into a red fire which burst forth from the earth, bringing with it deep passion and heat. And the first creatures came into being, coloured by the fire; the red salamander, the ruby hummingbird and the fiery bee. And the seed of the Goddess came into being, like a red pomegranate seed.

Mother Earth was full of love for the tiny seed, and the skies were lighted by her love and joy until they glowed orange. And in that time was born the glowing firefox and the orange lizards which roamed over the stony boulders.

And Mother was tired from her work, and she rested in the time just before the first dawn. And in that time of rest, she dreamed of the Goddess. While her mind rested, she saw what the tiny seed would grow to be. It was only in her dreams that she could imagine the future, for, until the world began, there was no time, no past and no future. In the golden shining light of that first dawn, the Goddess was born, born of a dream and a longing.

The Goddess was born shining with golden light, which encircled her head like the rays of the sun which now smiled upon the land. The baby Goddess smiled, and all around her marigolds blossomed and golden orioles flew from flower to flower. The Goddess was born at the very beginning of the very first day, when the sun warmed the land after its long night. And at the end of that first day, there came into being another God, Yael. For where there is life, there must be death, and where there is day, there must be night and where there is a beginning, and ending must come.'

I enjoyed listening to Gladia telling this story of how the Goddess had come into being. I had heard a shorter, similar version when I was young, but Gladia told it better. One day, I would have to ask her to tell it to me again, slowly, so I could scribe the words. It was a comforting and happy tale, and the thought of the little Goddess as a baby, surrounded by light and flowers and birdsong made me smile.

'Did you dream of a child?' enquired Gladia, still hoping for some hint as to whether I might be having a boy or a girl. For some reason, this was very important for her. There were so many old tales about how to tell before the birth whether the child was a girl or a boy that I had no patience with any of them, and as many gave me the hint that it was a boy as it did a girl. Gladia hoped for a girl, I think, like hers so she could see what it might have been like. I had no preference. Ravin and I had hoped for the Goddess's blessing for such a long time, it did not matter to us what the child might be. Achillea and Tarik had hoped for a boy after their two girls and had been overjoyed to have him. But I had not dreamed of a child that night, of course, only of half-remembered memories shrouded in the fog of uncertainty.

'I do not remember,' I replied, as honestly as I could. 'It was very confusing. How was your meal with Jan?'

Gladia preened. 'It was very nice. He traded with the owner of the honeywine dwelling near the harbour, and we had a spicy fish stew and then a fruit cake afterwards. And some honeywine,' she added triumphantly. 'I never had it before though I didn't much like it. Have you had it before?'

I hesitated, not sure what to answer, but Gladia was not interested in my answer anyway, and continued to tell me details of the time she had spent with Jan, what they had talked about, what he had told her about his life and how many times he had complimented her. I felt protective of her. I had seen her devastation when she had been confronted with the fact that Benakiell loved another and did not want to see it again.

'Be careful, Gladia. You will not be staying on Soora forever – unless you never want to leave again, and there is no sea near Mellia for Jan to sail his boat on. Do not become so close to him that it hurts you to part when we leave.'

Gladia chuckled. 'Listen to you, Talla, practicing your motherly voice on me! I can assure you I know what I am doing, thank you. When you reach my age, you will realise that you must take each new chance that arises. When I am so old that I cannot walk anymore, I want to look back on my adventures and enjoy the memories. Mellia is my home, where I have lived since I was born, but there is not a lot of adventure there. In any case, I told Bellis and Maren that I would be gone for months. It will do them good to look after everything on their own.'

She sighed, suddenly looking tired. 'They say they want to do it all but as soon as there is a problem, they send it to me. When I left Mellia to go to Gabez to see Jember, I told them I planned to stay with Achillea and Tarik and to visit you at least until the month of Flavus. They say it takes seven months to begin to see the future after a loved one has died, and I wanted to look after you until then. Of course, I didn't realise then that you were having a baby and that you would be planning on walking through Kashiq as a way of dealing with it, but it has certainly been an adventure.'

I thought about what she had said about the seven months, a year if you added on the three weeks of the Goddess throughout the year. Long before Ravin's death, I had learned of the Kashiqi way of coping with death. I had known that after seven years, the clay grave marker was broken and ground to powder in a ceremony of freedom, and that the Kashiqis believed that, in those seven years, the parts that person's soul was made of would be reborn in other people. There was a story that the Goddess made people like potters made clay pots, and that just as an old pot might break and become unusable, so it was with people. Just as a clay pot could be ground to powder and then mixed with water to make a new pot, so too could a person's soul. The Kashiqis had more interest in death than the Oramians, who just tried to bury people and forget them, ascribing it all to the will of the Goddess. Perhaps because the Kashiqis had Yael, the god of death, they were more able to acknowledge it and accept it. Death was an inconvenient fact when you worshipped the Goddess of life. A rhyme came to me that Ravin had told me, having learned it himself from his mother who was guided by Yael, and worked with the dying, and I said it out loud.

'Seven hours of disbelief,
Seven days of hard, sharp grief.
Seven weeks to rage and weep.
Seven months of long, dull pain,
Seven years till you live again.'

'And six months to have a baby to start it all over,' observed Gladia drily. 'It's a good saying though. Talking of leaving Soora, what are your plans exactly?'

I observed that she had moved the conversation away from her and Jan to me, but her question was one that merited thought. I had been so focused on getting to Soora to show Ravin that I was fulfilling what he wanted me to do, and then on saving the bees and then on finding out more about the powerful physics that they made here, that I had not thought beyond each day. Did I want to return to Mellia, Gabez or Pirhan for the birth of the child? I pondered, but with each option, there was a reason why not to go there. Mellia was where Ravin had died and would always now be associated with that for me. It was also too close to where Ambar might be, and I pushed that thought away firmly. Pirhan is where I would have been, had Ravin been alive, but he was no longer there. Gabez was the place of many happy memories, and my best friends Achillea and Tarik, but they had their own three children to care for and Achillea would be fussing over me too much.

'Do you want your child to be Kashiqi or Oramian?' asked Gladia after some time of me thinking aloud and going back and forth, arguing with myself. I stopped. I had not thought of this. I was of Oramia and Ravin had been of Kashiq. He was not here anymore so it became clear to me that this was what I could do to show my child in the future some of the things its father had treasured. A child born in Kashiq would be more likely to read and to scribe too. Not only that (and I kept this thought to myself), but the Court of the Queen had no power over me in Kashiq, and the old fortune teller's warning still held itself in my mind.

'Kashiqi.'

'I thought you might say that. But not Pirhan, you say. Surely not Arbhoun. It is much too far for you to walk as you are now; it is not good for the baby,' she ended triumphantly. 'I think you should wait and have the baby here, on Soora. This is where all the Birthmothers come from, they know better than anyone how to help you through it all. And the baby would be Kashiqi, but not born in Pirhan, born in a different place not associated with sadness, but with the joy of birth.'

It was an eloquent speech from Gladia, and I suspected she had been planning it, with an aim to seeing more of Jan. But what she said made sense, and, truthfully, I did not relish the thought of the long walk back from Safran to Pirhan. In any case, I might be able to find out more if we stayed for longer, and maybe even meet Hortensia, the one who might have been the Birthmother at my own birth. I felt safe here in Soora, safer than I had felt for a long time. And so, we agreed to stay in Soora until after the birth of the child.

Chapter 25

Jan found a dwelling we could stay in. He seemed to know most people who lived in Soora and was on good terms with all of them. The woman who owned it, Sashila, would let us stay there until the child was born, having checked with Estar, the Ray of Soora, that it was acceptable for us to stay. A note to that effect was scribed beneath our names on the scroll where they had been noted when we first arrived in Soora. Sashila had an interest in learning to stitch, and Gladia had agreed to teach her the basics in return for the use of the room. Jan had also procured sleeping mats for us and even two soft cushions which he produced with a flourish, presenting one to Gladia and one to me. They had been coloured with yellow dye and Gladia decided that she would embellish them further with different coloured silks and use them in Sashila's training.

'My sister used to live with me, when she was still on Soora, but she wanted to be a Birthmother and went to live on Rengat,' she told us. 'I work in one of the sailor's trading dwellings, where we trade honeywine and food, but I would like to do something different.' Her face fell a little. 'My sister, Riva, always seems to know what she wants to do, but I never do. I don't even know if I want to stay on Soora. Sometimes, I think I will leave here and go to Kashiq, that's what Riva wants to do. There you can trade for the things you make and there are so many more jobs to choose from. I like to make things but there is not much call for those kinds of things here. We all wear yellow clothes, unlike you.' She looked enviously at my dark red trousers and my orange robe, and at the purple netela Gladia had in her lap. 'Perhaps, if you will teach me, and I am good enough, I will finally take the courage to leave and try my luck in the lands beyond the sea.'

Gladia looked at her critically. 'Well, you won't be able to learn how to do fine embroidery straight away, you know. You will have to practice until all your stitches are fine and equal all the time. Can you sew at all?'

Sashila admitted that she could, but only so that she could repair her own clothes, only basic stitches, just like me. They agreed between them that Gladia would teach Sashila the stitching in the warm afternoons since Sashila worked in the evenings at the honeywine traders, and, although she did not say it, Gladia wanted to keep her evenings free for meeting Jan, since he was occupied with sailing his boat around the islands and back and forth to Safran during the daytime. As usual, Gladia made a keen deal with Sashila. She would supervise Sashila hemming up Gladia's fabric until her stitching was judged to be of good enough quality to move on to the decorative sewing that she wanted to learn. Then she would begin work on the cushions. Knowing Gladia, it would probably take Sashila about as long as it would take her to do all of Gladia's plain work for her.

'Talla, why don't you pounce a few patterns for her on these scraps of cloth, so she can practice simple shapes and flowers?' suggested Gladia. She had long pressed me to do more of the repeated patterns I had first shown her years ago when I left the Temple. I pricked a pattern out on plant parchment using a large thorn, and then laid it over a piece of cloth and dabbed charcoal dust over it. It left the tracing of the pattern on the cloth and could then be repeated. I was happy enough to do this as it kept my mind busy but was not at all tiring.

Sashila reminded me a little of Achillea in her love of bright colours and pretty things. She expressed irritation more than once that she was only permitted to wear yellow, as a Sooran woman, but then hastily assured us that she was very happy to do so. In her work, trading food and drink with the sailors, she heard many stories which they had heard from their passengers and relayed them to us in tones of wonder as she told us of the shifting desert sands and soldiers on horseback. Gladia smiled at her eagerness and told her stories of life in Mellia as they sat and stitched. She hung onto every word that Gladia said and frequently gasped and sighed. I listened too, enjoying the stories Gladia told, and occasionally joining in.

Sashila was a similar sort of age to many of the Angels who came under Gladia's care, being in the first age of adulthood, perhaps 23 or 24 years old. I could see that Gladia was practiced in talking with young women of this age, listening patiently and occasionally interjecting with words of advice carefully couched as suggestions. It was difficult for the women of Soora to show their individuality in what they wore, so Sashila liked to change her hair from day to day, one day wearing it braided, one day combed through, another day with a jaunty flower tucked into her curls. I showed her how Achillea used beeswax and a little Paradox oil to rub into her hair to make it shiny and soft. Even I had taken to doing this with my hair, and even adding a little scent to it too. Sashila sometimes wanted to do my hair before the stitching started and it was soothing to feel the hands of another tending to me. I drew the line at flowers in my hair though.

A couple of weeks after we had started staying there, we were visited by Nousha, the Ray of Rengat. She was making her regular trip to Soora to pick up any provisions needed by her island, including new supplies of physics for the women who were on Rengat, preparing to give birth. She was accompanied on this occasion by Riva, Sashila's sister, who took the opportunity to come and visit her.

Nousha smiled at me as they approached the dwelling, and greeted me in the Kashiqi way, putting her hand to her head and then to her heart. I responded with my hand to my heart and then to my head, and, as Riva went to chat to Sashila, she came to sit next to me.

Sashila's dwelling was on the edge of the settlement of Soora. Like all the dwellings on the islands, it was made of a mixture of palm wood and reeds, which must have been brought from Safran, for I had seen no reeds growing here, only in the wide river at Safran. Each Sooran island had at least one spring of fresh water, and there were rivers on Osh and Soora, but no reeds. These Sooran dwellings were quite different from the clay and mud dwellings in the rest of Kashiq, though we had seen similar reed roofs in Safran. They kept you cool, and there was the constant slight scent of something green, from the reeds. It reminded me of Oramia and of watching Benakiell thatching the roofs in Mellia. It was men's work in Oramia, but in Kashiq it could be done by any craftsperson guided by Maliq and here in Soora, it was done by women, of course. It was near the path up the hill to the sungold flowers and the bees and a peaceful place to sit, away from the hustle and bustle of Soora itself which was full of people trading and talking.

'How are you, Talla? I hear you will be staying here on Soora until the child is born. Will you want to have the baby here, or on Rengat?'

I had not thought of any choice in this regard and asked Nousha to tell me more. She explained that there was usually at least one Birthmother on Soora, but, that if I was to stay on Rengat, there would be many of them, all with different expertise, who could all join together their knowledge and help me better.

'There is no reason to think that there would be anything to go wrong,' she assured me. 'But I know how precious the child will be, given what happened to your husband. Your mother could come with you,' she added, turning to greet Gladia.

Gladia was just starting to settle into her very pleasant existence here in Soora and had no interest at all in moving again to Rengat, at least not yet. It took a couple of hours to sail from Soora to Rengat and Nousha pointed out that it was not advisable to make the trip once the birth had started. I pondered. The closer I got to this child arriving, the more I felt uncertain. I knew that Gladia had been present at the births of many children, almost all of them from the Angels who she had taken in to care for, but she tended to observe rather than be of practical use, leaving the birthmothering to Maren and to Bellis who often assisted her. The wisdom of those who had done this before seemed preferable, but I loved Gladia and that counted for a great deal.

'Would you like to come and visit the island first?' asked Nousha, sensing my indecision. 'You can see it all, and you could visit Hortensia while you are there. You have been to every other Isle of Soora except Rengat, after all. Then, if you want, you can come over to stay when you are nearer to your time.'

I agreed, and Gladia told me that Jan was going to Rengat the following day, taking Nousha and Riva and their trades, so I could go then.

'I was just about to tell you that,' laughed Nousha. 'Will you be coming along too, Gladia?'

Gladia declined the offer, which surprised me. I had assumed she would come along, if only because Jan would be sailing the boat, but perhaps she did not relish another trip on a boat. She had never really enjoyed the peculiar rocking motion of either riding a horse or being on a boat, and was much happier on land, with or without Jan. In any case, as she explained to me, Jan would be busy sailing the boat, and she would see him later.

'I have a lot of stitching to teach Sashila, anyway,' she said happily. She turned to her and asked her if she would like to start work on stitching a new netela for her sister, Riva. Sashila's face lit up at the thought of sewing something other than the tedious hemming she had been doing. Her sister Riva's face also brightened.

'Talla will make you a pattern before she goes, so that you can work on it tomorrow afternoon,' said Gladia firmly. 'Now Riva, come and look at my threads to see what colour you would like your design to be stitched in. We will start simple though, and I'm afraid it will have to be a yellow netela since that is what you all wear!' They went to look through Gladia's bag of threads, leaving me to talk to Nousha.

She was a short woman, edging towards being plump, soft around the edges. Her own clothes were plain and unadorned, the sleeves shortened for practicality. Her hair was neither short nor long, and again, it received little attention. Her eyes looked tired, and she rubbed them, apologizing for her lengthy yawn.

'I was up in the night, one of the women was giving birth. It was a long journey for the child, but he is just fine now. There are no more babies likely to be born now for some weeks. It might even be you next.' She smiled at what must have been a look of horror that came across my face. 'it won't be that bad! Remember that we are all born from a mother. It is the blessing of the Goddess Asmara who shares creation with us, and of the Goddess Soren, who heals us, who was herself born of the Goddess. Did you know that there is a story that is told on Rengat, of the Goddess Soren who was a DoubleSoul? With her brother, Maliq, the God who guides the crafting?'

I shook my head, fascinated by this. In Oramia, we only knew of Asmara the Goddess and of Ashkana, the one who started the Temples, and who had left behind her Aphorisms on working and life, the sayings that I had heard all of my childhood. When I had first gone to Kashiq, I had learned that there were more who were considered to be Gods and Goddesses, that there were six in total. But I had not heard much of Maliq, the one who guided those who crafted things, the stitchers and the woodworkers, the silversmiths and the tool makers, the cooks and the weavers, although those guided by him were all around us. It would be intriguing to hear this story.

'It was many ages ago, when the land was still new, and the Goddess Asmara, in her turn, dreamt of having children, ones like her who could make a better life for others. And so, her thoughts became her children. The first to be born were the DoubleSouls, Maliq and Soren. For it was only right that, just as men and women are equal in their skill, so they should be born at the same time.'

'But surely one DoubleSoul is born before the other, even if it is only by a few minutes?' I asked, thinking of the story Maren had told us about the Lady Paradox and the birth of the future queen, Lunaria, and her sister, who could be me. 'So, one of the DoubleSouls will perhaps always come first.'

Nousha smiled. 'Ah there is an answer to that, in the story. Though I do not know the truth of it, myself. It is said that when the DoubleSouls Soren and Maliq were growing in the belly of Asmara, that they argued about this very thing. And the Goddess grew tired of listening to their childish squabbles about who would be the most important, for she loved them both equally. So, she said to them, 'One of you will enter the world first in time, and one of you will be the firstborn. For the one who enters the world first will be first to ensure the world is ready for the first born, who will then be born.' And the DoubleSouls fell silent as they realised the wisdom of their mother, the Goddess. But then, as children do, they began to argue again about who would be born first and who would be the firstborn. And once again, Asmara showed her wisdom, for she took a stone from the ground which was white on one side and black on the other, and she told them that if the stone fell with the white side uppermost, then Soren would be born first, and Maliq would be the firstborn, and if it fell with the black side uppermost, then Maliq would be born first, and Soren would be the firstborn. Asmara threw the pebble high up into the air and it spun over and over as it came down to land on the earth. It fell with the black side facing and so it was decided who would be born first and who would be the firstborn. And ever since then, DoubleSouls have been born with one being the firstborn and one being born first. It was also the first time that the stone of choice was used to make a difficult decision. It is something we Soorans still do today; I know you have seen us, the Rays making the choices with the stones. But every woman who lives on Soora has her own choice stone to help her to choose where she cannot, given to her as she becomes an adult. Sometimes it is not the choice itself that is the difficult thing, it is the making of it. The stone makes that choice.'

I had never heard this tale before. How strange it was to constantly have to re-establish in my mind what I thought I knew. I had learned a lot about the Goddess, and about Ashkana and Lord Rao but had known little of either Soren or Maliq, save what I had learned when I asked Ravin. But even he did not know much of them, since he had always been guided by Rao. Achillea and Tarik knew a little more, since Achillea was guided by Soren and Tarik by Maliq. But while Achillea embraced Soren as her personal guiding Goddess and was much occupied with making small offerings at Kashiqi places of prayer to her, Tarik was more dubious, preferring to make no allegiance to any god or goddess. He obeyed the rules of whichever land he was in, but it meant nothing to him. In Oramia he made sure that all the crafts he made were only those allowed for men, and in Kashiq, he made sure all his work was guided by Maliq. It worked well for him, and I understood his ambivalence. But I loved to hear the stories of how the world began and how the people, made by the Goddess came about, and about the other gods and goddesses. Then, something else occurred to me, and I turned to Nousha again.

'I thank you for that tale, Nousha, I had not heard it before. But now I am curious about something else. You say that Maliq and Soren were brother and sister, DoubleSouls, born of the Goddess Asmara. But who was their father? And what of Ashkana and Rao? They were not brother and sister, surely, for they were lovers.'

'I see I have many stories to tell you, Talla,' smiled Nousha. 'I often tell the old stories to women who are waiting to give birth, so I have a good store of them. It calms them to hear them. It was the God Yael, the god of death and dying who was the father of the DoubleSouls, Soren and Maliq. Yael was the other side to the Goddess. Where she created, he destroyed. Where a child was born, someone else died. Where she was the day, he was the night. For one cannot exist without the other. There is no light without darkness to show the light. Asmara could only create new souls when Yael had brought them home to her, destroyed and ready to remake. Like a clay pot, Asmara and Yael were the two sides, and yet you could trace your finger over the clay pot and go from inside to outside without lifting your finger. Thus it is with life and death, Asmara and Yael. They are but seamless travelling from one to another and we are all on the same journey. As for Ashkana and Rao, they were not the children of Asmara and Yael, but ordinary people, who were elevated by the Gods. It was a game, they say, between Asmara and Yael, to give ordinary people special gifts, and to see which one would be the most useful. There must have been something in them that recognised the blessings in each other, for they fell in love. But that is a story for another time, now it is time for me and Riva to continue our business here on Soora. We will see you tomorrow morning at the dock, to travel to Rengat.'

Chapter 26

Rengat had none of the lush forest of Oshana, nor the dusty craters of Orish. It was a longer trip than I had been expecting, since the island seemed to be closer to Soora than Oshana but the whole of its northern shore was rocky cliffs and steep mountains. The birds flew overhead constantly, landing on those narrow, rocky shelves to rest and to nest. Some of them were quite large birds and as they swooped and dived into the water, I envied how freely they moved through the air and then through the water as they dived to catch the fish. They could fly directly to the island without being perturbed by the sharp rocks. The boat had to sail halfway round the island before it curved round into a naturally protected harbour which lay at the bottom of a gentle slope. To get into the harbour, the boat had to be steered through the narrow straits. Once through, the water of the harbour was calm and still, encircled with rocks which kept out the crashing waves. I was getting used to these journeys on boats now, and I think the rocking of the boat was comforting to the child in me, for it seemed to settle peacefully. I mentioned this to Nousha and Riva, and they confirmed that many infants liked to be rocked and we joked that perhaps the sailors could start a new venture by offering their boats as alternative sleeping places for babies.

One of the sailors on Jan's boat wanted to visit his family and got off the boat with us to make our way to the main settlement. Jan stayed on the boat, content to lie on the deck in the warm sun and doze. I asked the young man, by the name of Kir, about how the unusual arrangement between the sailors and the Soorans worked. It was unusual to me, at least. He seemed to accept it as quite normal, and I suppose that I would have thought nothing of it myself if I had been born and raised on the Isles of Soora like Kir himself had. He was born on Soora and told me that, after the first age of childhood, a choice had to be made by the mother of a son, about whether she would leave the islands with him, or whether he would be apprenticed to a sailor and learn the art of sailing himself and stay within the protection of the Isles of Soora. At the time of the second age of childhood when he was fourteen, he would move from his mother's dwelling to living on the boat of his mentor. This meant that naturally there were many more women on Soora since many who gave birth to boys moved to the mainland with them.

'Do all the sailors come from here or live here?' I asked, curious.

'No. Many of the mothers of boys move to live in Safran, with their families, where they can stay with their husband, who will continue to sail on the passages from Safran to the islands. Many of the sailors come from Safran, and some come from further up the coast of Kashiq, from the big cities like Lekan and Kafindim.' I had heard of the city of Kafindim up on the northern coast before.

'Some sailors also come from other lands', he added. 'There is a land beyond the sharp mountains south of Safran. You cannot cross into it from Kashiq, for the mountains are too steep and perilous. But if you are a sailor of some skill, like Jan, you can sail there in a boat. They trade sometimes in Safran, but also here in Soora. They call the land Jani – that's how Jan got his name.'

I had never heard of this place before. I had not ever thought of what might lie beyond Kashiq or Oramia. I wondered if there were many different lands which spread on and on forever, or if there were only a few. Perhaps in Arbhoun, in the Tower of the Wise there might be some scroll about this. I also noted that he had said that Jan came from there originally. It made me smile to think of Gladia who had been so stubbornly against Achillea and Tarik's relationship, and indeed had been dubious about my relationship with Ravin, and certainly of Benakiell and Shira purely because they were between people from different lands or backgrounds. And yet, here she was, spending a lot of time enjoying the company of a man from a land we had never even heard of before. It seemed that we all changed our viewpoints as we learned new things.

Nousha and Riva were walking ahead of us, their yellow robes lit up by the sun. The way that all the Sooran women wore robes of the same colour reminded me of the drabcoats we wore, as Maids, in the Temple. These were made of patchworked scraps of brown and grey cloth, so it appeared as if we all wore the same colour, even though, like the robes of the Soorans, each was subtly different from the next. We were not permitted to keep the same drabcoat all the time as we were told that the Goddess did not want us to be attached to things that were not important. Of course, this made the coloured robes and veils worn by the Priestesses even more alluring. I recalled how different I had felt when I wore the red robe of Flammeus before my Choice ceremony, and how different again I had felt when Gladia and Achillea looked critically at my drabcoat when I arrived in

Mellia. It did not seem to perturb the women of Soora, though. They only had interest in cloth in the colour of Soren, the colour of Flavus, the colour of the sun.

The light of that sun scattered over the dwellings. There were some gardens where vegetables and fruit were growing. Although there were mountains to the north and the west, the land around the harbour was gently sloped and green, presumably receiving exactly the right amount of rain and sun for the crops to grow. Rengat seemed a peaceful, happy place, but it was becoming clear to me that whilst I might stay on the Isles of Soora until I had given birth, I could not live in Soora forever. I did not want to live in a place which reminded me of the Temple. I grew up surrounded by women, and here it would be the same thing. I preferred my life in Kashiq, or my life in the Outer in Oramia, where men and women lived and worked together. I realised that Nousha was asking me something, and shook my head in apology, asking her to repeat her question.

'Would you like to rest now, or would you like me to show you how things work here on Rengat, or perhaps you would like to visit Hortensia? Riva can take you to her, if you would like, their dwellings are close to each other.'

Visiting Hortensia might be interesting, and it was quite possible that she was the Birthmother who had delivered me, if I was indeed Lunaria's DoubleSoul sister. This thought had stayed with me ever since I had first found out the significance of the brooch which had been pinned to my blanket when I was left on the steps of the Temple. If Hortensia could confirm that she had left both babies at the same Temple, it would make it much more likely. Lunaria and I had been found at the same time, but whilst we knew that she had the mark of the Queen on her, in the form of a birthmark, I was the one who had the Queen's brooch pinned to my cloth. That could have just been a story though. After all, I could not remember being a baby. I set off with Riva, not feeling tired at all.

Riva was around my age, perhaps a little younger. She was tall and sturdy, with an open face and bright, clear eyes. She wore her hair braided, and her netela lay draped on her shoulders and not on her head. The sun was not strong here. It was warm, but pleasant, and I dropped my own netela off my head. Riva admired it and admitted she was looking forward to seeing what her sister managed to sew for her under the tutelage of Gladia.

'It will be lovely to have a new netela, even if it will be yellow. Everyone else here seems to be quite happy to always wear yellow. I know it is the colour of Soren, bless her name, but I would love to wear different colours like you do. I would like to leave the Isles of Soora and find out what life is like on the mainland, but I am worried that I might hate it, and then I might never be able to return except when I am old, since I am a Birthmother. Sashila would not be allowed to come back at all.'

As we walked, I told Riva of my friend Maren who had been trained by Hortensia, and about how there would always be work for Birthmothers in Oramia and Kashiq. I did not mention how Hortensia had left Maren on her own to deal with the OutRiders who came looking for the Lady Paradox, nor indeed that the babies she delivered included the Queen of Oramia. Riva nodded thoughtfully and asked me more questions about life in Kashiq. It was not a long trip to sail from Soora to Safran on the mainland, but it was clearly the prospect of leaving the islands for good which was holding her back. Here, she was safe and protected, but she was also not free to do as she wished.

In the end, it depended on which one was most important.

'Hortensia does not always make sense,' Riva warned me, as we walked. 'She is past her seventh age and sometimes her wisdom is known only to the Goddess and to Soren, and probably not even to them. She has good days and bad days, and you never know how she will be. It is as if she has the Oblak always in her mind.'

I was disappointed that I might not find out the answers to my questions, but I knew that sometimes this happened as people aged.

Having arrived at the dwelling, Riva introduced me to Hortensia and then walked on to her own dwelling, a little way further down the path. Hortensia welcomed me and invited me to sit on the mat in the shade outside her dwelling and offered to make me tea. I greeted her and assured her that I did not need tea, but she insisted, and offered me a beaker of some sort of herbal tea which tasted a little dusty and stale.

I asked her about her health and made some light conversation before asking her if she remembered working in Oramia, long ago.

'Why yes, it was some five or so ages ago that I was in Oramia. I left here on a boat, looking to find out more about the world. Oh, I was young when I first left, and had a thought of living in another land, of having a family of my own and look now, none of it has come to pass. My dreams have passed into smoke. Why do you ask, are you from Oramia?'

'Yes,' I confirmed, hoping that it might make her tell me more. 'I have a friend, who I think you worked with in Oramia, called Maren. She told me that you taught her all she knows about birthing babies.'

'Maren, Maren...I think I know the woman you mean. She was learning her trade under me, I remember. But I cannot see her face in my mind at all.'

'It does not matter,' I soothed her. 'She will be happy to know that you still live and that you lead a contented life. She is contented too, now, although she led a sad life for a while. That only happened after you had left her though, so you would know nothing about it.'

Hortensia looked at me, at first through uncomprehending eyes and then as if a film had been taken away, much like the film that used to hang over Maren's unseeing eyes.

'Tell me what she told you,' she demanded. 'Tell me what she said about me leaving her.'

I was unsure. I did not want to cause distress, and I was naturally guarded, not wanting to reveal everything I knew to someone I did not. But I did not think I would ever meet Hortensia again after this visit, and her mind was muddled already.

'There was a woman of high status, who was giving birth, called the Lady Paradox. Maren was working with you at the time and the Lady Paradox had fled from those who pursued her, into the forest near Besseret. She was afraid but could not stop the birth. A baby was born, with a mark the shape of a bee, and then another child was born. DoubleSouls. Maren remembers the mother talking with you and then you wrapped the babies in cloths and left with them. You left Maren with the Lady Paradox and took the babies and left at least one of them at a Temple.'

Hortensia looked at me keenly.

'There is bitterness in your voice, girl. You have judged me by what you have heard, and yet you do not know me. Tell me more of Maren and then I will tell you my own story.' She sat back, waiting for me to do as she wished.

'Before I do, tell me if you left both the infants at the Temple together.'

'I did not leave them together on the same day. But I did leave them at the same Temple. They were very different in appearance, even as babies, so I knew they would not grow up as reflections of each other. Now tell me what I ask, and I will tell you the rest.'

What she said tallied with what we knew. We knew that Lunaria and I were both left at a similar time at the Temple, but that we had been allocated a different day of birth; Lunaria on Lilavis and me on Flammeus. Something Hortensia said had piqued my interest though and I could not resist asking another question of her after her answer.

'What do you mean when you talk about the babies not being reflections of each other?'

Again, the sharp look, but Hortensia was tempted to share her knowledge with me since I appeared to be so ignorant.

'I forget you are no Birthmother yourself. There are two kinds of DoubleSouls. One kind, like the first DoubleSouls, Soren and Maliq, are just like a brother and sister born at the same time, with no more resemblance to each other than siblings do. They don't have to be a boy and a girl; they can be two boys or two girls either. The babies I left at the Temple were much different; one was larger, they had different hair and different face shapes, even in their crying they were different. The other kind of DoubleSouls are what we call reflections of each other; they are exactly the same as each other, almost as if the same child were born twice over at the same time. They say they must be twice blessed by the Goddess for she chose there to be two of the same soul in the world.'

I had never seen DoubleSouls like this before. It must be very strange to see in front of you somebody who looked, and no doubt seemed, exactly the same as you, like seeing your own reflection in a still lake or a polished sheet of metal.

I was impatient to know more, to try to finally understand what had happened and if I really might be the sister of the Queen, but I could see that Hortensia had no intention of answering any more questions before I told her what I knew about Maren. So, I told her. I told her about how the OutRiders had come shortly after she had left, while Maren was still tending to Paradox after the birth, and how they had taken the Lady Paradox to an unknown fate, and how they had blinded Maren so that she could not see again to witness to the bee birthmark. I told her how Maren had been blinded for years, and how, eventually, we had cured her so that she could see again, and that she now lived happily in Mellia, with Bellis, still working with birthing mothers.

Hortensia showed little sign of interest or emotion when I told her of Maren's blindness and subsequent life. I did not tell her of the search for Lunaria that I had been drawn into, nor of my own belief that I was the second of the DoubleSouls born to Paradox, nor that the bee-shaped birthmark meant that Lunaria was now Queen of Oramia. She nodded a few times, looking satisfied, as if the events that happened after the babies were born were expected and inevitable. I did not take to Hortensia. She may well have been a skilled Birthmother, but she seemed to lack the kindness and understanding that others like Nousha and Riva possessed. Perhaps it was just her age.

'I had to take those babies away very quickly,' she said, a little defensively. 'We could not have taken the mother with us, she would have slowed us down, and Maren would not have done what was needed with the babies. The mother, Paradox, she told me that the soldiers were coming for her and her children, that she did not care for herself but that she wanted her children to grow up safe, protected from her world and those that sought her. It was her will that I take them to the Temple and leave them there, to grow up among the Priestesses as other abandoned girls do, in Oramia.' She shook her head. 'Why do so many people in Oramia want to get rid of their children, the blessings of the Goddess? In Kashiq, they do not do such a thing, so why do they do that in Oramia?' Her eyes filmed over, whether with tears or with a fogging of her mind, I could not tell.

I could not explain to her how the system in Oramia had grown from what seemed to be a genuine effort many ages ago to help those who could not care for their children and, for babies who were not seen as blessings from the Goddess, into an abhorrent system where babies were made to feed the demands of the Temple and the OutFort, and to work as slaves for the Queen. I still did not understand it myself. It was true that there was no such system in Kashiq. In most cases there, babies who could not be cared for were placed in the care of family or, often, of elder men and women. Ravin himself, though not a baby, was cared for by an elderly scholar after he had had to leave his home village under threats from his brother. I told Hortensia that I had no answer for her question, but that I had another question of my own.

'How did you leave the babies at the Temple? Maren always wondered whether there would be a way to identify them if their mother had wanted to get them back. She thought perhaps you might have left them with their names, or something else. Otherwise, how would the mother know where to find them? She has always wondered about that.' I had lied about Maren, trying to frame my own question in a more innocent way to Hortensia.

'I left them both well, and warm, wrapped in cloths. Each of them had the day they were born scribed on a piece of parchment pinned to their blanket. The mother said !Put the brooch on the blanket of the firstborn" – so I pinned it to the blanket of the firstborn, in the Sooran way. I wonder what became of them, those tiny little girls, I left them on different days, so they didn't know they were DoubleSouls....' Her voice trailed off and it seemed that she was treading on the long-shrouded paths of memory, trying to see clearly through what was hidden.

My heart was pounding faster. Although there was still no absolute proof of who I was, it seemed clear now that I must be the DoubleSoul sister of Lunaria. I had been told as a young Temple Maid by the old Priestess who found me that I had been found with a brooch pinned to my blanket and a note saying when I had been born. And now, it seemed, that tale really was true Only the day before, I had heard the story of the birth of the first DoubleSouls, Soren and Maliq. The Goddess had declared that one would be born first, and the other would be the firstborn. It was a story well known to all the Birthmothers of Soora, and Hortensia had interpreted the birth of Paradox's DoubleSouls in the Sooran way. To Paradox, the firstborn was the child born first, the one with the bee birthmark that showed her line to the Queen, but to Hortensia, the firstborn was the baby born second, the one who had pushed the other out first to make sure the world was ready for her. It explained why I had been left with the brooch, and not Lunaria. Even so, if there had been several babies left at the same time, the old Priestesses who cared for them could have muddled them up and told me that I had been left with the blanket and the brooch when in fact it might have been some other Temple Maid.

'Of course, I also left them with the DoubleSoul marks,' added Hortensia triumphantly. 'But you wouldn't know about them either, would you?'

'No, I don't.' I answered, trying to remain polite in the face of her scathing view of me, and hoping that it might work to my advantage and bring me more knowledge. 'Tell me more, so I can learn.'

'It's just something we experienced Birthmothers do with DoubleSoul children; in case their mother cannot tell the difference between them. If two girls or two boys are born, you cannot always tell if they are reflections or not, so we mark them in order of when they were born.'

'How interesting,' I smiled brightly at Hortensia, willing her on, and hoping that her clouded mind might stay clear for a few more minutes. 'How do you do that?'

'Well, we use a needle and a little darkberry juice. They are only babies, just born and do not remember any pain, but it is always there for their mother so that she knows which one was born when and forever links them as a pair. All you do is prick some small part of them with the needle and rub in the darkberry juice. It makes its own little birthmark, but just looks like any other little spot or freckle. Every Birthmother develops their own favoured place for the DoubleSoul marks, so sometimes you can even tell which Birthmother delivered a child if they have one of those marks.'

'Very clever! Where did you put your marks?'

'Always on the toes of the right foot. The one born first had a spot on the big toe, the one born second a spot on the second toe. Made it easy for the mothers to tell but it was small enough that nobody else knew.' Hortensia looked at me sharply.

'Do you know those DoubleSouls? Does Maren?'

I shook my head silently, unwilling to make up more lies, but unable to tell her the truth. I sipped the musty tea slowly. Hortensia smiled suddenly.

'Better not to know. We Birthmothers cannot carry every child we have seen into the world with us. There have been so many. Well, tell Maren my greetings and send her the blessings of the Goddess. I could not have known what might befall her when I left her, could I?'

I assured her that I would pass on what she said, though I had no idea when I might next see Maren. Privately, I thought that Hortensia probably did have an idea of what might happen to Paradox after she had left with the babies, and I thought that she might know even more than she had told me, but that she would not tell me more. Even though I had discovered more about Paradox's babies, and the circumstances of their arrival at the Temple, Hortensia's story left me with a sour taste. She looked up at me. Her hair was almost all white, and sparse over her head, but she did not cover it with her netela. There were lines between her eyes, deepened by frowning, and the skin hung loose on her arms.

'I'm tired of talking to you now,' she announced. 'Go away and leave me be, whoever you are. I have no time to deal with women and all their questions about birthing DoubleSouls. Go and ask one of the other Birthmothers if they think you will be having two. Always sending me the difficult ones...'

Hortensia had clearly descended into that clouded place where she could not match her mind to what was happening, and had tied a memory to it, as if with a fragile thread. She now seemed to think that I was a woman who had come to her for help about DoubleSouls, I suppose because I was so obviously with child.

SOORA SUN

I murmured my farewells hastily and got to my feet, glancing at my toes as I heaved myself up. There, on the first toe of my right foot, covered with a thin film of fine sand, was the spot she had described. I had never paid any attention to it before, or even noticed it. But there it was, proof that I was Lunaria's DoubleSoul sister after all this time. Hortensia remained sitting on the mat, waving me away irritably once I had got upright, travelling the twisted paths in her mind which only she knew. I walked away, breathing in the pure air as I went, grateful for its freshness after Hortensia's stale tea and sour words.

Chapter 27

Nousha took me on a walk around the settlement of Rengat. There was only one settlement on the island, and all the dwellings were there, since the north-western part of the island was so mountainous and inaccessible. Nousha explained to me that Rengat had become the island where the women went to give birth in part because of those mountains, which protected them from too many boats landing there and disturbing their peace, long ago. It was said that Soren, the goddess of healing had begun her work here, having been inspired by her own birth. She explained some of the old stories about her and why the place had come about as she showed me around.

'The Goddess Asmara was the first to give birth. She began by creating things, the things which filled the earth; the mountains and the rivers and lakes, and then she breathed life into other things, the fish and the insects, the birds and the animals. Finally, she created her children, the DoubleSouls Maliq and Soren with Yael and gave birth to them. They were also divine, like her. Asmara then created people and saw it as a lasting gift for them that they too would create new and unique beings, each time they gave birth. They too would create ideas, and objects and give birth to those who would do the same and grow from what had already been   created.

Her daughter, Soren, knew that people would need to be cared for as they in turn cared for their young, and so she began to train women in the art of being Birthmothers. Being the goddess of healing, it was natural to her; she worked with people who created and nurtured new people, and her brother Maliq worked with the craftspeople who created ideas which gave birth to new objects which were useful or brought joy, just as people do.

You may wonder why the Goddess did not make it easier for women to give birth. We cannot know, but they say that all that is created comes from a place of turmoil, that work is necessary to bring forth something new. Just as those guided by Maliq in metalwork work long hard hours which sap their strength in order to make a beautiful, jewelled necklace, so too do those who give birth to new people work long hard hours to produce them. Soren wanted only to ease their labours not to remove them, for when we work hard for something, we only love it more.

Soren wanted a place that was safe and protected for the mothers, where they could know they would get the help if they needed it. We can help you too, when your baby comes. It will not be long now.'

Nousha showed me the dwellings where the women stayed while they waited to give birth. Each woman stayed with a Birthmother who would care for her through her birthing. She also showed me the buildings where they stored the things they used, the poppy juice and the balms, the biting sticks and the cloths, the Oblak and the Iskra, as well as stocks of Soorai powder and Osh bark tea. Beside each one was a scroll, listing how many of each item there were, and of how much was taken out and by whom. A passing thought, like a small flaring flame in the emberjar of my mind came to me, and I wondered if I could somehow take some more Iskra, and properly recall what had happened on that night with Ambar. I blew it away, as you might blow out an oil lamp. Even if I could remember everything, it would not change much, surely, for Ambar still would not know what had happened either. The flame flickered again in my mind, and whispered to me that Ambar might have already taken the Iskra. I did not want him to know and me not to know, even though I could do nothing about it.

She also showed me the places where the Birthmothers learned their skill. Of course, mostly, they learned by watching those who already knew their skill, but there were scrolls with lists of what physics could be used and at what time, and drawings of ways in which mothers could be helped. It all seemed to be very well organised. I thought back to what had happened with the bees on Soora. It seemed as if Soora could have been better organised by Estar if she had taken some guidance from Nousha. I suggested to Nousha that she could help Estar to be better organised, and she looked at me in horror.

'Oh no, that would never do. There is one Ray for each island; it is not our job to tell the other Rays what to do or how to do it, for when we start to judge people, we are setting ourselves above them. We do not know what another person knows. We must just do our job the best way we can. If another asks for our advice, all we can say is what we might do if we were in their position.' She smiled at me, presumably aware of the disbelief which must have showed itself in my face.

'We know that how we live is not how all would choose to live. Many women leave these islands, but there are also many that wish to live here who come from other places. It could be that it would be a good place for you, Talla. You are good with the bees, you could help Estar. And who knows, in another five years' time, you could be chosen as a Ray, yourself, and then all your ideas for improvement would come to pass. We only allow as many women to come to live here as have chosen to leave, and there are just a few spaces left for suitable women - women like you.'

I laughed. However attractive the Isles of Soora might seem; I had no interest in confining myself again to one place for the rest of my life. And I certainly had no interest in being a leader. I had heard already from several Soorans who wished that they could travel beyond the world of their islands, to learn from others and about others. Once you left the islands, you could not return unless you were a Birthmother. Those who wanted to see other lands had to be very sure, for there was nobody who could tell them what it might be like in other lands. The only ones who could return were the Birthmothers who had once left the Isles of Soora. They were welcomed back if they wished to return but then had to stay for good. I had helped the Soorans with the bees and so I had had more chance to talk with the women than most other visitors to the Isles, but even then, I could not tell them what life would be like for them if they left their safe and protected islands.

'I think I can safely leave the governing of the Isles of Soora in the hands of the Rays,' I said. 'You do a good job.' I looked around, but although the isle of Rengat seemed so peaceful and so calm and comforting, I could not see myself staying here. It felt very remote from the other islands, perhaps because of those sharp pinnacles in the north. What felt like security to some, might feel like imprisonment to others, and I resolved to return to Gladia and Soora. I was sure there would be those who could help me when I needed a Birthmother, and otherwise Gladia would be there for me. I told Nousha and she told me that she understood why I wanted to be with my mother, and that in any case, she was sure everything would go well.

'But take this anyway,' she said, offering me a small yellow bag. It contained a soft cloth scented with jasmine, the scent of Flavus and of Soren. It brought to mind thoughts of warm evenings spent in the gardens of Arbhoun with Ravin. Its sweet scent soothed and wrapped itself around me. Nousha explained that the scent would calm me as I had the baby and would then calm the baby as it got used to living in the realm of people, coming as it did from the mind of the Goddess. In the same bag were some salves and some calming herb teas, and a smooth ring of wood for a baby to play with and to bite on. I thanked her and resolved to give the bag to Gladia for safekeeping until the child was born.

Having said my farewells to Nousha, I walked slowly back to Riva's dwelling. She was just leaving it as I arrived and explained that she was going to visit one of the Sooran women who had given birth recently, the one she had stayed up all night with.

'Come with me,' she urged. There was no reason not to, and Jan would not be sailing back until noon, so I followed her a little way along to one of the dwellings that Nousha had shown me earlier.

There I met the woman who had recently given birth, Panita, and her new child, a daughter she had named Sora after Soren, and the islands of Soora. I had seen Achillea not long after she had given birth, and this woman had the same sort of dazed look about her, a sort of disbelief that from her had come this new person. She offered the baby to me to hold. She was sleeping, wrapped in a faded yellow cloth, her head covered in soft, dark curls of hair and her eyelashes shut tight against her cheek. She sucked on her fist in her sleep, and as I held her, she stirred, pushing her foot against me much as my own child did from inside me. I could not believe that soon I would have one myself and would have to care for it, just as the Goddess cared for us. I handed the baby back to her mother gratefully when she started to whimper and left with Riva shortly afterwards.

We walked down the path, enveloped by the scent of jasmine, which grew everywhere here on Rengat, their starry flowers covering their twining plants. Again, it occurred to me that if hives were brought here, the women who lived on Rengat could produce their own honey without being dependent on the honey from Soora made by the bees who lived only on Sungold flowers. I had tasted some of the honey brought back from Aman and did not find it overly tasty. The sungold flowers made it taste somewhat pungent and salty and jasmine honey was well known to be sweet and flavoursome. But I knew from what Nousha had said before that on Soora each island was essential to all the other islands in some way, so that all were equally important, and that it was unlikely that they would ever change that. I talked with Riva about the scent of the jasmine, the scent of the day of Flavus, and its association with the colour yellow in Oramia and in the rest of Kashiq.

'Every day is Flavus here in Soora,' she told me. 'It is the scent of Soren, after all. We know that in Kashiq, each day is noted by a different name and a scent and a colour, but we no longer do that here in Soora. Some of those oils have to be brought from far away and are highly traded, so we save them for any physics we need them in. The jasmine grows everywhere here, so we can make our own oil to use every day in the Place of Prayer, so every day is the day of Flavus.'

I asked her how they differentiated between the days, to count the weeks, and she told me that on

Soora, they merely numbered the days up to seven and then began again. Each month was likewise numbered, so that instead of being born on the day of Flammeus, I would know that I was born on Flavus 1. This fitted with the Sooran love for order and for numbers and made sense to my mind, but my heart loved the way that each day of the week where I came from had a distinct name, and colour and scent. This system felt like the Soorans had, once again, narrowed their island world.

'Will you return to Rengat for the birth, then?' asked Riva, as we reached her dwelling. When I told her that I wouldn't, she asked if I planned to stay in Soora forever.

'That is the same question Nousha asked me, I replied. 'And the answer is the same. No, I want to return to Kashiq and to Oramia. I want to see familiar things as well as new things. I come from Oramia, but I live in Kashiq. My child's father was of Kashiq, and his child will live there too.' I paused, suddenly realising how much I really wanted to return to my own home to have the child. Despite Gladia's advice about not travelling at this stage, I realised that I needed to go back to the places and the ways of those I knew and understood. And I also knew that I needed Achillea to be nearby. I had relished my time with Gladia, but I needed my friend, too. Achillea's light heart and her kindness, the soothing sound of her singing as she worked, or her chuckles at her children, or the look in her big eyes when she looked up at Tarik, and the soft tenderness in his as he looked back at her. I knew that as I began a new and difficult life, she would be there to help me with any questions I might have about a baby. They were my closest friends, like I imagined a brother and sister might be. Certainly, I would rather have Achillea than Lunaria who was, it turned out, my

DoubleSoul sister. Lunaria and I seemed to have nothing in common at all.

'Do I have time before the baby is born to get back to Pirhan? It took me a week to travel down to Safran. It might take me more time now, I suppose.'

Riva's eyes lit up. 'Yes, it should be fine, I think. But you will need to rest a lot, and it would be better if you knew you could have a Birthmother nearby, just in case.'

My heart sank a little. I had felt at peace, having decided to return home, but now perhaps I had left it too late. 'Where can I get one of those?' I grumbled. 'If only Maren had travelled with me too.'

'Well, what about me?' burst out Riva, excitedly. 'This is my best chance to leave the islands and find a new life! I can come with you as you travel home and look after you until after you have the baby, and, in trade, you can show me life in Pirhan and how to live and work there. Sashila could come too! I know she would come with me if I left the islands. We could begin a new adventure together.'

I promised her that I would talk with Gladia when I returned and warned her that we would probably want to leave straight away. She waved away my concerns and told me she had little to pack up to bring with her, her Birthmother physics and herbs, some spare clothes and so on. She packed up her things quickly, and, as she said, there was surprisingly little. She went to tell Nousha, who did not seem surprised by Riva's departure, and told me that she was a good birthmother and that I would be well taken care of by her. She came down to the dock with us as we left and waved us off with good wishes. I spent the whole of the journey back to Soora thinking about how to break the news to Gladia, since she had just settled down into a new dwelling, fully expecting to stay there for at least the next few weeks. Perhaps she would want to stay here, on Soora, with Jan, rather than return to Pirhan with me, and I would have to journey home without her. At least I would still have Riva and Sashila to accompany me.

Chapter 28

Gladia had grumbled, of course, but was adamant that she would be returning with us too.

'You change your mind all the time at the moment, Talla. It's a good job I am here to look after you, who knows what you might do otherwise!' I did not mention that she was the one who had persuaded me to stay in Soora In the first place. I asked about Jan. Gladia sighed.

'Well, it was never going to last, was it?' she said finally, sounding surprisingly sanguine. 'Jan likes his life on the boat, and I like my life on the land. We always knew I would only be here for a while.'

She did go down to see Jan at the harbour, and then returned from her walk with suspiciously red eyes, but she was composed.

'When we get back, I want you to show me how to read and scribe, Talla. We have agreed that from time to time, we may scribe a message to one another and send it with that trader, Khadar, in Pirhan. Jan can scribe, so he will send me a scroll first. You will have your work cut out teaching me what all those little squiggles mean. I have said my goodbyes already, it will not be on Jan's boat that we travel to Safran tomorrow, that would be too hard. Now, I am going to talk to Sashila about life away from the islands. I have in mind that she might like to come to Mellia, where she can learn her stitching with the other women.'

So, we left the Isles of Soora, alongside Riva and Sashila, on a boat the next day. The sisters were excited about their new life now that they had made the choice to leave. Sashila told me that she had used her choice stone to ask if she should leave and that was why she felt so confident. I wondered if Riva's stone had chosen the same thing, or if she had even bothered to use them, and then what Sashila would have elected to do if her choice stone had indicated to her that she should stay. I felt sure that Riva, the elder sister was really the choice stone in Sashila's life. Sashila saw Riva's choices and followed them, trusting in her judgement more than in her own. I had not needed a choice stone myself, in the end, to decide where to go, and now the choice was made, I felt more optimistic about the future. It was not that I did not grieve for Ravin, but the constant dull pain was less now, and I remembered again the words of the Kashiqi saying about mourning. Now, Pirhan did not seem to be so much of a place of sad memory but a place of comfort and a foundation on which to build my future life.

The journey back to Pirhan was slow and arduous. I was frustrated by our slow pace, especially because I knew it was me who was slowing everyone down. Gladia assured me she did not mind walking slowly, and Riva and Sashila were so interested in everything they saw that it helped to distract me from my weariness. They were so used to always seeing the vast expanse of water all around them from the islands that they were disconcerted by the lack of water as we walked further north, through the hotter, drier, inner land of Kashiq.

'What do people eat instead of fish?' asked Riva. 'I know we are eating a lot of flatbreads and dates and nuts, but surely that is because we are travelling. What do people eat when they are at their homes?' Gladia sighed longingly, the memories of many past delicious meals overwhelming her, and described to the sisters the delights of spicy goat stews, and bean and pumpkin stew and sweet Kashiqi cakes made of honey, dates and oranges. She told them of strong Oramian coffee, of darkberries and chicken roasted over a fire. I never realised how well Gladia could describe things until I heard her descriptions of food. She made us all quite hungry, and when we stopped in Galdin for the night, Gladia took them to choose some food to trade for. The sisters had brought several hanging gourds of honeywine with them to trade, on the advice of Gladia, and just one small gourd brought them enough food for all of us to enjoy a feast. It was indeed good to taste a meaty stew, comforting and rich, mopped up with light and fluffy flatbreads, and to enjoy a piece of almond and date cake afterwards.

Galdin was a small town, but the sisters had only ever seen the settlements of Soora before, and they marvelled at the way that people seemed to be continually travelling through the land of Kashiq. Of course, they travelled in Soora too, but used boats to do it whereas here there were just lots of people walking to and from and through Galdin. Despite it being Ravin's hometown, I found nothing attractive in it except for the food we had feasted on.

'You don't get food like this every day, you know,' warned Gladia. 'That was a special feast to welcome you to the mainland. Most days, it is just a few vegetables and flatbreads. And certainly, no honeywine,' she added severely. Riva and Sashila had opened one of their gourds for themselves and had offered it round, but neither Gladia nor I had any desire for it; Gladia because it was not to her taste, and me because it reminded me too much of the evening that I had spent with Ambar, which I was trying so hard to forget.

The remainder of the trip was long and slow and forgettable for me. For Riva and Sashila, each day brought new chances to learn, and each evening, as we sat resting before we slept, Gladia would teach Sashila new embroidery stitches. Often, I would just sit and rest, but sometimes I would look at the scrolls which Riva had brought with her, which contained many of the lessons she had learned as a Birthmother and the recipes for the various physics they used. She asked me about the salves and tonics we made here in Kashiq, and I told her of Achillea, who also followed Soren, and who made most of them, using my honey and beeswax.

'The Soorabis use honey a lot, not just in making honeywine,' she commented. 'They say it is the food of the Goddess, that it was the only thing she ate when she first made all the lands. That the bees are like messengers of the Goddess. The lessons they give us are the lessons of life; to work hard and to make sweetness, to care and to nourish the young, to make and craft beautiful things like honeycomb, to make sacrifices for the good of others and to grow and make new hives.'

I pondered this. It sounded like the sort of thing that the Soorabis might say. Their devotion to Soren and to their role as her worshippers meant that they would see all these good things in the bees. But there were not only good things to learn from the bees. I had seen myself how the male bee would die after mating the Queen; how the bees would sting and hurt those they thought were threatening them without waiting to find out if it were true; how they would swarm together and work as a single mind for the purpose of protecting the queen, without ever querying whether she was right.

They would also oust weaker bees from the hive, by dragging them out of it and not allowing them to return.

There was much to be admired in the bees, for sure, but like all things, they were not perfect, and their good qualities were balanced by their bad. No doubt the Soorabis saw themselves in purely positive terms too, even if they were not themselves balanced in their views. Mina had been determined to keep as much of the honey they had as possible, even though the aim of giving it back was to help the very bees which she held up as perfect. No doubt the bees too, had their own good reasons for getting rid of some of the members of their hive and the other things they did that seemed unpleasant to me. My mind wandered on, contemplating whether the bees themselves were also guided by the Goddess, the mother of all. Whether they did or not, I was already eager to return to my own bees, having left them for too long on their own. Luckily, since I was not harvesting their honey, they would be fine on their own, unlike the bees of Soora, but I looked forward to getting back to the taste of that honey every morning; there had not been enough on this journey, since the Sooran bees themselves needed it all.

***

My dwelling looked much the same as when I had left it. My neighbour, Gurshan and his wife, Fari, had tended to the garden and harvested and used what they needed while I was gone, in exchange for keeping an eye on the place. I had locked the door with one of Tarik's complicated metal locks, and the key still rested in my underpocket. I spoke briefly with Gurshan, who welcomed me back, along with my companions and confirmed that all was well. He had a basket of beans with him which he had just harvested from my garden, and, although I protested, he insisted on leaving it with us, which at least meant that we would have an easy meal that evening.

On the journey home we had spoken about what would happen next. Gladia would return to Gabez the next day to visit Achillea and Tarik and tell them that all was well. Even though they had known of Gladia's plan and that it could be many weeks before they would see us again, they would have still been anxious about us all the time we were away, especially Achillea. Gladia was also eager to return to Oramia, her homeland, where she felt most comfortable, and to see Jember and the other children. Sashila and Riva would stay with me until after the baby was born, in the small dwelling on the other side of the garden, where guests could sleep. Gladia planned to take them both back to Mellia with her, eventually, to begin new lives in Oramia, far away from Soora. Really, she had need of another Birthmother to join Maren, and it was clear that Sashila was a quick learner when it came to sewing. She would learn well from Gladia, and Gladia would get someone to help her produce more of the items that traded well at the markets in Sanguinea and Gabez.

I had no plans now that I had returned, but it would be good to have the sisters nearby, and it eased my mind to know that I would be well cared for when the time came for the baby to arrive. I placed Ravin's scrolls about Soora back into his box of scrolls and promised myself that I would scribe my own scrolls of understanding about Soora soon, and perhaps even make a scroll to take to Arbhoun, to the Tower of the Wise, as Layla had wished.

Chapter 29

The sun was shining golden through the palm leaves as I made my way through Gabez towards the bridge to Pirhan. I had been to visit Achillea and Tarik, taking some honey and some beeswax for Achillea. I had a lot to spare since it had not been harvested while I was away, and I knew she would welcome it to use in her physics and tonics. It had been good to see her again, although in such a busy household, with Gladia as well as Jember visiting, in addition to three small children, there was little time for private chatting. She had promised that she would come to Pirhan to see me the next week, on her own, and I looked forward to that. I had a lot to talk about with her.

As I neared the bridge, I noticed the figure of a man, sitting on a low wall. The sun was in my eyes; all I could see was his silhouette against the brightness. When I walked past him, I heard him exclaim briefly, so I turned to look at him properly. Even though he might not have looked as if he came from the Court of the Queen, he did, for it was Ambar. Then it was my turn to exclaim in surprise. I had not expected to see him here in Gabez, so close to the bridge to Kashiq. I had steadfastly banished him from my mind since those half-remembered dreams and memories had surfaced.

'But how can this be?' Ambar did not even bother to greet me formally but gestured at me and my belly in bewilderment. 'You were not like this when I last saw you, months ago, and your husband is dead!'

There was much that made me suddenly angry with Ambar. He wandered in and out of my life, through time and place, and always it seemed to me that trouble or upset followed him. And yet he was the one demanding answers, even though he knew nothing of what had happened to me since we had last encountered each other, nor what I had found out on the Isles of Soora. In any case, it was not his business. I stopped walking and addressed him, speaking both bluntly and sharply.

'Yes, Ravin is dead. And yet he left me a part of himself as you have noticed with your clever eyes. You may not know, but a baby takes months to grow and last time you saw me was only a few weeks after Ravin was lost to me, when I did not yet know about this child. Are you not grateful that I will have a child as an everlasting memory of the man I loved so much?'

He winced. His face looked tired and worn, his eyes half shuttered by his eyelids. His forehead was beaded with sweat from the sun which glared at us in its turn.

'Can we start again?' he asked. 'Do you have time to talk with me, in the shade? I am on my own here, my men are working on the bridge today and I am supposed to make sure that they are working hard, but I think they will manage without me for a few moments. You will no doubt feel better sitting in the shade over there.' He pointed to a clay bench positioned under a group of palm trees. I considered refusing and carrying on with my journey home, but I wanted to see what he had to say. We sat down on the bench, and, as I looked up, I saw a little palm bird weaving its nest with long dry fronds of palm leaf, its thin feet and beak working together to make an intricate dwelling. There was the long shrill sound of

302

the palm cicadas. The bench was cool, and it was indeed a relief to get out of the sun.

'I am sorry,' he began. 'I was surprised that you were with child, that is all. I suppose I had thought that, like me, you might never have children, especially after Ravin died. You do look very different.' His face crinkled into a smile. I couldn't help smiling back. 'It must be coming soon, for it is five months since Ravin died and it is almost the month of Flavus already. Are you well?'

I confirmed that I was indeed well and that the baby should be here soon and then I asked him about Lunaria, remembering what he had told me when we last met about the need for her to have a child to carry on the line of the Queen. His face clouded over even more.

'It has not happened. I fear I have little time left at the Court, and who knows what will happen to me then. Silene has given the Queen physics from Soora to make the blessings of the Goddess more likely but still there is nothing. Lunaria trusts only the word of Silene, who never wanted Lunaria to marry me anyway. It is Silene who gives her the physic. They tell me that if the Goddess wills it, a child will be born, and if a child is not born, then it is I who is not the will of the Goddess.'

His mention of Soora alerted my mind. Without mentioning that I had been there myself, and knew all about the different physics they made, I asked him if he had seen the physic and what it looked like. I thought back to my time on Oshana, and the thick, sweet, dark-brown syrup made from the bark of the Osh tree, the very same physic that Ravin had read about, and had wanted us to go and get from Soora to increase our chances of having a child. From all I had heard, it was a physic which had very good results, and perhaps, if Lunaria had been taking it, even now she might be with child. After all, it had not been evident to me for some weeks after Ravin's death. And, since from what I had found out from Hortensia, I was definitely Lunaria's DoubleSoul sister, so perhaps we would also be similar in that regard. I had, however, no intention of telling Ambar about my relationship to Lunaria, nor how I knew.

'It is a strange-smelling powder,' continued Ambar, fretfully. 'It is a very dark purple colour. Lunaria takes it every day in her coffee, she and Silene call it the Blessing of the Goddess. Maybe it is called that in expectation of the happy event it should bring about.' He smiled tiredly. 'I can't help feeling that it should not be this hard. Look at Achillea and my old friend Tarik and their brood of children. They have three and I have none.'

I was speechless for some moments as my mind tried to understand what Ambar had told me. Up in the palm tree the little bird was pulling out one of the leaves it had woven wrongly into its nest, and I thought again of untangling silk threads in Gladia's sewing bag. So often you might pull on a thread and instead of it coming free it would cause a knot further down to tighten. Silene was not trying to help Lunaria to have a child but was trying to prevent it. And did the Queen know too? For it was the Priestesses who gave the Temple Maids the Soorai berry powder in their coffee, and Lunaria had been a Priestess, albeit for only a short time. But why was Silene trying to stop the Queen from having a child? Was it because she did not want Ambar to be the father of the child? Was there another plan? Ambar was looking at me with concern.

'Are you feeling unwell? Is it the child? Do you want water?' He pulled out a water gourd and offered it to me. I took it and sipped it slowly as I tried to frame my words well, admitting to myself that I would need to tell him about my journey to Soora.

'I have been away for some weeks from Pirhan. I travelled a long way south, down to the Isles of Soora, and visited them for myself. Why I was there does not matter for now. But while I was there, I learned a lot about the different Sooran physics, including the Oblak, that physic of forgetting and about honeywine, but also of two others. One of them is used to bless a woman and make her more likely to have a child, and the other is used to prevent women from having a child.' Ambar looked at me, more confused than anything else. I continued.

'The physic for blessing a woman with a child is a dark, sweet syrup called Osh bark syrup, but the one for preventing a woman from having a child is a strong-smelling, dark-purple powder, which is often added to coffee, perhaps to mask its bitter flavour. It is called Soorai berry. The physic Lunaria is taking is not encouraging the blessing of the Goddess but preventing it. I do not know why, nor why Silene is encouraging Lunaria to take it, purporting it to be the blessing of the Goddess, but I need to tell you something else too, that you need to know before you decide what to do.' And then I told him what I knew from my own experience about the practice of the Priestesses at the Temples, and of how they gave the Soorai berry powder to all the Maids in the Temples and called it the Blessing of the Goddess. I reminded him that Lunaria had herself been a Priestess and that it was likely that she knew what the effect of taking the Soorai powder would be.'

Ambar showed no emotion initially. There was just the tight clenching of his jaw, and the corresponding pulse in his temple as he worked through what I had told him. I had no reason to lie to him, after all.

'I am sorry to ask this, but is there a chance you could be mistaken? Could they have told you the wrong thing when you were on Soora, maybe even deliberately?' he asked, finally, running his hands through his hair.

'I might have thought that myself,' I admitted. 'But they did not know I used to live in a Temple and had smelled and seen the Soorai berry powder before, even though I did not know then what I know now. And what reason would the Temple have for giving the Maids some kind of physic that would encourage them to have children while they were in a Temple full of women? It does not make sense. But what does make sense, in the thoughts of the Priestesses, is to prevent them from having a child until it has been decided if they will be a Priestess or be returned to the Outer, from whence your men collect them and use them as the Angels. And then those children are used to fill the Temples and the OutForts with more!' I stopped speaking; my face flushed with anger.

Ambar sighed then, a long shuddering sigh, and put his head in his hands.

'You are right, as indeed you usually are, Talla. And now I will have to think what to say to Lunaria, the Queen, and to Silene, her DreamReader. Because, from what you say, they are united against the idea of my children being born to the Queen. And yet, I have always believed it was my destiny to father the next Queen of our land. I do not know what to do next, but I thank you for telling me this. Even though I have not always treated you as well as I should have, I have always trusted you to tell me the truth, Talla.' He smiled, a little sadly. 'If we believe in destiny, perhaps we have to question whether we can ever really know what it is. Are all things decided by the Goddess, or do we make our own destiny? Perhaps it is only that we

306

have a choice which might lead us to our destiny if we make the right choices. Like the set of stones that I showed you, perhaps I made the wrong choices somewhere in time, and now all my life is changed.'

I could not think of any useful words of advice to offer him, except to tread carefully in his dealings with the Court. His favoured position there was solely related to his relationship with the Queen, and he was unlikely to be able to easily escape from it. He frowned as I expressed my concern and then assured me that he would think carefully before he acted. I stood up to continue my journey, as it was clear that he was deep in thought and, in any case, I was tired and wanted to go home. There was a lot I needed to think about too, having learned this latest piece of information. He wished me well and then turned to walk towards the bridge too, but ahead of me.

I looked back as I crossed over into Kashiq, but Ambar had already disappeared from view.

WHITE

Chapter 30

I t was not many days later that my birth pains began. Riva was with me when the first sharp tightness began and knew that my time was beginning. She was well prepared already, and made cups of hot herbal tea, and rubbed ointments into my skin, and soothed me with songs and stories. She had brought with her several small cloth bags containing all that was needed for the birth of a child. It was a long and arduous time for me, but I do not have the clearest of memories of that time, since they were forgotten when I drank the Oblak physic for the second time in my life. I never intended to take it again, much less to take the Iskra afterwards for fear of what I might learn from it, but in the end it was Riva who gave me both. My memories are faint but insistent, like hearing the beat of a drum from far away, and even now, they build themselves. I scarcely know what is real and what has been created by my own mind.

Riva scribed short notes to herself on a scrap of plant parchment and read her scrolls of advice. She seemed calm and unhurried at the beginning as I paced the room and crouched and groaned, reassuring me that all was as it should be. She only looked anxious after some time had gone by and the pain was unrelenting. It was then that she gave me the Oblak in some tea, without my knowledge. She told me later that she was worried for me, in case something bad happened and she needed to act quickly. Because of that, some of what I now relate is from my own restored memory, and some of it comes from what Riva told me afterwards, and I have no reason to doubt any of it.

'Aureus: A child was born in the dark of night.'

I read later from her scribings. It was the Sooran way to record everything that happened. Riva told me it was so she and others could learn from the experience of each birth, that one day my experience might be mirrored by another woman, and that what she had learnt might assist that woman. That child, born in the dark of night, was my daughter, Amani, who emerged blinking into the light of the oil lamps. She cried then, fleetingly and Riva wrapped her up in a cloth and gave her to me. I looked down at her small, puzzled face and spoke to her of her father, Ravin, and how he would have loved her. As I spoke to her, there was suddenly more sharp pain, and Riva hastily took her from me, and laid her gently on a cushion in a basket. She ran her warm hands over me again, as she had done many times before, that night, trying to see what she could feel, and then she spoke to me urgently.

'Talla, there is another child to be born. They are DoubleSouls. You are doubly blessed by the Goddess. You must do it all again, for your firstborn, who is waiting to be born.' I could not comprehend what was happening to me, but whether I could comprehend it or not, another child would be born to me soon. I recall little of this, except that it seemed impossible to survive it twice in so little time.

SOORA SUN

'Flavus: A second child was born, at dawn.'

The simplest of facts, scribed by Riva. That child, the one born second but considered by the Soorans to be the firstborn, was my son, Ronai, who clenched his fists and howled as he came into the first golden light of the day.

Throughout all this time, Riva remained calm and spoke to me quietly, as far as I remember. As I have said, my memories of the birth of my children are softened at the edges, as if seen through a piece of fine silk. The babies were checked and then wrapped by Riva into a cloth. She wrapped them together since they had spent all their time until now together, and later she lay them next to me, and I slept. You might have thought I would have been awake, and looking at my children, but I drifted into a deep sleep, no doubt aided by poppy juice which Riva had also given to me in my tea. She never asked me if I wanted to take the physics, assuming that, since she was the Birthmother, she would know what was best.

Riva woke me as the sun rose higher in the sky, at around noon. Both the babies were crying, and she told me I must feed them and bathe them. I still could not believe what had happened. I knew that Riva would send a message to Gabez to Gladia and Achillea, and that they would be here later that day or on the next. There was a time when both babies were sleeping, and Riva spoke to me about them, and about them being DoubleSouls.

'They are very small,' she said. 'It does not seem as if they were ready to be born. And yet you were the right size to have a child, if it had been only one, and with the time you gave me.' She looked at me. 'Are you sure that the time since your husband died is right? Perhaps in your grief you lost some understanding of the time.'

'Perhaps,' I replied, uncertainly, but sure in my own mind of when Ravin had died, and now even more aware of a different possibility.

'The Goddess gives at a time of her choosing,' concluded Riva simply, willing to let the issue slip away. Her words rested heavily in my mind, though and I turned over the possibilities like the Soorans might turn a choice stone, flipping from one conclusion to another.

Despite their small size, the babies seemed to cry, feed and sleep with equal enthusiasm in those early days. I tried to spend time with each of them in turn, while the other was sleeping or being rocked by Riva. Her calm, quiet presence held me up, and she seemed able to manage to care for one of the babies at the same time as preparing a meal or washing the cups. We bathed them too. Riva showed me what to do with Amani, how to hold her and to wash and gently pat her dry with a cloth. As Amani slept, after her bath, I began to wash Ronai while Riva went inside. His small body lay in my arms, peaceful and compliant, quite unlike his mood as he was born. I spoke to him quietly about his father, and about all the things he would learn as he grew up, and about all of those who would love him; Gladia, Benakiell, Achillea and Tarik, Jember, Maren and Bellis. As I turned him gently over to wash his back, I saw something in the sunlight for the first time.

His skin was smooth and soft everywhere, but on his back, between his shoulder blades, there was a small dark mark, and as I bent closer to it, my heart jumped. For it was the same birthmark that I had seen on Lunaria's back. The birthmark in the shape of a bee, darker than the rest of his skin. Even though he was so tiny, you could still easily see that the mark was exactly like Lunaria's – if you had seen Lunaria's birthmark. That mark had been the way in which Lunaria had been identified as the future Queen. The Mark of the Queen. The same birthmark that Maren had been blinded for, and the reason that the daughters of the Lady Paradox, daughter of the Queen, were left at the Temple so swiftly by Hortensia, having been in mortal danger from the pursuing OutRiders.

But how could this be? Was it because I was Lunaria's sister, her DoubleSoul? Did these things happen to all the descendants of the Queen? I myself had no such mark, and besides, Ronai was a boy, and it should have been impossible. All the descendants of the Queen were women like her, so it made no sense for my son to bear the mark. And yet, bear it he did. I turned him back over and dried him off, wrapping him up in the cloth so that Riva could not see the mark, though it would have meant nothing to her even if she had, for she did not know what I knew. The next time I fed Amani, I examined her closely, too, especially on her back but she did not have any such mark.

Riva mistook my abstraction for weariness and advised me to sleep again if I could, with the babies lying next to me, on a mat in the shade of the courtyard. I took her advice, and she gave me some tea which this time contained the Iskra, for it was in my sleep shortly afterwards that some of my knowledge returned. The leaves of the tree shifted above me, as I drowsily finished the tea, and every so often, a patch of light would suddenly shine on me as the sun was allowed through the leaves.

I must have slept then, with the golden, shifting light flickering above me because my forgotten memories came to me in threads of dreams. I cannot, even now, tell you what was dream and what was memory, for perhaps what happens in a dream somehow becomes real and perhaps what we believe to be memory is, after all, just an imagined dream.

It was not that I remembered everything at once, it was more that memories drifted into my mind like wisps of smoke. Some I could trace back to the glowing ember in my mind, but others seemed separate and disconnected. I had sworn, after the first unsettling encounter with Iskra, that I would never take more but it was given to me without my knowledge, and that made it all the harder, for I could not prepare myself for what I realised.

***

The threads of warp and weft were woven in these dreams, with my memories of the birth mixing with my half memories of the time I spent with Ambar, after I had taken the Oblak for the first time. They circled back and around each other ceaselessly.

... *'How could I forget this?' said Ambar before he kissed me. 'And yet forget it I must.' He stroked my hair softly off my face. 'Some things are never forgotten, like the first moment I saw you, there at the market in Sanguinea. I knew there was something special about you.' I looked then, deep into his eyes, and saw their deep, honey sweetness...*

The sharpness of the beginning of my birth pains cut into the hazy memory of that night. It was as if I were being kicked in the belly, and as soon as I began to regain my breath and relax my muscles, I would be kicked again. It became almost rhythmic, a dull throbbing beat interwoven with the sounds I made. Riva rubbed my back soothingly, over and over. Or was it Ambar that I remembered, stroking my back, with light fingers? Or Ravin, who could always rub away the knots in my back after a hard day of working with the hives?

I could hear Riva's voice in my dreams, urging me to add my labours to those of the Goddess, who had

313

herself gone through the same thing. She told me that all babies are born of the sacrifices made by their mothers as they are born. There was no pause now; it was constant, unremitting pain and I was tired of it and wanted it to stop. Inexorably it continued.

'Breathe slowly, Talla.' Trying to make myself slow something down which wanted to go quickly was not easy, but through the waves of pain the child was born. There was stillness for a heartbeat or two and then Amani cried in protest at her entry to the world.

...I wept then, and Ambar held me as I wept. He said nothing, for there was nothing to say, and all of this should have been forgotten if only I had just taken the Oblak and not the Iskra...

There was a hollowness in my heart as I turned to look for Ravin, after both babies were born. He had told me once that to have both a son and a daughter would be his dream, and I turned to him forgetting he was not there. In that moment of remembering his dream and knowing it was too late. I wished that I knew if, somehow, back with the Goddess, he was aware that I had given him his dream. Or if his dreams died with him. For if he had not died, I would not have leaned on Ambar so much in my grief, and the longed-for babies would not have been born. I wept after the birth, and Riva soothed me, telling me that all women cry when they become mothers, for the Goddess makes their hearts more tender.

...'Let it be forgotten,' murmured Ambar, late in the night, so dark that I could not see him. 'We will not remember this; it will be as if it did not happen. It will be washed out of our hearts by our tears. But it is our destiny, surely, to be together, and even if we forget it happened, it will still be true.' He raised my hand to his cheek so that I could feel the wet tracks on his cheek where he wept...

***

There was not much more; vague feelings of pain and weeping, calm and pride and the gentle, warm darkness of sleep mixed with the savage, cold darkness of pain. It was some days before my mind stopped turning things over, trying to work out which memories were real, and which were just remnants of my mind. It could have driven me mad were it not for the fact that I had to care for the babies who took up every minute I was awake and most of the ones I should have been sleeping too.

Chapter 31

Make a straight line next to the circle. No not like that, like this.' I was trying to instruct Gladia in the art of scribing and reading some simple phrases. She was determined to learn enough so that she could send a scroll to Jan with Khadar the metal trader. She had asked me rather plaintively whether I couldn't just do the scribing and the reading for her, because Jan would never know, but I had firmly refused. I had already seemingly failed in my attempts to persuade Achillea to learn to scribe and read. Her attitude was that she did not need those skills in Oramia, and she had three young children to look after, as well as physics to make, and songs to sing, and had no time to learn something which seemed so difficult. I was determined that at least one of my friends should be able to scribe and read. Benakiell had started learning from me years ago but had lost interest and then had moved to Kashiq to live with Shira, and she did it all for him. Perhaps he had learned some from her since. I had not seen him since Ravin had died and I knew I should let him know about the babies because if Gladia was my mother, he was my father and yet he seemed so far away. I resolved to scribe him a scroll; Shira could read it for him.

Gladia dragged the sharp stick through the sand again. She was occasionally truculent, but she was stoutly determined too, and would keep on going until she had learned it properly. This time, she had done it right.

'Now read it,' I said. She squinted at the lines she had made in the sand.

'You...can...scribe...well.' Her face lit up. 'I did it! I am not too old to learn to scribe and read! Show me some more!' I took up my stick again, ready for the next lesson, but Ronai began to wail and just as I picked him up to feed him, his sister began her own determined complaint. I sighed. Gladia was staying with me for a couple of weeks to help and then I would be on my own as she would be finally making her way back to Mellia along with Riva and Sashila, who would, I suspected, soon be put to work. They were happy to have a place to go and eager for new adventures. Riva had remained with me, and Sashila had gone to stay with Achillea and help her with the children in return for a place to stay until Gladia and Riva returned for her on the way back to Mellia. Both sisters were eager to learn about life in Oramia, but I was not sure that they would remain there long. They were accustomed to Kashiqi ways, but they felt indebted to Gladia for offering them a home in Mellia, and perhaps, like many of the women who used to be Angels, they would stay for a while before they moved on.

I wondered what Gladia would find when she got back home. It seemed unlikely to me that any more Angels would have been left there to be cared for, especially after what I had discussed with Ambar. If he fell out of favour with Lunaria, he would have no sway over what happened to the Angels at all anymore. Without telling Gladia what I had discussed with Ambar, I asked her what would happen if the women stopped coming. She smiled.

'We do not only work with the Angels these days, Talla. Even if they do not come, there are always women who will need our help. Some of them are young women like I was, whose only option used to be to leave their child at the Temple. Now, they come to us and learn to care for their own children and learn a skill so that they can trade to care for their child and themselves and stay together. And there are those who come to us to learn a trade, who are not with child, but who have just lost their way in life.' I must have looked surprised, and she smiled again.

'We cannot always do everything we want to do. And being angry about something does not change it. We realised that one way we can stop the Temple Maids becoming Angels is to at least stop the babies from being left there by the women of the Outer. If they can look after themselves and their children, they will not be desperate enough to leave their babies to the Temple. If Ambar stops sending us the Angels, we will still have work to do. In any case, it will be Bellis and Maren who will decide on how things go. I am getting old now, and it is time for a younger woman to do all the hard work.'

Amani snuffled into my skin, her breaths gradually becoming more rhythmic as she fell asleep, sated. I gently laid her down on the mat next to her brother who lay with his little hands clenched, his mouth still making sucking movements even though he was asleep.

'But that just changes the problem, doesn't it?' I asked. 'We already know that the Angels are one of the ways in which the Temple and the OutFort get more children to raise to their requirements. They will just make it so that more babies are born to the Angels until they have the numbers they need.' I fell silent then, thinking of all the babies that needed to be born to keep the Temples and OutForts going, and of all their mothers. I looked down at my children, peaceful and content, and wondered at how a system had grown which had begun with good intentions and changed into that monstrous belief, that somehow it was the wish of the Goddess that this should happen to the women and their babies.

Gladia shrugged, and then looked a little ashamed.

'If I can protect the women of the Outer, then I will still have made a difference. Ambar letting us have a few Angels a year changes nothing, does it? Like you said, they will just make more. One person cannot change this system, at least not unless she is Queen. But even then, they would need to be very strong to change how it works. It should have been you who was Queen, Talla. You question things and want to change them. Lunaria could be told anything was the will of the Goddess and she would do it. But we of the Outer hear little of what happens in the Queen's Court. She may have a child herself now and it might change her heart if she did. Or maybe Ambar might change her mind.'

She got up then and went inside to fetch her stitching. She was making the headbands for Amani and Ronai, for when they were old enough to start wearing them, at the beginning of the third age of childhood. I could not imagine them being that old. Gladia had insisted that she should make the bands now, so that she knew that in fourteen years' time they would be wearing something that she had made for them, and that, with care, they would last their whole lives. I had shown her Ravin's headband and the one which I wore, although of course we had had to guess at the details of my parents. The only thing I knew was the day I was born, Flammeus. My children would not have that void of knowledge, I thought, for, unlike me, they would know who their parents were, and on what day they were born. And yet, for all they were DoubleSouls, they would have different coloured headsquares since they were born on different days; Amani at the end of Aureus, in the night, and Ronai at the dawn of Flavus. It pleased me that they would have this difference.

Achillea had been to visit several times, once with Tarik and all the children but at other times on her own, leaving the children with their father. It meant, she told me, that she could come and enjoy spending time with the babies without having to have any responsibility for her own.

'While they are with Tarik, I don't have to worry about them,' she said. 'It makes such a difference, having him there.' She stopped then, her wide eyes creased with concern that she had pointed out to me how much better it would have been if Ravin had been with me and his children to help me. As she stumbled through another apology, I wondered how long it would be before I would get used to this new and different life. I had once read a scroll, by the scholar Jasnat. She explained that just as there were seven days in a week and seven weeks in a month and seven months (and the Goddess weeks) in a year, so there were seven years in an Age and each Age was the beginning of some new gift from the Goddess.

'There are three ages to Childhood: the first is the age of growing, the second the age of learning and the third is the age of changing. There are then seven ages to live through if the Goddess blesses us with them all. In each one we grow, we learn, and we change. Each person has a path to walk, and at the change of each age, every person comes to a fork in the path, and must choose their direction. Everything that happens to a person will be the cause of growth, knowledge or change.'

So perhaps it would be an age before I could move forward and not continually feel as if I were looking back. Perhaps, as my children went through their first age, the age of growing, I would grow too, and learn and change. I knew I had changed a lot myself since I had first left the Temple. That young woman who had known nothing of the Outer, and who had made her choices impulsively and had guarded herself from attachment had changed a great deal. And now, two ages later, I knew much more about my world and about myself and the people I loved. I wondered if I would recognise myself if I could somehow meet myself when I reached the Age of Wisdom, or if I would have changed beyond recognition. Jasnat had not said much about what might happen after one reached the Age of Wisdom, but perhaps that was the point in life where one had achieved all one could hope for.

I had not yet been back to Gabez. I had made the excuse to Achillea that I was still not properly able to manage both babies; that carrying one on my back and the other on my front still felt strange and uncomfortable. Besides, they were still so small. She pointed out that I had been out with both of them in that way to the market in Pirhan, which I had, but I told her that it was only for a short time. The truth was that I did not want to go back to Oramia with Amani and Ronai. I still remembered the warning that had been given to me before, about bad things befalling me and those I loved if I did not flee. And I did not want to see Ambar again now that the babies were here. There was too much unsaid between us, and I knew that if he had told Lunaria what I had told him, that he would be being watched by Silene. All I could do was to try to keep the children in Kashiq. I felt safe here, under the protection of the Defenders of Yael, who would not allow any OutRider to cross the bridge – at least not dressed in the armour of the Queen of Oramia. It was the most I could do. But I could not explain all this to

Achillea who nonetheless professed to understand and said she could see why I would not want to go far just yet.

'There!' Gladia bit off the thread as she finished her sewing and showed me the finished headband. It was Amani's, orange with red circles on it, and she lay it next to Ronai's, which she had already finished. His was red with orange lines on it. Beside them was Ravin's headband, which she had been using as her pattern for the stitching, to make sure that the bands and the decorations on them were of the right size. It was considered lucky in Kashiq to keep the same headband all one's life, and Ravin had got his not long before he had run away from the village of Galdin. It was still bright, for he was a young man when he died, and his headband had not had the time to become faded and soft like the ones you saw around the markets on the heads of the old. I stroked it softly with my finger, as if it were his face and the stitches were his stubble. Gladia put her hand over mine kindly and then she rolled up the bands and gave them to me in a little carrysack she had stitched specially, so that I could keep them safe.

'Now we can get back to our scribing lessons,' she said. 'I would like to scribe a short scroll to Jan. Well, it would be longer if I knew more of my scribing. Could you help me and scribe some of what I want to say so that I can learn those words and practice them?' I agreed this would be practical although I was a little wary of what she might want to say but, in the end, she wanted to tell him more about my babies than about anything more intimate. I was just showing her how to scribe Ronai's name, when there was a call at the reed door into my courtyard where we were sitting.

Chapter 32

The caller was one of the men who traded in plant parchment at the market in Pirhan. I knew him well enough for I often needed to trade for plant parchment, and he had a need for my salves, since his hands were frequently chapped and cut from working with the reeds. His name was Narshin, and he was accompanied by another man, who looked like he had fallen on hard times, perhaps one of the beggars who used to sit forlornly outside the houses of Prayer, hoping for a blessing of food or prayer. He shuffled behind Narshin, his head bent low and concealed by his scruffy headsquare.

'Greetings, Talla,' said Narshin, touching his hand to his heart and his head in the Kashiqi way. I responded and waited for him to speak, wondering what he wanted of me, and hoping that it could be easily dealt with.

'I have brought this man to you; he says he is an old friend of yours and that he is visiting Pirhan and wishes to speak with you.' He looked concerned, and leaned a little closer to me, so that he could murmur quietly to me. 'If you don't know him, or you want me to take him away, just tell me and I will take him away. He looks very rough.' He raised his voice a little to speak to the ragged man who hung in the shadows near the courtyard wall. 'Come then, fellow, for Talla is here now, waiting to speak to you.'

The man was dressed in torn, filthy clothes, and held a similarly filthy carrysack. His beard had clearly not been groomed for some time, and he wore a Kashiqi headdress that was so faded and frayed that you could not even tell what colour it was. It hung over his face as he stepped forward.

He lifted up his eyes to me and spoke softly.

'I am a friend of Tarik, in Oramia, my name is Baram, do you remember me? I have come to ask you for your help. As you can see, I have fallen on hard times.' He smiled sadly. My eyes must have widened in recognition as I realised who it was and was just about to exclaim his name. Narshin looked on curiously. I lifted my netela up to my head and let it shield my face from him as I replied to the man.

'Greetings, Baram,' I acknowledged finally. 'It is a surprise to see you here at my home. Tarik did not tell me you were coming here.'

'It was...unexpected,' he said finally, 'My plans have changed, as has my life, as you can see.' He gestured to his robe with a hint of a smile. 'May I come in? I will only stay a short time, and then I will have to go again.' Narshin moved forward, eager to send Baram packing.

'Come on now,' he said. 'Talla is probably busy, and she doesn't want to be pestered by people who are down on their luck. Why not go down to the market? There might be someone there who needs some work doing, you look strong enough.' Baram looked at me, almost pleadingly, and, for the sake of curiosity if nothing else, I smiled and welcomed him to my home.

'Thank you, Narshin,' I said. 'Baram is an old friend, and I can give him some tea and some food before he goes on his way.'

'May the Goddess bless you,' said Narshin with a smile. 'Next time you come to the market, make sure you bring some of that marigold salve of yours for me, and I will throw in a couple of extra scrolls of plant parchment!' He waved as he set off down the path, and I opened the reed gate further, to allow the mysterious Baram in.

I knew who it was, but what I did not know was why he was at my door, nor how he had got there. It disturbed me that he had found me, but I really wanted to know what was going on, so I led Ambar, for that was who he was, to sit in the shade. Just as I was about to demand some answers to my many questions, Gladia came out of the dwelling, holding Ronai, who was crying with some vigour. From inside the dwelling, I could hear the sound of his sister joining in with the same determination.

'Who was that? Take Ronai, and I will go get Amani... Ambar, is that you? What kind of silly game are you playing at, dressing up as some kind of beggar?' She did not stop for an answer but swept off into the dwelling to fetch my daughter. I sat down helplessly with Ronai and began to feed him, feeling curiously self-conscious, and letting the edge of my netela drift over his face as he sucked, his wails quelled.

'Gladia is still in charge, I see,' he said. 'Now, do you have a son or a daughter, for I swear I heard Gladia say both him and her. I am glad to see you have had your child safely.'

'I have both,' I replied, smiling. 'I have a son and a daughter, for I was blessed with DoubleSouls.'

Before he could answer, Gladia returned with Amani, changing her cloths and muttering as she did so about unexpected guests and how they could at least have given warning. Ambar remained quiet, watching her and then me, and the babies.

'I suppose you will want a cup of good Oramian coffee and something to eat as well,' she grumbled. 'It's a good job I brought lots with me. Why do you look so awful anyway, are you in disguise or something?'

'I would be most grateful for something to eat and drink,' acknowledged Ambar. 'I have not eaten in a couple of days, and Oramian coffee sounds better than river water. I apologise for my appearance. If you have some water, I can wash.' Gladia wrinkled her nose up and gestured to the corner of the courtyard where the large clay pot full of water for washing stood.

'You can clean your hands and face in that,' she sniffed. 'More than that and you will have to find somewhere else to stay. Or at least go to the spring and wash there.' He got up and went over to the pot and poured some water into the clay pan which he then used, together with the soap ball to make himself clean. He tried unsuccessfully to smooth his hair and his beard. He still looked wild and unkempt, but at least he was clean. He had laid the Kashiqi headdress to one side, together with the carrysack, and as he returned to his place in the shade, Gladia came to swap over the children, leaving Amani with me to feed and taking Ronai who was now making small, contented sounds and looking around him with interest.

'Well, I suppose I had better make you this coffee and food then,' said Gladia, and thrust Ronai into Ambar's arms. 'Make yourself useful, there is a lot to do here, you know. Or probably, you don't know.' She bustled off to the fire leaving him holding Ronai awkwardly. He frowned at Amani and started to complain, so I told Ambar to get up and walk around with him to soothe him. I watched him as he walked with my son in his arms, his face bent down, talking to him in a low voice about what he could see, and pausing under the leaves of the palm tree which grew in the corner. They shifted in the sun and their dancing shadows moved across Ronai's face. He stopped crying and reached his hands out to the shadows, trying to grasp them. Ambar chuckled at the baby's attempts to take hold of the illusion and then plucked a leaf and dangled it in front of him, moving it around and keeping it out of reach as Ronai stretched for the leaf.

Gladia was unperturbed by the unexpected appearance of Ambar, whereas I was unable to explain it to myself with any satisfaction. And while she sat contentedly waiting for the water to boil for the coffee and for the flatbread to warm up, my mind bubbled like the water she watched. Ambar stole a glance at her from time to time but devoted more of his time to amusing Ronai who gurgled happily.

Amani had fallen asleep, meanwhile, and I laid her down on the mat and took Ronai from Ambar as he got his coffee and his flatbread from Gladia. She sniffed as she handed them to him.

'Well, I can't imagine this is a visit to see me, or to see the babies, and, by the look of you, you have a story to tell. I shall go to the market to trade for some more flour and food since you are so hungry, and some stitching threads that I need.' She looked at Ambar critically. 'Are you sure you wouldn't like me to get you some different clothes, Lord Ambar? Those ones could do with a wash.'

The flicker of a smile crossed over Ambar's face at Gladia's suggestion, but he declined, telling her that he still needed them for now. She sniffed again and bustled out of the door, leaving Ambar and me alone in the courtyard with the babies.

As soon as she had gone, I turned to him and demanded that he tell me what he was doing at my dwelling and in Kashiq, and what had happened to make him look the way he did. He settled down with his back against the wall, cleared his throat and told me his story.

Chapter 33

I thought about what you told me about what is made on the Isles of Soora, and what their effect is, all the way back to the Court. I convinced myself that it was impossible that Lunaria could know what the effect was on her of taking the Soorai berry powder, and that it must be Silene, the one who seems to live inside Lunaria's mind more and more, who must have deliberately told her the wrong thing. All Lunaria would need to do would be to stop taking it, and instead to take the Osh bark syrup, and then she too would have a child, and our destiny would be fulfilled.' Ambar told me as he began his recount of the events at the Court.

When he had got there, Lunaria was in her Temple, with Silene, offering her prayers to the Goddess. This Temple had become more and more important to her since she had first become Queen and was now enhanced with a new and costly statue of the Goddess. Expensive scented oils were used every day, and even the cloths for the days of the Goddess were richly embroidered, many by the Queen herself. Ambar waited for her in their chambers, hoping to talk to her about things in private, but she returned with Silene, looking shocked to see Ambar there.

'I thought you were in Gabez, working with the soldiers on the bridge,' she said. 'I was not expecting you to return for some days. Is your work already done? Those taxes will not collect themselves on the bridge.'

'The men are still there, working,' he assured her. 'But there is something important which I need to talk with you about - in private.' Silene raised a thin, grey eyebrow and looked at Lunaria.

'You may speak in front of Silene,' said Lunaria. 'I hold no secrets from her. After all, she is the DreamReader, and if she can read my dreams, she can surely read my mind too.' She smiled at Silene, who smiled victoriously back at her.

'Aye, well, you may have no secrets from her, but she may have kept secrets from you,' replied Ambar. Silene's eyebrows rose further, and her mouth tightened. Lunaria laughed, and Silene smiled with her, but her smile only reached her mouth while her eyes continued to spit fire at Ambar.

'Why would she have secrets from me? She speaks with the Goddess herself, and always delivers her messages to me, even the ones which may not be welcome. I do not think she would tell me unpalatable truths if she were keeping secrets from me but would instead tell me all kinds of flattering lies in order to keep her place here at the Court. I do need to talk to you, too, Ambar, about a matter of some importance. However, it can wait until you have spoken to me about this other matter, which is supposedly so urgent.'

Ambar explained about the different uses of the physics by the women of Soora, and how using one would make the birth of a child more likely, and the other would make it less likely. He assured me that he did not tell Lunaria where he had obtained the information, only that he had been talking to a man who traded with Soora. Lunaria listened to him but when he had finished explaining that she was taking the wrong physic and that, if she would only change her physic to the Osh bark syrup, she could well be with child quite soon, she turned away from him to her DreamReader.

'This is what you told me he would say,' she said, awed. 'You told me he would try to persuade me not to take the Blessing of the Goddess, and that he would use any reason he could to stop me from taking it and thus take away my connection to the Goddess.' Silene nodded virtuously.

'Do I not speak the truth?' demanded Ambar of Silene. 'Are the women of Soora who make the physics wrong? If so, perhaps we should stop trading at all with them. Who knows what could be in the physics they trade with us. Perhaps the Oblak does not work either on the Angels!'

The two women looked at him pityingly.

'You cannot expect him to understand, my Queen,' said Silene. 'He is not exalted by the Goddess like you are.' She turned to Ambar, her thin face outwardly impassive, but still glowing with zeal.

'You are not mistaken, if you talk of the people of the Outer. I can understand how an ordinary person like you might make that mistake. But these physics only work on lower people like them. Your Queen is not made of the same fabric as they are, she is of the Goddess. She is favoured by the Goddess just like the Goddess favoured our beloved Ashkana, who also worked tirelessly for the Goddess, and who taught us all we know about how we should behave.'

Ambar was silent for a moment, trying to work out what to say. He who always seemed to have an answer for anything, and whose charm added honey to any conversation, could not make the words of reply. Lunaria took up the explanation triumphantly.

'Any daughter I have will carry on the line of the Queen and must come from the Goddess. Otherwise, she will not be fit to rule. She must be blessed by the Goddess, as I was, before she becomes queen after me. And only when the Goddess decides that will happen, will it happen. The Blessing powder I take each day, takes me closer to the Goddess, as it did when I lived in her Temple. I will have a daughter through her, not through you. Silene has received messages from the Goddess in her dreams and in mine over recent weeks. The Goddess has told us that she has a plan and that a child will be born to me at the right time. She wishes me to devote myself more and more to her and, in that way, I will be more and more blessed. I do not need a husband to make me with child. The Goddess will do that, for she can do anything, and she brought forth life even when there was nothing to bring it from. And that takes me to the matter I need to discuss with you. You have been a good Vizier for me, Ambar, and your work has been noted, but your time here at the Court is over. You are no longer my husband, nor can you live here anymore. The Goddess finds you disruptive to me.'

Ambar turned on Silene, furious.

'I always knew you hated me and all that I stood for. I was the one who fought to bring Lunaria to the throne which belongs to her. You, no doubt, were here before, trying to stop her from being Queen and now you are trying to stop her from having children so that the power at Court will stay with you! You are a devious, nasty woman who has no thought at all of the Goddess and the goodness of her creation but think only of yourself and your desperate clinging to power.' Before Silene could open her mouth to reply, he addressed himself to Lunaria, pleading with her to come to her senses.

'Lunaria, all that I want is to be with you and for you to fulfil your destiny and to have children so that the future Queen of Oramia can be assured. For what will our land be without a Queen? How can you allow this poisonous woman to dwell inside your mind? Can you not see that she just tells you what you want to hear? All she has to do is tell you that she dreamed that the Goddess told her it, and you believe her. Because if you dared to tell her that you didn't believe her, it would mean that everything else you have decided, based on her advice, is also wrong. Have you forgotten what I have done for you, and the sacrifices I have made for you? How I have willingly put myself in danger for you, and how I have done all that you have asked of me? What would you have me do now?'

Lunaria looked at him coldly, any affection gone.

'It is clear that Silene has been right about you all along. It has taken me seven years, a whole age, to understand, but now I see that, in your way, you are just hungry for power. And it is you who has been the thing that has prevented me from having a daughter. After all, it is me, is it not, who is ordained to be the Queen and to produce the heir to the throne. You are misguided if you think that the destiny of our land of Oramia has anything to do with you. You have served your purpose and now you must leave. I warn you that, if you ever try to return here, my OutRiders, whose only loyalty is to their Queen, will remove you and punish you. And do not try to take anything of mine with you. Everything you have belongs to me after all. Silene, speak to the OutCommander and tell him of the changes. We will appoint a new Vizier soon. Ambar, you have until sunset to put your things together and leave.' And with that, she turned and swept out through the door, her robe trailing behind her. Silene smiled before she too turned to leave.

'You cannot change the will of the Goddess. Luckily the Queen understands that better than you. However, I am sure the Goddess will bless you in her own way.'

She paused and frowned, as if listening, and then shook her head. 'No,' she muttered. 'He will not be blessed in that way.'

'You may think you have won,' said Ambar. 'But as you have said so many times before, the Goddess knows what is to come. And when I die, and you die, and Lunaria dies, our souls will return to the Goddess, and she will know what has been done in her name. And then, like everyone else, the fragments of our souls will be reborn in others, and the Goddess will read what is scribed upon our hearts.'

Silene did not respond except to tell Ambar to wait at sunset by the path down the steep cliffs on which the Court was perched. Now that he was no longer of the Queen's household, he could not expect to use the basket lift that was used by the Court to easily move up and down and was guarded by the OutRiders. And to remind him that he could not take his horse, and that he should be grateful that his life would be spared.

I looked at Ambar when he had finished recounting this part of his story in complete disbelief. How could this have happened? How could Lunaria have acted like this, and what would Ambar do now?

'My story is nearly over now,' he said reassuringly. 'I got down from the mountain, although I did fall a few times since it was dark, and I had no guide and no lantern. Perhaps it was lucky that I had so little with me, though I have brought with me some useful things, and some small items to trade. As I left the mountain, I was set upon by a group of men. They were not OutRiders that I knew from the Court, and indeed were not wearing uniforms, but OutRiders they were, I could tell. They were waiting for me, and they beat me senseless and left me there. I pretended to be more hurt than I was, so they left me. When they had gone, I walked a long way until I found a place in the forest where I could rest and recover, near Besseret. When I was strong enough, I walked over the Osho mountains and crossed the Gabish river below Gabez and came into Kashiq. My first thought was to tell you all that has happened.' He smiled. 'There are very few people left in the world who I can trust but somehow, I feel like I can trust you.'

'But can I trust you?' I asked in a louder, fiercer voice than I had intended. There had been so many times in the past when Ambar had shown himself to be solely focused on his own aims, to the detriment of many.

'Would you trust my answer?' he asked finally, in return. 'Asking someone if you can trust them is a mistake. It shows them that you don't really trust them because if you did, you would not need to ask. Not only that, but it shows you do not really trust yourself either. After all, if I said that yes, you could trust me, and then did something to show that was not true, you would blame me for making your choice.' The old smile warmed his face briefly. 'Trust is something you feel, not something you are told. You will know the answer to your question one day.'

Chapter 34

When Gladia got back, I encouraged Ambar to tell her his story, but he only told her that he had left the Court because Lunaria did not want him as her husband anymore, not anything about the Sooran remedies or how they had been used by Silene. I left it as he had told it, reasoning that I could tell her the rest later, when he had left. Perhaps I would not, though. I had said nothing to her of the dreams and my slow realisations about what had happened between Ambar and I, and I had no intention of ever telling her, either.

'I don't suppose you will be going back to Oramia very quickly, then,' observed Gladia. 'Now you will have some idea of what it is like to be hunted by the Queen's OutRiders yourself.' She fell silent, remembering her own torture by the OutRiders and her rescue from them by Ambar. At that time, he was also being pursued by the OutRiders loyal to the old Queen, but Gladia had conveniently forgotten that. 'You could try going back to one of the most distant places in Oramia, to the far north or south where they would not know you, I suppose. Not many people would, mind, given what you look like now.' She sniffed disparagingly. 'Goodness knows who last wore that awful set of clothes!'

'The last owner of these clothes was an old man I met in a small village called Matir after I crossed the river from Oramia. I swapped my robe for his. He believed he had made a great bargain! I traded for the headdress in the market there with a trader. I think they have served me well enough, though I will trade them in again before I go; I must leave by tomorrow. It is not safe for me to stay here. I do not think that I have been followed, but it is wise to keep moving for some time, until I can change my appearance more. And please continue to call me Baram in the presence of others,' he added.

'I think it rather unlikely that anyone who knew you as the Vizier of Oramia would recognize you now,' said Gladia drily. At that moment, Riva returned, and both the babies began to cry again. Ambar said that he would go out to the market, presumably to trade his clothes again. Gladia told him to make sure he got back before sunset if he wanted to eat and gave him a basket of dates to add to his trades.

Riva looked at him curiously as he left and asked who he was.

'An old friend called Baram,' replied Gladia. 'He fell on hard times but is on his way to new things now and has called here to stay the night on his way.'

'He does look like he has had a hard time,' Riva replied. 'I may have something in my stock of physics that could help him with his bruises and grazes.' Her mention of this made me think of the Oblak and the Iskra which I knew she still had. Her stock would not last forever, she had admitted to me, and then she would have to learn to do without them and the way in which they eased difficult childbirth and softened memories of pain and distress. I had not thought much more about the night that Ambar and I had taken the Oblak since just after the children were born. I was so tired at night that I would immediately sink into a dark, dreamless sleep until I was roused from it by a demanding wail. I could not remember the last time I had dreamed – or rather, I could, because there was only one. It was the time after Riva had given me Iskra after the birth. I wondered what Ambar might recall if he took it. The thought sat in my mind, glowing like a hot coal.

'Perhaps Baram should take some of your Oblak to forget his hard times,' joked Gladia, seeming to read my mind. Riva laughed along with her.

'You would never give Oblak to a man unless he was sure he wanted to forget something forever,' she replied. 'And even hard times have a way of teaching us lessons. I am sure he would not want to forget the kindness of you, his friends, in hard times, for instance.'

'Well, could you not just give him the Iskra afterwards as you do to the women who take it during childbirth?' I asked, curious about this. I realised that nobody had really mentioned men taking Oblak on Soora, and why would they? Their purpose there had always been to ease any difficulties in a woman's mind during birth, which was, after all, something only women could do, and Soora was populated by women.

'Oh, the Iskra does not work on men at all!' she said, laughing again. 'They tried it a few times on men, especially the sailors, if they had been badly injured and needed painful work doing on broken limbs or deep wounds. The Oblak worked fine on helping them to forget but they could not remember anything at all even if they were given the Iskra straight away. That day of their life just disappeared from their minds as if it never existed.'

There had been, glowing in my mind, the thought that I could have given Ambar Iskra, and compelled him to remember what had happened that night and then I could have asked him what he recalled. My own memories were so fractured and insubstantial that, as soon as I concentrated on them, they melted away into the shadows, much like Ambar himself. I knew now that there would never be another person who would have those memories or be able to weave their memories together with mine, to try to produce a stronger, more reliable memory. When Ravin had been alive, we would often talk together of experiences we had shared, and somehow that would make the memory even stronger, as if a layer had been added to it. Now that he was gone, my shared memories with him were diminished. I had made a choice to take the Oblak when I was full of grief and anger and now all my mind wanted to do was remember clearly what had happened. Relying on dreams and half retained moments was not an answer to my questions, and now it seemed there would be no more answers to those questions at all. It would be better to forget all of it and, once Ambar had gone, get on with my new life wherever it might lead me.

Later that evening we sat near the fire. There was the faint scent of jasmine on the breeze. Many people in Kashiq would have their own little oil lamps scented with the days of the week and then would light each one accordingly. My neighbours, Gurshan and Fari, would light a lamp every evening when the sun went down, and the scent of it drifted pleasingly into my courtyard. I had found that Ronai and Amani slept better if they had the scent of jasmine oil around them, so I put it on their blankets to help them to sleep and gave them the scented cloth from the bag that Nousha had given me. Perhaps it was because they were born as we crossed from Aureus to Flavus, and that scent was around them when they were born. Or perhaps it was because on Soora it was the only scented oil that people burned and somehow they had taken that in while they were inside me. In any case they both slept peacefully, lulled by the scent and by the gentle noises around them of people talking and palm leaves rustling. The palm cicadas had settled their buzzing call to a low hum, and the moon was half full in the sky with the stars blinking near her. Riva had gone inside the dwelling after we had eaten, to allow us time to spend with our old friend Baram. I was grateful for that, since it meant that Gladia and I could speak more openly with him before he left Pirhan.

He had returned from the market in different clothes. These ones were better quality, but still very ordinary; some Kashiqi trousers in a dark green and a light brown robe with a simple embroidered collar and cuffs. He had also acquired a new headdress and headband and had had his hair cut so it was much shorter, and his beard was trimmed to a new shape. Gladia nodded her approval at his change of attire and at the more groomed look.

'So, what will you do now, and will you ever return to Oramia?' she asked him.

'Gladia is always the one asking the hard questions straight away,' replied Ambar with a faint smile. 'It makes a change to the people at the Court trying to find out their answers without actually asking me the questions.' His face fell, perhaps thinking back to his time at Court and to his old life, and to his wife, the Queen, who had turned against him. I couldn't help feeling sorry for him while, at the same time, feeling somehow pleased that he had his own troubles and that he had not been able to talk his way out of them. Ambar, with his implacable faith in his destiny and his ruthless pursuit of it, had come up against something that he could not sway: Lunaria's faith in her own destiny and the way in which she believed the Goddess would direct it. Ambar had faith in himself to fulfil his

339

destiny and Lunaria had faith in the Goddess to fulfil her destiny. It remained to be seen which one of the two would be proved more accurate.

'I would not tell you even if I knew,' he said. 'If I told you where I might go and what I might do, it is possible that one day someone might ask you.'

Gladia looked at him with concern. 'Are you saying we might be in danger in Mellia? Or in Gabez? Surely not here in Kashiq where Talla lives?'

Ambar told us that he was just being careful, but both of us knew what the OutRiders were capable of once they were sent on a mission by the Queen. Ambar then told Gladia that there would be no more Angels delivered to her in Mellia, for that had been his own commitment, and that the Queen would never continue with it, and, in fact, did not even know that it had ever occurred. Because she had never known about it, she would not know much of Mellia nor have any reason to think that it would have any connection with Ambar.

'I never told her about the bargain I made with you for the Orange of Kashiq,' he said. 'I never intended to. The arrangement we had for the Angels to come to Mellia was only between us.'

'But you told us that it was the Queen who had ordered the Angels to be given the Oblak,' I said. 'You said that it was she who wanted the Angels to be given it, you made us think that she knew about the Angels coming to Mellia.'

Ambar looked abashed. 'I told you that so that you would be more likely to understand if our arrangement ended. It was becoming hard for me to find the right women to leave with you and it involved a lot of difficulty.'

'Difficulty!' Gladia exclaimed. 'Difficulty? I tell you what difficulty is, it is what those women are forced to endure by the Court of the Queen and her servants the Priestesses and the OutRiders! Anything you have to put up with is small compared to that!'

Ambar nodded. 'I know. But I could not ask the OutRiders to get them for me, I had to find them myself and then pretend they were being taken to other OutForts when I was actually delivering them to you in Mellia. I was careful to only take one at any time from one of the OutForts, so that they would not be noticed. Often I said they were being taken somewhere to have their babies. But without me at the Court, there is no one to know about it, and no one to continue with it. I am sorry for the pain that causes.'

We were silent, all thinking of what it meant. Gladia spoke again first.

'Well, I never thought it would carry on after the seven years we agreed anyway. And this forgetting stuff you give them now is not good for them, they still hold their pain inside, hidden away even from themselves. It is time now for us to look at other women we can help, for it seems clear that we will never make a difference to the Angels. Talla will get the scroll of agreement that was scribed by Ravin, and we will burn it now, for it might be dangerous to us all to keep it.'

I felt very sad to hear Gladia say this. She had said it to me before, but to hear her say it to Ambar somehow made it feel more real, that she was now admitting to someone who had been at the Queen's Court that the power they had over how people lived was too great. But now, of course, Ambar was no longer part of the Queen's Court and was as powerless as the rest of us. And perhaps that was why Gladia had admitted this, because it would have no effect. I thought of all the women, like Bellis, who were used by the OutFort and by the Priestesses and who had ended up being rescued by a woman of the Outer, one who had no learning nor status, but who had nevertheless fought for them, and for the right thing to be done. I reached over and put my hand on hers, feeling her plump, warm fingers underneath mine, and the love between us flowed just as the thoughts had once flowed from the Empath Erayo into my heart. We did not need to speak for it to be real.

Gladia was right about the scribed agreement though. It was the downfall of scribing, that it recorded for many years things which might have otherwise fallen into the fast-flowing river of memory and been swept away. They could be read by others who might understand something completely different from what the scholar or scribe intended. I got up and retrieved the scroll from the scroll-box inside the dwelling. I ran my hand over it, regretting that it would be something else of Ravin's that would be lost forever. His small, tight scribing had covered the parchment and was proof of him and of a piece of time which he had lived. I dropped it into the fire and watched as the flames took it and the darkberry ink spat flames that were pink and purple as it curled and crumbled to ash.

'I am sorry,' Ambar repeated. 'I did not think about what would happen if the agreement were ended, truthfully. At first, I just agreed to it because I really had no choice, but then it became important to me, it became something that I could be proud of in myself. My OutCommander told me when I was in my Third Age of Childhood that we should all keep something in our hearts that we were proud of. Not something that others are proud of, but something we are proud of in ourselves. He told me that it would be the light that would shine in the darkness, for it would always be there. It is something that we can all be proud of, I think. But this system will exist for as long as they want it to.'

I was frustrated. Two ages had now passed since I left the Temple where I has been raised, and I had been full of righteous anger when I first found out about the Angels. I had believed that something could change, that when Lunaria ascended the throne she might stop them being used, that a new way of being might begin. I had hoped that Ambar would have had power at the Court and that he might have influenced things for the better and he had not. And now, I was angry at myself for not doing enough, for not trying hard enough. For moving into another land where it did not happen and allowing myself not to think about it much anymore. And yet, what could I do, I who lived in another land with two tiny babies and no husband? I had to raise my children safely and to do that, I needed not to draw attention to myself. It seemed even more crucial to me now that I had seen the bee mark on Ronai. If anyone found out about that, then it might become more dangerous for me and for those I loved. I thought again of the warning that had been given to me by Silene, the DreamReader, masquerading as a fortune teller. Even though I was angry about the Angels, I was more worried about my friends and my small family.

'Where will you go?' repeated Gladia. 'You cannot stay here, and you cannot go back to Oramia, at least not straight away. So, what will you do?'

'I am planning to travel south,' said Ambar. 'I will not tell you more than that, and even then, it may not be true. I do not want you to know where I am going, as I have said.' Gladia rolled her eyes. She had little patience with Ambar's ways, but knowing what I knew, they seemed sensible.

'I just wanted to make sure that you would not be trying to stay here, with Talla,' she continued. 'It would be just like you to try to find another place where someone else could look after you. Well, Talla has far too much to deal with looking after my grandchildren to have to be concerned about someone else, so I am hoping that Baram will have left by the morning.' She looked at him pointedly.

'I promise you that I will leave at dawn, or just before,' he said. 'I am grateful for the chance to stay the night here before I go on, but do not worry, I will leave the house in peace – or in as much peace as is possible with two babies!' He grinned as we all heard the insistent noise of two demanding babies battling for attention, and Gladia and I went inside the dwelling. Ambar stayed outside in the courtyard, sleeping on a mat so that he could leave early the next day. I had wanted to speak more to him before he left but there seemed no chance to do so and I went to sleep knowing that when I next woke up, he would be gone.

Chapter 35

It was an unsettled night. The kind of night where, even though you long for the nothingness of sleep, the time is filled with tossing and turning and worrying about this and that, startling to every little noise. And the time that was not occupied with that was filled with strange, unsettling dreams in still pictures. Normally, when I dreamed, what happened ran on in my mind as if it were happening; people moved and sang and talked. This time it was as if I was looking at some of the diagrams and pictures that Ravin used to make. Nothing moved at all.

There was a picture of me with Ravin and our children, an impossibility, and yet it seemed quite real. There was another picture of Gladia with two children, a boy and a girl of the same age, who I knew to be Ronai and Amani even though they were past the First Age of Childhood in the picture I saw. Another picture was of Hortensia as she was now but holding the DoubleSouls of Paradox in her arms and looking from one to the other as if weighing them up. There were pictures of me as a child in the Temple of The Goddess' Blessing where I grew up, and further pictures of a small solemn boy in a dusty OutFort sitting alone with a pile of pebbles and a sling, who I knew must be Ambar. And then there was a picture of me, sleeping in Ambar's arms under the tiny, bright stars of that black night.

I woke in the flat greyness that comes just before dawn, when the colours seem to have been leached out of the world. Ronai and Amani slept, tangled together. I got up, wrapped my blanket around me and went out into the courtyard. Ambar was still lying on his mat, asleep, despite it being almost dawn. One could not, after all, make oneself wake up at any given hour, and the sun that was about to rise would doubtless wake him soon. I sat down on the other mat and leaned against the wall. So much had happened in this single year. If I had thought, a year ago, to scribe my life as it would be in a year's time, it would not have contained any of the events that had occurred. The death of Ravin, the journey to Soora, the birth of my children and the actions of Lunaria, my sister, the Queen, seemed as unlikely to me now that they had happened as they would have seemed before. We could not predict our future lives nor how or why we would make the choices we did.

I looked across the courtyard as the first weak light began to appear and cross over the space as the sun rose higher in the sky. There was an orange tree in one corner, which Ravin and I had planted in memory of our meeting and of our efforts to find the Orange of Kashiq. The sun hit that corner first and I watched it travel across, landing on Ambar's face. His eyes suddenly opened, and he looked surprised to see me sitting there. I wondered if he had sat in the same way looking at me after that night, before he went, having left me the sun pendant which I still kept in my underpocket.

Ambar yawned and sat up. He had slept in all his clothes, ready to leave, so there was very little for him to pack away in his carrysack.

'Do you need anything to eat?' I asked, quietly, so as not to wake anyone else up. He shook his head and picked up his things as he stood up to leave. It had only been a few minutes since he was fast asleep and he showed no signs of exhaustion, looking alert and determined.

'I had hoped you would be asleep when I left,' he said finally, as he stood next to me by the reed door of the courtyard, which was by now flooded in sun. The colours had been reborn into the day by the sun, brighter and cleaner. 'It would not have been so hard.'

I looked at him, understanding that sometimes it is easier to leave without saying goodbye, for there is a finality in those last words, even if you expect to meet again. If you never acknowledge you are departing, perhaps you never feel like you have left.

'I thought you would already be gone,' I replied. 'Sleeping is no longer easy for me. If the OutRiders ever need people to stay awake on guard at night, mothers of babies would be a good choice!'

Ambar smiled. 'I might have suggested that if I was still an OutRider.' His face clouded. 'But I must set my mind aside from that life now and become somebody else. It seems very difficult to me to leave half my life behind me, and yet you have managed to leave your life in the Temple behind you, and Tarik also seems to have managed it. I must learn new things just as you both have done. I wish I could still talk to Tarik as I used to.'

I felt sorry for him. It had not been easy for me or for Tarik to grow into ourselves as new people separate from our upbringing, but we had been helped by those we loved, by Ravin and Achillea. Ambar, on the other hand, had never had the chance to get away completely from the world he had grown up in like Tarik and I had, and had nobody to support him in that new life. It would be good for him to live in Kashiq, a place that was quite different from Oramia, while he started his new life, far away from Lunaria.

'You must,' I agreed. 'Maybe now you are in Kashiq, you will learn to scribe and to read. You will have no need for that silent language of the OutRiders here. But you will have more choices if you can read and scribe if you stay in Kashiq.' He nodded thoughtfully, and then opened up the gate and paused, halfway between leaving and staying.

'Do you still have the necklace in the shape of a sun? I left it for you on that other morning when I left at dawn.'

'Yes, I have it,' I replied, reluctant to get into any conversation about that night with Ambar just as he was leaving. He looked at me as if he was waiting for me to say more, but I remained silent.

'Think of me when you look at it sometimes,' he said, finally. 'There is a power in the sun. We notice it when it is there, shining on us with every new day, bringing us colour and warmth, and we notice it when it is gone, in the darkness and in the cold. I always wondered if the Goddess Asmara lived in the sun.' He smiled and then raised his hand in farewell and touched it to his head and his heart.

'May the sun's light shine upon you and upon your children forever.'

ACKNOWLEDGEMENTS

Thank you, my lovely readers first of all! Reading books often reminds me of meeting new people and each time that somebody reads and enjoys one of my books, it feels like meeting a new friend. If you like my stories, please recommend them to someone you know who might like them or lend your copy to a friend!

My deep gratitude goes to the small crew of 'Alpha' Beta readers who volunteer to read my books first. They answer my questions with wisdom and understanding and are my deep foundation and strongest support. Those who believe in my writing make such a big difference.

My thanks also to Amy Yeager, the artist of all of my front covers, who listens carefully to my words, examines my rough scribbles, and produces lovely, evocative pictures to grace the covers of my books. You can find her on Instagram at @amy_art.illustration.

If you have enjoyed this book and the ones which came before, you may like to visit my website www.emberjar.com where you can find maps, glossaries, pronunciation guides and a whole range of supplementary information and news about all the books in the Emberjar series.

See you in Book 4!

SOORA SUN

Printed in Great Britain
by Amazon

24224932R00202